PAR FOR THE CORPSE

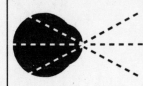

A MAY LIST MYSTERY

PAR FOR THE CORPSE

T. DAWN RICHARD

WHEELER PUBLISHING
A part of Gale, Cengage Learning

GALE
CENGAGE Learning·

Detroit • New York • San Francisco • New Haven, Conn • Waterville, Maine • London

LIBRARY OF CONGRESS CATALOGING-IN-PUBLICATION DATA

Richard, T. Dawn.
   Par for the corpse : a May List mystery / by T. Dawn Richard.
   ISBN-13: 978-1-4104-3721-1 (pbk.)
   ISBN-10: 1-4104-3721-3 (pbk.)
   1. Older women—Fiction. 2. Murder—Investigation—Fiction.
3. Country clubs—Fiction. 4. Large type books. I. Title.
PS3618.I335P37 2011b
813'.6—dc22   2011003254

Published in 2011 by arrangement with Tekno Books and Ed Gorman.

Printed in the United States of America
1 2 3 4 5 6 7 15 14 13 12 11

For my children, Calin,
Summer, Genny, and Jesse.
Every day is precious because of you.

ACKNOWLEDGMENTS

This book was made possible because of the inspiration provided by the hardworking grounds crew members of the Spokane Country Club in Spokane, Washington. While the events depicted in *Par for the Corpse* are fictional, and all characters are also fictional, there are times when this author meets people so unique their personalities stimulate ideas for a truly entertaining tale.

Many thanks to Mr. Jeff Gullikson who gave me the words to use when I didn't understand all of the golf terminology, and who made it possible for me to spend a memorable summer working with the crew at the Spokane Country Club. And a big thank you to Alice Duncan and Scott Kirkman for their suberb work in editing this book.

CHAPTER ONE

If old man Pendersnack hadn't gotten his lure all tangled up in Moira's hair, we'd still be guessing what became of her. As it was, ol' Snack's peaceful day of fishing turned out badly and not just because he'd dredged up the trout-nibbled body of the late Mrs. Finch. Sadly, during his efforts to knock Moira free, he lost one darn-good lure.

After Snack realized what was hanging at the end of his line, he checked briefly to see if the coast was clear and considered shoving Moira back down with an oar so he could continue his morning of casting and reeling. He already had three fish in his creel, and it was looking like he'd hit a sweet spot. But he paused. There was something curious about the way the woman's head bobbed and twisted in the calm swells, so he decided to take a closer look.

Pendersnack bent down, clutched the rim of the aluminum boat and leaned over the edge, teetering on knobby knees. He dragged his fishing net though the water until it clanked against a metal object shimmering near Moira's neck. At first he thought it was a chain necklace or some kind of brace. He'd worn one years ago while suffering a bad case of whiplash. However, when he grabbed the net with two hands and hauled up the sodden head of Moira, he was startled so dreadfully he almost pitched his own face into the murky drink.

Shaking like a dog passing peach pits, Snack secured Moira to the back of his boat and dragged her to the bank of Moody Lake. In his panic, he forgot about his outboard and rowed furiously, skimming right past the dock. Momentum slid his boat up onto the sandy shore of a busy campground, a place called Candy's, where you could pitch a tent or hook up your RV for a reasonable fee. Snack bounded from the boat and raced toward Candy's Bait and Tackle Shop, hollering for all he was worth.

Naturally, news of Snack's discovery immediately became a hot topic among the campers and within minutes the Harvest Police Department's dispatcher was juggling calls from thirteen ready cell phones. Time to investigate.

That's where I came in. My name is May Bell List, I'm sixty-eight years old, and I'm a detective. The title is honorary, but with a couple of huge busts to my credit I'm hoping to get a badge pretty soon, thanks in part to my new friend, Mike Murphy, a guy who should be listed in the Who's Who of Law Enforcement, if there is such a thing. Mike had taken me along on some of his shifts and he'd taught me a thing or two about perp management. I'm sorry to say I did demolish his patrol car once but everything turned out well in the end, so fiddle-dee-dee.

I live just a few miles from Moody Lake in Harvest, Washington, a cozy, wooded town just north of Spokane. I keep tabs on what's happening in my neighborhood, which is why I was privy to the news of Snack's find when it came across a police scanner I keep in my bathroom.

Just out of the shower, I cut my morning constitutional short in anticipation of another good murder case. While wrestling with my drawers, I lost my balance and careened over sideways. I grabbed for a towel rod and hung onto it for a second, slowing my forward momentum, but it ripped away from the wall with a loud, grinding *pop!* and I hit the floor with a

11

fleshy thud.

"May? You okay in there?" My husband Ted poked his head in the bathroom door. No time to prepare for company, so I swiftly did a Marine-style roll and snatched up a towel to cover what I could. Unfortunately, when I whipped up the towel I also spun the aluminum rod into the air. It ricocheted off the toilet seat, changed trajectory, and thumped me hard between the eyes.

"I see you have everything under control here, May Bell," Ted said. The twitch in his upper lip told me he was trying very hard not to laugh. Good thing he held it in, too. The metal rod wasn't far from my reach.

The police scanner squawked out more of what was happening at the lake, something about a dead woman with a foreign object shoved through her neck, orders to send the medical examiner, fresh plastic bags, and a couple of ham sandwiches, double up on the mayo and hold the olives. I was missing all the fun.

"They're playing your song, Maybe Baby." Ted held out a hand, and I accepted it, blinking back tears of pain while keeping an ear to the police scanner. At that time, there was no news of the woman's identity. But I assumed she was someone by the name of Victoria or Vickie, and it sounded like she

12

was of some elevated stature because the police kept referring to her as the Vic. Well, I just had to get over there to get a look at our little Miss Vickie. Sheesh. Murders were happening all over the place, and I still hadn't made it out of the bathroom.

"Can you straighten up for me here, Ted? I've got to get over to Moody Lake before they haul the body away."

"No problem, sweetie pie, I've got a few minutes. Mrs. Daly's labor pains are only five minutes apart last I checked . . ." Ted looked at his watch and raised an eyebrow. "Guess I'd better hurry." He helped me to my feet, kissed me on my throbbing brow and picked up the towel. He swung it around by his knee, locker-room style, as if he were going to smack me with it as I passed. A glare changed his mind. Ted's not a bad guy; in fact he's pretty handy when I need him. A doctor, the son of a doctor, the grandson of a doctor, Ted specializes in the field of female medicine. Despite some quirks, I like him a lot.

No time for the complete beauty regimen, I scraped a comb through my wet hair, rolled on some pink lipstick, pulled on some sweats, and headed out the door with my purse on my arm. Ted jogged after me and stood on the front porch, motioning that he'd packed a sack breakfast. What a nice guy.

I jumped into my car, slammed the door of my Camaro and motioned for him to toss the grub. There was little time to lose. He cocked back an elbow and threw a dandy spiral. Since I hadn't gotten my side window down fast enough, my breakfast slammed against the glass. Eggs and bacon broke through the soggy paper bag and slid down the glass leaving a greasy trail. Never mind. I'd get a McMuffin or something after my investigation. I waved to Ted, signaling it was okay, and turned the key. My car rumbled to life and after slamming the shift into reverse, I was on my way.

Our country driveway was long and windy, full of holes from a late spring rain. My teeth clacked together over the bumps while I jockeyed the car onto the adjoining dirt road. More corrugated lane jiggled a little flap of loose skin under my jaws, but minutes later I peeled out onto a paved road and mashed the gas pedal. My car was old, a convertible, cherry-red sixty-seven Camaro, but full of horsepower. Three twenty-seven under the hood, Hurst three-speed on the floor. I stole it from Ted a couple of years ago, but he's content with his yellow Hummer. Calls it his big banana.

I got to the crime scene in fifteen minutes when it would have taken twenty for any law-abiding citizen. It was still early morning, which meant there wasn't much trouble with crowd control, just the few campers who had wandered from their nearby tents with sleepy eyes and coffee mugs in hand. I pulled into the gravel parking lot in front of Candy's Bait and Tackle Shop and tried to crank down my window to ask a passerby if he knew what was going on, but a piece of hog fat was lodged in the window frame, jamming the window, so I got out of the car to have a look around for myself.

The tackle shop was a small, rustic structure with a huge wooden fish affixed over its door. On the fish in black sans serif type was the word "Candy's." On the shop's weathered front porch stood a wooden sandwich board outlining all of the services and products available at the lakeside camping spot — live bait, boat rentals, and campsites by the day, week or month, along with their corresponding prices. Potted plants added color and cheer.

I followed the sound of chatter around to the back of the shop. The smell of campfire smoke drifted through the air, reeling me back in time to happy days of childhood camping trips. But there were no happy

15

campers here. Yellow crime-scene tape was wrapped around the trunks of trees and tied to a couple of picnic tables, making a large square at the edge of the lake. Quite a bit of police activity was happening inside the barrier. One officer was standing beside something which I assumed was *the Body.*

I scanned the uniforms for Officer Murphy. He would be a good source of information when it came time for me to gather data. There'd been four cruisers parked in front of Candy's Bait and Tackle Shop; just about every car in the Harvest Police Department's modest motor pool. I saw no sign of Mikey, so I turned back to the tackle shop. It was here that customers could rent boats or purchase postcards and toilet paper, among other things, but shopping for toiletries wasn't my main interest. The campground proprietor, a lovely woman named Candy Schultz, had recently installed a cappuccino machine. I walked up to the shop's dusty back door and pushed through, in need of a caffeine fix. The door's hinges creaked pleasantly.

Snack was there and he had an audience.

Several elderly men dressed in heavy flannel and sporting morning stubble sat in rickety chairs forming a semicircle facing Mr. Pendersnack. They were a picture of rapt attention. One man poured steaming brew from a paint-faded red-and-black-plaid thermos, counting it out in equal shares to three outstretched Styrofoam cups. Nodding to the men in passing, I made my way to the coffee counter just a few steps away. It was impossible not to overhear their conversation. I glanced back occasionally to match voices with faces.

"What was that thing sticking out of her neck?" Thermos Man asked, leaning toward Snack. "Did you get a look?" He wore a floppy blue hat decorated with flies. He closed his thermos, twisting the plastic stopper until it squeaked.

Snack was basking in his newfound celebrity status. "I got a look awright, and at first I thought it was one of them harpoons like the kind you spear fish with. Ya shoot it off sorta like a rubber-band gun, ya know. I used to make those when I was a kid." Snack cocked his head, closed one eye and squeezed an imaginary trigger with his index finger. "But then I think to myself people don't really use 'em much in these parts so it didn't quite fit."

"Course not," said Mr. Thermos. "Spear fishing means you have to get right down into the water, swim around, go all the way under. You go swimmin' around in that lake,

17

even in the summer, and you'll come up missing a few important features. Freeze 'em right off."

Snack nodded somberly. "That's why I knew it couldn't be a harpoon."

"So . . . what? A suicide you think?" Another man with a face as stiff and weathered as cardboard, plenty of sun wrinkles and chapped lips narrowed his eyes and rubbed the back of his hand over his scruffy chin.

I did a mental eye roll and ordered a latte from Candy, keeping tabs on the men in my peripheral vision.

"You can forget that," said a third man. He crossed his legs and showed a lot of white ankle above polished loafers. His face was brown too, like Mr. Cardboard, but his tan was too orange to be natural and I suspected it had come from a bottle. He wore a sweater vest under a sports jacket. No shiny worm residue on his pants. "She was skinny-dipping," Ankle Man said. "Goin' for an early splash, and all the while you get some healthy young guy, maybe an athlete-type who's built up a tolerance to the cold down there knife fishing, thinking he had himself a shark or maybe a manta ray. Could've happened."

"Where are you from, man?" Cardboard

Face asked, turning in his seat to stare at Mr. Ankles.

"California," Ankles said with a sniff. "And just in case you never heard of it, it's the home of Hollywood, fine wine and the best darned president this country ever had. You got a problem with that?"

Cardboard looked at Snack with an expression of amusement. He turned to Ankles. "Ya know, with a chip that big on your shoulders, I'm getting the idea there ain't much room for anything in the noggin." Cardboard tapped the side of his own head with a knuckle.

Mr. Thermos tipped his head back and roared while Ankles went crimson.

"Ah, don't take it personal, guy," Snack said, and nodded toward the lake. "It's just that you aren't gonna find any sharks or manta rays out there."

"Or any skinny-dippin' little lads, if that's what you're fishin' for." Cardboard leveled a stare at Ankles.

Snack lifted his chin toward Cardboard's face. "Don't mind him. He thinks everyone from California is a little fruity."

It seemed impossible, but Ankles turned a deeper shade of red.

I groaned inwardly. Ankles should have known better than to cozy up to the good

19

old boys of Moody Lake. Snack did have a point, though. In order to spear someone in the water, you definitely had to be *in* it, and I just couldn't fathom paddling around those icy waters. But wait. Who says you have to be in the water to get a spear through the jugular? The body could have been dumped, and if you were out in a boat . . .

I shifted my attention from the men and looked through the wide windows, checked the police activity, and caught sight of Officer Murphy out back near the yellow tape. He stood with his hands on his hips while a woman in a pink robe chatted his ear off. I couldn't hear her, but I could see her mouth going a mile a minute. I silently urged Candy to hurry up with that latte.

"Now I was confused at first and I got to wondering." Snack shifted in his chair and crossed his legs, the side of one foot on the opposite knee — man style — and scratched the back of his head with the hand not holding his cup. "What the heck is that thing in her neck? I helped haul her onto the beach, of course, and stared at it a long time because it looked familiar, but unfamiliar all at the same time."

"I know just what you mean." Ankles was back in the game and he was eager. "Like when you see someone at your thirty-year college reunion and you think you should know them, right? But they've had work done so you're not sure."

"Whatever," Snack said. "So I'm looking and looking at this thing and *whammo!*" The audience of men jumped. Two Styrofoam cups jerked and coffee flew. The thermos cracked against Ankle's knee. "I figured it out."

I watched Murphy and held my breath while waiting for Snack to reveal his discovery. What did he figure out? I felt cold fingers press against my wrist and that startled me so badly that I squealed high in my throat. It was a quiet peep because my mouth was closed and, remember, I was holding my breath. I whirled around to see Candy smiling at me. She held out my latte and said softly, almost cryptically, "Be careful."

I furrowed my brow and leaned in. I whispered, "What for?"

She nodded her head toward the drink. "It's hot."

Oh.

I thanked Candy and plunked down a five. I left her to attend to a gesticulating Mr. Ankles, who suddenly had an urge for a skinny iced vanilla caramel macchiato. I

21

exited out the back of the shop and ambled over to the crime scene, tired of waiting for Snack to reveal his find, guessing he probably didn't even know what had killed the poor woman. I'd just figure it out for myself.

It was nearly seven o'clock and the sun was rising higher now. The lake shimmered in silver ripples. A few more campers had come to see what was happening. It gave me an opportunity to slip past a uniform who was busy taking statements. Near the yellow tape I looked around quickly, saw that I was in the clear, did a deep knee bend sideways, swooped, and went under. The woman was lying just a few feet away so I shuffled over, sucked at my latte, and observed.

The body wasn't covered yet. Even though she was pretty bloated, I recognized her immediately. Moira Finch was on her back; her cloudy eyes watched a V of honking geese overhead, and aside from a large metal rod protruding from both sides of her neck, she looked quite peaceful. Sure enough, just as Snack had said. The thing looked familiar — but not. And then I had it. This was not a traditional weapon but lethal just the same. I pulled a tissue I'd tucked under the strap of my bra and, using it, I lifted the end of the rod noting its sharp jagged edge.

An inch or so from the end of the hollow tube I found a neatly carved hole in its side about the size of a dime, clearly made by a machine of some sort. I could even see the tool marks without my reading glasses. What in the world?

I dropped the end of the rod, then reached into my purse and pulled out a pencil. Using it as a tool, I probed Moira's skin. A little of it sloughed off onto the eraser, which indicated she'd been in the water a few days at least. Her fingers and feet, I saw, were pruney. Washer woman hands. I jabbed at the rod, and it vibrated. I pushed at it with more muscle, and Moira turned her head to look at me. Her eyes were a dull blue, almost colorless, and that was pretty creepy, her staring at me like that, so I sucked at my latte and squatted down closer to examine the body. Fully clothed, and aside from the thing in her neck, no sign of trauma, blunt force, or gunshots, and no indication she'd been ravaged, save for the ragged chunks of meat that feathered out along her bare arms, picked at by scavengers no doubt. Her ears were pretty much gone, and her nose was a mess, again chewed on by turtles or bottom feeders. Since she was on her back, I couldn't tell if the bottom feeders had done that literally. Hmmm. I sucked at my latte again, keeping the smell of coffee close to my nostrils. The smell of Moira was hovering.

"Mrs. List, what are you *doing?*" Someone whispered loudly behind me. A voice I recognized. I stood stiffly, turned and smiled.

"Mikey! I was wondering where you were. So good to see you. Homicide, you think?" A pretty silly question really, but it's hard to come up with small talk when you've got a bloated floater under your feet.

Officer Murphy took my elbow and pulled me away from Moira. "You can't be in here. It's a crime scene." He glanced around fretfully.

"Oh, I know that," I said, and ducked under the tape before either one of us got in any real trouble. "Heard it on my scanner." I held up my pencil close to his nose. A tag of skin was attached to the eraser end of the number two. "Down two days? Three? I'm saying four, tops. Otherwise, her whole face would have fallen off by now."

"You shouldn't be poking around the corpse like that."

Mikey looked very nervous at what I'd just done, but I patted his arm and said, "You can forget any kind of footprint evidence, dear. It looks like the whole Harvest Police

24

Department did the Texas two-step through there. Only evidence you should be concerned with is that five iron sticking through her skinny throat."

Mikey took a step toward Moira and cocked his head. "Is that what that is?"

"Well, as you can see, the head's been broken off, or sawed off, but sure. Or it could be an eight or nine. But looky see. There's the handle right there." I pointed to a slightly greenish rubber end. Some mossy substance was clinging to it, so it could have been difficult to identify if you didn't know what you were looking at. "Of course it's a golf club. Take a look yourself if you don't believe me."

"Pretty good, Mrs. List."

"Oh, you'd have figured it out. So, have you questioned all the bystanders?" I narrowed my eyes and scrutinized the crowd. Mostly tourists who would go home with a story to tell. A large woman in a pink ragged bathrobe, the one I'd seen earlier giving Mikey an earful, was snapping photos with a disposable camera. A uniform stepped up and sent her away. At least she'd have a four-by-six glossy to paste in her photo album back home. Maybe she'd even print up a few wallet sizes to pass around. Now that the uniform was attending to other

25

business, a dad gathered his family and had them pose, smiling, with Moira's body in the background for creative effect. That one would be for the Christmas card.

"We're still canvassing the campground to see if she knew anyone here. Maybe she was a guest with a hot-tempered husband."

"Oh, no, Mikey. That woman's a local. Her name is — was — Moira Finch. And she wasn't married. Widowed."

Mikey raised his eyebrows, paused, and then took my pencil. He scratched something in a notebook. The little tag of skin dropped off and plopped onto the ground.

"Evidence," I said, motioning to the skin.

Mikey grimaced, reached into his pocket for a little paper envelope — a bindle is what it's called — bent down and scooped up the piece of Moira. He dropped the piece of Moira into the envelope and tucked it all into his breast pocket and said, "At least now we've got a name to put to the victim."

Ah . . . the Vic! "You might want to take a look at her golf clubs, you know, to see if one's missing."

Mikey pondered this latest bit of information while I smugly slurped my latte. Then he asked, "How did you know Mrs. Finch?"

"I didn't really *know* her. But I did run into her at the country club now and then."

I waited, and then pointed at my pencil. "Write that down."

"Oh. Of course." Mikey scribbled quickly on his pad. "The Northside Country Club?"

"Um-hm. Not that I have any use for that sort of thing generally, pretty hoity-toity and not my style, but Ted, you know, my husband, he's a doctor. Remember you met him that time I was in jail? Anyway, Ted is always getting invited to golf, and all his doctor friends belong to the club, and it's sort of like expected that he'll golf, and so it's expected that he'll join the club, which he did, but I don't golf so the only thing I do is go to the occasional benefit, which is where I met Moira. We all had to wear those ridiculous sticky name tags on our clothes and write our names with a black felt marker, you know? That stuff never comes off. Ruined one of my best dresses."

Officer Murphy cleared his throat. "Did the decedent have any enemies that you know of? Anyone who might have wanted her dead? Anything she may have been doing that would have put her at risk?"

"Like I said, I didn't really know her, but . . . wait."

I held up a finger and passed my latte over to Mikey, after which I dug around in my purse. I always carry a notebook in there, something every good detective should have in events just like these. Remembering not to lick my fingers, I flipped through it and came to a page dated May twenty-fifth. The last time I'd seen Moira alive.

"Here. Right here. This was the day of the benefit luncheon at the club." I held out the notebook.

Mikey looked interested. He squinted some and read through the entry, then looked at me with an expression of great sympathy. Poor May.

"What?" I looked at my scrawl. Eggs, bread, cat food, dog biscuits, paper towels . . . "Oh, for Pete's sake." I flipped the page and held it out again. "Here. Read this."

Mikey read again and this time I had his full attention. Something on those pages of such significance that it couldn't be denied, just as a dark cloud slipped through the sky and blotted out the warm rays of the sun.

I frowned and stared at Mikey. "Oh, I'd say she had plenty of enemies, my dear boy. Plenty."

Mikey's eyes widened. He started breathing a little faster and chewed on my latte straw. "Yeah?" He sucked on my coffee straws until his cheeks formed dimples. "Who are these people?"

"Oh, Mikey. Don't get ahead of yourself here. Could be nothing." I reclaimed my latte, shook it, and noticed Mikey had finished it off. A little bit of my pink lipstick was in an oval on Officer Murphy's lips. Mikey realized what he'd done, blushed and apologized.

"Tell you what," I said, dabbing at his mouth with my tissue. "You wanta make lieutenant? You buy me another one of these and I'll get back in that club. I'll work my magic, and before the end of the first forty-eight, you should have an exclusive. Until then, I'll tell you what I do know."

"First forty-eight?"

"Forty-eight hours! First forty-eight hours! I know how these things work. You gotta solve a murder within the first forty-eight, right?"

Mikey's shoulders drooped a little and he said, "It should be so easy."

CHAPTER TWO

I loved the idea of helping the police again, and my heart hammered a gleeful drumbeat in my chest. I could already see the words "Confidential Informant" added to my ever-growing list of bona fides.

Officer Murphy was interested in what I had written on my notepad, and more importantly, what I hadn't. But, like a man who really knows how to hook a woman, he baited me with the promise of two drinks if I really could dig up anything worthwhile at the club. The names I'd jotted in my trusty notebook were all members, all associates of Moira's to one degree or another, and I can say (although I hate to gossip) she wasn't the most popular socialite in the lot.

Mikey escorted me into the tackle shop to order a replacement latte from Candy. The place was hopping so we pushed our way in behind a cluster of groggy tourists all shouting their orders in the manner they were accustomed to, from lands near and beyond.

The woman in the bathrobe muscled her way to the front of the crowd amid groans and loud protests. "Where's your biscotti?" she hollered in a thick Brooklyn accent, unnecessarily because Candy's face was just inches away.

"I'm sorry, ma'am, I don't carry biscotti." Candy steamed milk and smiled sweetly.

"No biscotti? What am I supposed to eat with my *cooahfee?*"

"We have some homemade cookies. Just took them out of the oven an hour ago." Candy wiped off the metal steam tube with a hand towel and deftly spooned foam onto the top of a brown drink.

"No biscotti? Are you saying you don't sell no biscotti here?"

Candy was patient. "No, ma'am, we have chips and donuts over by the front, though. Why don't you try some of those?" She pointed with an elbow.

Robe huffed. "Why don't I try some chips? Do I look like I need chips at seven o'clock in the morning? Some biscotti I can use. What about some hummus? Got any hummus?"

"Hey, lady, why don't you get back there where you belong and wait your turn like everyone else?" A young woman standing nearby frowned at Robe. She had one of those phone things in her ear and a head of wild blonde hair that looked very much like it had been cut by a dull lawn-mower blade. Her fingernails were painted black and she wore a tiny diamond stud on the left side of her nose, which actually looked rather attractive despite my old-fashioned prejudices.

Robe pulled herself up to her full height and was prepared to go at it when I spotted an opportunity to quash the inevitable melee. I sized her up in a flash. The older woman was directly in front of me, about my height, and with a fast bend, I thrust my knees forward into the soft place behind hers. Her legs buckled and her head snapped back before she caught herself. I sidestepped quickly just before she whipped around to see Officer Murphy behind her, the picture of surprise and innocence. Robe cut Mikey down with a smoldering stare.

"You pull something like that again, buster, and I'll get you for police brutality." Robe huffed and gathered her lapels in her hands. She tossed her tousled head and stomped off to check out the chip and donut rack.

Mikey glared at me but said nothing. I looked straight ahead.

Wearing a badge did have its privileges,

and together with the fact that there was a dead Moira now being prepared for a loading into the ME wagon, the crowd moved off to watch the fun and gave Mikey a clear path to the cappuccino bar. He ordered a small latte for me and a regular Americana for himself.

After fixing the drinks and pushing them across the counter, Candy said, "No charge, officer. Always do what I can for the men in blue." The sweet woman smiled. You'd think she was catering a wedding party instead of playing hostess to a murder investigation.

"In that case, I'll have a super large," I said, pushing my cup back across the counter with splayed fingers, smiling even more brightly than Candy. She frowned and I quickly changed my mind. "Or this one would be good, no prob."

Mikey ushered me out the back of the bait and tackle. We stood on a covered porch, sipped, and watched the other cops do their jobs. I knew Mikey was missing all the excitement keeping me company, but I'd promised information and he had sense enough to know where he was needed most. First, though, I wanted to know what *he* knew before giving up the goods.

"So, Mikey, what's the sit rep?" I asked. It was still chilly out there and I held the paper coffee cup close to my cheek.

"Sit rep?" Mikey sounded amused but he didn't look at me. He was watching and cringing while the pros tried to zip Moira into one of those plastic bag things. They got it zipped all the way to her neck and then couldn't figure out what to do with the golf club. They twisted it this way and that, causing dead Moira to do head-to-shoulder nods and cranes. Finally, a cop I recognized as one Officer Sherman drew a pocketknife from his pants and stabbed holes in either side of the bag. The men got the club through the holes after that and zippered her the rest of the way. Done.

"Yeah. Sit rep. *Situation report*. I know Mr. Pendersnack found her. Got that from my scanner. Heard he snagged her with his fishing line. Did he then pull her into his boat?" *Sip, sip.*

The cops squatted and grabbed Moira's bag. It was slippery from all that slime on the bank.

"Nah. Actually Snack cut her loose but then thought better of it, lashed her to the side of the boat and towed her in."

"Hemingway would be proud," I said.

"Hm?"

"Never mind. Look, Mikey. I really checked over Moira's body. Other than the

34

obvious, there were no signs of injury, no bruises, ligature marks or anything. A few fish bites, but that's to be expected."

"Snack was gentle with her, I suppose." Mike looked almost wistful. "And fish need to eat."

"She was fully clothed, too. No sign of sexual assault, I take it." *Sip, sip.*

"We'll get swabs and know about that soon enough."

"Being in the water all that time, I don't imagine swabbing is gonna give you much."

Mikey brooded over this probability while blowing on his coffee. "The toxicology and autopsy reports will give us a place to start."

I nodded slowly, pushed my little straws around for a while and watched another formation of geese flying over our heads. They honked a chorus and I heard Sherman shout an expletive. He brushed at his shoulder, then shook his soiled hand and rubbed it on his pant leg. When he did that, he lost his hold on Moira's bag. The sound she made when thudding back into the wet sand reminded me of the mess of cooked noodles I accidentally dropped on my kitchen floor last night.

"I see Sherman doesn't have his gun. Still got that nervous tic?" I shifted my cup to the other hand and waved away a fly crawling across my forearm. I scratched where its little feet had been.

"A nervous tic, and now a leaky bladder, thanks to you."

"He'll get over it." I couldn't really be blamed for Sherman's ticks and bladder squirts, but my past deeds with the police force had played havoc on the more robust in the bunch.

Mikey squinted into the sun. His jaw pulsed, a sign of deep concentration. I knew this from past cases with the officer. He was a credit to any police force, a stately six feet tall with a blond flattop, buns of steel, arms of ripped muscle, and the scruples of a minister. He was a good cop.

I chewed at my straw and put a foot up on the ledge of the porch railing. My joints were stiff and this took a couple of tries, but soon I was striking a pose. "What I can't figure is how she ended up here," I said.

"I told you. Pendersnack rowed her ashore."

"No, how she ended up here *at the lake.* What was she doing here? How did she get here? I didn't see her car and she loved that car. Wouldn't go anywhere without it. She'd pull that big thing into the club parking lot, always the same spot like it had her name on it, shoved it right up against the bushes which, I'm told, made the landscape people pretty steamed."

"Pretty steamed?"

I scoffed. "Shyeah, *really* steamed. I heard some say that Moira rolled right over the zinnias one time, and you have to jump a curb to do that. It was almost like Moira did it on purpose."

"Maybe Moira just had trouble handling her car."

"Not that woman. She used her car like a . . . passive-aggressive weapon. Pretend to mow down a hedge or park on top of a dogwood by accident, all to say to the help, 'I'm important, you're not.' So the question remains. Where's her beast of destruction?"

"We haven't checked the whole lake yet. She could have been floating a while. I'll have the guys do a walk-around."

"You'll be looking for a white car. Early model. Quite ostentatious and a long sucker, so it shouldn't be too hard to spot even if it's hidden in the trees."

"Right." Officer Murphy listened intently while keeping his eyes on the crowd.

"Did anybody hear a commotion, an argument, some kind of struggle?"

"I'll check the statements later. Sherman got all those. But ya gotta think, Mrs. List, most of these people are on vacation. That lady in the pink robe is from New York, and those guys over there by their hibachi are from Vegas. Those people smoking weed are from Taos . . . Hey!"

"Not now, Mikey. What's your point?"

"This kind of thing probably happens every day where they're from. I doubt if they'd even think it strange to hear a woman screaming."

I noticed the fly had jumped from my forearm to Mikey's nose. I reached over and killed it with my palm. Mikey's eyes pooled.

"That's for being cynical," I said.

"It's my job." Mikey gulped his coffee, tossed the dregs over the ledge and crumpled the paper cup.

"Another thing," I said, while watching a spider crawl over the porch rail. I flicked at it with my fingernail. "I'm thinking she's been gone a couple days at least. Didn't you get a missing-person report on her?" I watched the spider spin itself a line and rappel to the dew-heavy grass below. Then I finished my coffee and felt my stomach churn. I wondered if I could talk Candy into giving up some of those chips of hers.

"You know there's only so much I can share with you in a case, Mrs. List."

"But you'll check out the missing-person report, right?"

"I just found out who she is." And then in answer to my question, he added, "You made a good suggestion. Don't worry; we'll take care of things. All I want you to do is give me a list of names of the people you heard talking about Moira at the country club, and why you think they had reason to kill your friend. You promised."

"Not my friend. Just an acquaintance." I held up my cup. "Another?"

Mikey cocked an eyebrow, crossed his arms, and squared up. Sheesh. He could be intimidating when he wanted to be.

"Okay, okay. Don't get your panties in a wad. Here's what I've got." I set my cup down on the rail, pulled out my notebook again, tried to pull my foot off the rail but my hip was locked up good, left my foot hitched up like a cowgirl, licked my thumb (immediately thought of Moira's skin tag, regretted the lick, but heck it was too late anyway), and flipped through pages. I went back a few pages before the country club benefit.

"Like I said earlier, Moira and I went to the club for things like benefits and luncheons. She was a golfer though, that much I do know. As for me, I don't know the difference between a putter and a wedgie."

"Wedge."

"Huh?"

"Wedge. Not wedgie."

"Right. As a matter of fact I do know what a wedgie is, speaking of wadded panties. It's when you stop by the lingerie department and you get a size six by accident when what you really need is a fourteen, and after you walk a couple of blocks it's like . . . anyway, I don't golf."

Mikey tilted his head as if to say "no kidding."

"So I'm at the last luncheon, a benefit for the animal shelter, complete with a slide show, and don't get me going because in a moment of weakness I'm gonna want to adopt every kitten and puppy, you know me, and there's no way Ted's going to stand for that because we already have my little Torch and Trixie and they're a handful."

"Your grandkids?"

I paused, looked at Mikey, wondering how someone could be so cruel. I said quietly, "No, no grandkids yet. You have to rub that in my face?" I started to tear up.

Mikey blanched. "Honestly, May, I wasn't being facetious."

"Well, who would name their kids Torch and Trixie? Okay, Trixie I can understand, but Torch?"

"I remember now. He was that little hairless dog you rescued from the meth-lab case."

I relaxed some then, knowing he hadn't really meant to make fun of the fact my daughter still hadn't given me any babies to carry around on my hips. "He's a darling, and never sheds."

"Bald does have its benefits," Mikey said.

"Ted still has a full head of hair."

"I thought we were talking about your dog."

"Naturally. I was just a little emotional there." I dabbed at my eyes with the back of a knuckle and continued. "When they started flashing those pictures on the screen, I had to zone out a little bit because it was a tough lunch to get through. But in a way to distract myself, I started paying attention to the conversations around me. I've been thinking of writing a novel, and I just read this book by some famous author that said you should listen to conversations and write down things that are noteworthy. You know, not commonplace, but things that would make for good dialogue. So I scribbled the stuff I heard. And then I wrote a donation check for five thousand dollars." I handed my notebook to Mikey.

I looked out over the lake as Mikey read through my notes. Mr. Pendersnack was back out in his boat. The other guys I'd seen in the shack were riding along. Ankles wore a snorkel and mask, and as I watched, he leaned over and put his head in the water. Snack was rowing, looking back over his shoulder, and as he drew the oar up out of the water, he brushed against Ankles's face. Up came the oar with the snorkel and mask hanging from its tip, and the Californian was screamin' mad. I heard him yell something like "Nearly ripped off my ear!" The other guys laughed hysterically, dangerously rocking the boat.

I stared at the crew of misfits. "They think they can find the missing iron head."

Mikey looked out at the men. "Too late. We picked him up last week."

"Who?"

"Iron Head. He jumped bail but we got him."

"Are you kidding me?"

"Yes."

"Come on. We've got to get serious here." I'd been standing on the porch in my cowgirl pose for some time and my joints were getting stiff and really aching now, so I tried to pull my leg down off the rail again. It didn't budge.

Mikey noticed my discomfort and reached down to disengage my leg from the rail.

I thanked him.

"You're right. Let's get serious." Mike cleared his throat. "From what I'm reading here, Moira was a regular at the club, golfing at least three times a week with a foursome."

My stomach lurched and I thought at the moment *regular* was an appropriate word. Too much of the bean and I shoulda known better. "Always on Ladies Days, always with the same women, and always a pain in the putter, if you get my drift."

Mikey pointed to a word I'd written on the white pages. "Grumpy doesn't get you killed."

"Get with it, my friend, these are fine upstanding ladies of the community. You have to translate. Grumpy means witchy. Witchy means — you use your imagination. Annoying, well, that could mean downright obstinate."

"And what does 'cheat' mean?"

"She cheats."

"That still doesn't get you killed."

"It does if she cheats *off* the golf course."

"Ohhhh."

"And I thought you were cynical." I turned my attention back to the lake. Snack was having fun with Mr. Ankles, waving the oar holding the snorkel and mask in front

43

of the Californian's outstretched grasp. Ankles kept trying to grab it but Snack jerked it away just out of his reach. The other guys must have been beside themselves with laughter, because all I could see of them were their legs kicking and flailing while they were rolling around in the bottom of the boat.

"May." Mikey got my attention. "I don't see any names here, uh, by the dialogue."

"Huh?" I took the notebook. "It's simple really. They were smart enough not to ruin their good blouses with sticky tags and felt markers. Besides, I didn't think it was important to write down their names and I didn't really care. I was just looking for tidbits. Snippets."

"Tidbits. Sure. Would you recognize them if you saw these ladies again?"

"Probably."

Mikey closed the notebook and handed it back to me. "I need names. Do you think you can get them for me?"

"Plan's in motion, my good boy."

Mikey pulled some sunglasses out of his pocket, shook out the stems, and put them on. He looked at me over the tops. "Remember, Mrs. List, yours is an informal, uh, investigation, you understand. We'll get out to the country club and canvass the members, ask some questions, and do cop stuff. You've been helpful, but all I need are some names. That's it. Just names."

"Right." I stuffed my notebook back down into my purse. Somewhere along the way I'd lost my tissue. Now where was that thing?

Mikey directed his attention to the lakefront again when there was some commotion. The guys had made progress. Moira's bag was hauled under the police tape and was well on its way to the waiting ME wagon when Sherman accidentally got tangled up in the golf club, stepped on a corner of the bag and jerked the parcel out of the hands of the other officers. Moira probably got a good case of postmortem whiplash. Big wet spaghetti sounds again. Off to one side I caught sight of a poodle, dashing past with something white fluttering in his mouth. My tissue. Robe woman was chasing him, her nightwear flapping out behind her. The dog made a quick fake left, then right, and zoomed around the hibachi. Robe, in close pursuit, bumped it with her leg sending the portable cooker crashing onto its side. Coals spilled out, caught a tent on fire, and within seconds the whole thing went up in a four-alarm blaze. Lots of running and screaming.

"I think you might want to give them some help out there. Things are getting out of hand, and Sherman is making a mess of things, as usual. I'll tell you what. I'll get a complete report and bring it over to the station as soon as it's done."

Officer Murphy put his hand on my shoulders and looked at me. I saw my reflection in his sunglasses. What a fright! I'd forgotten how quickly I'd left my house. With my hair drying in the wind and lacking makeup, I looked like a ghoul; not to mention that coffee was whipping along uncomfortably through my intestines.

Mikey said, "Bring that report directly to me, okay? We don't want it to get into the wrong hands. Now run along. There's work to be done here."

I should say so. In the distance the wail of fire engines announced their approach while the tourist crowd did laps around the crime scene shouting directives to the attending officers. "Move her this way! No, you're stepping on her! Slide her by the feet! Anyone got a fire extinguisher?"

What a circus.

"Right." I started to go back through the bait and tackle shop then turned quickly, remembering something important. "Get a look at the end of that golf club, Mikey. See

46

if you can figure out how it was broken — or cut."

"I was just thinking the same thing." Mikey said, and though his glasses were covering his eyes, I was sure he winked at me. Were we a good team, or what?

CHAPTER THREE

By the time I got back to my car, the tent
had burned down to a black patch on the
campground's lawn, and Moira was safely
loaded into the ME wagon. I followed her
out of the parking lot and shook my head
because Sherman had obviously been in a
hurry when he closed up the back. A piece
of the body bag was hanging out the side of
the door.

There were plenty of suspects, but as Mike
had pointed out, no clear reason to kill
Moira. I had my work cut out for me. There
was so much data to collect, and I would
have kicked myself for not buying one of
those little tape recorder things if my feet
weren't busy with the clutch and gas pedal.

And speaking of pedals and clutches,
where in the heck was Moira's car? She
loved that car. Wouldn't have been caught
dead without it. Could that have been a
clue? Was she in the car when she was

killed? Oh, my. Why hadn't I thought of that before? I had to get Mikey on the phone and ask if they were planning to take a look at the bottom of the lake. It was deep in places, optimal for getting rid of a body, or a car. I couldn't imagine any murderer wanting Moira's body to be found floating around on Moody Lake, but there was no indication that she'd been weighed down in any way. Could she have been in her car? It was logical; one would think she'd never be found if that was the case — if the car was at the bottom of the lake. But something had brought her bobbing to the surface, and that might possibly mean she'd squeezed her gas-inflated body out through an open window, or maybe when the car hit the muddy lake bottom, a door popped open, or the trunk — wherever her last resting place had been.

All conjecture, I had to remind myself. But I had a gut feeling that car would offer some important clues. There was just so much to do. I could hardly wait.

In my excitement I lost track of the speed limits and barreled down the road. I wasn't half a mile from the campground before flashing lights appeared in my rearview mirror. Drat and double drat. I rolled to a stop on the shoulder of the road, grabbed my purse and plucked out my wallet. If Mikey was behind this, he'd get a good tongue-lashing from me. How in the heck was I supposed to file my report if I couldn't motor?

It wasn't Mikey. It was Sherman, and he was on a mission. We hadn't made nice since the last time I flooded his precinct with a toilet plug, and he really didn't find it funny when my friend's ferret took refuge up his pant leg. *Sheesh.* No wonder the guy couldn't use his gun. He was still holding a grudge with both hands.

Sherman exited his police car and crouched down in a sumo wrestler stance.

Good grief, Sherm.

The officer scuttled along toward my car, still in that bent-over shuffle like he was expecting to dodge gunfire. By the time he got alongside my Camaro, I'd dislodged the soggy bacon and had my window down. I screwed on a smile and waited.

"Hello, Sherm. What's the charge?"

Officer Sherman narrowed his eyes. His face was flushed and he had a streak of white excrement on his shoulder. It's hard to see someone as an authority figure when they're covered in goose poo.

"Oh, I think you know why I stopped ya, Mrs. List."

"Could it have been jaywalking? Or perhaps underage drinking. Let me guess. You want to look and see if I have another body in the trunk of my car. I can assure you I checked it before I left and it's clean."

Sherman crouched lower and took a step away from my car. Then he held out his hand. "Driver's license and proof of insurance."

"Oh, Sherm. You don't have to get testy or anything. I'll give you what you want." While Sherman scrutinized my license and insurance card, I caught my face in the car's mirror, again thinking I did look a mess. I reached into my purse to pull out my lipstick, just to touch up, you know.

"Freeze!" Sherman took a quick jump back and slapped at his pant leg where his gun used to be.

That gave me quite a fright, but what could he do with no gun? I held up my lipstick, waved it at Sherman, twisted the top off of the tube, ran the pink gloss over my lips and smacked at Sherman. Kiss, kiss.

"You certainly are tense today, Sherm. I know just what you need. Hang on. I have something for you." I reached again for my purse where I kept a good supply of Mentos. "These always take the edge off for me."

"Freeze! I say, freeze!" Sherman was slapping at his pant leg again, and looked pretty much like a winged chicken.

I rolled my eyes and tossed the Mentos at Sherman. He shrieked, dropped to all fours and scrambled back toward his cruiser.

Leaning far out my window I hollered at Sherm's retreating back pockets. "Does this mean I can go?"

The poor officer dropped my license and insurance card like he'd been scalded, threw himself into his cruiser, and had it roaring to life before I could demand he retrieve my things. He backed out of there with a lot of gravel spray.

I had to chase down my insurance card because it was blowing down the road, but at least I got out of a costly speeding ticket. Taking better care this time, I drove home where I could work up my plan of action in relative solitude.

Not a formal investigation, Mikey had said, but I did have an idea. A great idea! I was going undercover, and I was going to bust this case wide open.

CHAPTER FOUR

I got to my home without any additional problems. After I smooched my dog and got the cold shoulder from Trixie, I opened my address book. I turned to the page with the Northside Country Club listing and put my fingernail on the phone number. Just as I reached for the receiver, my phone rang.

It was probably Mikey, and I hadn't done anything to help the investigation. He'd be so disappointed. I prepared to offer my apologies.

"Mrs. List?"

"I'm so sorry." I turned my back to Trixie who was stalking me now. I spoke quietly. "I'll get that suspect list to you as soon as possible."

"Never mind that right now. I just wanted to let you know I've cleared the way for you to view the autopsy on Moira Finch. You've mentioned before you were interested in this part of police work. You still game?"

Interested? This was police work Big Time. My heart started thudding again. An autopsy! "Of course! Sure! I mean, if you think it's appropriate."

"I wouldn't have suggested it if I didn't think so. You're not family, and you said you weren't particularly close, right?"

"Yes. I mean no. This is very exciting news." I was breathless. Such an important part of crime investigation. I'd already experienced high-speed chases and gun usage, but an autopsy? In spite of my excitement, I suddenly felt like a little girl standing on the end of a high dive board, happy I'd had the courage to take that step, but once I looked over the edge it was an awfully long way down. I wondered, could I hack it? Poor choice of words.

Mikey continued. "I'll log it in as part of your citizen's police training." He must have noticed the silence on the line. I was holding my breath. He gently asked, "You sure you're up to it?"

I let my breath out, hoping I sounded exasperated. I didn't want him to think this gal didn't have the courage to get through a simple ol' autopsy. "What do you mean?" I threw out the challenge.

"You're going to be watching some pretty gruesome things. Body fluids, organ extraction, cutting, snipping, sucking, stuff like that."

"Body fluids? Organ extraction?"

Trixie stared at me.

"Blood, intestines, brain matter."

"Blood? We get to see her brain?"

Trixie extended her claws.

"Naturally."

"Now, Mikey. You know me well enough by now. You've seen me in action and I assure you, cutting up dead bodies won't intimidate me, not one bit. Not in the least." I swallowed hard. A little dribble of bile was working its way up my throat. "I've done my homework and I know what goes on during one of these things. Don't you worry about me." I leaned out over that high dive and wanted to scurry back the way I'd come, on all fours like Sherman if need be, but there was a line of expectant faces behind me screaming, "Jump! Jump!" "Let me set your mind at ease," I said firmly. "I'll be fine."

"Great. Get over here in a hurry then because the coroner's just about ready to do the Y incision and I won't be able to hold him off for too long. You've got about thirty minutes."

On the other end of the line I heard the buzz of a saw. I took a few tentative bounces on the diving board. Trixie drew a bead, lowered her front and wiggled her bottom.

"What should I wear? I'm not sure I have anything appropriate." *Bounce, bounce.*

"Whatever you had on this morning is fine. They'll put a gown over your clothes anyway." Mikey covered the mouthpiece of the phone and I could hear him yelling in a muffled way. "Put that guy over by the sink! And don't forget to bag his hands."

"You've got another body? Another homicide?" Incredible. Two in one day.

"Oh, yeah. Might be nothing more than a few too many pulls on the happy sauce, but there's some suspicious circs involved so we've gotta check it out, just the same. Can't say any more than that. The investigation's ongoing. We're at Spokane General, basement level. Look for the sign that says *Morgue.*"

"Gotcha. I'll get there as soon as I can." *Bounce, BOUNCE.*

Trixie wiggled, wiggled.

"I'll do what I can to stall Dr. Sawbones until you do, but you'd better hurry. He's in a pretty foul mood since he's got two back-to-back cases. Don't think I've ever seen him this worked up."

Again the saw revved like an angry hornet.

"Dr. Sawbones?"

"Don't call him that."

"Just wait for me, Mikey. I'm comin'."

Bounce, hang, plunge.

And Trixie was on the move.

CHAPTER FIVE

I hung up the phone and got a full frontal attack by my demon cat, all claws extended. I tossed her aside like I would an ugly shawl, apologized, and hurried to my task.

After a quick bathroom break, I was on the way to the door with my purse on my arm, my cell phone in my purse, and a big hollow spot in my stomach, so I paused by the stove and swept up the skillet Ted had left sitting there from the morning. It still had the remnants of breakfast. Two slices of bacon, a rubbery fried egg and a slice of toast. No time to pack it neatly into a paper bag, I'd just eat on the fly.

I zoomed down the hill, fishtailing around the switchbacks leading out of Harvest, and after I hit pavement and raced toward Spokane General, I forked breakfast from the skillet I had sitting on my lap. Some days nothing happens at all and I can go for hours puttering around fighting boredom.

Today this was not the case. I had a murder to solve and when things pile up like that, it's easy to get indigestion and a case of nerves. I drove and scooped eggs, bacon and toast into my mouth while keeping an eye on the road. Most of the time.

Harvest isn't big enough to have its own morgue, so Moira's body had been transported to the hospital where Ted works in downtown Spokane. Spokane General, a towering, impressive old building, is in the medical district south of Highway 90, and like everywhere else in Spokane, parking is at a premium. After circling the parking lot three times and getting more and more frazzled, worried that I'd miss the all-important Y incision, I slapped myself on the forehead. What was I thinking? My Camaro, (because it was Ted's until I stole it) has doctor's privileges. I pushed the gas and drove into the underground parking reserved for medical staff. There. Ted might not be happy about that, but I was on official business.

I caught the elevator to the hospital's basement and followed the arrows and signs until I saw Mikey at the end of a long, narrow hall. He waved at me, urging me to hurry up. I guess that meant Dr. Sawbones had lost his patience. That thought struck me funny for some reason and made me think of the old joke, *not much of a doctor if he keeps losing his patients.* The giggly feeling that overtook me was undoubtedly from fear and nerves, but Mike didn't seem to notice my apprehension, so the fake smile of confidence was working.

"Come on in," Mikey said. "Hurry up and get a gown on and put one of these things on, too." Mike held up a face mask, one of those flimsy cotton things. I'd assumed wrongly that I would have a full-face shield made of tempered plastic. I'd seen *Silence of the Lambs* and asked Mikey about some of that cream to put under my nose. The good cop looked puzzled, which surely meant he didn't know a thing about Special Agent Starling. He just held the door open and I went through.

The smell of the morgue rushed up through my nostrils — a mixture of death, chemicals, stainless steel and formaldehyde. I gagged, and then coughed to cover my reflex. I'd left my purse in the car, but quickly felt around in my pocket and found my lip balm. It was the best I could do under the circumstances so I rubbed it back and forth under my nose. Too bad it was the cherry-flavored kind because, though I didn't know it at the time, I later noticed traces where it left a rose-colored skid mark along my upper lip. No one seemed to mind, or if they did they were polite enough not to point it out. The balm helped. A little. I was sorry I'd left my peppermints in my purse. Shove a couple of those up the schnozzle and I'll bet you don't worry much about reek.

The room was brilliantly illuminated, equipped with metal tables, shelves, and equipment of all sorts, and . . . there was Moira. She was nude, positioned on her back on one of the tables with her head resting on a block of some sort. I thought how uncomfortable it must be on that cold table, but Moira wasn't complaining.

A short man with a large mustache and no hair at all on his shiny, pink head glanced up from something he was doing with a metal tube. He grunted a hello. Dr. Sawbones.

Mikey whispered to me. "Another minute and he'd have blown a gasket. Good to see you."

"Thanks for holding him off," I said, trying to smile, but that little trickle of bile was working again, crawling up my throat, and I thought that quick breakfast of cold eggs and undercooked bacon had been a bad idea. Despite the lip balm, the smell was growing stronger and my stomach started to go into hard spasms. The lights grew dim and I thought it would be smart if I moved around a bit just to take my mind off the churning feeling right below my diaphragm.

"You all right, Mrs. List?" Mikey gently touched my shoulder. "Your face is really white." There was concern in his eyes, but I waved him off.

"No worries, Mikey, I'm just fine." I took some deep breaths to regain my composure, which turned out to be a big mistake. Saliva pooled under my tongue and I nearly drowned in my own spit, so I swallowed three or four times and looked for a distraction. "I think I'll just see what's over here while the doctor gets ready." I swished away in my paper gown and worked the mask over my mouth and nose. I looped elastic bands over my ears. At least if I were starting to look green around the gills it was covered.

"Hey, Mike!" A uniformed officer burst through the morgue doors and hurried over to Officer Murphy.

Mikey turned. "Hey, Paul."

Paul's interruption elicited a low, unintelligible grumble from Sawbones. The doc scowled as he snapped blue rubber gloves over his stout fingers.

Paul was flushed. He bent his head toward the stiff under a sheet at the far end of the room. "Did you get a look at the guy in the corner? It's Skinny Carl! Can you believe that? I never thought his body would turn up. To tell you the truth, I figured he'd be out floating around Puget Sound or locked in a fish barrel on his way to Hong Kong. What a stroke of luck, huh?"

"Hey there, Paul." I waved a limp hand. Paul was one of the Harvest police officers and Mikey's partner when I wasn't on a ride-along. He was a few years older than Mike, which put him in the mid-thirties range. He was a little more high-strung, but equally competent and good-looking too, in a dark, frantic sort of way.

"Hey, Mrs. List. Good to see you." Paul acknowledged me, but he was in a hurry to discuss the body spread out under the sheet. "They started Carl's autopsy right after he came in but I had to hold 'em up on account we got a tip."

"Yeah. I was here when they wheeled him in. I wondered what the holdup was. Now I know why the doc is in such a bad mood. Your fault."

Paul snorted. "You don't have to give him a reason to be grouchy. I suggest you just stay out of his way when he stabs that scalpel thing through your vic's chest."

My curiosity was moderately aroused with talk of the other body, some guy named Skinny Carl, but at the mention of a knife going through Moira's wrinkled old bosom, the trickle of bile began to rise freely. I glanced around nervously for a trash can and wished like anything I'd thought to bring along my spacious purse. I swallowed, swallowed, breathed, swooned, sweated, and got more than a little dizzy.

"Hey, Mrs. List. You a'right?" Paul turned his attention away from Mikey, and now both of the guys were eyeing me with honest concern.

I mumbled behind my mask. "Fine, I'm fine, Paul. No problem."

"Can't stand around all day!" The doctor held up some instruments and walked briskly over and took a stiff-legged stance beside Moira's body. "Are you gonna get over here or what?" He slapped down a full-coverage face shield. At least *he* got one.

Mikey held up one finger as if to say "wait," and nudged Paul close to Carl's gurney. Like an obedient puppy I followed, mostly because I wanted to get away from Moira until I could get that stomach problem under control. I huffed and puffed and massaged my stomach, which only made matters worse. Some new smells were breaching the lip balm wall of protection.

Paul was excitedly explaining some things to Officer Murphy. "We got a call right after the doc took out Skinny Carl's organs."

Organs? My stomach convulsed.

Mikey took a peek under Carl's sheet at what I knew would be an irreverently disassembled torso. "I've never heard of the doc stopping an autopsy for nothin'," he said. He tilted his head while looking at the body. "That's Skinny Carl all right. I thought he looked familiar."

I turned away to concentrate on something else, anything but the naked body of Moira and the chopped-up body of Carl. There was a long counter along one wall where little pans were arranged containing what looked like organs and body parts. Red, runny stuff was in a large industrial-sized sink. My cheeks began to puff out and I gulped very hard, fighting the urge with all of my might.

"He had to stop the autopsy," Paul was saying, "because we got an informant spilling her guts on the phone. She told us everything. We got it on tape if you want to listen . . ."

Guts. More about guts. Why did everyone

have to mention guts? Oh, dear, my stomach contracted into a rigid little ball. Saliva gushed into my mouth.

"I will now make the first incision!" The doctor lifted his arms in the air.

My thigh muscles turned to warm pudding.

Mikey was irritated. "One minute — please!"

Paul continued in a rush. "*She* said Skinny Carl had been kidnapped by a local terrorist group out of Idaho. They kept him in a box underground for four days without food or water. They kept him sedated by dosing him with small amounts of horse tranquilizer and some other potentially lethal drugs. The informant said they were the ones who'd put out a ransom demand to the family after the family posted a missing-person report complete with a reward offer, but when they got the money and went to pull Carl up out of the box he was dead. So they dumped him in an alley, which is where we found him."

"Good work, Paul. This is great. Great! We can put this case to bed at last. Just a shame it turned out the way it did."

"Yeah, it's been a tough one. Thought I'd never know what happened to him. The girl's promised to testify and name names.

She'll get the reward money and we should have some bad guys behind bars by tonight."

"So why'd you have to stop the autopsy? Seems pretty clear-cut."

Oh, there he went again. Guts and cuts. Uhhhh. I started seeing double.

"We stopped it as soon as the woman placed the call. We wanted to get his fluids tested for the drugs. You really need to know what you're looking for if you don't want to miss anything, and we need an airtight case on this one. We couldn't afford to screw this up. Some of this stuff they were using doesn't show up in normal tox screenings. She said it was what they use to sedate patients during surgery. That's probably what killed him if they doped him up good enough."

"I've heard of that," Mikey said. "You can go a long time without food, but that stuff is lethal."

Drugs and guts and cuts and murder. I tried really hard to take it in professionally while sweat rolled down the sides of my face in rivers. *No problem, Mikey! No problem!*

Mikey looked to the ceiling in concentration. "If he was drugged with that stuff, it means we've got at least one perp with access to it, and whoever sent the ransom demand probably never intended to let him

67

go. We might be looking at a hospital worker, a pharmacist. Someone who knows someone who can get the drug. Don't forget to follow up on that." Mike put his hand on Paul's shoulder. "Good work, partner. One step closer to putting this one to bed."

Mike nodded affectionately at Paul, and I could see he was proud, but that wasn't the most pressing thing on my mind right then because I had reached maximum tolerance. I clenched my teeth so hard that my jaws locked. One more second and I'd be squeezing cheese through my molars.

"That's it. Time's up. We're goin' in!" The doctor, his patience finally exsanguinated, began the Y cut, plunging his scalpel through Moira's flesh just below her collar bone. I heard a thud followed by a slushy, juicy sound. We weren't close enough to get a really good view of the procedure, so Mikey loped across the room to look over the doctor's hunched shoulder. He fell into deep concentration and motioned me over without looking up. Paul headed for the door and was met there by a young-looking professional dressed in a white lab coat. They greeted each other and became involved in a brief, animated conversation. I couldn't make out the words because my ears were ringing. To add to my discomfort,

I had oceans of sweat soaking my under-wires, my underarms, and my underwear.

"Come on, Mrs. List, you're missing it!" Mikey glanced back at me and then back to Moira's body. The doctor was good at his job. He cut, split, snipped, cracked, and pulled out things along with a whole lot of splashing, sucking wet noises.

That did it.

No, that almost did it. What finally caused my chunks to fly was what I did next. While frantically looking around for something to throw up into I staggered over toward Skinny Carl who was just a couple of steps away, stumbled, and put out my hand to steady myself. I clutched his sheet in a moment of dizziness and pulsing nausea, fell forward, grabbed another handful of the sheet and pulled it off of Carl's face. The man was gray, his eyes slightly open, his tongue hung out and lolled off to one side, stuck dryly to his cheek.

That did it. My stomach launched my breakfast forcefully into my mouth. Thankfully, Mikey and the doc were busy, Paul was looking the other way, and it only took three steps to get to the counter. I pushed up the little mask, opened my mouth and . . . plop. Everything fell out into a little bowl on the shelf. There was some stuff in the container already and it mixed together with a soupy, wet splash.

Slap. The mask went down over my mouth and nose. I swallowed again and felt much better.

"Come on, Mrs. List!" Mikey gestured wildly. I moved on unsteady legs over to him.

"This is the good part," Mikey said.

Sawbones had extracted a large square of chest bones and ribs and they were set off to one side of Moira. My stomach lurched and lurched, but I'd left my eggs and bacon back on the counter so I let my gut muscles spasm away.

"See? He's opened up her chest and removed the organs. He'll take each one, weigh it, examine the stomach contents, send samples of blood to tox, check for levels of alcohol, look for any foreign substances like drugs or medications, that sort of thing."

The doctor was in his element. For the first time he wasn't frowning — far from it. There was an unmistakable expression of delight in his eyes. Couldn't see his mouth behind the mask thingy because of splatter, but I was sure he was grinning — big, yellow teeth. Probably had a couple of sharp canines in there the way he was enjoying himself.

"Now," the doctor said, "what we need to do next is peel away her face. To accomplish this, I'll start by cutting a long incision over the top of her scalp . . ." He explained everything in a pleasant way, even hummed as he worked, but my ears started up that ringing sound again and all I heard was *wha, wha, wha, wha, wha.* I continued to sweat from every pore in my body, and I was seeing double. My upper lip went rigid and then it lost all feeling completely. The doc was having the time of his life. Body fluids and bits of bone and sinew covered his rubber gloves.

As the room swayed and dipped around me I heard a loud expletive coming from the back of the room near Skinny Carl where Paul and the young attendant were standing. "What the — !" Paul shouted. "That's not right. That can't be right. Check it again." The attendant started to say something, but Paul cut him off. "Check it again!"

The attendant glowered but obeyed Paul, who was now cursing a blue streak.

While the room yawed and my legs buckled (I felt strangely like I was on Mr. Pendersnack's rowboat), the argument between Paul and the attendant got heated. I swiveled my bobbing head around like a drunken sailor and tried to focus on the guys. They were standing in doubles. Two Pauls, two technicians, and the doc continued to cut and peel, and Mike, apparently accustomed to Paul's outbursts, didn't flinch. He was busily handing Sawbones instruments like a seasoned OR nurse.

"That's not possible," Paul said. He shook his head. "What did you find in his stomach contents? Bacon?" More cursing.

The attendant nodded. "And eggs. And toast," he said. "Undigested, and he must have been in a hurry when he ate his last meal because they were hardly even chewed. Guess that blows your buried-in-a-box theory. Sorry, sir."

"Skinny Carl ate bacon before he died?"

Mikey perked up at this. He paused while Sawbones had his hand outstretched, then called back to the other officer, "Shucks, Paul, I thought you had something there. Too bad. Better discount your caller and make sure she doesn't get her hands on that reward money — she's a kook."

I should have fessed up and told Paul and Mike the stomach contents in Skinny Carl's basin were mine, not his, but I didn't get the chance. Because when the doc started peeling back Moira's face, I went out like a forty-cent flashlight.

CHAPTER SIX

I woke up on the floor of the morgue staring at the underside of Moira's stainless-steel slab. What a treat.

Mikey peered down nervously while there was still quite a bit of activity going on above me. "Gee, Mrs. List, you must have the thickest skull in the world. Didn't bust it or nothin'."

"Thanks loads," I said, massaging a sizeable lump on the back of my head.

"She coming around?" Old Sawbones bellowed.

All I could see of the doc was a gown from the knees down, pant cuffs and cloggy black boots covered in yellow paper booties. I dodged just as one of his bootie-covered heels nearly took off my left ear. He must have problems with his own ears the way he shouted everything. His mood sounded greatly improved, and I'm sure it was because he'd had the pleasure of seeing me flop. I hadn't known him for more than a couple of minutes, but there was no question: he was one of those guys who took great joy in his job, going bravely where no other human could stand to go while those around him dipped and dove and puked up their eggs.

Oh, dear. Thinking of eggs, I decided it was time for me to come clean, and — aside from wanting a toothbrush in a really bad way — I'm talking about fessing up about Skinny Carl and his mistaken stomach contents.

"Mikey?" I called weakly from under the table. "There's something you should know." I didn't want to try standing just yet, and besides, the guys had made me quite comfortable on the floor. I had a paper gown balled up under my head, and my feet were propped up on a phone book.

Mike's head appeared below the table and he looked at me. "We're almost finished here. Just got to get the shaft out. Someone already came in and took X-rays with a portable machine and I'm really sorry you missed it. Why don't you just hold on and I'll help you up. Do you want a Coke or something?"

"Wrench!" Sawbones hollered.

Mikey popped to attention. He disappeared from my view except for his feet which shuffled off and then came back again.

Wrench?

The doctor barked instruction. "Now you just put a little pressure here, son, and I'll give a tug, and . . . yes. Ah. There she is."

I heard some juicy, sticky, liquid sounds followed by a metallic *clang!* when something fell into a pan. Must have been the golf club. My imagination is good, and the idea of what was going on over my face made me want to slip back into my happy place. Some detective I'd turned out to be.

"Now, you see here? It cut right through the carotid artery and severed the trachea. A couple things could have happened. The projectile could have done enough damage to her windpipe and asphyxiation would follow in that case, but see here? There's tearing around the entry and exit wounds. Scavengers didn't make these. These are purposeful rips in her dermis. Someone jerked up and down on this thing while it was in her neck, probably so she'd bleed. Otherwise, the projectile would possibly have staunched the blood flow like a finger in a dike, so to speak. In any case, this is a fatal wound. Even without the bleeding there would have been an obstruction to blood flow leading to her brain, but it does appear that she bled out. It wouldn't have taken long, no time at all. Everything else seems to be in order; in fact she was quite healthy for a woman her age. Still, whoever did this would have gotten buckets of blood everywhere. Cut an artery, and it's like shaking up a warm can of beer and then stabbing it with an ice pick. Except it's not one long spurt. It pulses. With every beat of the heart, it shoots out. The blood can really travel. Until the victim dies, of course."

"Of course." Mikey was taking it all in.

I was holding it all back. But with nothing left in my stomach, I just did a dry heave and left it at that.

"Buckets of blood," Mikey said wistfully. "Should make my job easier when it comes to figuring out where she was killed, at any rate. You can't completely mop up a crime scene like that. We'll check the drain trap in her home, the laundry, spray a little luminal around on her floors and wall . . ."

"And don't forget the ceilings. A real gusher," the doc was quick to add.

"But the point could be moot if she got stabbed while in the lake." Mikey paused to think. "And there's no possibility she was impaled after she was already dead?"

"I didn't find any other fatal wounds. Her

77

heart looks in good shape, no brain abnormalities, no water in the lungs. Nope, this did the trick. Unless something strange comes back from toxicology, you've got your murder weapon."

I heard more clanging and the swish of a sheet.

"All done?" I asked hopefully.

"We're finished here." *Snap!* Rubber gloves coming off. "I'll send this stuff off to the lab and you'll have my written report by tomorrow," the doc said. *Click.* Sounded like a button on a tape recorder. I'd notice that earlier and wondered if they had video cameras too, recording the event. The doctor's lounge would be having a hay old time watching May Bell's bloopers by evening. Very funny. Yikes. If there had been video, then surely someone would catch me upchucking in Skinny Carl's emesis basin. Not good. Better warn Mikey.

I wormed my way out from under Moira and stood, trembling like a newborn fawn. "Officer Murphy?"

"Mrs. List! You should have waited for me to help you up. Wouldn't want you conking your head again. You're still looking a little unsteady. Want some water or a sniff of this?" Mikey snapped an ammonia capsule and waved it under my nose. I jerked my head back and reflexively swatted it out of his hand.

"No. But thanks. Listen, Mikey, there's something I have to tell you."

Sawbones wheeled Moira away to her drawer, and I took the opportunity to pull Murphy aside so I could spill my guts. Figuratively.

"Earlier, before I passed out, I wasn't feeling too good. I was a bit nauseated."

"Nooo." Murphy gave me one of his "you don't say" looks.

"I need you to be serious for just one second, okay? When I smelled all that stuff and saw the bodies and Skinny Carl's tongue stuck to his cheek and everything, I thought I could handle it but . . ."

The morgue door flew open and Paul rushed in, moving like his hair was on fire. "Mike. You're never gonna believe this. We checked out the informant. You know: the one who told us what happened to Skinny Carl. And guess what?"

"What?" Mike was calm.

I was silently screaming. *I did it! I confess. I confess!*

"She was lying after all. It took a little creative counseling, but she finally cracked after we said she'd be an accessory to Carl's murder if she didn't tell us everything, and

79

she said she didn't know anything about any terrorists. In fact, she just moved here from Hawaii and needed a little extra cash. She'd heard about the reward money and thought she could play us."

"So," Mikey said, "we're back to square one."

Paul's face fell. "Oh, yeah."

"Wait a minute," I said. I could feel a hot flush working its way up my neck. *Think fast, May, and you might just save your bacon.* "If that's true then how did she know about the ransom note?" I asked.

"Good point, Mrs. List. Paul, have you gotten the toxicology reports back yet?"

"Nope. And my bet is that we aren't going to find any of those things she told us about now, but we still have a discrepancy when it comes to TOD. I just can't figure it out. Coroner puts the time of death around ten o'clock last night. But the undigested bacon and eggs? Who eats bacon and eggs at nine o'clock at night?"

"Lots of people do!" I shouted out. "Sure! When I get hungry, and I'm up looking for a snack, bacon and eggs, toast, grits. It's all good."

Paul gave me a glance and I was thankful for the thigh-covering material of the gown because I was reading his thoughts, like,

*May, you might want to cut out those late-night
snacks if you know what's good for your waist-
line.*

"Hey," I said to Mikey, tapping a finger
lightly on his arm. "Does the doctor usually
tape his autopsies?"

"Yeah, sure."

My heart fell.

"I prefer the written reports, though.
Sometimes it's hard to understand what
he's saying over all of the noise."

"Yes. Of course." My mood brightened.
"And he only uses audio, and not video?"

"He only takes video if he's doing some
kind of training film. It's not really necessary otherwise."

Whew.

"Hey! Hey!" Paul was feeling ignored.
"We've got a real problem here, Mike.
Skinny Carl's been into some bad stuff, and
I figured this was a hit after his parents
reported him missing. It would have been
sweet if it had been a hit, because I'm thinking we could maybe get a twofer but — get
this. His girlfriend just called. She doesn't
get along with Carl's parents and didn't
bother to let them know where he was, but
after she heard Carl's body showed up in
the morgue, she says she's been nursing him
for the past couple of days. Bad case of the

81

flu." Paul shouted out toward Sawbones, "Can you get me cause of death on that DB over there ASAP?"

It was like Paul to talk in acronyms. Most of them I could figure, but other cop-speak I was learning as I went.

"A twofer?" I whispered to Mike.

"Bad guy gets whacked, he's out of our hair, and second guy goes down for the crime. We've got two bad boys off the streets without even trying."

"Except you gotta catch the killer, and that's got to take some work."

"All in good time."

"No whacky here," Paul said. "At least not in the traditional sense. Now this is really weird. The girlfriend says Carl decided to drive himself to the emergency room. Left her house last night and he ends up in the alley. He's got a bullet in his chest, but the doc says that's postmortem, not what killed him. And there are no other injuries."

"Did you find a gun?"

"Girlfriend is bringing it in. Says one of her ex-boyfriends brought it by her house after confessing he whacked Carl."

"Oh, how sweet. He's trying to impress her?" Mike asked. "Why would he give her the gun?"

"It's her gun. They used to live together,

82

and he ended up with it when she moved out in a hurry."

"Man. All right. We can check that out easy enough. You'd better hold on to the girlfriend. She has some explaining to do."

"I'm on it." Paul raced away.

Mikey looked at me. "You probably want to go home and take a nap. You've had quite a morning."

I glanced at the clock on the wall. It wasn't even noon yet. "Oh, no, officer. I have a report to finish. But I have to admit I haven't had this much fun since the last time you found a body rolling around in the trunk of my Camaro."

"The last time?"

"The only time." I peeled off the paper gown, removed the mask that was hanging off of one ear and threw them in the trash. Before I left the morgue I told Mikey that when I got to my car I'd take a look in the trunk just in case.

CHAPTER SEVEN

Rarely do I intrude on my husband while he's at work. Almost never, as a matter of fact, but I was just a few floors below the maternity ward where he spent more time than at home, and right across the street was his clinic. I couldn't remember him mentioning any pending deliveries, C-sections, inductions, or plain-ol' push-and-catches, so he must be over at the clinic seeing women for various medical reasons. It would be a nice surprise if I dropped in.

I checked the lobby for his name, felt a little proud when I saw him listed with the other doctors — a hematologist named James R. Flyseed, an osteopath named Greg S. Needles, a gastroenterologist named Craig N. Winny, and a proctologist named B.G. Pucker. Oops, I'd read that wrong. It was Plunker. Must have been the power of suggestion.

Ted's office is on the fourth floor. My, my,

my. I'd been married to Ted for so many years and it still made me proud to introduce him as *Doctor* List, and although for a time it was enough to feel proud of being *Mrs.* Doctor List, I realized almost too late that it was important for me to find my own entertainment. That's why I had just finished puking my guts out for forensics. What a thrill.

But . . . I was becoming my own person, whatever the heck that means. It was just something I've heard a lot about and I'm beginning to understand. Gone was the wallflower, the prim and proper trophy wife. (We weren't called that back in the day, but I fit the bill just the same and the memories are good ones. Sigh.) Every stretch mark and wrinkle, every liver spot and gray hair I sport as a badge of honor because they were a testament to hard work and motherhood. I'd earned every last one. But then . . . there was this cosmetic surgeon on the board . . .

Never mind. I punched the elevator button to the floor of Ted's office. His waiting area was bustling. Lots of women with swollen bellies, one with an infant carrier by her feet, and a few who looked like they wouldn't need any cosmetic attention for several years. Then I remembered why I didn't often go see my husband at work. I assured myself he was a strict professional, but I didn't need to watch his work to know he was intimately familiar with these ladies and it made me just a little bit uneasy. And, yes, in an odd, ridiculous sort of way, jealous. There was one woman, early twenties if I had to guess, a bombshell: high heels, long blonde hair, full lips, full everything where it needed to be full, and here I stood in gray sweats, reeking of embalming fluid and DB.

I hurried up to the receptionist's desk and waited patiently for the girl on the other side to slide a little glass window, opening the area for conversation. I didn't recognize the young woman and that meant she didn't know me. That was good. I thought quickly, searching for a way to get into Ted's office without giving my last name.

"Yes, ma'am? How may I help you?" The young lady was probably a temp. She was way too happy to be an entrenched member of the working class. Perhaps a college student earning money during spring break.

"Um, yes Miss . . ."

The girl stared down at her lapel and tapped an index finger against a plastic nametag that hung crookedly. I cocked my head and read, "Hannah."

I bent over, placed my elbows on the counter, laced my fingers under my chin and looked left and right. I spoke very quietly. "I don't have an appointment. But I do need to see Dr. List about a very important matter. I'm fairly sure it's an emergency."

"Oh." One of Hannah's neatly plucked eyebrows arched. "What is the nature of your emergency?"

"Shhhh." Again I looked around as if I had something going on that required the utmost confidentiality. "I'm pretty sure I'm pregnant."

"Excuse me?" Both eyebrows reached for her hairline.

"Pretty sure. I need to see the doctor immediately to confirm or deny."

Hannah coughed into her hand, shuffled some papers and then regained her composure. "Well, ma'am, what makes you think you might be?" She couldn't even bring herself to say it. Pregnant.

"I'm late."

"Um. Okay. How late?"

"About fifteen years."

Hannah got busy rearranging pens, peeling sticky notes, and glanced repeatedly at the phone as if she were hoping it would ring and rescue her from dealing with this nut in front of her.

For Pete's sake. Just let me see my husband already!

"Dr. List is with a patient at the moment but his next appointment didn't show. I'll see what I can do. May I have your name please?"

"I'd rather not."

"Beg pardon?" the girl asked.

"I'd rather not give my name. I'm a member of the First Baptist Church choir."

The girl made a circle with her mouth that looked like she wanted to say, "So?"

"I'm not married."

"Uh-huh." Hannah looked around, searching for reinforcements, or security, or an escape hatch.

"And I'm a virgin."

"All righty then." Hannah smiled, waiting for the punch line.

"I don't even watch R-rated movies."

"That's . . . very commendable. Okay. Fine. Why don't you . . ." — Hannah pointed to the waiting room — ". . . have a seat and we'll see what we can do."

I pushed myself away from the counter and watched Hannah rearrange more office supplies.

"You can have a seat, really," she said. The phone rang and she practically jumped on it. I moved over to the magazine rack and

88

stared at the movie stars.

"May?"

I whirled around. Ted was escorting a very large woman to the receptionist's window. He held up a "wait" finger to me and said a few words to the lady, probably making arrangements for the upcoming event. Hannah waved her hands around, trying to get Ted's attention. She was pointing at me and actually bounced up and down in her chair.

I didn't wait. As soon as Ted's back was turned, I hurried down the hall and entered his office. This was where he did his report writing and research; his exam rooms were separate. Ted was quick on my heels. He hurried over, grabbed me up in a big hug. "Is everything okay?" He suddenly stepped back and held me at arm's length. "May. You smell like corpse."

"Good to see you, too."

"Sorry. But there is this pungent . . ." He moved the air around him with a cupped hand.

"I know, Ted. I apologize for stopping by unannounced like this, but I had to tell you. I just came from an autopsy, and you'll never guess who was on the slab."

"You attended an autopsy? Good for you. Good, good. Officer Murphy still has you keeping up with your police training, does he?" Ted walked around his desk and took a seat. I plopped down on the leather couch across from him. I looked down and noticed I still had little booties over my shoes. I worked them off just using my feet.

"I know you think this is a waste of time, but you will never in a million years guess who was out floating in Moody Lake this morning."

"You're twittering, May."

"Perhaps." It's true, I was smiling really big.

"And I think you got a little something . . ." Ted pointed to his front teeth and sucked with the tip of his tongue.

"Her name was Moira Finch. She was the DB!" I rubbed a forefinger over my front teeth.

"I'm just guessing here," Ted said, tossing me gum. "But it wasn't a simple drowning. She was murdered, wasn't she?"

"No question." I popped the gum in my mouth and swished it around. Minty fresh.

"And you think you can figure out who killed her."

"I have to do a few things, but, yeah, I'm on the case."

Ted looked dismayed.

"That name doesn't mean anything to you?"

"Should it?"

"She's one of the ladies from the North-side Country Club. And, Ted, at that last benefit I went to, I heard quite a few people gossiping about her and how she'd really teed some people off."

"Was that supposed to be a golf joke?"

"Hm. I guess it was." More smiling.

"Okay, babe, you do what you gotta do. Drive on."

"Good try."

"I'll just stay here and putter."

"Not any better."

"It was a long shot."

"I'm going now."

CHAPTER EIGHT

I didn't know much about Moira. She was a widow; I did know that because there was a plaque dedicated to the memory of Mr. Colin Finch on the pro-shop wall. He'd been a charter member of the Northside Country Club, and that meant Moira had been a member by default for at least forty years, since the eighteen-hole course was established on Spokane's hilly northwest side.

The sprawling course was beautifully landscaped with hundreds of towering pines, spruce, willows, and immaculate, multicolored flower beds. Water features bestowed a sense of serenity, and the grounds were spotless and groomed to immaculate perfection. Everything a golfer wanted — and what members of such an exclusive club paid for. I needed to learn more about Moira, but if the killer were a member, namely one of her golf partners, which seemed the most likely, I'd alert the perp by asking too many questions. No. I needed to get inside. *Undercover.*

Back at my house I cleaned up, changed into a wispy skirt and blouse and tied a scarf around my poodle fro-do. (Note to self: no more home-perms.) Then, I steered my Camaro toward the country club. Instead of pulling into the members' parking lot in front of the club, though, I turned down a narrow road, went through an open gate and stopped near the club's maintenance shop where the grounds crew stored their tools and machines. Club golf carts were parked here and there, but the shop looked empty of workers. Large sliding doors were up, and as I wandered through the neatly appointed shop, a gruff-looking man drove up on a huge machine. He wore blue mirrored sunglasses and a sneer.

"You look lost," he mumbled.

"No, actually, I'm looking for work."

The man peered over the top of his blue sunglasses. "Can you operate a rough mower?"

I shook my head.

"Work an edger?"

No.

"An aerator? A blower? A gosh-darn weed whacker?"

93

Again, no.

"Hmph. What good are ya?" Blue stalked off.

"But, sir." I ran after him, my purse swinging on my arm. "I was thinking more in the lines of gardening. I know a thing or two about flowers."

Blue shoved a dollar in the Coke machine and out popped a Coke. "What are you asking me for? I'm not the boss." The man grabbed his drink, jumped on his mow machine and took off without a backward glance.

I yelled after him, "Who's the boss, then?"

"That would be me."

A tall, tanned, good-looking man walked from the office area of the shop and held out his hand. Charming. He was clean and dressed in pro-shop garb. Immediately I could tell he was a winner with the club members. He took my hand with both of his, putting me at ease. "What can I do for you, Mrs. List?"

Drat. I should have known he'd recognize me. Part of his job was schmoozing with the members. He was the eyes and ears of the club — keeping the grounds to the members' liking, making adjustments, putting out fires, making everybody happy. Not an easy job.

"Mr. Gullikson." I was so proud to remember his name, but for the life of me I have no idea how I did it. Sometimes wires connect at the right time and in the right way. "Can I talk with you about something? Behind closed doors?" I asked.

"Call me Jeff, please. My office is right this way."

I followed him down a white hall, past a lunchroom, through an outer office and into his inner sanctum. It was a small tidy office. My eyes darted around picking up clues so I could learn something about this man. On his desk sat a worn Bible, on his wall a framed copy of the Lord's Prayer, and there were a couple of church bulletins lying atop the trash in his gray metal wastebasket. A virtuous man. He would be sympathetic to a woman on the outs. He closed the door to his office and after briefly touching me on the elbow, he walked around to the other side of his desk, waiting to hear what I had to say. Before he could sit, though, I let out the wildest, loudest banshee scream I could muster. Mr. Gullikson whirled around and put up both of his hands, stepped back and sat down on his keyboard. His monitor scrolled fast letters spelling ffjdklshgagjgjksldkldkka;;.

"Oh, Mr. Gullikson!" I blubbered. "I

don't know how to thank you for this opportunity." I squeezed out tears and made my face go really red.

Jeff bounced up off his keyboard, and his computer settled down, but I don't think I've ever seen a look quite like the one on his face. He gauged the distance to the office door; no doubt calculating how fast he could get over the top of his desk and past me, but I didn't give him the chance.

I tipped my head back, waved it back and forth, and squealed in mortal anguish. "It's my husband. Oh, my sweet, sweet heavenly days. Lord, help him!"

"Did something happen to him?" Jeff grabbed a handful of tissues and held them out to me. I took the wad and blew my nose loudly into them and then tucked them into my bra.

"Did something happen to him? Well. I should say so! He's a sinner, is what he is. A dirty no-good, backsliding sinner. And God forgive my impertinence, but he's squandered all our money, is what he did, and we're in some serious financial straits. Don't ask me what he spent his money on because . . ." I worked up some really fine hitching sobs, but it was hard to bring forth more tears until I pinched myself under the arms while pretending I was giving myself a comforting hug. "Oh, I don't even want to think about it. Women? Gambling? Binge-ing? Blogging? Who knows?"

Jeff clucked his tongue. "Um-hm. These things happen. I never would have thought Dr. List, though."

"Heck, yes, Dr. List. The father to my dear sweet Patty who, with her husband Jack, is doing the Lord's work in Belize. Missionary work, mind you. *That* Dr. List. And may the Lord have mercy on his soul!" I didn't have to lie about my daughter; she *was* doing im-munization work with her husband in Bel-ize. As for my dear Ted, I'd have to do atonement later. He'd understand — it was for a good cause.

"Oh, Mr. Gullikson, I have to find work and fast." I hurried over to him and grabbed fistfuls of his maroon shirt. "I'm desperate, Mr. Gullikson, just desperate!"

Jeff put his hands over mine and gently pushed them away. There were two clench wrinkles on his chest. He held my hands and escorted me back to my side of the desk. "Please have a seat and we'll talk about this, okay?"

"I can't have a seat. Just can't!" I paced back and forth. "It's so humiliating." I whirled around and pointed a finger at him. "You won't tell anyone, will you?"

97

Jeff shook his head vigorously. "No, no, ma'am, but how can I help you?"

I slapped my hands together. "You can give me a job."

"Uh."

"Yes. You can give me a job. Nothing permanent, you understand, just something to hold us over until we can get this financial thing sorted out. I know there's been some trouble here lately with one of your members getting murdered and all, and some of your help might need time off for bereavement."

Jeff paled. "Someone was murdered?"

Oh, drat. He wouldn't have known that yet, of course. Stupid, stupid me. "I — I heard it on the news this morning."

"Oh, my. I had no idea. I get here at five, so I miss the morning news. Still, I don't know why I wasn't notified by our manager, but I suppose he'll be calling me soon enough. At any rate that is bad news."

"Five in the morning?"

"That's when the crew starts work."

I did the math in my head. Five o'clock. Thirty minutes to shower and dress, a twenty-minute drive, give or take, and . . . criminy. Reveille at four A.M. There had to be a better way. But it was too late. The die was cast.

Mr. Gullikson had calmed quite a bit and resumed the posture of a kind peacemaker. He clasped his hands near his face, all but for his two forefingers. With these, he tapped his pursed lips and spent a few minutes thinking. Then, making his decision, he said, "I think we can find you something, Mrs. List. Please don't worry."

I had to do it. Again, the banshee screams, this time of feigned joy, with the whole head-waving thing, and I got to him before he could post any more bum notes on his computer. I grabbed his shirt with clenching fists and squeezed and twisted the fabric, banged my forehead against his chest (which hurt a little after the bathroom incident), and popped out some more tears, all of which dribbled onto his formerly pressed shirt. "Thank you, Mr. Gully . . . gully . . . gully . . ." And there it went. The wires that had earlier connected in my brain short-circuited and I lost his name.

". . . son."

"Yes, father?"

"Gullikson."

"Oh, yes. I just thought . . . I mean. Yes. Oh, dear. Look at what I've done to your shirt!" I wiped my hands over his chest, trying to make things better.

"It's okay. That's not necessary." Jeff

leaned back as far as his spine would allow and would have escaped, but he was cornered.

"No. I should fix this." From my purse I pulled a lint roller and ran it up and down the front of his shirt. "Don't you worry." I did quick little up-and-down rolls on the places where the wrinkles were most evident, followed by long rolls from his collar to his waist. Long, short, short. Long, short, short, short. "Now, turn around." I made twirling motions with my forefinger.

"Honestly, I'm fine!" Jeff took me by the shoulders, spun me away in an oddly gentle manner, and got to the door in a jiffy. "Why don't I give you a tour of the, uh . . . grounds?" He sprinted to the garage. I ran after him as quickly as my heels would carry me, slipped on the concrete floor and snapped one of my heels right off. Luckily I was wearing simple pumps so I was able to grab the other shoe without messing with straps or buckles. I smacked it on the side of the Coke machine as I ran past. By the time Jeff had the golf cart running, I matched.

"Ready?" Jeff handed me a white hard hat. "You'll need to wear one of these. Hop in."

And we were off.

CHAPTER NINE

Moira's body had been pulled from her watery grave that morning, and within hours I was sitting inside a golf cart wearing the kind of ridiculous hat that would only look suitable on a sweaty construction worker in a stained wife-beater T-shirt.

May Bell, what in the heck are you thinking? I could hear Ted already, and my usual "It's for the mission" wouldn't work this time, especially after he showed up at the club for his game on Friday. Mr. Gullikson, while I'm sure he would show discretion, would never again be able to look my husband in the eye. I just hoped he didn't call Ted in for a golf-buddy intervention.

"So, Gully." (It felt good to use my own nickname for Jeff; made me feel like part of the team already — and it would be a good cover, just in case I forgot his full name again.) "What do you have in mind? For work, I mean."

"Do you have a preference? Any special skills?" Jeff steered the golf cart along a gravel road. We were heading down the back way toward the course, and in the distance I could see the driving range. A skinny elderly man in plaid pants bent over, wiggled his hips and raised his arms in the air. He came around with a fast approach. The head of the golf club struck dirt and a huge clod flew through the air. The man shielded his eyes from the sun and stared down the range. The little white ball remained at his feet. When he looked down and noticed his failed drive he shouted, cursed a blue streak, jumped up and down and threw the club end over end. He turned, hopped into his cart and spun a U-turn back toward the clubhouse.

"Special skills?"

"I need to know where to place you," Jeff mentioned, as he continued along the road. The driving range was in full swing and golf balls whizzed past my head. I ducked and dodged and pulled my head down even with my shoulders like an anxious turtle, but Gully didn't flinch even when one of the balls put a dent in the golf cart. We passed the driving range and came out onto a paved cart path. Gully pressed the pedal and we gathered speed. As the wind picked up, so did my skirt. I squeezed it between my thighs and wished I had a seat belt or something to keep me in place, because the only security I had was this little metal rail pressing against my lower right hip. The vehicle, as I saw it, was nothing more than a short couch on wheels.

Skills. Skills. I'd been a mother and wife before becoming a detective (okay, Ted, *in my own mind*), so aside from an education in television forensics, a recent shot at writing a novel, and baking the best manicotti on this side of the Mississippi, there wasn't much on the old résumé. "Gardening," I said. "I've always been an avid gardener." Lie, lie, lie. I couldn't tell an azalea from a zinnea, but Jeff didn't know that.

"Then I'll put you on the landscaping team. You'll like the ladies you'll be working with — two cousins but they look like twins. I can't ever keep 'em apart." Jeff scooted between cars, weaving this way and that, explaining that we were passing through the club's parking lot. I knew that, but I kept my mouth shut. "They're grandmotherly types like yourself."

So now I'm a grandmotherly type. Shoulda seen me dragging the sheet off of Skinny Carl this morning, my good boy — shoulda seen it. But it was good to know

I'd be working with some gals who were domestic. Nothing too strenuous, because I wasn't in terrific shape and had never been an athlete, but I could manage plucking weeds and deadheading a few marigolds. It would be healthy to spend some time outdoors. And by the looks of the golf course, it would put me right in there with everyone else. I could weed and observe and chat it up with the members.

Then I had a moment of panic. There were two Harvest police cars in the parking lot. Officer Buns-o'-steel Murphy was standing by his car, one hand on his belt, the other resting on the top of his open door. I scooched way down in my seat and lowered my head. When Gully slowed to see what was happening, I could tell we were going to stop and I adjusted my scarf, wrapping it around my face until only my eyes showed. I brought the hard hat down even with my eyebrows.

"Hold on a minute, Mrs. List." Gully did a double take when he saw me swaddled up like an Egyptian mummy, but he remembered our agreement of secrecy and didn't say a thing to me while he drew up alongside Mikey's police car. "Can I help you, officer?"

I turned my head away just in case Mikey

could recognize me under the makeshift disguise and wondered if he was as good an officer as I thought he was. Would he be able to identify me by my perfume? Because now I was really working up a good sweat, and the fumes were wafting around me like a steaming soup of lavender and roses with a little DB thrown in.

Mikey came away from the car and walked over to Gully. "And you are?"

"Jeff Gullikson. I'm the grounds supervisor here. What's going on?"

I heard the shuffle of papers. Mikey was taking notes. "I'm Officer Murphy, sir, assisting in a homicide investigation. I'm afraid one of your club members was murdered. We recovered her body this morning, although she was more than likely killed two or three days ago, and we're talking to some of the people she associated with. Just asking a few questions."

I stole a glance at Mikey. He was flipping through a small notebook. When he looked up I quickly turned away.

"And you are, ma'am?" Oh, holy crap. Mikey was addressing me. I had to do something. When I turned my face ever so slightly, just enough not to appear deaf or rude, I caught my reflection in his sunglasses. Featureless. Just a space where the whites of my eyes showed through. Would he know it was me? No way.

Gully, remembering his manners said, "Pardon me. This is . . ."

And I nearly crawled under the golf cart.

"Mrs. Uh . . . Li-ktish. Yes. Mrs. Liktish. She's considering joining the club and I'm just giving her a tour." Good boy. Gully was a quick study.

"Did you know a Mrs. Moira Finch, Mr. Gullikson?"

"Of course. A fine woman. Was she the one who was murdered?"

"Afraid so, sir."

"Goodness. That is a shame. How was she killed? Where was she killed? Who . . . ?"

"I can't really give out any details at the moment," Mikey said. "Ma'am? Mrs. Liktish? Did you know Mrs. Finch?"

I vigorously shook my head.

Mikey studied me for a long, agonizing beat before finally turning back to Gully. "Can you think of any reason someone would want to murder Mrs. Finch?"

"Of course not. She's been a member here for years. I guess at times she did get a little cranky and short-tempered but that's understandable. She took her game very seriously and golf *can* be stressful."

Really? I thought it was supposed to relieve

stress, but what did I know?

"Do most members store their golf clubs here at the country club, or do they take them home?"

Good question, Mikey. I had just taken for granted Moira would keep her clubs at home or in her car. I had to be sure Jeff took me by the pro shop so I could do some digging around the storage area. Naturally the cops would look at Moira's bag, but you probably had to have a search warrant to dig around everyone else's property. As an employee, I could speed things up a bit. Mikey was keeping things close to the flack vest and that was understandable, but if he didn't move things along it might give the killer time to dispose of evidence.

Since Moira had been murdered by a golf club one could only assume that if it was hers, the killer would have had access to it whether it was in her car, home or at the country club. Storage was an important issue. On the other hand, if the golf club belonged to another golfer, the police would have to find out who was missing a club and that was going to be next to impossible — unless it had been stored at the pro shop along with its mates. Once I established ownership of that club, we could move the investigation forward. Unfortunately, no matter how hard I tried to recall the exact brand and description of the club, all I saw was a mossy, broken-off spear.

"I know Mrs. Finch kept her clubs here — has for as long as I can remember," Mr. Gullikson told Mikey. "But you can go down and talk to one of the bag boys just to be sure. You follow the sidewalk over to the west side by the sign that says 'cart wash,' and they'll be happy to help you there. You see, the normal procedure here is for a member to call in a tee time. Their name appears on the schedule, and the bag boys know to pull that member's clubs. One of the boys puts the clubs on a cart and parks the cart outside the pro shop. If the member prefers to walk, the bag boy will put the bag on a pull cart and leave it over there under the hanging baskets."

"Thank you very much." Mikey scribbled. "Did Mrs. Finch usually walk the course or did she prefer to use a cart?"

"Depends," Mr. Gully said. "In good weather she walked, but lately she'd been complaining of some knee problems."

Mikey nodded; all business. He scribbled some more while I watched discreetly, stealing glances when I could. "When did you see her last?" he asked.

"Can't remember exactly, but talk to the

guys at the pro shop. She would have called for a tee time before her last golf game and they'll have those records. Or you can ask the ladies she usually golfed with. All that information will be there."

"Thank you very much. Oh. One more thing. Please ask your crew to keep an eye out for Mrs. Finch's car or for any pieces of golf clubs during your work around the course, or just anything else you feel might be . . . off."

"Certainly."

"And if you see anything, please don't touch it. Call the Harvest Police Department and someone will come out to pick it up."

"Of course."

"Thank you, Mr. Gullikson. Here's my card. If you can think of anything that might help us, please let me know, okay?"

A gust of wind flew through the parking lot, and my skirt billowed. I slapped my knees together but didn't catch it in time, and the darned thing flew up over my head. I clawed at it, scraped my scarf away and was in great danger of blowing my cover. I swatted and wrapped and had everything back in order just in the nick of time, because just after Gully assured Mikey he'd contact the officer if need be, I could hear boots coming over to me. Mikey.

My favorite officer reached into his breast pocket and brought out a card for me as well. I kept my eyes averted like some harem girl and took the card. Then Mikey bent over as if he were picking up something off the pavement. "You must have dropped this, ma'am. But don't worry, I found it." He placed something small in my hand. It was the tube of red lip balm I'd used to grease my upper lip back at the morgue.

Mikey winked at me. "You be careful out there," he said.

I shriveled up a little then as we pulled away from the police cruisers. I could almost feel Mikey's eyes burning holes in my hard hat. Must have been my perfume. I unwrapped my face and decided I was not going to mess up this investigation. I owed that much to the Harvest Police Department after all they'd done for me. Just as I was about to pepper Gully with all the questions I had regarding our dear friend Moira, he cranked the wheel and jetted the golf cart up a steep hill. I rocked back in my seat and looked for something to hang on to but there was nothing.

It was a whirlwind tour. The golf path was narrow, so when we encountered golfers coming at us Jeff did the gentlemanly thing and gave the right-of-way to the club members by pulling over onto the grass. Most of the members were kind and waved or said a thank-you, but there were a few who had crazy looks in their eyes, seeing nothing but the hole in front of them. We wound around trees, alongside a wide, beautiful river, up and down gently rolling hills, and Jeff never took his foot off the gas. His running narrative was impossible to follow. "This is hole ten. That's hole nine. Putting green, practice green, twin beds over there" — referring to identical gigantic flower beds — "and hole twelve."

We weren't going in any particular order. There were golfers all over the course, some pulling golf bags, some driving carts, and some hunched over little white balls. And as we flew past, I even heard one guy singing. Golfers are a strange breed.

"You don't see anyone from the crew working right now because everyone's down at the shop eating lunch," Gully spoke softly. We'd stopped out of respect for some ladies at the fifteenth hole. "We do most of our work early in order to keep out of the way of golfers, and most everyone's finished with their work by two or three. If you look over to your left, you will see one of our most impressive flower beds."

And that was when I got this really bad feeling. The flower bed was huge! It must have covered half an acre, was surrounded by landscaping rocks, dotted here and there with bushes, decorative grasses, trees, and the most beautifully choreographed flower arrangements I'd ever seen. A narrow creek gurgled happily through its center and ran under the cart path to continue on where it eased out into a gentle river. And Jeff had said it was only "*one* of our most impressive flower beds." *Ted, what have I done?*

"We also have a good-sized pond near the middle of the course, fed by an underground spring. A pump pulls water from it to keep the grass green. We're self-contained here."

"A pond, too? Wow."

"Why don't we head down to the shop now? I'll introduce you to our crew, and you can grab a bite to eat. How does that sound?" Gully asked.

The ladies had moved off to the next hole so we could talk freely now, although my throat was a bit tight. This landscaping business might be tougher than I thought. *Buck up, May Bell. Quit yer sniveling.* "I'd like that very much," I said.

Jeff looked me over. "You okay?"

"Um-hm."

"Good." Jeff looked at his watch. "Oh, my.

112

It's late."

I don't know how, but the man could make a little golf cart fly. We went up on two wheels coming around the first corner, then burned rubber and flew down the straightaway. Pretty soon we were close to the hill and there was no slowing this guy. Straight down we bombed, hit a tree root and took another corner at right angles. Since I was up about two inches off my seat after the bounce, I hadn't reconnected squarely when we took the corner, and everything went sideways.

"Oh, chicanery!" I screamed, having the presence of mind to edit my outburst. I flipped and hung over the side of the golf cart, my hands wrapped around that blessed little bar. My hard hat grazed the asphalt path; my feet whacked poor Gully on all sides of his face, and it was quite fortunate I'd already knocked off my heels back at the garage or he'd be full of holes. I hung onto that little bar for my life. Forget my skirt. Who cares about a skirt at a time like this?

"Mrs. List!" Jeff slammed on the brakes and ran around to assist me. I looked up at him, my eyes bulging. With trembling hands he pulled me back up into the seat.

"Hey, buddy." Behind us, a group of men

pulled up in their cart. "Mind if we play through?"

CHAPTER TEN

Mr. Gullikson apologized all the way back to the shop, but I told him it was nothing — I'd been in fixes before and he shouldn't worry at all, and by the way, "You got your shirt messed up a little, and would it be okay for me to smooth it down with my lint roller?"

Before Gully had a chance to answer, we were back where this whole fiasco began. Things looked very different. The shop pulsed with activity. Dozens of unidentifiable machines were crammed into the building and what had before felt vacuous and cold was now a thumping hub of life. Music blared from a dusty boom box. Thump, thump, thump. A few guys were sprawled across work vehicles of every sort, taking a short siesta. Some of the machines had rollers, some had blades, and all looked intimidating and quite frankly, all looked quite capable of cleanly, or messily, eviscerating any and all body parts. I said a prayer that Jeff wouldn't decide to put me atop any one of them. I was slightly relieved to see there were no wood chippers in the lot. For some reason, and I can't say exactly why, those things always give me the heebie-jeebies.

We were at the tail end of lunch. Tooth-picks all around and I'd missed the formal feast, but Gully was a chap and put together a paper-plate meal for my empty belly before introductions. I ate fast, hardly even tasting the mini corndogs, pasta salad, coleslaw and bratwurst because I was so hungry by this time, and then the tour began.

There would be no social disgrace as-sociating with the grounds crew because they couldn't know who I was, so I told Gully he could use my real name but keep to himself the fact that I was a member. The only one I'd been worried about any-way was the Harvest Police Department, and Mikey wasn't fooled at all, so as far as everyone was concerned, I was just a "grandmotherly type" here to work a few hours a week. If things went as planned, I should be out of there in no more than forty-eight hours. Moira deserved no less. Or, no more. Time, that is. I didn't want this murder to go to the cold-case files. The police could only do so much. So here I was.

First stop: the garage, aka the mechanics' hovel. Two guys peeled themselves away from their screwdrivers and stuck out grease-slick hands. Dave and Joe. Dave was a man of few words but had, to his credit, a spontaneous chuckle that was quite endearing. Don't know why he would have a need to chuckle; maybe he knew something I didn't. Anyhoo, he was all right in my book. Joe should have been photographed and placed on a Monthly Mechanic's poster. Gray overalls, red rag in the back pocket, an expression that spoke of serious wheels and cogs, and if ever there was a man who knew engine parts, it was Joe. He even smelled of octane. The introduction could be summed up as one of grunts and nods. A large black dog appeared from a dark corner and circled my ankles. Joe reached down and called to his dog. "This here's Jake. It takes him a while to get used to strangers."

I smiled nervously and said, "I'm stranger." What a dumb thing to say. I just didn't know how to connect with these guys. I reached my hand out toward Jake. He curled his lips and snarled low in his chest. I pulled my hand back. "I'll just give him some time."

"Good idea," Joe said. And I swear, while I looked at him, he curled his lip up just slightly, and the growl I heard could have been coming from him.

Dave chuckled.

Of course I was taking mental notes this whole time, keeping in mind the task at hand. There was a dead Moira, and I wasn't there to make friends. Gather data, pick some weeds and get the heck out.

"So nice to meet you, Dave." I bowed ever so slightly in his direction. He chuckled. He definitely knew something. I turned to the other guy. "Joe."

Joe made a little dismissive hand motion and went back to his engines. Dave crossed his arms over his chest and kept an eye on me. As I left the garage I could hear him chuckle again. What was with that guy?

Outside of the shop a group of young men were tossing around a football. Jeff explained they were seasonal employees and would head back to college in the fall. A clean-cut, good-looking bunch of about five guys, friendly and innocent-looking; just kids really, and I didn't see any prospective murderers in the bunch. But as they say in the world of crime, it's always the last one you would expect. So I wasn't going to discount anyone.

"Verticillium wilt!"

A strapping young man hurried toward Jeff. He had a thick shock of sandy hair, a well-groomed goatee and a handful of branches. "Verticillium wilt! Not to mention Phytophthora root rot and slugs. Look!" The man slid to a stop in front of Mr. Gullikson and waved the branches under Gully's nose.

"Hmmm. Yes." Gully took a leaf between his fingers and examined it closely. "How many trees?"

"Isn't that the question of the week?" the man said. "I found this by the practice green. But you know it's only a matter of time. Only a matter of time. You get one diseased tree, the infestation spreads and before you know it . . ." The man was flushed, sweating and in quite a dither.

"Mrs. List, I'd like you to meet Tim Kholhauff."

I held out my hand and got a branch. There was this professorial air about Tim, a look that spoke of his serious nature.

Jeff said, "Tim's our local tree expert, holds five degrees in horticulture, teaches out at the colleges, hosts extreme-gardener competitions, and has worked here for the past three years. Anything you want to know about trees, this is your guy." Jeff smiled up at Tim.

"Very impressive, sir. Extreme gardeners?" I asked.

Tim came through some sort of fog and realized I was standing there. He looked me over good, took his time processing, and I put him in the category of a man who is so organized and intellectual that an old woman shaking his limbs might just push him over the edge. I did not compute.

Tim looked at Jeff. "Is today the retirement home tour? If so, Mr. Gullikson, that's a large measure of cruel soup you just poured on my head and I'm feeling the burn." Tim's complexion darkened. "That's just dandy. Just dandy. Did I get a memo? No. Did I get a text or even a *minute* to prepare? My gosh, man, you've got verticillium wilt!" Tim grabbed the branch out of my hand and walked away, his arms raised in a "why me" fashion.

Dave lumbered past and chuckled.

"Tim is a very important asset to the country club," Gully said. "We have fifteen hundred and eighty-five trees on the course and they all need special care. Tim knows all of their names."

"Wow. I didn't even know there were fifteen hundred and eighty-five different varieties of trees."

"No, I mean he named them all."

Oh.

Shouts and warning hollers came from the football gang, and I squinted toward the noise just as a dark blob rocketed toward my face. Inches before it struck my nose a grimy hand swung around from behind me and grabbed the ball from the air with a resounding *smack!* I turned to thank the hero. It was the first guy I'd met, Mr. Blue Sunglasses.

"Hey, lady. Can't even catch a football?" he huffed. He squished the ball hard, prompting sounds of dismay from the football team when the ball popped and fizzled out a long whine of escaping air. Mr. Blue slammed the ball to the ground like he'd just scored a touchdown, and then jumped on his machine and zoomed out of the shop parking lot. Temper, temper.

Wow. That guy had just made it to the top of my list. The only reason I was hanging out with this odd group of people was to get data on Moira's murder. And the only reason I thought I'd get information was because of one little golf club. Oh, and then there was the matter of the impression she made with her lady golf-buds. I feared that I was spinning my wheels and that, if I

121

didn't hurry up with something concrete, Mikey would solve this crime before the inevitable indigestion from my hasty lunch.

"That's really sad." One of the young men who'd been playing football squatted down and stared at the deflated ball. He brushed his thumbs under his eyes and I do believe there were a few tears. "Poor, poor little thing." His voice trembled with emotion. He stroked the ball with the back of his hand while Jeff and I locked eyes.

I leaned over and whispered in Jeff's ear. "Is he okay?"

"Elder, you okay, son?" Jeff put his hand on the young man's shoulder.

Again I whispered in Jeff's ear, "He's an elder? He looks so young."

"No," Jeff whispered back. "His first name is Mike but we had three Mikes last year so we got used to calling him by his last name."

I had so many names to learn I thought it would be best to just try to remember the important details and worry about names later. Football Mike. Elder, if I could think of it.

"He was so young." Elder sniffed and then snorted loudly. "Why? Why? *Why?* Why did he have to kill him?" He craned his neck and looked up at Mr. Gullikson. Moisture dotted his long lashes; lashes that framed caring eyes — dark-brown, sensitive eyes. Some gal was really lucky to have him if there was a gal in his life. He was a little older than the college kids, no ring on his finger, and I was moved by his loss. "Why didn't I do something?" he asked.

"It's not your fault," I said, putting my hand next to Gully's. I patted Elder's back. "You never know when it's someone's — something's time."

"No, no, no," Elder moaned. "I was careless! I torqued too late, I flicked too early. I cocked too high. I stepped with my left when I always go right. What have I done?" He scooped up the ball and cradled it against his chest, and then he stood and left us, moving like the undead.

Jeff shook his head and clucked his tongue. "He really loved that ball."

"You want me to pop a cap upside Riley's head?" A meaty, foreboding guy stepped up and punched the palm of his left hand with a gloved right.

"No, no, Jim. Mrs. List, this is Jim. A former member of Spokane's finest, now one of our drivers."

Oh, goodie. An ex-cop. Once he hears about Moira's murder he'll be poppin' caps all over the place.

"I could open up a can of woop —"

123

And opening cans.

"Woops, Jim, you know the rules." Jeff wagged his finger. "Keep it clean. But, yes, I believe Riley has gone too far this time and he needs to be taken down a notch. He killed Elder's ball."

Jim smiled a menacing grin. "Let the punishment fit the crime." Obviously no stranger to barbells and weight machines, Jim flexed his right bicep, gave it a kiss, and then did the same with his left. Then he leaned forward and did a classic bodybuilder's pose, pumping up his shoulders, arms in parentheses, hands in fists, muscles quivering. He pivoted at the waist a smooth move left and right like he was playing to a swooning audience. I have to admit he was quite impressive. Then he strained too hard, tooted, and — now, embarrassed — stood up quickly.

"Just remember we need Riley to mow the surrounds tomorrow," Jeff said.

"I won't leave any visible marks." Jim left us, walking away with short staccato steps and stiff legs.

"I guess he strained too hard," I said.

"Huh?"

"Never mind."

"Now I want to introduce you to Marcia and Teresa. They're the two women you'll be working with. I'm surprised they haven't come out to greet you already, but maybe they're in the greenhouse. Why don't you follow me and we'll make our introductions."

Finally, I was going to find some feminine presence amongst all of this masculine good will. I equipped myself for small talk, for conversations about hair gel and flat irons, designer jeans and expensive bags. Then, I'd get to talk of Moira and what they knew about the woman.

Suddenly, a golf cart nearly took off one of my thighs. The speeding green machine skidded around me in a wide arc and came to rest in a spray of gravel and dust. I waved my hand through the air.

"Oh, good. It's Heckle and Jeckle," Gully said.

"Hey! We be Bonnie and Clyde. I'm Clyde," said the cart driver.

"I'm Clyde, you clod." The smaller of the two shoved the driver and nearly unseated him, but the driver held fast to the steering wheel.

"I'm Clyde, and you must be Betty, because my Bonnie lies over the ocean."

"You couldn't get a Bonnie with a hundred bucks and a good health plan."

"Are you saying I can't deliver the package?"

"I'm saying you don't have the package to deliver."

Gully wasn't amused. "Guys, guys. What are you doing off the course?"

"We just came to tell you Marcia and Teresa are on hole one. They heard we have a new lady on the landscaping crew and they want you to bring her out there." The smaller man turned to his partner and said, "Hit it!"

The driver shoved his foot down onto the pedal and they flew away.

"Apparently, that's Bonnie and Clyde," Gully said. "Real names are Marlin and Dave but we already had a Dave, so it's Clyde. Two retired postal workers. You rarely see one without the other, but as long as they're getting the work done I stay out of their way."

Postal workers? Hmmm.

"It's getting late. Why don't I get you some work clothes, I'll quickly familiarize you with the tools you'll be using, and then we'll go meet the ladies. Okay?"

My mind was reeling. This was turning out to be a much bigger challenge than I'd anticipated. "Fine," I squeaked.

The shop was empty once again, all carts

and machines having made their way back to the course, and I was impressed with the order and cleanliness of the place. Not a spot of oil stained the concrete floor. Tools of all shapes and sizes were neatly hung along the far west wall. Gully began his well-rehearsed recitation, pointing out various items of hardware much like a flight attendant would gesture to exit signs or airsick bags. Two fingers per hand, point there, out, back, up, down.

Most of the tools I recognized; they were fairly common even for the gardening novice. Rakes, shovels, pruning shears and trowels; not much of interest there. Some things I wasn't familiar with. There was a thing that had been (as he proudly explained) modified by Gully, a three-pronged rake with two of the prongs cut off turning it into a nice long-handled pick. "We call this a crack tool. It's used to scrape grass out of the cracks on the cart paths. Works great, and I've been thinking about having it patented."

"You continue to impress me, Mr. Gullikson."

Jeff hung the crack tool up with the others and moved along. "Nothing special here, a regular old hoe, but next to it are these: the workhorses of the landscaping business."

Jeff handed me a wooden-handled instrument with a metal flat-edged ring attached to its end. "The hula hoe. You push and pull like this." Jeff demonstrated, scraping against the cement floor with a most annoying sound. "And the weeds don't get bunched up. The metal ring cuts underneath, making the job far less wieldy."

"You mean weedy?"

"Wieldy. Wieldy. As in difficult, cumbersome, resistant."

Oh.

"What did you call it? A hula hoe? I've never heard of this before, but it makes so much sense." Not only had I never heard of one, I don't even remember the last time I put my hands on a rake, shovel or pitchfork. Didn't matter what it was used for.

"We'll get you a cart, some gloves, and your uniform, but you'll be responsible for equipping your cart every morning. I suggest you buy a pair of safety goggles and pick up several packages of ear plugs from the box on the counter."

My puzzled expression must have told the tale.

"In the morning you'll use a backpack blower to clean off the parking lot with the other ladies."

Grandmotherly types, my eye.

Gully pointed to the blowers, menacing contraptions that looked like they weighed at least fifty pounds apiece, and then he put his hands on something in a dark corner. "Here's another one of my inventions."

Gully turned. What he held in his hands made the hairs on the back of my neck stand at attention. Oh, my.

CHAPTER ELEVEN

"Let me see that." I grabbed the tool from Gully's hand. "What is this? What's it used for?"

"I was just about to explain."

"Explain quickly. Where did this come from? How did it get here?"

"I made it."

"You made it. Why?" In my hand, I held a broken golf club identical to the one I'd seen thrust through poor Moira's neck.

"You certainly are interested in our soil probe."

"Soil probe? What's a soil probe?"

"Come with me and I'll show you." Gully walked out one of the bay doors and onto a patch of grass. "Come here, Mrs. List, come on now." Gully beckoned, drawing me toward him with an outstretched hand. "Now, just stand right there in front of me."

I did as I was told and slowly walked over to stand in front of Gully but something gave me pause. I got this sudden, anxious feeling deep in my loins.

"So you want to know what this can do, huh?" Gully ran a long finger over the shaft of the truncated club in a loving stroke. The metal shimmered in the sun. "Tell me, Mrs. List, are you sure you really want to know? Because I'm not getting the feeling you're all that interested in gardening."

"No. I mean, yes, I am, I really am, Mr. Gullikson. That no-good husband of mine, well, he, he . . ." I took a step back and glanced over my shoulder.

Gully continued to run his finger along the metal of the club. "Are you up to it? This . . . business? It can get downright messy at times."

My lungs were the size of peas. "Honestly. I'm interested. I want to hoe and rake and weed! It's the truth, Mr. Gullikson, I wouldn't be here for any other reason."

"I'm not so sure. But I'll show you what this can do just the same." Gully lifted the club with both hands high over his head, and as he brought that club down in a swift aggressive manner, I knew I'd found my killer, and I knew he knew I knew. It was a simple deduction when you think about it.

"Oh, no you don't!" I shouted. I wrapped my hands around the broken shaft and wrestled with Gully until we went to our knees. Using all of the old-lady mustard I could find, I wrenched the club from Gully's hands and swung it hard against his temple. Gully's eyes rolled up and he dropped onto his side.

"That'll teach ya," I said.

I got to my feet and wiped the dirt from my skirt hem. I pushed at Gully's limp body with the toe of my broken pump, and then I heard the sound of an approaching golf cart. Thank goodness. Help had arrived.

"What's wrong with Mr. Gullikson?" Blue Sunglasses walked over and spit a little chaw juice onto the ground by Gully's head. Gully moaned.

I was breathless and shaking. "He had this." I handed the club to Blue.

"Heyyyy. I been looking for that." Blue took the club and looked it over. "Darn Chris lost one on the course last week, and this's the only one that's left." Blue jabbed the shaft into the ground and brought it up just as Gully started to come around. Blue then lifted the club and examined the soil he'd jammed into the broken shaft. There was a small hole in the metal tube, and the soil showed through. "Looks like we need to water today. This lawn's dry as dust. Tell Mr. Gullikson I took this one, okay? What's wrong with him, anyway?"

I began to feel really sick, then, even worse than before when I'd tainted Skinny Carl's emesis basin. What a horrible mistake I'd made. "He, uh, fainted. Must have been the heat."

"Hope he's okay. Did you take his pulse? Give him a cold compress? Massage his temples?"

"No."

"What good are ya?" Blue spat again and lumbered back to the shop with the soil probe over his shoulder, and I soon heard the clatter of a Coke dropping in the machine. By the time Jeff woke up, Blue had sped away.

Jeff didn't remember a thing. As far as he knew he'd been overcome by the afternoon's heat, had fallen against a rock (that I placed conveniently by his head before he was fully conscious), and had been out for a few minutes. He didn't even remember how we got outside of the shop and I didn't care to remind him about the soil probe. I'd figured it out. Thrust the thing into the ground, look through the hole and gauge the depth of moisture. Brilliant. Still, Jeff did say it was his own invention and undoubtedly he knew where to find one in case it was needed as a murder weapon. But, I had to admit, there were all kinds of tools in the shop and most would require much less force or accuracy. What had Blue said? One was lost on the course recently?

I really needed to think, but we had one more stop to make before I could beg off and go home to write down what I knew. Walking like he was a little bit drunk, Gully helped me once again onto his cart and handed me my hard hat. We headed back toward the clubhouse.

At the backside of the clubhouse I took in the full magnitude of the place. I couldn't remember ever seeing the course in the middle of the day since all of the dinners and benefits were evening affairs. I'd really missed a treat. A bricked patio with umbrella tables overlooked acres of green grass, mammoth trees and winding paths. We paused for a minute before moving along toward a short tunnel covered in vines and flowers. At the edge of the tunnel, Gully came to a stop.

At first, I was not sure why we weren't moving forward, but then I saw two dark forms walking through the tunnel, moving in tandem strides. Behind them, the sun shined brightly, making it impossible for me to make out their features. Time oozed like molasses. The silhouettes reminded me of terminators moving through a swirling fog, or like Pete, Link and Julie in the opening scene of the *Mod Squad.* Step, step, step. Joints swung easily, knees bent and straightened over well-functioning shock absorbers. They each carried heavy-looking machines on their backs. Safety goggles covered their eyes and they wore tool belts around their waists. No designer footwear for these ladies, their combat boots struck the pavement with commanding thuds.

Marcia and Teresa. Grandmotherly types. Sure. They stopped in front of us, close enough for me to take a half step back.

"Is this her?" One of the women pushed her goggles up onto the top of her head. She looked from Gully to me.

"She's a little puny." The other lady addressed the first. "What do you think, Teresa?"

Gully was right. They were nearly identical. Cousins, he'd said. Amazing.

Marcia considered me for a minute and then broke into a wide grin. "She'll do." She thrust out a gloved hand. "Welcome to the landscaping team."

"Mr. Gullikson! Mr. Gullikson!" Tim raced through the tunnel and skidded to a stop. "Sucking spider mites! Just found 'em down by the bathroom. You have to do something!"

Jeff sighed. "Mrs. List, I'm afraid I'm needed at the bathrooms. I'll let the three of you get acquainted. If I don't see you again today, I'll leave your time card in the holder. Don't forget to punch in tomorrow."

"Now, Mr. Gullikson! Before it's too late!" Tim sprinted away.

Gully touched the brim of his hard hat as he drove off, weaving a little as he went, and I felt sort of bad about what had happened before, but how was I to know? There was a murderer skulking around somewhere and quite possibly it was someone I'd met that very day. You can never be too careful.

As I followed Marcia and Teresa to their carts, I mentally went over what I'd learned and who I'd met. I glanced at my watch. I needed to get to Mikey fast. I had a feeling the cops were looking at the wrong people, partially thanks to what I'd already told Officer Murphy. I was beginning to think the members weren't at fault; it was just too coincidental that the tool used to killed Moira was missing from the grounds crew shop. Hurry, hurry, hurry, I wanted to say, but instead, I followed the ladies, putting on a new-employee smile.

When we got to Teresa's cart, I saw how tidy and efficient she was. Tools were aligned in a custom-made rack in the bed. Hoses were coiled to precise and exact circles. She had a watering can, a bucket and a utility basket, all placed in squares she'd drawn on the metal floor of her cart. My gosh. She could have been an actuary. Hmmm. I pulled one of the tools out of the holder. Teresa shrugged off her blower and dropped it into the cart bed. She came over to me after Marcia did the same with her machine. Teresa was just about to tell me something but I was caught up in my new environment. I love it when I learn something. I looked at her and said, "Crack hoe."

Teresa was wearing a smile. That disappeared.

"Say again?"

"Crack hoe," I said, this time with more gusto. I wanted to impress her. "Crack hoe!"

"Why, I oughta . . ." Marcia barged over and placed herself between Teresa and me. "What'd you call her?"

"Call her? Nothing," I said, perplexed. I held out the tool. "Crack hoe. That's what Mr. Gullikson called it."

"Crack *tool*. Crack *tool*. *Not* crack hoe." Marcia grabbed another tool and waved it at me. "This — is a hula hoe." She shoved the other one in my face. "And this — is a crack tool. Kapeesh?"

137

"Kapeesh." *Sheesh.*

Jim rocketed toward us in his cart and slammed on the brakes. "Problems over here, girls? Need me to pop anything?"

"No, Jim. Keep on truckin'."

"Ten-four," he said. And off he went.

"You know anything about a dirt probe?" I wasn't going to be cowed by these girls, even if they looked strong enough to bench-press two Jims apiece. Their muscles were so well-defined, they could have posed for pictures in an anatomy textbook. They had ropy veins sticking out all over their fore-arms. Even their necks looked ripped.

"*Soil* probe. We don't say dirt. We say soil. Dirt is what you get under your fingernails."

"Got it. Soil probe. You use those?"

"If we have to, we're not doing our jobs. Are we, Marcia?"

Marcia pushed her goggles up just the way Teresa had. Now that messed me up, be-cause the goggle difference was how I could tell them apart. "We have a routine and keep the gardens watered on a precise schedule," she explained. "Once you get the hang of it you can tell by looking at the plants whether or not they're getting adequate time under the sprinklers."

"So you're saying you don't use them at all."

"On rare occasions, but I have to say neither of us have handled one this year at all. Right?" Marcia checked with her cousin. Teresa nodded.

"Just one more thing," I said. "Have either of you ever been fingerprinted for, say, any kind of criminal activity? Anything like that?"

"Excuse me?"

"Oh, nothing. Say, are those junipers?"

CHAPTER TWELVE

Even though Marcia and Teresa looked like twins, I learned over the next hour that they were nothing at all alike. *And* they were nothing at all like any grandmothers I knew. First of all, their eyes were different; Teresa had the longest, darkest lashes I'd ever seen, and Marcia had one blue eye and one brown eye. She told me she wore one contact lens, and the optometrist messed up her prescription but she hadn't had time to correct the problem. Second, Teresa had one front tooth that slightly overlapped another in an adorable way, giving her smile a charming quality. Also, Teresa ran marathons every other weekend, held nearly as many horticulture degrees as Tim, wrote weekly columns for the gardening section of the *Spokane News,* and had five daughters.

Marcia had a multitude of talents and skills. She had a private pilot's license and was a retired Marine. She wasn't a professional gardener; just happened to love flowers. And, oh, yes. She had twelve grandkids. As we were getting to know one another, I didn't dwell on the grandkids part because I'm a little sensitive about that. Darn Patty and Jack. Get busy already.

Anyhoo, to them I was recovering from a severe brain injury. I had to have some reason to explain my complete lack of gardening knowledge, and it was the only thing I could come up with. The bruise on my forehead gave me some credibility I suppose, and on occasion I would rub my temples in little circular motions. My memory would come back, I told them, and I'm surprised I'd never used this ruse before because the sympathy was wonderful. I also said because of the injury I would occasionally have verbal outbursts or ask inappropriate questions. And, oh, yes, it made me fall into a one-sided paralysis without warning. (I'd use this when the work got really hard.)

This didn't seem to bother the ladies, and by the time we were back at the shop we were all talking about shoes. Everyone was punching their time cards, Elder was sitting against the outside wall, dabbing at his eyes with a tissue, Jim was hefting rocks, one in each hand, and Bonnie and Clyde were in a leg-wrestling match out on the lawn.

Mr. Gullikson was nowhere to be seen, probably on the hunt for bark beetles or verticillium wilt, so I said my good-byes and hopped into my Camaro. It had been one busy day, but I wasn't finished yet. Before going home I stopped off at Candy's again. The question of Moira's missing car, and why she'd been dumped at Moody Lake had been bothering me all day. Nothing was coming together yet, but I'd made an important find with the soil probe, and I needed to relay what I knew to the police department. As I sat in the parking lot, I looked through my wallet for Mikey's business card. Before I could call him, though, three Harvest police cars rounded the corner with lights flashing and sirens wailing. They slid into Candy's parking lot and surrounded my car.

I threw my hands in the air, spilling my purse out onto the floor, and felt my bowels start to give way before catching myself. What had I done?

Officers poured out of their cruisers and ran past me and into Candy's shop. I exhaled loudly and dropped my hands onto my lap. Whew. Hey. Why was I just sitting there? I jumped out of my car and raced after the officers. One of whom was Mikey himself. I wouldn't need to call him after all.

Once inside the shop I understood the reason for the police presence. Snack sat calmly where I'd left him earlier that morning, but he had a cooler beside him now and his clothes showed signs of a day of fishing. His buddies were there, and Ankle Tan had a trout lying across his lap. Pretty healthy fish, too, and by the puffed-up way he was showing it off it was probably his first catch — ever. They were watching the show. A crowd of campers shouted at the cops, all clearly upset to judge by the looks on their faces and by their hand-waving, but there was so much noise it was difficult to understand what they were saying.

"Okay," Mikey said, while pushing a woman back. "One at a time, please."

"Right after I find they had no biscotti, I go out, snap some pictures of you guys doin' your jobs, ya know?"

That was Mrs. Robe, the one who'd been talking a mile a minute that morning, getting in Mike's face, complaining about her chips and cookies.

"Then, I go rinse off in the community showers, don't ya know, and let me tell ya I ain't takin' my time in there. Then, I get my stuff packed up and ready to go because

143

checkout is by noon, or ya get charged an extra day if you're late — a rip-off if you ask me, but then what happens when I get back to my camper? I don't notice at first, but eventually I see something's out of place. I go looking for my computer. And of course, it's gone. Gone, gone, gone. Somebody came in there when I was in the showers and stole my laptop. Shebang! Let me tell you, I'm not leaving here without my computer, and I sure ain't payin' extra."

Shouts rang out.

"And my camera's missing."

"My purse was stolen, too!"

"Someone lifted my wallet!"

"Fifty dollars is missing out of my back pocket," Snack shouted, and then he laughed. "Naw, just kidding. I've been out on the boat all day."

Ankle Tan was intently focused on his trout. He opened its little mouth, played with its gills, and picked at the scales until some came off on his finger. That bothered him and he stared at the little colorful disks for a time before wiping them off on the underside of his chair.

Ew.

Candy stood behind the counter smiling while steam curled around her hair. She had paper cups lined up along the countertop, and the cappuccino machine hissed pleasantly.

Just then another police car skidded to a stop in the parking lot, the last one in the Harvest motor pool, and Paul jumped out. He ran into the bait and tackle shop and grabbed Mikey by the arm. I floated around the two of them, listening. Paul was practically quivering with excitement.

"You will never believe this."

Mikey said, "Hurry up, Paul. We're getting close to a riot here, and I might have to call in for reinforcements. Whatcha got?"

"We held Skinny Carl's girlfriend and took the gun in for testing. Sure enough, the bullet found in Carl's chest was from the gun. But the bullet didn't kill him. We knew that. He was shot after he was dead. What we'd first heard about him being held captive, poisoned and finally shot for good measure was dismissed, as you know. Then we hear he's been at his girlfriend's house with the flu, and on his way to the hospital he's killed in an alley by the girlfriend's ex. That's according to the girlfriend."

"Not true?" Mikey asked, splitting his attention between Paul and the angry crowd behind him.

"No. After Sherman leans on the girlfriend, she fesses up. She says he did have

145

the flu. That much was true, and she's been hiding him because of all the warrants out on his head. She doesn't want to take him to the doctor, knowing we'll be able to arrest him as soon as they get an ID. So she's been pumping juice and applesauce into him and he can't keep it down. Finally, he dies on her, she knows about the reward money Carl's parents put up, and she's got a grudge against an ex-boyfriend to boot.

"So," Paul continued, "girlfriend dumps the body in the alley, shoots his dead body with her gun, hoping it will look like a hit, and she doesn't want us to know she's been hiding him. She's planning to call and claim the reward money, framing this old boy-friend, but when we put things together she admits she's the one who shot him but she swears she didn't kill him."

Mikey said, "It was the flu."

"Riiiight. We'd already started the autopsy before we had to hold up, because of the story this Hawaiian lady phones in. Then we get the word that Carl's got bacon and eggs and toast barely digested. So somebody's lying. What's a guy with a raging case of the trots and heaves doing with a whole breakfast floating in his stomach?"

Mike chewed on the stem of his sun-glasses. "What are you thinking?"

146

Paul was flushed and excited. "We take a closer look at the girlfriend."

"She did admit she shot him, right? After he was dead?"

"Yeah, but she said he died from the flu. And if that's the case, there's no way he'd have a full stomach. Not with bacon and eggs in him at any rate. And another thing. There was a ransom note sent to Carl's parents, but the girlfriend didn't write it and she didn't know anything about it. So she says. Carl's parents were wealthy and Carl's girlfriend just wanted the big fat reward. But they posted the reward after they got the ransom note. That part wasn't public knowledge, and she doesn't mention the ransom note, which says to me she didn't write it. I'd like to tie this up before the feds get here."

"Keep on the girlfriend. I think you're right. We still don't have the full story. And we still don't have the full autopsy. Check those tox reports."

"Got it."

"By the way. Did you find out how the Hawaiian learned about the ransom note?"

"I'll check on that." Paul headed for the exit, but thought better of it when the young woman with the weird haircut grabbed him around the knees. "I guess you can use some help here," he said.

"That would be nice," Mike responded.

"Mind if I talk with you a minute?" I touched Mike's shoulder, and when he saw me standing there he looked like he'd just stepped into a cold shower.

"I can't right now, Mrs. List." Behind Mikey tempers were heating up and the crowd was getting downright nasty. Paul had the girl by the wrist, her arm pinned behind her back and she was cursing him out. The robe lady slammed her fists against the counter, screaming about her laptop. The paper cups danced and toppled onto the floor. Candy smiled, set up another line of cups and poured cappuccinos. I pulled Mike's nightstick from his belt and handed it over.

"Here," I said. "Bust some skulls if you have to. Pop some caps or open up a can of woop-woop if it will hurry things along because unless you've found Moira's murderer, I've got information that you're gonna want to hear and it can't wait."

"Oh? Something good?"

"A case breaker."

As I was taking a breath to tell Mikey about the soil probe, the two Hibachi Boys got into it. Fists flew and much to my surprise they fell to the floor and rolled around in a tangle, biting, spitting, jabbing elbows, pulling hair. They tumbled right across the room and smashed into Ankle Tan who jumped to his feet. His trout slipped from his lap, and when he lunged into the fight to make a grab for it a swinging right hook caught him in the jaw.

Snack, in a calm, controlled manner, lifted his ice chest and dumped its contents, ice, water, beer and all, on top of the dog fight. The Hibachi Boys howled and split. Then they scooped up beers and took chairs beside Snack. All better. Ankle Tan found his fish and kissed it on the lips.

But Mrs. Robe wasn't so easily pacified. Sherman had given her some paperwork to fill out, but instead of putting pencil to paper, she'd torn it into tiny bits and tossed it in Sherman's face. Sherman was twitching. His gun hand kept knocking against his thigh, his trigger finger pulsed in a repetitive spasm.

"Mrs. List, I'm afraid I have to go. And, sorry to burst your bubble, but we've already got a suspect in the Finch case."

"What?"

"Yeah. A darn-good suspect with solid evidence and I doubt if we'll have any trouble getting an indictment."

"When did that happen? Who?"

"All I can say is that you were right about one thing. It was someone from the club. Someone rather high up, as a matter of fact. We just had to follow the money."

The Hibachi Boys had finished their beers and after smashing the empties against their foreheads they decided to play keep-away with Ankle Tan's fish. It was ugly.

"I can't tell you anything else. I'm really sorry. Now, why don't you just go on home and enjoy the rest of your day. We'll catch up later, okay? Run along now."

Mrs. Robe was now riding piggyback on poor Officer Sherman. She kept trying to bite his ears, but he jerked his head out of the way, spun in circles and tried valiantly to shake her off — with no success.

"Run along? Run *along?*" I crossed my arms over my chest. "Fine, Officer Murphy. You don't deserve to hear about the soil probe."

"Soil, huh?"

"Right. I guess I'll be running along." I turned on my broken heels. Mikey grabbed my arm.

"What's a soil probe?"

The girl with the wild hair had scooted out of Paul's clutches and — despite the fact she was cuffed — kicked at his head with first one foot and then the other. Her legs were as nimble and as flexible as an emu's. She made contact several times.

"A soil probe, you ask?" I waved my hand dismissively. "Oh, nothing, except it's what the killer used to skewer Moira. A landscaping device made out of the golf club. You didn't know that, did you?"

"Okay. You got me there. Still, it probably won't change anything."

"But what if it does?"

Ankle Tan (I think he was actually whimpering now) chucked pieces of cooler ice at the Hibachi Boys. Surprisingly, he had a pretty decent throwing arm, although his aim wasn't too good. One piece whizzed by my face and smashed through the expansive front window of Candy's shop. Glass shattered in a spray and cascaded onto the front porch followed by a horrific, drawn-out creaking sound. The large wooden fish sign came loose and swung for a minute on its brackets, a big fish-eye peered into the shop, and then the sign came crashing down onto the wreckage. The cappuccino machine stopped hissing. I glanced over at Candy. I swear I saw steam blowing out her nostrils.

Mikey looked across the room, thinking. He hadn't even jumped when the window exploded, and I counted this as his incredible ability to compartmentalize. Either that or he just couldn't multitask. "All right," he said. "You'd better tell me what you've got."

"When do you get off work?"

"As soon as the National Guard gets here."

"Harvest Inn. Sixteen hundred hours. Don't be late or you'll get a personal demonstration of what a soil probe can do."

"Ream on."

CHAPTER THIRTEEN

The Harvest Inn is just down the road from my home. It's a renovated farmhouse, two stories, converted into a charming bed-and-breakfast. The sleeping quarters are upstairs, with a sitting area, library and, of course, a coffee bar on the main floor. An oversized fireplace crackles to life during the winter months, but now it was dark, cold and lifeless.

For some reason, as I considered that dead fireplace I had a moment of melancholy. What if the police department *had* sewn up Moira's case? What then? More needlepoint and country club benefits? When I was younger there was always something to look forward to, something to get my pulse thumping and my stomach fluttering. And now? Hypertension and heaves.

I ordered my customary vanilla latte and took a seat at one of the tables in a quiet dark corner. I took out my notebook to record what I knew so far. But instead of listing my items of data, I scrawled *boredom is death* across the top of my notepad. Then I added six exclamation points after it. Then I wrote *carpe diem* under that. It felt good. I lifted my cup and blew gently at the foam then took a slurp. A young man at a table nearby glanced at me. He'd been mesmerized by his computer screen, so it was nice to see I could still draw the attention of someone from the opposite sex. I smiled at him, batted my eyelashes and slurped again, then lifted my cup as a gesture of introduction. The man blushed, pulled his ball cap down over his eyebrows and hunched lower in his chair. He disappeared behind his laptop. Fine. Talk to your dumb computer.

Then I scribbled on my notepad: *What's going on at Candy's? How did Moira end up in Moody Lake? Who's ripping off tourists? What happened to Moira's car? Who wanted to kill her? How did she end up with a soil probe in her neck? Was anyone in the landscaping crew a possible suspect?*

Then I knew with absolute clarity that the killer was still out there and Mikey had the wrong suspect, whoever it was. Why would someone, anyone, from the country club use something that could so easily be traced back to its source? Pretty obvious, wasn't it? Sure, the killer probably hoped Moira's body wouldn't be discovered, but how hard could it have been to pull out the murder weapon, clean it off and put it back where it belonged, or at the very least tossed it into a trash bin? Dumping Moira's body in Moody Lake had muddied up the waters, so to speak, and given the killer a little time by throwing some confusion into things. But why leave the weapon in her neck?

"So boredom killed Moira?" Mikey stood behind me. He was still in uniform but both of his front pockets were ripped and hanging.

"You know it's rude to read over someone's shoulder."

"Sorry."

Mike took a chair and adjusted his belt.

I asked, "Everything under control back at the lake?"

"We took statements and told everyone we'd send their stuff if it was recovered. Not much else to do. We only made two arrests."

"The Hibachi Boys?"

"Their complaint was that someone stole their dope stash. Then we found it."

"Here's your brain on drugs."

"Right. Anyway, everyone was cooperative, and things settled down eventually with the exception of one woman who wouldn't give us her personal information and says she's not leaving until we find her computer."

"The robe lady from New York City."

"That one. How did you know where she was from?"

"You told me this morning. Besides. Who else would pitch a fit over hummus and biscoooatee? Let her stew. I don't really care about her; what I want to know is what's going on with Moira's case and why you think you have a suspect."

"I can't tell you that. I just came here to find out about that soil probe thingy."

"Listen, Mikey, whoever you have is probably the wrong guy, and I'm getting really weary of your 'I can't tell you's.' That thing in Moira's neck was a golf club, that's true. But it was customized by the manager of the grounds, one Mr. Jeff Gullikson. You met him in the parking lot today right before you handed me my lip balm, thank you very much."

"Customized how?"

"You take a golf club and cut off the head. Then you use a grinder to make a hole in the side of the shaft. It's a tool that the landscaping crew uses for measuring moisture in the soil. It's *not* something you're going to find lying around the country club pro shop. It's either going to be down at the maintenance shop or, from what I learned today, it might have been left on the course by some careless grounds crew worker. Now, what would someone in management — and, by what you said, I'm assuming it *is* someone in management — what would they be doing with a soil probe?"

"The manager golfs, too. Everyone who works there golfs. He could have picked it up as easy as anyone else."

"The manager?"

"Forget I said that."

"You think the club manager killed Moira?"

"I did not say that."

"What's the connection, kiddo?" I asked sternly. "And you'd better fess up now because since our last case together I've been working out and I'm taking self-defense classes. I can put some hurt on you."

Mikey suppressed a laugh. "Really? Like martial arts or what?"

"I do chai tea."

"Chai tea?"

"And feng shui."

"If I ever need my furniture rearranged I'll give you a call."

I clasped my hands in front of my bosom.

157

"Come on, Mikey, please."

Mike looked down at my notepad, and his eyes traveled over the *carpe diem* line. Guess he saw himself at my age and a flitter of understanding passed over his face. He sighed, rubbed his chin and dropped his shoulders. "Okay. But this stays here, you understand? I'm only going to tell you this because you've got me thinking, and I need to know more about that soil probe. I'm starting to see your point, which is really scary, but I do want to make lieutenant eventually, and if we arrest this guy and he's innocent I can probably kiss my career good-bye."

I locked my lips with my fingers and threw an invisible key into the fireplace.

"Moira had no family, but she did have a lawyer on retainer," Mike explained, "who had power of attorney over all of her affairs, and Moira was a very rich woman. Her will stated that all of her money would go to the country club after her death. Her life insurance policy named the country club as the beneficiary, too."

"How much money are we talkin'? Big bucks?"

"Big, big bucks."

"Okay," I said. "But the manager wouldn't get any of that personally. At best he could improve the grounds and give himself a raise, but I'd like to think it would take more than upgraded umbrella tables to turn someone into a killer."

"It would. And it probably did." Mikey put his hands behind his head. "We started doing a little digging. It didn't take much really, and I have to thank Sherman for being anal-retentive because he spotted it right away. The manager was embezzling funds from the club, blowing the stolen money at the casinos and — after losing it all — embezzling even more. It was just a matter of time before he was caught, fired and jailed. With Moira's money he could crunch some numbers and make everything right. Otherwise, he was just about to push the club into bankruptcy. Can you imagine all those members finding out where their money was going? He'd have been *lucky* to go to jail."

"Hmm." I squinted my eyes.

"Hmm, what?"

"That's pretty good. And I guess he could have gotten his hands on the soil probe."

"Could have. He had access to everything. He could go anywhere he wanted."

"Guess it doesn't get much better than that, does it?" Disappointment was an understatement. "But did he have opportunity?"

"When we questioned him, he said he saw Moira checking in for her tee time early morning two days ago. He says she told him she was golfing with someone special, not her usual golf lady friends, and it was a day she doesn't normally golf. But of course he didn't see her partner, he said, and from what we've learned he's the last person to see her alive."

"Opportunity. Or big lie. Or both. Nobody else saw this mystery partner?"

"Nope."

"Was it supposed to be a man or woman?"

"Can't say."

"But Moira did check in?"

"According to the tee sheet, but the guy in the pro shop says he was out sick that day and the assistant pro doesn't know Moira personally."

"Convenient timing. Moira golfing with a new partner when the pro was out sick. *Perfect* timing. The manager must have been waiting for something like that. So there's no reason to think her partners had it in for her after all." So much for my list of suspects.

"They might have, but we aren't looking at her lady friends. They weren't even golfing the day in question. Just Moira 'and guest.' And the coroner is certain she's been dead for two days. No more."

"And no caddies?"

"Moira always drove her cart or pulled her own bag."

"Damnation!"

The young man at the other table jumped and banged his knees under the table.

"Mrs. List!"

"I guess you've solved it, then." I wiped my hands together. "But . . . something just doesn't feel right. I don't know, Mikey, I have this really funny feeling in my gut. We're missing something. I don't know what, but I know we're missing something. Of course the manager didn't confess."

"To the embezzlement? Yes. To murder? No. And we didn't have enough to hold him so we had to let him go. For now."

"Wait a minute. Wait a gosh-darn minute, Mikey. Think about it. If this guy was really in trouble. I mean, if he were just about to, as you say, get caught, fired, and jailed, then why in the world would he put Moira's body someplace where it wasn't found for two days and may have never been found if it weren't for the misfortune of Pendersnack's hook? She could have disappeared *forever*. He'd want his money right away, wouldn't he? Hey. Have you found her car yet?"

161

"Not yet. We're still looking."

"I've got a hunch. It's just a hunch, you understand, but if that car is at the bottom of Moody Lake, then she was probably in it when it was dumped. Again, if she hadn't bloated up and floated out of it, she would have disappeared and no one would have ever found her. You have to find that car, Mikey, and you have to see if she was killed in it or transported in it after she died. The killer didn't want her to be found. But that manager *most certainly* would have wanted her body to be discovered, and quickly. Otherwise, no body, no money. It doesn't sound like he had a lot of time to wait before his little money problem was discovered."

"That makes sense."

"Of course it makes sense!"

"But we're still back to — who wanted to kill Moira if it wasn't the manager? Financially, he was the only one who would benefit from her death. Of course the members would be happy to see her money, but kill her for it? I don't see that happening. Club membership fees are steep and these people are willing to pay. They aren't hurting for dough-ray-me." Mike ran his hands through his hair.

"And the murder weapon. Don't forget

that. Someone from the grounds maintenance staff?"

"Because she mowed down some aza-
leas?"

"You should see how some of them act
when you say verticillium wilt," I said.

Mike stretched out his legs and rubbed
his thighs. "Do any of them have connec-
tions to Moody Lake? Maybe one of them
lives around there or did some landscaping
work for Candy. That sort of thing."

"I don't know. I'll ask around tomorrow.
In the meantime, don't be too quick to arrest the manager."

"I'll stall."

We stood and bumped fists. "I'll give you
a call tomorrow after I ask some questions . . . do some probing."

CHAPTER FOURTEEN

When I got home I didn't even spend time with my Trixie or Torch. I went straight to the garage. My daughter and her husband left boxes of their stuff at my house before they went to Belize, and as a Christmas present I'd given them both new scuba equipment. In my younger years I'd enjoyed the sport but I hadn't been diving for years. I hauled a cardboard box from the rafters, and when it was too heavy to carry down the ladder I let it fall to the floor below where it broke open.

All of Patty's old dive gear was there. Fins, snorkel, mask, BCD, and wet suit. The suit was pretty small but I could squeeze. There was no time to buy a new one and I was only going for the one dive. I figured I could save a little time and help Mikey by finding Moira's car for myself. I'm sure there are papers to file and procedures to go through before you can get taxpayer money to go on an expensive dive expedition, so it was up to me. Only one problem. I didn't have a dive tank and I'd need to rent one.

I gathered up the gear and made a phone call. There's only one dive shop in Spokane and it was closed. Drat. I'd have to wait one more day. Just as well; I was about to drop where I stood. I looked at the clock. Where had the day gone? My, oh, my. It was nearly six o'clock. Torch was in the living room pulling the stuffing out of my couch pillows, and Trixie was hanging on the drapes again. Anything for attention. Okay, babies, Mama's home.

Ted walked through the door at seven-thirty. By that time I had sogba cocktails chilling in the refrigerator and shrimp piri piri ready to go. To make the meal complete, I had whipped up some tomato chutney, Aleppo meali bread with hummus on the side (I'd had a hankering for it ever since the morning's events) and a nice couscous fruit salad. I quickly hid my self-improvement magazine in the towel drawer. Thank goodness for inspiration. Otherwise, it would have been meatloaf and fries that night.

Over dinner I gave Ted a brief synopsis of my day. He already knew about the murder and the autopsy (sans the part about my puking and fainting or the bit where I took on a job naming him as the reason for our fall into a pit of financial ruin, and I left out the assault on my new boss), and of course I couldn't tell him anything about a suspect. I just said the case was ongoing.

"You've certainly had a full day, Maybe Baby."

"And another one tomorrow," I said quickly, my words muffled by bread.

"What's going on tomorrow?"

"Thought I'd head out to the golf course."

"You taking up golf? Terrific! I've been trying to get you to go with me for years. Why the sudden interest?"

"I don't know. Guess I just want to see what's so exciting about whacking a little white ball around."

"That's great, honey." Ted dropped his napkin on the plate and stood. He gave me a kiss and a thanks and shuffled off to the showers.

"Don't suppose I could interest you in running the dishwasher?" I shouted at his back.

"That's great, honey," Ted said. Soon after, I heard the sound of water.

I looked at the table full of dirty dishes, the overflowing garbage can, the pile of stuff in the sink, and then I looked at Torch, now working on his third pillow, and at Trixie, chewing on the phone cord. "You think I'm gonna let him get away with that?"

The look on Ted's face when I joined him in the shower was one of happy surprise. "You want I wash your back, sir?" I spoke with an accent, something I hoped sounded sexy. It came out like a mixture of Croatian and Puerto Rican. I was aiming for Italian. I rubbed the soap around in my hand.

"Woops! Silly me, I dropped de zope." I leaned over, taking my time so Ted could appreciate my assets, and I made a big production of letting him know how little space we had in the shower by sliding my naked body down his legs. My knees popped like gunshots when I knelt to retrieve the soap bar. "Here we go . . ." I worked my way up his body, starting at his ankles. "Oh, my, deez need zum little rub, no? What's diz? Are we starting our golf game early? Looks like you've chosen de finest golf club, yes?" Ted closed his eyes and put his face in the stream as I worked my magic, then he started to giggle when I found his ribs. I pressed him against the shower wall so he couldn't fend off the soap tickles but when he started to squirm I thought it was best we get out before we both repeated my slam dance from that morning.

"Come, my darling," I said, "I vill light the candles. You start the music, ya?"

Ted twisted the shower knobs to off, raised his leg high and kicked the shower door open. His breathing was labored. Just where I wanted him.

I sashayed over to the side of the bed through a cloud of steam, dripping on the carpet as I went, but the devil with that. I'd already thumbed off the bedroom lights, and the soft glow of the candles did wonders for my curves. Ted literally ran across the room to the stereo and with trembling, excited hands grabbed the first CD he could find. He broke the case when he hurried to get it open, shoved it into the player and what came out was the most awful thumping disco music I'd ever heard.

"Vat is dat?" I shouted over the din.

"Sorry, babe, aerobic music. I was doing my workout this morning."

"No vorries, let it go." I then went to the dresser while Ted turned the music down to a tolerable thump and I felt around until my hands found something I'd been saving for the occasion. "Dis is for you!" I held up a leopard-patterned thong I'd bought Ted at a lingerie sale.

"Ohhhh, no." Ted fell onto the bed, got up on one elbow and shook his head.

168

"Oh, yesssss!" I slingshot the thong over to him. "Oh, yes!"

"Okay, but I don't know . . ." Ted squirmed into the form-fitting gear and leaned back, hands behind his neck. "You like?"

"I like!" I pounced, caught him off guard and knocked the wind out of him, but after a few minutes he was back to some healthy panting.

"Oh, phooey. The dog," Ted said, or wheezed might be a better description.

Beside the bed, Torch wiggled and looked at me with pleading in his eyes. He needed to go out. Now.

"Hold that pose," I told Ted.

I grabbed Torch, ran to the front door, shoved him out and left the door slightly ajar so he could come in on his own. Then I ran back to my bedroom and did another flying dive, but this time I was more careful with my aim. "Ted, remember when we could do this all night?"

"On the kitchen table?"

"In the pantry?"

"On the stove?"

"I've still got the scars."

"In the backyard?"

"I miss that." Ted ran his hands all over my body and gave me soft little kisses on

169

my neck. "I miss the way you used to squeal and shout."

"I did that?"

"Especially when I did this." Ted nibbled on my neck and earlobes, used his teeth occasionally and because I hated to think I was getting too old for that sort of thing, I let out a scream that made Ted stop, but then he realized I was showing my appreciation and continued. I screamed and squealed and screamed some more. I even banged my fists against the headboard and kicked the walls.

"You're a maniac!" I screamed. "You're so bad! You're such a bad man! Eeeee! Oooooo!"

"Mrs. List, are you all right? Mrs. List!"

I shut up and stared at my husband. He stared at me. I whispered, "What was that?"

A man's voice called out, "Is everything okay in there?"

I heard heavy footsteps race down the hall toward our bedroom. A head poked through the door followed by a second, then a third. This time when I screamed it wasn't for pleasure. I grabbed the sheets (the blankets were on the floor) and crawled under. Poor Ted was left blowing in the breeze with his leopard-skinned thong straining against his husbandly duty. "Pastor Jerry? Deacon Wall?

Deacon Ambrose?"

"Your front door was, er, open."

I poked an eye out from under the sheet. Our pastor was standing there with an entourage. "And I almost ran over your, er, little dog here," he said. The pastor had Torch under his arm. "I'm so sorry. I thought I heard someone in distress." He placed Torch on the floor. "I'm guessing you forgot tonight's Bible study was meeting here . . . tonight."

Ted swung his long legs over the bed and sat there with his hands clutched in his lap. "No sir, no, not at all."

"Fine, fine." The pastor was looking at everything in our room except for the bed. The ceiling fan seemed to be especially fascinating to him. "We'll go ahead and get settled in the living room then and let you, um, finish up with your quiet time."

"That would be good. Thank you." Ted jumped up and crossed the room, hand extended. The pastor reluctantly took his hand. "Good to see you, Brother Jerry. I'll be right out," Ted said.

Footsteps retreated down the hall. Running footsteps. And, although Ted and I argued about this later, I could swear that I heard some manly giggles.

I poked my head out from under the

171

sheets. "Bet they're jealous, no?"

"You betcha, my little chickadee."

The Bible study began without my husband. I gave him a little spiritual guidance of my own.

I don't remember falling asleep or even closing my eyes. I woke up the next morning with bed-head, and sometime in the night my sweet husband had covered me with blankets. It was still dark out when I dressed for my first day of work. My objective that day was to learn everything I could about the landscaping crew, who had used the soil probe last and where, and whether or not anyone had seen the "guest" Moira had checked in on her last day on earth. I also wanted to know if anyone had seen Moira with the manager — at any time. If he had anything to do with her death, he must have known about her financial situation. But how had he known her money was going to the club after her death? That was something I'd failed to ask Mikey. If the manager did know, then maybe he'd cozied up to her off the course, or maybe she was just one of those ladies who liked to garner favors with the promise of an eventual payoff. Plausible, but I just wasn't sure. I needed to know more about the lady.

I dressed in khaki work slacks, maroon

shirt with an attractive gold club symbol over the left breast and some old shoes I used for hiking (they were like new), and I found an old pair of gloves in the garage. I left a note for Ted, kissed him good-bye, and thought it was funny when he snorted and made kissing motions in the air. I grabbed a breakfast bar from the cupboard. Trixie and Torch sulked and pouted but I gave them each an extra can of food so they were pacified, at least for the time being.

As I drove away from my house, I dodged four deer, a porcupine and a wild-eyed coyote. I was the only car on the road for miles. I couldn't remember the last time I'd been out this early. Stars were still winking in the sky, and I felt like I was the only one alive on planet earth until I turned onto the highway and nearly got sideswiped by a semi. Think I might have dozed off for a minute.

Lights were on at the country club maintenance building when I got there. I trudged up the long driveway, breathing in the crisp morning air. Dave and Joe drove golf carts out through the open bay doors and parked them in neat rows along the fence line.

I walked into the hall and punched my time card. People I'd met the day before were shuffling in. Football Mike had dark circles under his eyes and said a quiet hello. He looked like he'd been crying all night, poor guy. He punched his time card and wandered into the break room. Marcia and Teresa came in together looking fresh and energetic. "We all meet in the break room for a brief staff meeting every morning. Coffee should be on," Teresa said brightly. "Cups are over the sink."

I filled my mug and took a chair at one of the long tables in the break room. Jim came in and slapped me on the back in a friendly way. I choked on a mouthful of coffee but got things under control right away. Bonnie and Clyde were playing thumb wars. Marcia and Teresa got their coffee and immediately sat down to play a vigorous game of cribbage with Joe and Dave. The young guys were sprawled and draped over chairs everywhere. Some looked like they hadn't been to bed yet, and there were a few guys I hadn't met giving me a curious once-over. Nothing like being the new kid on the block. A guy named Chris introduced himself then curled up on the counter by the sink and started snoring immediately.

We all wore the club uniform, khakis and maroon shirts, which filled me with a warm sense of camaraderie. This was a fraternity of sorts; a club, a group, a brotherhood. The representation of female workers was so small that we were a group apart, but not left out in any way. In fact, when I noticed Teresa's muscles flexing as she shuffled the cards, I knew she didn't slack off where the heavy lifting was concerned. I thought about that and got a nervous feeling again. If I had to pull my weight, I really had some heavy lifting to do. The partial paralysis excuse might be needed in a big hurry.

I scanned the group looking for shifty eyes or fresh scratches — signs of a struggle. That wasn't very helpful since just about everyone had a bruise or scrape somewhere on their bodies — these were hard workers after all. As for the shifty eyes, all I noticed were the morning bags and red rims common at this inhumane hour of the morning. Chris snorted, jerked, and tumbled onto the floor.

The guy with the blue sunglasses wandered in. He swung a chair around and sat in it backwards. He held a Coke in his hand, took a slurp, and grunted a hello through a burp to no one in particular. I waved. When the clock said five, a ruddy-faced gentleman made his way through the room. He was of the husky variety, tough-looking, and in no mood for conversation. His dog, a boxer that looked disturbingly like his master, walked at the guy's flank. The man nodded to the group. Chris quickly took a chair, the cribbage board disappeared, conversation stopped, and all eyes went to the white board on the wall upon which was scribbled our names and the day's assignments. Teresa leaned over to me and said, "That's Mr. Stamper. He's our assistant supervisor. He'll be giving out assignments."

That seemed rather redundant to me since everything was clearly written on the board, but I didn't want to be difficult so I listened patiently.

"Good morning," the man said with no enthusiasm at all. He looked as tired as I felt. "First, I would like to welcome our new member of the team, Mrs. May Bell List."

I didn't know if I should stand, or what, so I just raised my coffee cup, which must have been a violation of company policy because everyone gasped. Then I noticed all the other staff members had hidden their coffee cups under the table. Guess I was breaking some sort of rule, but since I was new that gave me an excuse and I wasn't fired or anything.

"Okay," Mr. Stamper said with a sigh, like he was happy to have that chore out of the way. "Today, Aric will be on the rotary mower . . ."

Before he could continue, in rushed Tim, looking disheveled and quite upset. "We have an emergency!" he shouted. "The pump shut off in the middle of the night, and the irrigation system quit. Nothing was watered! Oh, my goodness. Did you know about this, Stamper?"

"I'm giving out assignments, Tim," Stamper said, clearly aggravated. "Now I'll have to start all over again. Elder is on the rotary mower, Marty's on the triplex, Chris is on the surround mower . . ."

"This can't wait!" Tim grabbed his hair with both hands. "Roots are withering as we speak!" He ran out, leaving boot rubber on the linoleum.

". . . on bunker duty . . ."

Tim stuck his head in the room. "Now, Mr. Stamper, now!"

Stamper grabbed a handful of dry-erase markers and snapped them in half, one at a time. His eyes were clamped shut and his face color changed to a glowing crimson, so red in fact that I was quite concerned he'd stroke out.

"All right!" he finally said, ink dripping from his hands. "Go. All of you just go. Nobody listens to me anyway."

The crew raced out of the break room, hooting and hollering. Stamper took his dog by the collar, stomped out and locked himself in the men's bathroom.

"Where are they going?" I asked Teresa and Marcia as they calmly collected all the discarded coffee cups and put them in the sink.

"They're going out to the pond where we get all of our irrigation water. It's pulled up through a filter and pumped around the golf course. I'm guessing something is stuck up against the filter. Probably leaves, pine needles or a branch. Someone's gonna have to go in the water."

I hoped it wasn't Elder. He was so distraught about his football I was quite concerned about his mental state. He might decide to go under — and stay. I heard golf carts race out of the parking lot, and then . . . silence.

"Ready, Marcia?" Teresa asked.

"Ready."

"Come on, Mrs. List. You can ride in my cart."

"What's up?" Mr. Gullikson met us at the door.

"Clogged filter. I guess the irrigation system broke down last night," Marcia said.

"That's not good," Gully said. "Oh, hey, Mrs. List, good to see you. How's your first day on the job?"

"I don't know yet, but it's starting out pretty interesting."

"Fine, fine."

"We're going to take her over to the pond. See if we can help."

"Sounds like an opportunity," Gully said with optimistic gusto. "I've got some paperwork to finish up here so I'll be in the office all day. Let me know how it goes."

"How are you feeling today, Mr. Gullikson?" I asked. A nasty purple knot had formed near his left eye. "Any more fainting spells?"

Gully rubbed his temple. "Darnedest thing. I've never passed out like that before. I'm sure it was the heat." Then he smiled in his charming way and said, "Today should be nice and pleasant, though. The forecast mentioned rain."

"Rain?" Marcia looked at Teresa, then at Gully. "Are we talking about a thunderstorm or just an ordinary run-of-the-mill downpour?"

Gully frowned. "I'll get on the Internet and look at the weather patterns. Better hurry on over to the pond and . . . if you hear the sirens, you know what to do."

Sirens? As we left the shop I asked Teresa, "What do we do?"

Teresa shrugged. "Run for your life."

CHAPTER FIFTEEN

I wondered why Marcia and Teresa were in no hurry to follow their comrades until I learned a new little tidbit about the cousins. They were absolutely fearless. They had a shortcut, they explained, something about working at the club for eight-plus years and how that had given them unrestricted access to every blade of grass on the course, and how they could find their way from hole one to eighteen with their eyes closed. They were going to beat the guys to the pond or die trying.

"Get your hard hat on, May Bell!" Marcia and Teresa were already hoofing it toward Teresa's large utility cart — a much more beefy contraption than the little golf carts everyone else had ridden off in — and they leapt into the two available seats. "It's against club policy to ride in the back but we're breaking the rules today. Hop in and hang on." Marcia twisted around in her seat and shoved aside a coil of hose. "Come on, come on, time's a-wastin'!"

I clambered over the side of the cart and tumbled down into the little metal box usually reserved for tools and landscaping equipment. As I reached for a handhold, Teresa shoved the gearshift into drive and slammed her foot on the gas. I toppled onto my back, my feet flew up in the air and I got tangled in the hose. I wrestled around with it like I was fighting off a family of snakes, twisting it this way and that, bumping painfully along the floor of that cold, hard metal box. Before I could get loose of the hose I was on my hands and knees in search of a comfortable position, but that certainly wasn't it. "Hey," I yelled. "Hey, I don't mind walking to the pond, I really don't."

Marcia and Teresa, however, were busy arguing about the best route to the pond and I was all but forgotten. Teresa drove, but that didn't stop Marcia from grabbing at the wheel every time she thought they should be going in a direction contrary to the one Teresa had chosen. Teresa deflected Marcia's hands and they struggled for control, which caused the cart to veer wildly back and forth, and then we left the cart path altogether and things went from bad

181

to worse.

It was only five-thirty in the morning, but already golfers were out swinging away under the overcast sky.

"Hey!" I shouted. "I thought first tee time wasn't until eight o'clock!"

Marcia hollered back. "I guess they're trying to beat the weather. Stamper's gonna have a fit!"

We flew over the first tee right in front of a guy who checked his swing at the last minute and blasted a dirt clod high into the air. Uh-oh, it was the guy I'd seen the day before on the driving range. He screamed at us, cursed a blue streak once more and threw his club straight up in the air. It didn't come down because it got lodged in a tree branch. When I turned to give him an apologetic wave I noticed several golf clubs were stuck in the same tree. I wondered if Tim knew about that.

Teresa veered again, I fell hard onto my left shoulder and grazed my ear on a bucket and we sped straight down to the second green. Three members of a foursome stood by calmly as they watched an older gentleman square up to his ball. Teresa shouted but didn't swerve. The men dove left and right, landing hard on the dew-soaked grass. I'd gotten to a seated position by this time and watched as they ran after us, fists raised. I held up two fingers making a peace sign.

We bombed along, serpentined between a row of trees, jumped a curb along one cart path, and eventually came out to a wide clearing. In the middle of the clearing I saw a pond, a small utility building and the rest of the crew standing around with their hands in their pockets, staring out over the water.

"You didn't do it right!" Marcia yelled. "You should have taken the back way like I told you."

Teresa skidded to a stop near the water's edge and elbowed Marcia in the ribs. "Hey, Marshmallow, did you show them our short-cut?"

"Don't call me that."

"Marshmallow, marshmallow, marshmallow."

"You're so mean." Marcia's chin quivered.

I'd found my way out of the cart and took Teresa's hand. I led her a few feet away. "Is this really necessary? She seems to be rather sensitive about the nickname."

Teresa looked at her feet and shuffled around a little before saying, "It's not as bad as what she calls me."

"Let's just concentrate on the job at hand, okay?"

"Oh, all right. Sorry, Marcia."

"That's okay, Tinkles."

"Why, I oughta . . ." Teresa turned and would have gone after her cousin if I hadn't grabbed her by the back of the shirt.

"The task at hand?"

The guys were talking and I wandered over. Three of the bigger men were stripping off their shirts, taking their time because I guess they'd lost the paper-rock-scissors contest and had to go for a dive. I tried not to stare, but my goodness. They were all at least six feet tall, muscle-bound and young. One was a redhead. Another, from what Marcia quickly explained, was from the land of Samoa and had the smooth chocolate complexion that was the envy of every red-blooded American white male and the admiration of every living woman from anywhere. The third had the mysterious, tall-dark-and-silent look of a man who never knew a challenge he couldn't wrestle into submission. Teresa ticked off their names. James, Jesse and Aaron. Chris, the biggest of all the guys in the crew, sat on the ground laughing at the three cabana boys, then fell back and started snoring again.

The guys should have moved faster but . . . that water was cold.

After about five minutes of watching the

slo-mo strip show, my tolerance had reached its limit. "Oh, for Pete's sake," I said, and dove head-first into the pond.

Bad idea, because it was a shallow edge and I scraped my face against the bottom and stopped short, crumpling like an accordion with my backside sticking up in the air. Thankfully it was muddy at the bottom of the pond and not too rocky. I didn't want to embarrass myself, so I kicked and flailed and moved out toward where I'd noticed the drumlike filter before diving in. Unfortunately my movements stirred up the silt and soon it became virtually impossible to see anything.

I raised my head out of the water to get my bearings. Everyone was crowded along the edge of the pond, their mouths agape. I raised a hand, gave a wave and shouted to ask which way to go. I swallowed a mouthful of water but not before I saw a lot of waving and pointing. Down I went again, and kept swimming. I opened my eyes now and then, saw a fat frog gazing at me before shooting off, closed my eyes and kept swimming toward the big metal object that was the source of our water troubles.

Soon I found the object and felt around it. It was a drum all right, at the end of a long metal tube. The drum filtered anything big enough to clog the pipes. Its sides were metal with tiny holes drilled through. The drum rotated as I pushed on it. I felt around it, swam around it but could find nothing that would staunch the flow of irrigation water. I reached down toward the bottom, reached around, felt around, and felt a cold, rubbery hand.

I shot to the surface, sputtering, scraping weeds out of my hair. "Hey!" I shouted. "Did someone else dive in after me?"

The group all shook their heads in unison.

"I think I know what's clogging your filter. Hold on a minute and I'll get it for you."

CHAPTER SIXTEEN

Now this is something I've wanted to do my whole life. Scare the bejeezus out of someone. I took a deep breath, closed my eyes, and went under the water again. It was a task that made me cringe and feel really creepy, and I was shivering like mad both from the cold and from what I was about to do, but I was dying to see the shocked faces of everyone when I brought up the clog, so I suffered through it.

I felt around again, and this time ran my fingers through hair, then raked my nails over a face (nose, mouth, eyebrows, the works), and that made me really feel goobery, but when I bumped against the hand again, I swallowed a little nervous spit and wrapped my fingers around it and squeezed. The hand was rather slimy and hard to hold onto. I gave a yank but the corpse was stuck tight. I had to come up for one more breath before going back under.

Patting the body down like a cop on an arrest, I did a thorough search until I found the source of the problem. A belt buckle was caught on a filter screw. I jerked the belt this way and that and pulled, feeling my face turn blue from lack of oxygen, then, duh, I unbuckled the belt and slipped it out of the pant loops and freed the body. I hoisted the limp form over my head and kicked for the sky.

We broke surface with me gasping and panting for a lung of air, spewing pond water, while the corpse roiled up like an emerging submarine, and you should have heard the screams. First from the trio of cabana boys, then from the rest of the crew. The only ones not screaming like little girls were — the girls.

"Whoa! Take a looka that!" Marcia hollered.

"Who is it?" Teresa had produced a pair of binoculars from somewhere and peered through them.

While I was under water, Tim had made his way onto the scene. His hands were cupped around his mouth and he yelled, "Do you know how many diatoms and microbes are in that water, Mrs. List? You're gonna need shots for sure, and I wouldn't be surprised if you don't get a flesh-eating

188

bacteria up in there. Whatever you do, don't get it in your sinuses. I saw this show once where this guy had a fungus in his sinuses after fishing in contaminated water and . . . hey, is that guy dead?"

"Looks that way, Tim," Marcia said. "Who is that, anyway?" She grabbed at Teresa's binoculars and they tussled.

"Marshmallow," Teresa said.

"Tinkles," Marcia countered.

I swam, pushing the body in front of me. "A little help here?" I pleaded, but the guys were all backing away from the pond. I guess I should have known. This was bad juju.

I was getting tired, and my water-soaked clothes made it hard to stay above water. I rolled over on my back, held the corpse's hand and paddled in a long, steady, one-armed rhythm. It was going to be hard to fake paralysis now. I'd just say I was having a good day.

Marcia and Teresa waded into the water up to their waists. They took the body from me. I was spent and dragged along after they grabbed the corpse by his clothes and hauled him out onto the grass. They laid him out on his back beside the big guy named Chris. Chris woke up, took one look at the body and jumped to his feet, eyes wide.

"Oh, my gosh!" cried Marcia. "He's got a crack tool sticking out of his chest."

"What?" I crawled out of the water, once again on my hands and knees. I was beginning to wonder if I'd ever walk upright again. "What's that you say? A crack tool? I didn't notice that before."

"Step back everyone, this is a crime scene."

Did I say that? My body was so numb with approaching hypothermia that I was having an out-of-body experience. No, it was Jim, the retired police officer, finally stepping up to do his duty.

The guys all crowded around, taking slow, cautious steps. They peered into the face of our body. "Wow," Jim squatted and stared. "I can't believe it."

"Do you know this man?" I asked.

"Sure," Jim said. "It's Buddy Shields."

A collective "Ooooh" went up from the rest of the guys.

"Who's Buddy Shields?" I asked Marcia.

"He's the club manager. Guess we're gonna have a down day."

Just then the sirens went off.

Thunder rolled in loud eardrum-shattering blasts, and the sky opened up on the Northside Country Club. Rain pummeled my already-soaked head.

"We can't leave the body unprotected!" I shouted, but to no avail. Everyone hopped in golf carts and sped away, cutting across the golf course with no thought to keeping on the designated trails.

"Hey," Teresa said to Marcia. "You *did* show them my shortcut!"

"Did not."

Terrified golfers raced hither and yon; carts peeled out, some were abandoned. Chaos and commotion propelled by panic swirled around me as people in bizarre apparel made a panicked rush to shelter. In the distance I saw umbrellas unfurl, and then on the club's porch, the umbrellas on the tables toppled as the panicked athletes rushed to get into the banquet room.

"We should cover the body," I cried. "Protect the evidence."

"You have to go, Mrs. List," Jim yelled at me. "It's too dangerous to stay on the course right now. We'll call the police and let them deal with it."

"Come on, come on!" Marcia and Teresa grabbed me and tossed me in the back of their cart. Their muscles weren't just for show, I discovered, and away we went. A flash of lightning blasted the top of an enormous ponderosa pine. The branch flashed briefly into flames and then toppled down, landing in front of us. "Look out!" Marcia screamed. Teresa expertly twisted the wheel and skidded around the smoking branch. Naturally, I bounced around in the back, rolling from side to side, feeling every bruise and wishing I hadn't thought of this really dumb idea. "We can't make it back to the shop in time," Marcia shouted. "Plan B!"

We took a side road and managed to stay one second ahead of the falling branches and lightning strikes. Finally, we slammed to a stop in front of a large, old, dilapidated building. Marcia and Teresa hauled me out of the cart and we raced inside while lightning blazed ribbons through the sky. The inside of the building was dim and dusty but safe. Along a wall was a soft, comfortable-looking couch. An old TV was in a corner near a card table. On the card table sat a tattered Monopoly game, a deck of cards and a cribbage board.

"Where are we?" I asked, my teeth chattering. I dripped a small puddle around my feet.

"This is the old shop," Marcia explained. "We only use it to store excess or broken equipment and other stuff now, but it's sturdy enough. There's a working bathroom in the back and all the drinks left over from tournaments are stored here as well. It's sort of a refuge in times of need. Hey, Mrs. List, we've got to get you into some dry clothes before you freeze to death."

Standing in the door of the old shop, I watched the tempest and was awed by the sky in all its turmoil. "I've never seen anything like this," I said dreamily.

"Like what?" Marcia and Teresa joined me.

"I've never seen a thunderstorm like this so early in the morning."

"How often are you up this early?" Teresa asked.

"Good point."

"Come on now. Let's find something to get you warmed up." Teresa's concern was touching. She didn't even give a thought to her own discomfort. She, too, had wet pants and must be cold, but she didn't mention it.

Marcia shuffled off and returned with a six-pack of beer. She peeled one off and tossed it to me but I couldn't feel my fingers and it landed on the concrete floor where it made an awful clutter.

"No, I mustn't," I said around a mouthful of chattering teeth.

"Do you know your lips are blue, Mrs. List?" Teresa got right up into my face and scrutinized my features. "And your chin is trembling so hard. You're definitely in the first stages of hypothermia. I suggest you take that beer. It'll warm you up while we strip off these wet clothes." Teresa started yanking on my shirt and got it untucked, but being a little on the prudish side, the last thing I wanted to do was stand nude in front of these women who didn't have the word cellulite in their vocabulary. Besides, I barely knew them. I batted her hands away with my numb fist clubs.

"Mmmm, mmmm, mmm," I said.

"See?" Teresa put her hands on her hips. "You can't even talk anymore. You're like an ice cube! Marcia! Help me get her out of these clothes."

I wasn't frozen, except with fear. Standing behind Marcia in the shadows was the silhouette of a man. He crept slowly toward Marcia with one hand extended and in his grip was some sort of object. First a soil probe, then a crack tool. I didn't think the object was as big as a chainsaw but it could have been. We'd found the killer's hideout, and Marcia was a mere five strides out of his reach.

"Mmmm! Mmmm! Mmm!" I struggled

to shout, to scream, to point and warn Marcia but she tipped a can to her mouth and didn't understand a thing.

The man suddenly jumped from the shadows and screamed, "Armillaria root rot!"

Marcia turned calmly. "Oh, Tim. How'd you get in here?"

I withered like the dry roots on the golf course and sank to the floor. My legs just couldn't support me any longer.

"The Douglas firs are infested with it. Next it will be phytophthora root rot, then the maples will be destroyed. Oh, this is so bad." Tim shuffled over and sat beside me. "Mrs. List, you're like a glacier!"

So now it was a glacier. Before, I was an ice cube. A cute little ice cube. I was thankful Teresa hadn't gotten my clothes off or perhaps Tim would be calling me Antarctica.

"Tim, forget about the firs and maples." Teresa grabbed the branch out of Tim's hand. "Do you even care there's a dead body lying out by the pond? Who, I might add, is our very own club manager? Wilt can wait. For now, we've got bigger problems."

"Hear, hear," I said and crab-walked my fingers over to the beer can. Maybe it would be just the thing.

Tim snatched the branch away from Teresa, clucked his tongue and wagged the leafy stick at me. "That will only make your condition worse, Mrs. List." He looked off into the distance. "Oh, sure, you'll feel warm for a few minutes, maybe even all powerful as the beverage seeps its way through your veins. You might even feel euphoric, like you can take on the world, and after half a can you might feel like you're the best-looking man in the room, able to hold deep intelligent conversations with the hot girl dancing with her hot friends, who wouldn't otherwise give you a second look — until you open your mouth before remembering to swallow . . ."

"Tim," Teresa said loudly.

"Huh?"

"Back to the body."

"Oh."

Outside the storm boiled and knocked out power as far as the eye could see. The wind blew and the rickety building creaked and groaned. It was terribly dark and drafty in there and I was so stiff I couldn't bend any of my joints. My situation was hitting the critical level.

"B-b-b-b-blanket?" I asked.

"Here." Tim shrugged out of his rain gear and handed it to me. "Change out of those clothes and put this on. It's dry inside and very warm. I had it custom-lined."

Marcia gave Tim a beer-can salute. "You're a class act, sir."

"Put that away," Teresa scolded. "If Mr. Gullikson finds you sucking suds you'll get fired." She turned to me. "She was always the rebel. Her dad, my uncle, was a Navy man. My dad was a sergeant in the Army. What does she do? She goes and joins the Marines. No respect."

"Ah, don't get all twisted, cuz. We're off the clock," Marcia said. "Did you forget our boss's boss got whacked?"

Outside the wind continued to howl. By now I'd lost all feeling in my extremities. I moved my arms by sheer will and positive thinking. There was no way I was going to be able to walk to a discrete corner so I rolled around on the floor and somehow got Tim's rain gear wrapped around my body. It was a poncho with slits for armholes, and, as Tim had said, the lining was a quality product still warm from his body heat. Once I was covered in a shroud of privacy, I squirmed out of my wet clothes and kicked them aside.

I didn't mean to shed everything, but with no feeling I couldn't tell cotton from denim, and I watched in horror as my undies sailed a good twenty feet across the dusty floor. Tim was a gentleman and pretended not to notice. Marcia and Teresa, on the other hand, turned their backs to me and shared a good silent laughing fit at my expense. They regained their composure quickly enough, but when I tottered to my feet and my king-size bra fell around my ankles they exploded again, turning away quickly, as if I couldn't tell what they were doing.

"Why don't you have a seat over here, Mrs. List," Tim offered. He pulled a wooden box through the dust and tossed a tarp over it. (Guess he didn't want me to get his comfy couch soggy.) He glanced through the open door. "We're not going anywhere for a while, so we might as well get comfortable."

I thanked him and took careful baby steps over to the crate.

"There you are, then," Tim said. He reached out and patted my head. I could hear my hair crackle. "Oh, my. Your hair is frozen right to your head."

"Wonderful," I mumbled.

Tim grabbed more tarps and bundled me up nicely. I was just a head poking over a mountain of brown-and-green canvas.

"You were pretty darn brave, May Bell," Marcia said. She chewed on a breakfast bar and sat cross-legged on the floor. "I mean, to go in the water like you did. That was pretty brave."

"Where did you get that?" Teresa asked Marcia. She patted her pockets. Little squirts of water sploshed out.

"To tell you the truth, I don't really know what you were thinking, diving in like that. You could have broken your neck or something," Tim said.

"Is that mine?" Teresa squinted and glared daggers at Marcia.

Marcia popped the last of the breakfast bar in her mouth. She chewed fast and then opened her mouth. "You want it back?"

Tim took a seat beside Marcia. "There's a food stash back there in one of the old ice chests," he said to Teresa. "Sometimes I have to work late."

Teresa wandered to the back of the shop.

My teeth chattered, but I could finally speak without shaking too badly. "Were you working late last night, Tim?" At least I could get some work done here. I'd seen the wild look in Tim's eye when he was disturbed about his root rot or wilt or whatever had him in a dither, and he was a passionate guy. Maybe he was capable of losing control. The manager must have been killed during the night because Mike and company had questioned him yesterday. Surely someone would have noticed if he'd gone missing during the afternoon. He had a club to run, after all, even if it was under a cloud of suspicion and accusations. If he'd been thrown in jail he wouldn't have ended up in the pond.

"I was teaching a class at the community college last night," Tim said. He sniffed at the branch he held in his hand.

"Oh? On the west side then?"

"Yeah," Tim wasn't acting nervous so I pressed on.

"And how late does your class run? I mean, maybe I should take one of your classes. Except my husband likes his meals on the table around six or seven."

Tim licked the stem of his branch. "I learned to cook for myself by the time I was ten."

"Yes. I suppose Ted could fend for himself. So you're saying your classes run rather late."

"I rarely get home before ten-thirty. Questions, always questions after my lectures, and then there's the paperwork and I have a thirty-minute drive home. Sometimes I have to take a nap in the parking lot before I leave the campus."

"I guess it's hard for you to keep these

early hours, then." I was barking up the wrong verticillium-wilted tree. Tim had an alibi. But I'd ask Mikey to check it out just the same.

"Hey, May Bell," Marcia said. "How did you have the nerve to haul up the body?" She was now chewing on a hunk of jerky. "If it had been me, I'd have been walking on water as soon as I knew what I had in my hands."

"How do you do it?" I asked.

"What?"

"How do you eat so much and stay so skinny?"

"You think I'm skinny?" Marcia beamed.

"You're a reed." Tim nodded in agreement.

Teresa came back then, dragging a large cooler. She reached in and hauled out three sandwiches.

"Quite a stash," I said.

"I didn't have time to thaw my lasagna before work this morning," Tim said.

"So you made sandwiches? Before work?"

"Don't tell Mr. Gullikson or the kitchen staff. I just can't eat another mini corndog or bratwurst, although the coleslaw isn't half bad. I usually fake my way through lunch and then duck in here afterwards."

Definitely no time for murder, I thought.

I mentally scratched Tim off my suspect list. Teresa handed sandwiches all around and I munched the avocado-bean-sprout delight while thinking. I had to hold it through my wraps. Quite a chore but I managed.

"Did you all know that one of the club members was murdered a few days ago? A woman named Mrs. Finch?"

"Shame," Tim said.

"Shame she wasn't killed earlier," Marcia said.

Teresa gasped. "I can't believe you."

"Like you weren't thinking it."

"Was not."

"Was too."

"Okay, so I take it she wasn't very well liked," I interrupted.

"She was the worst," Teresa said, and then looked like she was sorry she'd been so insensitive. "I'd like to say I didn't have anything against her personally, but she really was horrible."

"How so?" I asked.

"Do you know what she did every year as soon as the flowers bloomed? She'd drive her cart around with her very own personal pruning shears and cut bouquets. Bouquets! Last year she cut so many flowers the beds looked like they'd been hacked to pieces. No respect. She had no idea how hard we

202

worked, planning, planting, pruning, weeding, and she just came along and chopped down what she wanted, sometimes even while we were working in the bed she was taking the flowers from. We asked Mr. Shields to make her stop, but he said we had to do whatever was necessary to keep the members happy. But what about the other members who complained that the beds looked awful? It was her fault, but *we* had to take the blame."

"Yeah," Marcia agreed. She grabbed a Coke and popped the top.

"And she was doing this for years?"

"As long as I've been working here," Teresa said. "But I got used to it and kept my mouth shut. I like my job."

"And Mr. Shields let her get away with it," I said, knowing exactly why he wanted to keep this member happy — she was going to be his meal ticket, and he didn't want her moving on to another country club. But I couldn't tell them that. It had all been so simple. He was stealing from the club, her money would get him out of trouble, but now he was dead, too. My hunch had been right. He didn't kill Moira. They were connected all right, and the money issue probably had something to do with it, but someone else wanted them both dead. I had nothing.

I looked through the door. The storm hadn't subsided a bit and the power was still out. My eyes had adjusted to the dark interior of the shop, but it seemed like it was getting even darker. I thought of the two bodies I'd seen in the last couple of days and everything turned spooky.

"I guess you all saw what was sticking out of Buddy's chest, didn't you?" I said, and even my own voice sounded ominous.

"A crack tool," Marcia said. She broke off a piece of chocolate and popped it in her mouth.

"What do you usually do in the evenings, Marcia, I mean, after you leave work?"

This certainly seemed like a non sequitur, and Marcia stopped nibbling on her chocolate for a minute. Then she choked a bit and sputtered, "You think I used a crack tool on Buddy? Whatever for?"

Darn. That was really subtle, May Bell. *And what do you do in the evenings, Marcia?* Why hadn't I just said, *Where were you when a crack tool speared the heart of your manager, Marcia, and were you on the business end of the thing?*

"You do have access, Marcia," Tim said. He carefully folded his sandwich baggy and tucked it under his thigh.

"And so do you," Marcia shot back.

"But not opportunity. I was home in bed last night."

"And if you've got any bright ideas," Teresa said, giving me the stink eye, "Marcia and I were holding a late-night cribbage match with our husbands. Then Marcia left — with her husband — and I went to bed. With *my* husband."

"And just so we get the record straight, Mrs. List, where were you last night?" Marcia asked.

I pointed to my chest (only nobody could see that because my arms were still under Tim's poncho.) "Me? I didn't even know Mr. Shields. And why in the world would I want to kill him?"

Tim looked at Marcia and Teresa. A silent message passed between them. Marcia nodded at Tim.

"We've all been sort of wondering, Mrs. List. How did you get this job so easily, anyway?"

"You're insinuating I knew somebody?"

"Mmmm," Teresa muttered.

"That I'm lying about not knowing the manager?"

"It just seems awfully convenient," Teresa said. "You waltz in, and the next thing we know you're on the staff. No screening, no consult by Mr. Gullikson, just — there you are. We don't even know anything about you."

I huffed out a short laugh. "I am certainly no killer."

"I thought it was strange that you just *dove* into that pond like you knew what you were going in after. Right, Teresa?" Marcia had found a fistful of red licorice and she waved it around.

"And I used a crack hoe to kill him?"

"A crack *tool.*"

"See? That just goes to show you. I had no idea what that thing was before this morning." A minute ago I was freezing. Now, I was sweating.

"You don't have to know what something is called to use it to kill somebody. A tool of opportunity."

"Yes," Tim said. "Opportunity. Like, say, you have to stay late after class and some coed forgets her book and comes back unexpectedly while you're wiping down the chalkboard and . . ."

"Tim." Marcia slapped him with her red licorice whips.

Tim flinched. "Ouch, Marcia."

"Focus, Tim."

"And how, pray tell," Teresa asked, "did you know about the other murder? About

Moira Finch, if you didn't know anyone here at the club before you so conveniently landed this job?" Teresa's brows were furrowed. Her eyes glistened ominously, catching a streak of lightning's reflection through a grime-streaked window.

"Oh, bugger," I said.

Tim jumped to his feet. "Where? Is it a bark beetle? Let me at him."

"Bugger. I said bug-ger. All right, I suppose you should all know. I need someone to help me out here and I honestly don't think any one of you had anything to do with that crack hoe."

"Tool," they all chorused.

"Tool — sticking out of Buddy's chest. And, I don't think you know anything at all about Mrs. Finch's murder."

"Just that she wasn't killed here. We don't even know the details."

"I believe that." Of course I believed that. The cops were keeping things quiet for now. Unless the beachcombers at Candy's were talking, which was highly possible. I didn't think Moira's murder weapon was public knowledge, though, and thankfully there hadn't been enough time for that information to be leaked. Two tools from the country club grounds equipment inventory, and then I had a horrible thought.

"That tool. That crack tool was custom-made wasn't it?"

"Sure. It's quite an ingenious invention, really."

"And" — my breath was coming in ragged gasps — "is Mr. Gullikson the only one who modifies the tools?"

"Mr. Gullikson? Of course; he does all the alterations around here."

Oh, my.

CHAPTER SEVENTEEN

So Mr. Gullikson did all the alterations. And he had opportunity. He admitted he often stayed quite late; it was his job to keep the members and the staff (especially the management) happy, but did he have motive? I certainly hoped not. He was such a nice young man and, oh, so handsome. I'd considered him the picture of stellar principles and of the highest repute. He'd protected me, after all. Could it be? Could he be protecting someone else? Would he stoop to murder?

"I think," I said, pushing off the tarps, "these two murders are connected. I just don't know why. First Moira, then Buddy Shields? And both with gardening tools? It's just too fluky to ignore."

Tim's mouth dropped open. "Moira Finch was killed with a garden tool, too?"

"I did not say that." Ooooh, Mikey was gonna kill me.

Marcia's eyes grew wide. "What kind of tool, May Bell?"

"Did I say she was killed with a garden tool?" I chuckled nervously. "How would I know that?"

Again, Tim, Marcia and Teresa shared a look. "There's something going on here, May Bell. Spill it." Teresa crossed her arms over her chest. Muscles quivered along her biceps. Wow. My feng shui would be useless.

"Yeah, Mrs. List, spill." Tim waved his branch under my nose.

I poked my arms through the slits in the poncho and squirmed out from under the tarps. I waved Tim away. "Okay. You got me. I'm not really an employee here."

Marcia sucked in a long breath. "You lied."

"I had no choice." I put on a regretful, if not-resolute expression. "I'm undercover."

"Undercover," all three said together. They liked the idea.

"Who are you?" Tim asked. He pursed his lips and cocked his head. "CIA? FBI?"

"It would be best if you didn't know," I answered, speaking in a low, controlled voice. "Suffice to say I'm working the murder of Moira Finch, and now it looks as if I've been unwittingly thrust into the investigation of Buddy Shields's murder as well. Sometimes it just shakes out that way."

Marcia bit off a chunk of licorice. "Can we help?"

Teresa clapped her hands and gave Tim a high five. "What can we do?"

How in the heck did I get myself into this mess? If I dismissed them now, they'd probably get mad and squeal to the rest of the crew. If I took them into my confidence, I would get in real trouble with the Harvest Police Department. Mikey would never, ever take me on another police ride-along, not that he was eager to do it anyway after I messed up his last cruiser, but that window would be closed forever. Not to mention I might even be convicted of obstructing justice, tampering with evidence, the whole shebang. I remembered the last time I spent a night in the gray-bar motel, and despite the fact that I'd made a couple of new friends (Spanky and Leather were nice girls, even if they did make a living in the world's oldest profession), I wasn't eager to repeat the visit. But I was at a loss. I needed these people and they were more than ready to join my quest.

"Okay, but everything I tell you must — I repeat *must* — be kept between these walls. You can tell no one. Understand?"

Tim was grinning and I saw what a difference it made to his face. I'd thought he was distinguished and handsome before, but this spark turned him into a dashing babe magnet. Whew. Smart *and* good-looking.

A loud boom made all of us jump, then chuckle nervously. Strobes of lightning continued to streak through the sky.

"You want me to shut the door?" Tim started toward the entrance but I stopped him.

"Don't worry about that. Nobody's coming in, and I'm sure nobody can hear us. I'm going to make this quick, so listen up." I leaned over my knees while Tim, Teresa and Marcia gathered around. They sat on the floor in front of me.

"Yesterday morning Moira's body was found floating in Moody Lake. Mr. Pendersnack, a fisherman, snagged her on his line. She'd been in the water about two days according to the coroner. From what I've learned so far, she has no family and spends all of her free time here at the golf course. Golfing during the day, attending benefits and functions when they occur in the evenings."

"That's right." Teresa nodded. "She told me once, right after she made herself a corsage, how many miles she has on her car.

212

She loved that car, by the way, and she bragged that she only drives it to the club, the grocery store and once in a while to run errands. She was a real homebody. Didn't do much but golf. This place was her life."

"Well, she'd need all that time at home to arrange her bouquets, now wouldn't she?" Marcia said.

"Let's not speak ill of the dead, Marcia."

"You brought it up."

"Did not."

"That's a really good point about the car, Teresa, because to the best of my knowledge it hasn't been found yet. I just got started with this investigation, of course, but so far, no car."

"It's at Moody Lake," Tim said with such certainty I was immediately alarmed. Maybe I'd read him wrong. Mikey was really gonna be mad.

"How do you know that?" Teresa turned to look at Tim.

"She never, ever, went anywhere without it. I think it was somewhat unhealthy, to tell you the truth, maybe some sort of obsession thing, some sort of psychiatric disorder or something and I thought a few times about talking to her, because if someone can't part with a piece of machinery, then that piece of machinery becomes an enabler. A form of codependence. Not that there's anything wrong with codependency if it makes you feel more secure and at peace with the world, because heaven knows this world can be very scary and critical if you're not a conformist, even if your ideals are above the understanding of the masses. It can be a higher calling and —"

"Tim." I cut him off. "Her car. You really think she wouldn't have gone to the lake without it?"

"No, I have to agree," Teresa said. "Once we offered a tour of the gardens in Spokane. We had a bus and everything. Everybody except Moira rode the bus. She insisted on taking her own car. Really strange, too, because she had to follow us all over town and made me call her on her cell phone every time we stopped so she could hear my commentary. No, she would have taken her car."

"So what?" Marcia asked. "So what about the car?" She bit into an apple and crunched loudly. "Who cares about the car?"

"May Bell?" Teresa looked at me expectantly.

"I have this . . . hunch. I don't think Mrs. Finch was supposed to be found when she was, and I think she might have been dumped in the lake in her car. There might be some evidence in the car if we can find it. At the very least, if her car isn't in the lake, then that means someone stole it. That someone would have to be the one who killed Moira."

"Or, think about this now," Tim said. "Moira was killed and dumped in the lake, then her car was ditched at the campground and someone came along and stole it. Someone not even related to her murder. The killer might even have left the keys in the ignition to be sure it was stolen to throw suspicion off of himself. Or herself. Equal opportunity, you know."

"Good point, Tim." I had to agree it was a great theory. "But we won't know until someone finds that car."

"What are the police doing about it?" Marcia asked. A little drop of spittle stuck to her chin. She wiped it away with the back of her hand.

"Right now I don't know, since we have another murder to investigate." I used the "we" and it felt right. The three were buying it. "I've decided I need to look for the car myself."

"How are you going to do that?" Teresa asked. She looked at me with wide, innocent eyes, and I noticed again how long her eyelashes were and how blue her eyes were even in the dim light of the old shop. Stunning. She was quite a beautiful woman.

"I know." Tim looked smug. "She's goin' in."

Marcia squealed. "I wanta go too, Mrs. List, take me with you!"

"We're all going." Tim said firmly. "We're in this together. Right, Teresa?"

"Wild horses . . . ," Teresa said.

Oh, crap. Mikey. What have I done?

The wind had died down somewhat at this point and I glanced through the door. The lightning had slowed and flitted high in the clouds. We were getting a break from the storm. In the distance I heard the sound of sirens.

"The cops are here," I said. "Remember. Undercover."

All three nodded somberly.

"Okay." My plan was formulating and took shape as I talked. "Meet at Candy's Bait and Tackle Shop tonight at midnight. I'll find a boat and bring my scuba gear. Oh, drat. I just remembered. I need to rent a tank."

"You'll have time," Tim said. "Even if we have to stay here till the end of the shift, that should give you a few hours before the dive shop closes."

"You dive?" I asked Tim, excited that I

216

might be able to pass off the task.

Tim looked sad. "Another missed opportunity. One little mistake and you're decertified forever."

I wanted to learn more about what could have possibly gotten Tim stripped of his dive card, but the sirens, which had been growing louder, suddenly stopped. I gauged the distance and decided the police cars had actually driven right up to the crime scene. No more golfing today, then. Enough that lightning had pushed everyone indoors, now there'd be yellow tape and questions. This wasn't in the Harvest jurisdiction anymore, but since the Harvest PD was already investigating Moira's murder and had made a visit to the club the day before, I was sure they'd be involved to some degree. It just made sense.

"We've got a break in the weather," Teresa said, standing in the doorway. "I'm going to make a run for it."

"What? Why?" Marcia asked. She had a bag of Fritos in her lap. "It's not even done out there. This is just the eye of the storm."

"I'll leave the cart and cut over the hill. I should be able to make it in about five minutes. Mr. Gullikson will be wondering where we are. You all stay put, I'll get over there, tell him and get back before you know

I'm gone."

And then she was gone.

"She can run a mile in four minutes," Marcia said. "Show-off."

I reached down and pulled my cell phone out of my wet pants pocket. "Why didn't she just call him?"

"Oooh, Mrs. List, that's against the rules," Tim admonished.

I flipped my phone open and frowned. "Doesn't matter anyway. It's completely waterlogged." I snapped it closed. So. No cell phones on the golf course. No coffee cups at morning staff meeting. I had a lot to learn.

Tim stood and paced, glancing nervously at the sky. The thunder rumbled like my hungry stomach. I motioned to Marcia and she tossed me a piece of jerky.

"I sure hope she hurries," Tim said. "I don't think we've seen the worst of the storm yet." He wrung his hands and then absently started picking up my clothes. He first folded my pants and draped them neatly over a sawhorse. Then he did the same with my shirt, and still glancing toward the door, folded my bra. When he reached for my panties I jumped up.

"As long as we have five minutes, I'm going to go see what's happening out at the pond." I grabbed my underwear out of Tim's hand and scooped up my other clothes. Thunder rumbled more intensely outside. I had to hurry.

I dashed to the bathroom and got into my clothes, squirming a lot because they were still sopping and uncooperative, and made a break for the golf cart. I must have looked like I was in control of this situation and exuded confidence because Marcia and Tim didn't make a move to stop me. It didn't take long to find my way back to the pond. Just as I imagined, police cars were parked there and yellow crime tape was wrapped around several of them, cordoning off the body of Mr. Shields. A wave of déjà vu washed over me.

I parked behind a tree and slithered out of the seat, leaving a wet streak on the vinyl. Switching to my stealth mode, I dashed from one tree to another, staying in hiding as I made my way toward the scene. Surprisingly, nobody even noticed and I got all the way to the edge of the tape. There was a place between two cop cars where I could sneak under. I leaned back, bent my knees and began a limbo approach. I held my arms out to my sides and scooched forward, an inch at a time. Scooch, scooch. My feet were under. I was up too high. I bent back farther. Scooch. My knees were under with very little clearance. I needed to go lower. I tipped my head back. Scooch. I teetered, off-balance, and with quivering thighs, held it, held it, and then lost it. I sank down to the ground, my knees bent and my feet hinged back even with my hips. I had to do something. I put my feet out in front of me, staring up at the yellow tape fluttering over my face and dug my heels into the sod. I shoved down, gaining leverage, and pulled myself forward ending up again with my feet even with my hips. I did it again. The going was slow but I was making progress.

"Mrs. List!" Again, the hissing reprimand. "*What* are you doing?"

I looked up into Mikey's face. "I can tell you what's in that man's chest," I said, smiling like I was being helpful.

Mikey squatted behind me and repeated the scene of the morning before, looking nervously over his shoulder. He poked me in the nose. "You can't be in here."

I remained in my supine, bent-legged position. "I know, I know, it's a crime scene."

"And we've got folks from the Spokane PD here. If I allow this, they'll think I'm a hick or, worse, an incompetent."

"Oh, Mike, I know you're not incontinent.

But I'm a little worried about one of the grounds workers . . ."

"Mrs. List! Get out."

I rolled over and did a sliding low crawl back under the crime-scene tape. "Relax, Mikey. Sheesh."

Mike followed me, lifting the tape over his head. That was easy; I'd have to remember that for next time. My knees were killing me.

Mikey took my elbow and guided me behind a thicket of nearby trees. "Why are your clothes all wet? Were you out in the storm?" Overhead the sky rumbled. "It's very dangerous out here." Flitters of lightning zigzagged and blossomed in the dark clouds again, but the storm was taking a breather.

"Didn't you hear? I hauled out the body!" I was really proud of this, but Mike just looked dumbfounded. "So, I think I have a right to some answers."

"Everybody has to get off the course, and that means you."

"So you don't want to know what's in the guy's chest?"

Mike rubbed his chin. "Actually, that would be helpful." He looked toward the group of police officers. A flash went off and startled me, but then I realized it was a camera flash. Someone was taking pictures, someone else was writing a report, lots of cop activity and no one was looking at us. That was good.

"You'll need to look for prints on the murder weapon but I'm not sure that will do any good. Probably washed away."

"Doesn't matter. We're not going to get any prints off that — whatever it was."

"It was a modified rake, called a crack hoe."

"You think a crack ho was involved? Some sort of drug connection?"

"I mean a crack tool. Crack tool. No crack hoes down here."

"I sort of wondered."

"About what?" I craned my head around but couldn't see Buddy's body from where I stood.

"When you took the body out of the water you left him on his back."

"Right. But then the sirens went off and we had to leave him. Sorry, but we couldn't stay and protect the body. I trust you found him just like we left him, right?" I asked.

"Yeah. Except, Mrs. List, he was in rigor, and the cold water just made him stiffen up even more when he was laid out like that. The tool kind of, well, stuck up in the air."

I put my hand over my mouth. I was getting the picture. "And then the lightning started."

"The handle acted like a lightning rod. It was wet, and just splintered on impact."

"So no prints." I shook my head sadly.

"Not only that, but the current followed the handle down to a metal object pierced through Mr. Shields's heart. It superheated and just, well, literally blew the man's chest to pieces."

"Oh. How horrible!"

"It gives a new meaning to the term blowing chunks."

For the second time that day my blood turned to ice water. Was Mike hinting at something? He didn't smile or even look at me when he said it, so I caught my beating heart and willed it back to a steady rhythm. He didn't know about my mishap at the morgue. Yet.

"It means," Mike continued, "we can't even know cause of death for sure. Of course we'll assume it was from the sharp force trauma, but, hey, it could have been a heart attack for all we know and the stabbing could have taken place postmortem. The ME will take a look and we'll find out soon enough."

"You, uh, always trust his findings?"

"Sure. No reason not to. Ol' Sawbones is

good at his job. Top notch."

"Good."

"Thanks for telling me what the thing was, though. I assume it was a tool you might find in the grounds crew toolshed?"

"And custom-made, just like the one you found in Moira's throat."

"No, Mrs. List. That was a soil probe, remember?"

"I mean, they were both altered. Changed to meet a need. Both right here in the grounds shop."

Mikey put his hands on his hips and stared out over the grounds. "I guess we're looking in the right place, then."

"I agree you shouldn't waste time looking at Moira's golf buddies, and I guess now you can rule out Buddy as Moira's killer."

"We don't rule out anything or anyone at first."

"I knew that."

"Now you've really got to get out of here."

"Say no more, lieutenant," I winked at Mikey.

"Maybe someday."

"You'll be the first one I call when I find out anything new. Don't you worry."

"Bye, now." Mikey patted me like he would a little kid. A dismissal. "Mrs. List.

Do you know your hair is frozen right to your head?"

Chapter Eighteen

When I got back to the shop, my clothes were still wet but at least they were warm and wet. I'd pushed through the hypothermia, and the little bit of exertion had heated me up nicely. I *used* to be able to limbo like nobody's business in my younger days, and now the best I could manage were some hiney scoots.

Even though the storm gained strength for another blow and the lightning jagged around me, the power had been restored and the old shop was alight. Also, it was humming. I heard the unmistakable sound of a boom box, and the parking area in front was crowded with golf carts. I walked through the door.

"When did you all get here?"

"Hey, Mrs. List!" Tim shouted. "Grab a Coke over there on the plywood. Ice is in the cooler! We've got the day off. Isn't that great?"

"Yeah, nice. But what are you doing?" I looked around me, not sure I was seeing what I was seeing. I held out a cup, distracted while someone poured me a Coke. All of the grounds crew had come down to the old shop for an old-fashioned hoedown. (They might call it a hoe-down but that would be taking it too far.) A space had been cleared, and bluegrass blasted out of the radio. Marcia was dancing a jig with Jim. Teresa twirled around, very graceful and athletic, while the college boys twisted and spasmed in the circle of her personal space. The gruesome twosome, the postal workers, were dancing cheek to cheek, fighting for the lead in a rather impressive tango.

I took a long draw of my drink and wiped a hand over my upper lip. This was amazing. Mr. Stamper held his dog's paws and pushed him back and forth across the floor. Jim and Dave leaned against the wall, one foot up, arms crossed over their chests, watching the show. The three tall cabana boys were break dancing and once in a while they'd take out two or three of their coworkers when their long legs swung around but it didn't bother anyone a bit. Football Mike was doing the robot, and I was pleased to see he looked much more cheerful.

The guy in the blue sunglasses sat on my

discarded pile of tarps whittling a wooden chain with a big knife, while off to the side Chris juggled at least six golf balls. I finished off my Coke and tossed the empty plastic cup in a trash can. I'd worked up quite a thirst and signaled for the guy manning the soft drinks to pour me another.

I felt a tap on my shoulder and turned around to see a guy I'd never met before holding his hands out to me. "My name is Jerry," he said, "and I think you're pretty."

"You got into the beer cooler, didn't you?"

Jerry smiled lazily. "Would you mind if I put my head on your shoulder for a while?" He leaned toward me and I poked him in the sternum. I expected to feel bone but was pleasantly surprised when my finger pressed against a generous layer of ropy chest flesh. I took note of the massive, broad shoulders and wondered how long it had been since I'd cuddled up to anything that, well, teddy-bearish. Oh, snap. What was I thinking? I blushed crimson. Speaking of Teddy, I had a hardworking husband who'd never strayed even when temptation draped itself over every available piece of furniture at his clinic. There was the one time when I thought he'd been courting his nurses but that was just a stupid moment of delayed menopausal angst. But look at me now. I should be ashamed. I gazed at my wedding ring and then pressed it against my lips and gave it a good hard kiss.

"Good-bye, Jerry." I sighed, reaching up to rest my hands on his shoulders. He gazed longingly into my eyes with his expressive brown ones. "And . . . thanks for that," I added. Then I walked away. Behind me I heard Jerry pleading.

"Just one little hug?"

I collected my drink and wandered into the celebration. I found Tim leading a dance I knew as the Electric Slide. Two guys, Matt and Brandon, who until now had kept such a low profile I was beginning to think they were ducking social contact, *commanded* the dance floor. They moved like pros. Everyone behind them followed their moves, all in tight lines, and they were snapping, kicking, turning and shuffling to the music. I tossed back my second Coke and then scooted up next to Tim and talked as I faked it. "Remember," I whispered just loudly enough for him to hear, "midnight at Candy's. You got that?"

Tim was flushed and sweat glistened on his forehead. "Gotcha, Mrs. List. I won't be late."

"Good." I wiggled my way toward the back where Teresa and Marcia were working their stuff. Down, up, kick, twist side to side, shuffle back, back, snap. "Twelve o'clock. Midnight," I said in a low growl. Both girls nodded without looking at me.

"*What* is going on in here?"

Uh-oh.

Mr. Gullikson stood in the doorway. His face changed color about three times before it settled on a blazing garnet shade. His ears were literally glowing. I heard a sound in my head like a record-player needle scraping hideously across vinyl. The music stopped abruptly. The crowd stopped, frozen in whatever pose they'd held before our boss started screaming.

"You have turned a respectable workplace into a den of iniquity!"

Off in the corner I heard the rattle of dice. The guy I knew as Aric hadn't been able to stop his throw in time and he got busted playing craps with Joe and Dave. Gully glared at him. Our poor boss was shaking in a supernatural way, sort of like the really creepy dude in the movie *Scanners*. I thought Gully might have a coronary or shatter his teeth, because he was clenching his jaw so hard. Something had to be done and fast. I'm quite sure if there had been some roulette wheels going around and around, Gully would be tossing the tables and cracking a whip if he had one. The man was livid.

Jerry took that opportunity to let loose a roaring belch.

Oh, my gosh.

Chris froze. All six of the golf balls clattered onto the floor.

"Out! All of you out!" Gully had his finger pointing toward the door. "Jerry. Are you drinking beer?"

"No, sir," Jerry said. "Huh-uh. No way, sir. Nope." He held his beer can behind his back.

"We were, uh, doing calisthenics, Mr. Gullikson!" I flapped my arms and kicked my legs in, then out. Jumping jacks, I think they're called. "Keeping fit, Mr. Gullikson." I got down and did some squat thrusts. Man, that burned.

Marcia did an aerobic grapevine move behind Jerry and grabbed the can out of his hand. Then she twisted and turned and passed the can off to James who in turn slid it over to Dave. In no time I'd lost sight of it.

Teresa, the athlete, ran toward a wall, ran *up* the wall, did a backflip and landed soundly before giving it another go, and then another. Flip, flip, flip. "Just keeping fit, Mr. Gullikson!" The college kids quickly

231

formed a cheerleading formation. Matt and Brandon tossed one of the guys — I think his name was Derek — way up into the air, spinning him on the release. But the ceiling wasn't quite high enough, and Derek took out a fluorescent light before coming down in a spray of white glass. He landed with a thud on the floor because all of his buds had scattered when the light exploded. Some friends they were.

"Out! Do you hear me? We'll talk about this tomorrow at the staff meeting. Stamper!"

Mr. Stamper lumbered across the room, his dog Billips at his heel. "I told them to stop, Jeff. I've got a list of names right here, and all their corresponding infractions." Stamper looked at all of us and smirked. He held out a sheet of yellow legal paper but before Gully could take it I heard Joe give the command under his breath.

"Git it."

Joe's dog Jake growled, lunged, and grabbed the paper. It was confetti in seconds.

"Good boy." Dave chuckled. "Huh, huh, huh."

"Out, out, *out!*" Mr. Gullikson was shaking really hard now. Some of his hair actually fell out.

The place was empty in seconds. The party was over. But it hadn't been a total loss; Mr. Gullikson proved a point I'd been wondering about. In his moment of righteous indignation he showed his true colors. And now as I turned to glance at him as I ran past, I saw that color was a seething purple. His blood pressure must be pegged at maximum voltage. Without a doubt, the man had a volatile temper. Opportunity. Capability. But motive? I was getting close. I could feel it.

"I can feel it," I said as I tumbled over the edge of Teresa's golf cart. We sped off and I barely even noticed the jarring bumps and fast turns. I just rolled with them now. My bruises had bruises, as they say, and it just didn't matter anymore. I was too deep in my own wonderful thoughts.

"What's that?" Marcia turned around in her seat.

"I can feel it," I shouted. The wind was whipping around again and rain hammered us and pelted my face but I didn't care. "We're getting close to solving this Moira-Buddy thing. I can feel it!" Oh, I had that funny, fluttering feeling in the pit of my stomach again. It was truly delicious, finding a higher purpose in life, living the dream, sailing above the humdrum of everyday life. I couldn't fight the grin that spread across my face. "I can feel it!"

"Oh, that," Marcia nodded. "Yeah. I guess I should have told you. Jerry spiked your Coke."

CHAPTER NINETEEN

I sat in my car for a while, waiting for my head to clear, before I left the country club. Everyone else had gone home by that time, and the drive toward town was under a preternaturally dark sky. The clouds hung over me like a pall, and the rain washed my Camaro in an onslaught of waves, shoving away my earlier good mood and replacing it with a sense of confusion and doubt. As I listened to the cadenced thumping of my windshield wipers, I wondered: what did I know about Moira's murder? What did I really know about Moira at all? I'd never even met Buddy, and all I knew about him was what Mikey had told me.

The best way to catch a killer is to find out everything you can about the victim. It's usually someone close to the victim. After all, that's why detectives always start with the ones closest and work their way out in ever-widening circles. First spouses or lovers, then family and friends, then acquaintances, neighbors, coworkers, and finally, people who happened to be in the area. There had to be a reason to kill someone, and aside from the occasional sociopath who didn't give a whit about who they killed, there was always a motive. And even sociopaths had their own twisted motive. They just liked to kill. They were the hardest to catch because there was no way to easily link them to their victims, short of physical evidence. Unless there was some forensic proof or an eyewitness, it was almost impossible to get a handle on that kind of case, but that's not what we had here. There were two murders, and they were related; no doubt about that. They were even connected by the murder weapons. Both killed with tools that came from the Northside Country Club maintenance equipment stash. They were custom-made, after all, and truly unique.

My thoughts went back to the hoedown. These were good people. Could there be a killer amongst them? Did I make a grave mistake inviting Tim, Marcia and Teresa to join me in the hunt at Moody Lake? I searched my innards for a sense of worry or fear, one of those female intuition things we're supposed to have, and I didn't feel a niggle. Not one instinct sounded a warning bell. I trusted these guys. I hadn't known them long, but I counted them as friends. Tim had been so thoughtful, offering me his custom-lined rain gear, folding my delicates, even sharing his sandwiches. No, he was one of the good ones. Teresa? She said she liked her job and she was disciplined, driven and responsible. She wouldn't be so careless as to do something that would ruin her life in one fell stroke. Marcia? Too happy. Nope, nothing on the internal alarm meter. I'd done the right thing taking them into my confidence.

I changed lanes and kept my eyeballs peeled for signs of the dive shop. It was early still and there was no need to hurry, but I felt compelled to get everything ready for our midnight venture. I still hadn't tried on my daughter's wet suit, and if there were problems I'd have to hoof it back to the dive shop for a rental. Never mind. I survived the chilly pond and I'd survive the lake even if I had to go in naked.

I had to wonder about that — two bodies in two bodies of water. It was strange, but maybe the murderer knew something about forensics. Water could mess up a crime scene, fingerprints could be destroyed, evidence washed away. So the killer wasn't stupid. Not stupid, but not especially bright either, since we'd recovered both murder weapons. Then again, they might have been intentionally left with the bodies in order to throw off the investigation and point the finger at someone working at the club; someone in the grounds crew, to be exact.

What did our murder victims have in common? There was the money connection, but with Mr. Shields dead, we couldn't say he'd killed Moira for her money. They both spent an inordinate amount of time at the club; both had personal problems, Buddy with his money situation, Moira with her unsavory personality. But it doesn't make sense to kill a guy if he owes you money, thereby ending any chance of getting it back, and you don't kill a woman for being a grumpy, flower-grubbing, bouquet-making golfer. There had to be more. Something bigger. Something none of us had uncovered.

I hurriedly rented a tank at the dive shop and got back in my car in record time. It was nearly four o'clock when I headed toward home, and that gave me eight hours to prepare for the evening. Once again I drove out to Candy's.

A large section of plywood covered the shattered front window. The campsite was quiet. Most of the tourists had moved on,

238

with the exception of a couple of RVs and one new tent. I guess the Hibachi Boys had made bail after all and then found a replacement for their burned shelter. They were out front grilling something good-smelling. One of the RVs belonged to the Robe Lady, and the other I couldn't place. I went through the door of Candy's shop looking for Pendersnack. He wasn't in his usual place. When I asked about him, Candy motioned toward the lake.

"He's having a pretty good day," Candy said. "Been fishing since early this morning. Wish I could say the same for my other customers." In an uncharacteristic change of mood, Candy scowled. "The police recovered almost everything that was stolen. That little blonde gal with the crazy hair had been sneaking into tents and RVs when their owners were in the showers. There's one thing they didn't find that I wish they would. A laptop computer, and I'm here to tell you that woman who lost it probably faked her theft so she could squeeze out a free week. She's telling me she won't leave until it turns up, and she won't give me her address, and she won't pay me for the time she has to wait here."

"Mrs. Robe." I nodded, all knowing.

"Who?"

"Well, I don't know her real name but she was asking for biscotti and wore a pink robe all the time."

"Mrs. Smith."

"Naturally."

"Yeah. I should have asked for identification, but it's not easy making a living doing this sort of thing. She paid for her first week and then all this stuff happened. Now she's making life impossible for me."

Poor Candy. "Did you ever think she might make a living doing *this?* I mean, going from campground to campground, claiming to have something stolen, sneak in a couple of free days before moving on to the next job?"

I shouldn't have said that, because Candy's face fell and she looked absolutely miserable. No one wants to believe they've been bilked.

"I've been a fool. I just want to believe people are honest with me." Candy went to work making coffee, wrenching things this way and that. "Should have known when she said she'd misplaced her glasses when she registered and would fill out the paperwork when she found them."

"I'm sorry, Candy. But people really did have their stuff stolen, so maybe Mrs. Smith is telling the truth." I backpedaled as quickly as I could.

"True, true. And there was that awful thing that happened yesterday. Something spooky is happening around here so I shouldn't go jumping to conclusions. Maybe Mrs. Smith is a victim like everyone else. Yes. She's probably a good soul, and those other two boys out there, just as nice as can be — and the police hauled them in for a little bag of weed. Can you believe it? It's something that should be legal anyway." Candy started humming.

I grinned. *Candy,* I thought, *you're a throwback hippie!* "I'm sure her computer will show up. Maybe she thought she'd brought it along and it's sitting safely on her desk at home. It can happen that way. I forget a lot of things."

"Just the same, I wish she'd move on. I wish they'd all move on. I could use a little break. Mr. Pendersnack said he'd take over for me, and I need a vacation." Candy ran her hands through her hair and left a streak of foam on her bangs. "Here." Candy handed me two lattes. "One for you, just the way you like it. And would you mind taking one over to Mrs. Smith? I feel really bad thinking those things about her. It would really help soothe my conscience."

"Sure, Candy," I said, taking the cups.

"And don't worry. The police are working the Finch case, and I'm sure everything will work out."

Candy looked out over the lake with a faraway gaze. "I don't think I'll ever be able to look at the lake the same way again," she said. "Makes you wonder what else might be floating around out there."

I patted Candy's arm and headed out the door. She had managed to give me a good case of goose bumps. Yeah. I wondered what might be floating around out there, especially since I was getting ready to take a look under cover of darkness. I added a few "needs" to my list. Waterproof flashlights, diving knife, boat. Which reminded me why I was there in the first place. I'd need a boat. But I didn't want Candy to get any more worried, so renting one from her was out of the question. As I wandered over toward Mrs. Smith's camper, I saw Snack hauling his boat up onto the beach. I called out to him.

"Hey, Mr. Pendersnack, ho! Hey. Yoo hoo!"

Snack shielded his eyes and looked up at me. I don't know why he'd be shielding his eyes since the sky was still a dark purple, but perhaps it was out of habit. "Hey there!"

I hobbled over the sand. "How are you?"

Snack looked at me, curious. "I'm not selling my fish."

"I just need to talk to you. Not looking for dinner, thanks. Say, I was here yesterday after you pulled Mrs. Finch out of the water."

Snack scratched the back of his neck. "Darnedest thing, wasn't it? Hooked her, just like that." Snack yanked on an invisible line and I winced.

"I noticed your boat and what I was wondering is . . . do you ever rent it out? I mean for a day or a . . . night?"

Snack studied me, his eyes closing down to small wrinkled dots in his face. "You can rent one from Candy, here."

"I know, but, see, yours is bigger."

"Not by much," Snack said. "In fact, hers are nicer."

"But I like yours."

"Why?"

I sighed. "Just because."

Snack shrugged. "I guess I could rent it out. Same price as Candy's though, and if you trash it, you buy it."

"Absolutely," I said, my face breaking into a smile.

"When do you want it?"

"Later. Uh, later today if that's all right."

"I was gonna quit for the day anyway. Had

243

one heck of a time fishing around all that lightning this morning."

"You were out in that storm?"

"Best time to catch fish!" Snack said. "I caught so many, Mrs. Pendersnack'll be cookin' fish for a year. If you're really lucky and the lightning hits water, yee hah. The fish just float on up to the surface. Dip, dip, dip, and you've got yourself a shipload!"

I glimpsed at his boat and cringed. There were fish guts and slimy stuff all over the bottom of it. "Good for you."

"I'll just leave it up there next to the shop. You ain't going out by yourself are you?"

"No, actually." I worked up a blush. "It's for a romantic evening. A surprise."

"That's real nice, Mrs. . . . ."

"Liktish. Mary Liktish."

"Well. Really nice, Mrs. Liktish." Snack winked at me. "You take as much time as you'd like. Just leave it where you found it, awright? And if you don't mind, hose it down."

"Thank you, Mr. Pendersnack." I handed him a latte so I could get to my purse. "I need to get some money, then." I reached in for my wallet, and Snack gulped at the latte. Oh, well. He told me how much, and we made the deal. I hurried off toward Mrs. Smith's trailer before her latte got cold.

Mrs. Smith answered her door — in her robe. This time in a nice blue fuzzy thing, and she wore matching blue bunny slippers on her feet. She didn't say a thing. Just stared at me, and it was an awkward moment, to say the least. At her feet a poodle barked, barked, barked. Mrs. Smith didn't even shush him.

"Mrs. Shultz asked me to send this over," I said.

"What for? She trying to butter me up?"

"I guess she's sorry for your troubles." I shoved the latte at her, eager to get home.

"She needn't bother. I'm packing up and I'll be out of here within the hour. I think I made a mistake." Mrs. Smith's voice softened. "I guess I left my laptop at home. I could have sworn I had it with me, but . . . we do make honest mistakes sometimes, don't we?" Mrs. Smith bent down and picked up her dog. At last he was quiet but kept a wary eye on me.

"Yes. That's just what I was saying to Candy."

"You were talking about me?" Mrs. Robe appeared agitated.

"No, no, we were just talking about stuff in general." I held out the latte. "Please. Take this."

"I don't drink that kind. But, oh, well. Tell

her thanks." Robe took the cup and by the way she handled it I was sure it would be going into the sink as soon as I left. I mourned for the two lattes that had been so close, but so far away. "I really have to get going." Mrs. Robe started to close the door.

"Mrs. Smith." I stopped her. "I just wanted to know: how long have you been here?"

The woman bristled. "What business is that of yours?"

"Pardon me. I'm not being nosy, just curious. I was here when that body was pulled out of the lake and I saw you taking pictures, and I was just wondering if you heard or saw anything that could have been a fight or a scuffle or anything unusual a couple of nights before the decedent was found."

A look of fear crossed Robe's face. "You a cop?"

"No, ma'am, just a frustrated citizen. She was a friend of mine, and the police don't seem to know much."

"Never do, do they? Nah, I didn't hear anything," Mrs. Smith said, a little too quickly for my trained ear.

I took a step closer to Mrs. Robe. "Is something wrong?"

"No. No, I don't know nothing." Robe glanced around, obviously nervous. "Now

246

I've got to get going."

"You did hear something, didn't you? Please tell me." I took a step closer.

"I don't know nothing. I didn't hear nothing. Now, please go. I have to finish getting my stuff together."

Mrs. Robe slammed the door in my face and would have taken my nose off if I hadn't jumped back, nearly tumbling down the stairs. How odd.

As I walked back to my car I was sure of one thing. Something had spooked Mrs. Robe. The sudden change in her story about forgetting her laptop was too handy. She was leaving, and in a big hurry, and she was scared. Scared now, but not after the body was discovered or after she learned her laptop was missing. So what had happened in the meantime to give her such a fright? What had happened between Moira's murder and now? Buddy's murder came to mind. Did she know someone at the camp who'd talked about Moira and Buddy, and had Mrs. Robe made the connection? It was just too much. I was getting a headache.

With nothing else to learn at Candy's, and with my boat tied up and ready at the dock, I left. In no time I found myself driving up my long dirt road toward home and noted the enlarged potholes caused by the earlier deluge. I had to wind around fallen branches and loads of pine needles and labor through the mud, but I got home safely enough. I was deep in thought, troubled by the reaction of Mrs. Robe, and prayed silently that the weather would clear up before the night's dive. I pulled the tank out of the backseat of my car and walked slowly up the porch steps with the heavy thing knocking against my knees. I couldn't believe how tired I was, and I hadn't even worked my landscaping job yet. Too much nervous energy finally catching up to me, I guess.

I got to the front door, plunked the tank down with a metallic thud, pulled out my keys and inserted them in the lock. Before I could turn the key, the door swung open on its own. My heart started beating in double time. I glanced quickly toward the garage, already knowing Ted hadn't made it home from work yet; there were no fresh tire prints in the mud, only mine. I backed away from the front door. Something was wrong. My dog hadn't come through the door as was his custom when I got home. There was no reason for it to be open, and I was getting the heck out of there. I turned to run then heard a noise behind me. My heart moved up to a chaotic triple-beat rythym, and I wasn't going to stop for introductions. I pinwheeled my arms, and churned my legs, crossing the lawn. My car was a short distance away, but not close enough. I thundered toward it, hearing fast footsteps behind me. The hot breath of my pursuer scorched my neck. I lunged for my car door, fumbling with my keys.

A strong hand gripped my shoulder and spun me around.

I screamed and swung.

Marcia ducked, avoiding my fist. "Why are you running, May Bell?"

I couldn't breathe. I bent over and sucked wind. "Oh, my gosh. Oh, my gosh. Oh, my gosh! You scared me to death. What are you doing in my house?"

Teresa stood in my doorway and called out, "We would have called, but your cell phone is dead."

I grabbed at my knees, panting like a rabid dog.

"You okay, Mrs. List?"

I looked into Marcia's face. "Why does everyone keep asking me that?"

"You look like you're about to pass out. Or hurl or something."

"Considering my stomach is tickling my tonsils, yeah, maybe." I stood. "Again. Why are you two in my house?"

Tim poked his head over Teresa's. "Me, too, Mrs. List."

I rolled my eyes. "Well, okay! Come on in, then. Why don't you all make yourselves at home?"

As we walked back, Marcia supported me with a hand on the small of my back. She explained how she'd tried to get in touch with me but when she couldn't, she and Teresa got on their bikes and, using my employment form, found my address with "no effort at all." They'd hidden their bikes in the bushes.

"And Tim?"

"He drove through the trees and parked around back. We wanted to stay undercover, just like you said."

"And you broke in?"

"Not technically. Your door wasn't locked."

Darn Ted. I guess I couldn't blame him, though. He wasn't used to me being gone when he woke up, and if I had to guess, he probably didn't even realize I wasn't home when he left, which made me wonder who, or what, he'd kissed on his way out the door. I'd have to talk with him about that.

Then a thrill of fear ran up my spine. "My dog."

"What?" Marcia and Teresa looked at each other.

"My dog. My little doggie. Did you let him out?" I was starting to panic. There were coyotes and mountain lions roaming the hills around my house and he never stayed out for long. "Where is he?" I ran into the house.

"Here he is." Tim had disappeared and came back holding my Torch wrapped in a yellow towel. "I gave him a bath."

"You gave him a bath."

"It was so easy because he doesn't have any fur. Just like a little baby. I like bathing things. We really bonded." Tim rubbed the towel over Torch's head. The tiny tuft of hair my puppy did have stood up when the towel came away, reminding me of Don King. My little dog actually smiled like he enjoyed it. "A little no-tears shampoo, some warm water, it's surprisingly good for the mood."

"Yours or his?" I asked under my breath. Then I cleared my head. "So you three just walked into my house. Just like that."

"We couldn't stand outside, and we didn't know when you'd get home. The UPS man stopped by and we all got down on the floor. He left this package for you." Teresa held out a brown package. Oh, good. Patty and Jack sent some trinkets from Belize. At least they were thoughtful in that regard. Just wish they'd send me a baby announcement one of these days.

Teresa led me into my living room. I was still having trouble processing a breaking and entering by my new friends (but not technically), and I was still shaking a little bit. "Sit, May. Should we fix you some tea or something?"

"Just tell me why you're here."

Marcia, Tim and Teresa took chairs. "After you left we started thinking. Maybe we should go to Moira's house before we search the lake. We could snoop around and . . ."

"And what?" I asked.

"Snoop around and find something that might give someone reason to kill her. We still have a few hours left in the day, and none of us could just sit around."

"Sit around? You rode your bikes fifteen miles to get here. Do you ever get tired?"

The three looked at each other like I was speaking in Urdu.

Marcia pulled a candy bar out of her pocket and peeled back the wrapper. "At least we should come up with a game plan. Even if we do find something in the lake, what will that get us? No, I think we should start with her house. It was my idea."

I stood up and rubbed my chin. "You might be right. Let's just think about this for a minute. I can see you all have no problem breaking into someone's house, but we could get in big trouble rummaging through Moira's stuff."

"No one will know." Teresa held her hands out, palms up.

"We can get in and out of there without leaving fingerprints or anything." Tim pulled out a wad of blue rubber gloves.

"But don't you think the police already searched her place?" I asked. Mikey wouldn't like this at all.

Teresa said, "If they did, they didn't find anything . . . um, what's the word?"

"Probative?" I asked.

"Something like that." Tim blew into one of the gloves and rubbed the inflated hand over Torch's mop. Then he released it and we all watched in somber reverie as it sputtered around my living room. It landed on one of my lamps and started to smolder. I hurried over and peeled it off.

"I guess it couldn't hurt," I said hesitantly. Everyone smiled with glee. *But.* Everyone frowned. "We do this the smart way. We form a game plan. A foolproof game plan, all right?" I wadded up the glove and dropped it in the trash. "And don't leave anything behind. Understand?"

"Whatever you say, Mrs. List, you're the secret agent."

I closed my eyes tightly. "I'm no secret agent. But I did do a stint in the pokey and it's an experience I hope never to repeat. Okay." I opened my eyes and looked around the room. Then I started giving orders.

"Tim. Turn on some lights. It's downright gloomy in here. Teresa. Put on the coffee. Marcia. Come with me."

I hurried off toward my office with Marcia in tow. Tim gently placed Torch on the couch and went about the business of lighting up the house while Teresa clattered around in my kitchen. The sky was still dark, but the rain had stopped and I could see some sunshine trying to break through the clouds.

"Help me move this," I told Marcia, taking the end of a bookshelf. We shoved it into the middle of the room leaving a clean white section of wall. "Grab those markers over there."

Marcia snatched up some dry-erase markers and handed them to me. I pulled off the top of one and drew a line on the wall. "This is the road to Moody Lake." Then I drew something that resembled the outline

254

of the lake as I remembered it. "Here's Moody Lake." Then I drew a small building and some little squares around it. "And here's Candy's and a few campers — from what I saw today."

"That doesn't look like a camper," Marcia said, cocking her head to the side.

"Use your imagination. Now. This up here . . ." I drew an X in the upper-left-hand corner of my wall. ". . . is the country club. We all know how to get there, right? So I don't have to draw the roads or anything."

"I think it's a little bigger than that."

"It's an X. Again, you have to use your imagination."

Marcia took a marker from me and walked up to the wall. "And down here . . ." She quickly drew a beautiful rendition of a Victorian house. ". . . is Moira's house. I know because we followed her home after our tour. She insisted because she wanted to show off her peonies."

"Wow." I looked at the lovely drawing. "You're quite an artist."

Marcia blushed. "Actually, I was a cartographer for the Marines. Didn't see much action, but I learned to draw."

"And you can plot a back azimuth I'll bet."

"Just give me a compass." Marcia sniffed.

255

"What's the plan?" Teresa came in with coffee cups balanced on top of a platter I couldn't remember ever seeing before. I really needed to go through my dishes one of these days. Tim followed her in, cradling Trixie.

"Be careful, Tim," I grew alarmed. "She's not a very nice kitty."

"This adorable thing?" Tim cuddled my psychotic cat under his chin, and I could hear her purr with contentment. I was amazed. "I've never seen that before. I've never seen her do that."

"She was great in the shower."

"You took a shower with her?" I shuddered, remembering the last time I'd tried that.

"You've got all this mud and stuff outside."

I shuddered. "Just stop. Let's concentrate here." I took a cup of coffee, looked at the board, and explained everything again quickly. "First, let's synchronize our watches." We all looked at our wrists. When I looked at mine I dumped my cup of coffee onto the floor. Oh, well.

"Uh-oh," Marcia said.

"What?"

"Mine's got water in it. Guess when I reached in to pull Buddy out I got it wet."

256

"Mine, too," Teresa said, putting her watch up to her ear.

"Yup, mine's dead as well." I pulled off my watch and tossed it onto the desk. "Never mind. We'll all be together anyway. If we need to know the time, we'll ask Tim."

"Right-o," Tim said, nuzzling Trixie's nose with his own.

That was just too weird. I tried that with my cat once and could have worn a diamond stud for a month after. She pierced me with a fang right through the left nostril.

"Tim, what kind of car do you drive?"

"Hmm?" Tim looked up. His eyes had a dreamy quality. "I have an SUV with plenty of room. We can all ride together."

I drew a little car resembling a grasshopper on the board. Marcia gently took the marker from my hand. "May I?"

"I guess you'd better," I said. "We leave here in an hour. I have to get my dive gear together, and I need a little time for that. Then we drive to Moira's house by way of Day Road."

Marcia drew little arrows.

"We'll come up this way and park over here," I continued.

Marcia drew more arrows.

"We don't want to be right next to her house. We'll pretend we're joggers, moving in pairs, then duck around to the back of her house. Marcia, are there other houses next door?"

"She lives on forty acres." Marcia said.

"Scratch that plan," I said. Marcia rubbed across the arrows, erasing them. "We'll drive up to her house, get out, break down her door and go in."

Everyone stared at me.

"Kidding, guys. We'll just drive up, see if anyone is looking and find the best point of entry. No breaking anything. And if anyone comes a-calling, we'll say we're there to clean her carpets. Tim, you and Teresa can load up some cleaning supplies, vacuum cleaner, towels and that sort of thing while Marcia helps me with my diving gear."

"What are we looking for?" Tim asked. Trixie was licking his goatee.

"I don't know exactly. Anything that looks out of place, strange, interesting or unusual. We'll know it when we see it, I guess."

Tim wrapped Trixie around his neck like a muff. He said, "One of us will need to check her files, her paperwork, letters, that sort of thing. Bank statements, you know: the good stuff. And, I can get into her computer if she has one, and do some checking there."

"I'll go through her refrigerator," Marcia

said. Silence. She laughed. "You thought I was serious, didn't you?" Then she grew sober. "I was."

"You'll go through her trash, Marshmallow," Teresa said firmly.

"Fine."

"And Teresa, you can have a look around the grounds. Check the outbuildings if there are any, and see if she left her car in one of them."

"I know the police would have found that," Teresa said.

"Probably. But we're just looking, right?"

"And what will you do, Mrs. List?" Tim had his hands in his pockets. Trixie was still wrapped around his neck. Her tail hung down like a necktie.

"I don't know. I'm just going to look. I'll go through her drawers, her cupboards, whatever." My cat was distracting me. Tim had somehow managed to cozy up to my pet in one hour, when I'd been unable to get her to love me in years. I almost got a little weepy. Maybe I just wasn't lovable. Then Torch ran up to me, tongue hanging out, grinning and begging for my attention, and everything was all better.

Marcia tapped on the wall. "That's the end of phase one, right? Then, we have to go over to Buddy's house."

"Hold on a minute," I said, alarmed. "Who said anything about Buddy's place? He was married with a family, right?"

"I got that all figured out," Marcia said, all excited. "Tim will call the wife and tell her she's won a TV or something, at some made-up address, but only if she comes down right away to claim it."

"Ah, that won't work," Teresa said. "She's planning her husband's funeral. Are you crazy?"

"I thought it was a good idea." Marcia pouted. "You don't always have the good ideas. Sometimes I can have some, too."

"That was a stupid idea," Teresa said.

"You're stupid."

"Girls. Let's not fight. We have to be completely on our game tonight. No Buddy's house. Not tonight at any rate. From Moira's we're going straight over to Moody Lake to look for her car or anything else that might be in the water."

Marcia went back to the board and, from memory, drew Moira's place — bushes, trees, fences, barn, outbuildings, pump house, well cover, drain field, stumps, and even a herd of grazing deer. "We don't want any surprises," she said.

Wow.

Soon, Marcia was drawing in details about

Moody Lake as I relayed them, and also from the time she'd been there to help with some landscaping. She even used shading and everything.

We decided to start our boat trip near the shop and work along the shoreline. If someone had dumped Moira's car in the lake, it wouldn't be far from the edge. There was an area on the far north side of the lake that was shadowed by a dense forest with no access to the lake, and we'd search that last. I had to remember I didn't have much time to look: an hour on the tank at most, and I'd have to use my air sparingly. We studied the drawing of the lake, pointed to places where we thought someone was most likely to dump a car, and committed it all to memory. There were about fifteen little red Xs all over the wall. Tim would row the boat while the girls would use flashlights to help me navigate. I searched my house until I found three flashlights, and then replaced the batteries. I wrapped them in plastic baggies, since I hadn't had a chance to buy the waterproof kind.

"Are we set?" I asked, flushed and slightly out of breath.

"Just about. It's time for you to get your dive gear while we get the cleaning supplies together," Tim said. He unwrapped Trixie and set her on the floor. "Marcia, you go ahead and help May. Meet us in my SUV when you're ready. Break!"

"Break!" Marcia and Teresa said in unison. *Oh, Ted. Rescue me.*

CHAPTER TWENTY

I should have known. You can't fit a size fourteen into a size six wet suit. But I was going to try. I was in my spare bathroom in the hallway because I thought it would save some time and it was close to the garage where I'd been hiding all of Patty's scuba gear. The bathroom was tiny and nearly impossible to move around in, more so when you had to wiggle and squirm into a clingy neoprene straightjacket.

I got the pant legs up to my knees, and then everything stuck. I couldn't get them down and I couldn't pull them up. In desperation, I opened the medicine cabinet and rummaged around for something with "lubrication" on the label. I couldn't walk more than an inch per step and had to hang onto the walls for support. I grabbed a bottle of baby oil and squirted it all over my bare body. It helped quite a bit, and with more squirming, panting and grunting I had the wet suit up over my torso. I poured more oil up and down my arms and thrust them into the sleeves. There's a long zipper pull in back and I reached over my back, then around without success, and then I started to get very hot. More than very hot.

My skin burned like I'd been dipped in lava. I clawed at the wet suit in desperation, trying to get it off. I caught a glimpse of my face in the mirror and was alarmed to see how red it was. Even the whites of my eyes were crimson. My ears were glowing and my hair was frizzing.

I tamped down the screams rising up my throat, but my skin grew hotter and hotter, nearing what must have been the boiling point because little wisps of smoke escaped from my cleavage. (I swear.) I could take it no longer and shrieked long and loud, ruining my fingernails as I clawed and scraped at the suit.

"Mrs. List!" Tim hollered from the other side of the door. He sounded as horrified as I felt. I grabbed for the door handle and threw wide the door. He jumped back, startled by my appearance. Behind him, Trixie dashed for the drapes.

"Get me out of this!" I yanked at my collar, holding it away from my raw neck. Tim's eyes were wide with shock.

"Are you suffocating? What's wrong?"

"Aaaah! I'm on fire! Eeeeeee!"

Tim dashed into the fray. He moved my hands away and grabbed at my collar, and tugged downward. Then I came to my senses. I'd rather boil in a wet suit than stand exposed in front of this young man. "Go get the girls, and hurry!" I yelled. I could feel my throat closing. I was gasping for air. "And bring ice!"

Tim hesitated, unsure, until I screamed at him again. He raced away shouting for Marcia and Teresa, who were already on their way to the bathroom after hearing me shriek. They spun me around, each grabbed the top of my wet suit and had me stripped down to the ankles before I could warn them that I had nothing on underneath. Again, Tim the gentleman turned his back, squatted down and played with something on his shoe.

I took a long, recuperative gasp and stumbled backward. My calves connected with the sides of the bathtub and I pitched over and in. Marcia lunged for the faucet handle and showered me with ice-cold water. My gosh, that felt good. After I rinsed off, Marcia handed me a towel.

"What happened, Mrs. List?" The girls were beside themselves with worry. I glanced down at my exposed skin and saw it was cherry red and by the feel, close to blistering. "I don't know. I put some baby oil on to help get this stupid thing pulled up and I just started burning!"

Marcia reached over and lifted the bottle off the sink. "You used this?" She held it out for Teresa to see.

Both girls turned and had another laughing fit at my expense. They pawed at each other with each spasm. Teresa chortled loudly while Marcia did one of those I-can't-breathe things. When they turned, Marcia's eyes were squirting tears.

"What is it?" I grabbed the bottle and squinted. "Oh, my." I read the label. "A warm sensation will occur with friction. For added sensual pleasure . . ." *Ted, you're gonna pay.*

I patted myself down while the girls cleaned out the wet suit. They found the real baby oil and eventually with all three of us working, I got suited up. It was snug, but since it was old, it stretched. And I compressed. As long as I was breathing, I didn't worry too much about positional asphyxiation or ruptured blood vessels. Then I tried on the snorkel and mask, slapped around in the fins, and grabbed the tank and BCD. All ready. I gave the girls a thumbs-up and they helped me get my gear to the car. I wore tennis shoes and left the other stuff in the back but didn't dare undress. I'd just have to suffer for the cause.

I was surprised to find Moira's house silent and undisturbed when we got there. No yellow crime-scene tape, no orange cones, no SWAT vehicles out front, and no neighbors. This was going to be easier than I thought.

First we did a canvass of the outer perimeter. The lady did love her peonies. Not to mention her roses, her daisies, her irises and so many other flowers I couldn't name them all. But of course Teresa, Marcia and Tim could, and we wasted time while they admired her gardens and spouted technical terms until Teresa screamed an oath after realizing the plants had all been pilfered from the country club. When I asked her how she knew, she just said, "A mother knows her own children." Since I thought that was just too weird, I wandered out to Moira's backyard. I could tell the grass was usually tidy, but she'd been dead long enough for it to grow tall, and if I hadn't been shining my flashlight around I would have missed it.

"What's all this stuff?" I hunkered down and ran my hand over the grass. Scraps of paper covered a section of the back lawn, but since it had rained hard earlier in the day they were little more than mush. I tried to scoop up a handful, but the paper scraps disintegrated and stuck to my fingers like mashed potatoes.

Marcia knelt beside me and did the same but she, too, came up with slop. Teresa was busy yanking out Moira's garden until I called her over. Tim wandered around the outside of the house looking for a point of entry.

"Hard to tell," Marcia said. "But I think I've got an idea." She pointed to a bale of hay standing on end just feet from the paper mess. Attached to the hay bale was a well-perforated paper target. The target was weathered and faded, but since it was laminated it hadn't been destroyed by the rain.

I walked over to the target and pointed my flashlight at it, only because I'd forgotten my reading glasses and the light was fading. The target had a number of stickpins through it, like something had been hanging there. I looked back over the white paper goo.

"She was blasting something off this target," I said.

"What would someone stick on a target

and blast with a shotgun? Who does that?" Teresa asked.

"Wasn't a shotgun," Marcia said. She held two shell casings in her hand. "I found these about fifteen yards away. I wouldn't have, but I dropped my Tootsie Rolls and there they were."

I pointed my flashlight beam on Marcia's hand. "Looks like a forty-five."

"So she tacked something up on the target and fired away."

"Papers? Documents?"

"Love letters?" Tim leaned over my shoulder.

He startled me so badly I spotted. "Geez, Tim. Give me a warning, why don't ya?"

"Everything's locked up, tight," Tim said. "We're gonna have to break something."

"Look at this. Does it mean anything to you?" Teresa poked at a slip of paper still hanging on one of the stickpins. I pulled out the pin and held the paper in my flashlight beam.

"Looks like part of a . . . letterhead. Yeah, there's some typing, a word . . . can't really make it out but we'll take it as evidence. Did any of you think to bring any extra baggies?"

No baggies to spare, so I secured the sacred piece of evidence in a blue rubber glove and locked it in Tim's SUV. There was nothing else of interest outside of Moira's house, and darkness had fallen before we decided the best way to get inside was for Marcia to shimmy down the chimney. We climbed to the roof using a ladder we'd found in Moira's barn. We'd also found an old rope, and we wrapped it around Marcia's chest, just under her armpits. We all sat on the roof's peak like we were riding a horse. Tim braced his feet against the fireplace and gripped the rope in both hands. Teresa scooted in behind him and held her part of the rope and I took up the rear. The peak of the roof took up my rear, but I don't even remember why that made such an impression on me.

Marcia eased herself over the lip of the fireplace, and we carefully lowered her down hand over hand. Her head had just disappeared below the edge when the rope began to fray at the point where it scraped against the sharp bricks.

"It's rotten!" Tim screamed. "Haul her back up! Come on, girls. Heave!"

Like we were sculling for the gold, all of us leaned back against the rope until Tim was lying on Teresa's lap, Teresa on mine, and I was pressing my back against the roof edge. I felt another hard tug.

"It's coming apart, girls! Put your backs into it!"

We ran our hands up the rope and pulled back again, straining against the struggling Marcia. The muscles in my arms burned, the veins on my neck puffed and grew dangerously close to exploding. The rope slipped a little in my hands, burning my palms. I gritted my teeth, closed my eyes and . . .

"We've almost got 'er girls! Heave!" Tim leaned forward for another section of rope and pulled, digging his heels into the shingles.

Another hard jerk.

For a split second I saw the hair on the top of Marcia's head fluttering in the moonlight, and then . . . the rope gave way. Tim and Teresa were thrown back and I was knocked off balance.

Marcia screamed on her way down the chimney, an awful, hollow sound, and crashed through the flue at the bottom, which was a good thing, really, because we hadn't thought about that part.

As for me, I fell sideways, flipped onto my stomach and slid face-first over the wet shingles at breakneck speed. The rain, the oiled wet suit, and the steep pitch of the roof combined to turn me into the perfect roof luge. I couldn't even call out, because I was so compressed.

When I got to the edge of the roof, I flew out, arms and legs extended, caught some hang time, and then dropped hard into a thick, spiky hedge of junipers.

"I'm okay!" I called out weakly. "Think I ripped my wet suit, though."

Tim and Teresa scrambled off the roof and we all ran to the front door, where we were met by a soot-covered Marcia, who, by the way, wasn't in a really good mood. There were black footprints from the hearth to the threshold and I told her it was probably best if she hosed herself down in the back and let us do the searching. She grumbled and stomped off.

"Okay, everyone, turn on your flashlights. Let's make this quick."

I reported nothing of interest in the kitchen, bathrooms, bedroom or living room. Just old-lady stuff.

"Nothing good in here, either," Marcia said, her backside sticking out of the refrigerator.

"Are you out of your mind? You're gonna leave smudges all over the place. And where are your gloves?" I was so irritated that I was shouting, but when Marcia held her hands up, she was wearing oven mitts so I couldn't get too excited. She'd also hosed off well enough, although she'd missed everything above her neck and when she turned to look at me, I saw her face in the light of the refrigerator and nearly died of laughing fits.

"Missed a spot," I said.

"Oh, yeah?" Marcia misunderstood, and pulled out the crisper drawer. "Oh, yeahhhh." She pulled out a withered carrot and a black banana. "Thanks, May."

"Looky what I found." Teresa came into the kitchen and flipped on the lights. "Don't worry, there's nobody out there and you need to see this." She swung a thin black cord until it wrapped around her index finger, and then swung it off again. "It's a cell phone charger, but no cell phone. Do you know if Moira had one on her when she was pulled from the lake?"

"I can assure you she had nothing on but what she was wearing. Good job. Unless the cops took it, we'll be looking for it along with her car. Unfortunately, it won't be much good if it's been under water. Bad break. That would have told us who she's been talking to. Would have been a good clue, Teresa."

Teresa's cheeks flushed. "Thanks, May. But, then again, the cops can just check her

273

phone records."

It was my turn to feel a flush work its way up my neck. How stupid of me. Of course the cops could check Moira's phone records. I hadn't done any good here at all. But. Maybe they didn't know she had a cell phone. Or maybe — it was someone *else's* cell phone! Ah, I was reaching.

"Anyway, anything we take from here will be considered fruit of the poisoned tree. Can't be used in a court of law *unless* we get it back here without telling anyone we touched it."

Tim came in, looking flustered. "They were here. The cops. They were here. I found her file cabinet but it was cleaned out. Her computer's gone, along with her address book and any calendars or date books she may have had."

"Shoot." I gnawed off a fingernail. "So we have nothing." And, I thought, if the police collected all of that stuff, they are wayyyy ahead of me. Of course they would have searched her house. What did I think *I* was going to find? I so wanted to solve this murder for Mikey. "Nothing at all?"

"Nada." Tim creased his forehead. "I said this was a waste of time."

Marcia pushed a bite of banana into her

cheek. She opened the freezer. "No, you didn't."

"I thought it."

"So we have nothing." I bit off another nail.

"Nothing," Marcia said. "Except this."

Chapter Twenty-One

Marcia put her hand to her mouth and spat into it.

"That's disgusting, Marshmallow."

"You're not allowed to use that name, Tim."

"Can I if I tell you what kids called *me* in school?"

"Hey!" Marcia spat into her hand again. A glop of banana fell out, and along with it, something shiny. Marcia sort of mumbled something but it sounded like "Are you paying attention here?"

Marcia reached into her mouth and pulled out a long, gold chain.

"I think I chipped a tooth," she said.

I crossed over to Marcia. In her hand, amid the banana goo, were two rings and a gold chain. They all looked expensive.

"She hid her jewelry in her banana?" I was flabbergasted.

"Brilliant," Tim said. He examined the

black banana skin. "She cut a slit in the side here and shoved 'em in. Absolutely brilliant."

"Cops missed that," I said. "What else did they miss?"

"So she did have some secrets." Teresa stuck her flashlight in Marcia's face. "Open up," she demanded. "Let's see if you lost any fillings."

Marcia slapped the flashlight out of Teresa's hand and it flew across the room. Teresa pressed her lips together and flared her nostrils. "I'm telling your mom."

"I already told your mom."

Fuming, Teresa turned on her heel.

"Tinkles," Marcia added.

"Okay, then!" Tim jumped in before fists flew. "So we know the cops checked all the usual places. That means we have to check all the unusual places."

"Exactly," I said. "She was shredding documents in the backyard, forty-five style. That meant she was angry about something." I paced around the kitchen. "Angry at something on those papers. What?"

"Taxes? An audit?"

"She was plenty wealthy. Money wasn't a problem," Marcia said. She sucked on a popsicle, and her black face was now sloughing off down to her collar. Her forehead was perfectly clean.

Teresa leaned against the counter. "Maybe they were love letters. Jilted by an angry lover?"

"I don't think so," I said. "What little I saw on that scrap of paper looked official. A love letter would have been handwritten."

Tim followed me around the kitchen. "A lawsuit? A subpoena? Jury duty? What about a doctor's report? Maybe she was ill and she couldn't face it."

"Again," I said, "I don't think so. There were lots of papers, and lots of pins in that target outside. And some of the pins looked old, rusted, while others looked like they haven't been there more than a couple of months at the most. So she's hanging up these papers over a long period of time and shooting them full of holes."

"Her monthly utility bills?" Marcia bit into the banana again and spat out another ring. "This one's really nice," she said, and popped it back into her mouth, swished it around a bit and plucked it out all clean and shiny. A huge diamond glinted under the soft kitchen light.

"Wow," I said. "Can I look at that?"

"You can't keep it, Mrs. List. Fruit of the poisoned tree." Tim shook his finger at me.

"I know that. I just want to take a look.

And maybe try it on . . ." I took the ring from Marcia and studied it. It was exquisite. I turned it this way and that, catching the beauty of the stone in the light. When I checked the band to establish the karat weight I saw something written there. "Teresa, can you shine your flashlight on this a sec?"

Teresa locked eyes with Marcia. "Why don't you tell her to get it?"

"It's your flashlight." Marcia was now peeling back the wrapper of a popsicle.

"And you knocked it right out of my hand!"

"Why should you get all the good stuff?"

Teresa rolled her eyes. "Oh, now, here we go."

I was guessing the girls' history went back a long way, and I wasn't in the mood to mediate so I picked up the light myself. I aimed it at the inside of the ring and squinted. Still no good. "Marcia? Can you read this for me?"

"I can with my good eye."

Okay . . .

Marcia took a bite of her popsicle, closed one eye and tilted her head. "Yes. I see it; there's an inscription. It says, 'To my dear M.F. from J.G.' " Marcia waved a hand in front of her face then, hopped up and down

279

and closed her eyes tight. "Oh, oh, oh, cold headache."

"You can't freeze air," Teresa mumbled.

"J.G.," I said. "J.G. J.G. J.G." As if by mere repetition I could crank over an epiphany.

Teresa pulled on her earlobe. "Those aren't her dead husband's initials."

"You said after her husband died her whole life revolved around the country club. So whose initials are J.G.? A golf pro? One of her golf buddies? A caddy? It's pretty personal, with the 'my dear' part, and jewelry is always a romantic, intimate gift. Since she was married once, I'd probably eliminate her lady friends but she has been single for a long time . . ."

"Jeff Gullikson." Tim looked out through the front window.

"Yes. Could it be?" I had that happy feeling in my stomach again. Now we were getting somewhere. "I thought there was something fishy about that guy. He's way too nice to be good."

"No. Jeff Gullikson! His truck is pulling up in front of the house!"

Teresa went rigid.

Marcia gagged on her popsicle.

"Turn off the lights!" I shoved the ring down the front of my wet suit.

"No! If we do that, he'll know someone is

in here." Tim looked around frantically. "Out the back. Come on!"

Teresa was a blur. I'd have sworn she was wearing cleats if I didn't know better. Marcia was last because she paused to grab another popsicle. Tim was ahead of me, pulling on my hand because it's really hard to run in a wet suit. There was a danger of starting a fire between my thighs.

"Up here, quick!" Teresa headed for the ladder and scurried up. Her flashlight bobbed along and there was no time to argue. We followed like lemmings. Tim pushed me from behind. Running is hard in a wet suit, but climbing a ladder when your legs are sheathed and shaking is even harder.

"Tim," I whispered loudly. "What about your SUV?"

"I parked it in the barn. No worries," he said, and continued shoving.

Marcia grew impatient and swung around us, stepping on my head on her way to the rooftop. When we were all at the top, she kicked the ladder away from the house.

"What did you do that for?" I cried.

"Can't get him thinking," Marcia said. "Now it just looks like an old ladder stuck in the juniper bushes." She licked at her popsicle.

Tim studied her. "You might have a tape worm."

"I don't have a tape worm."

"Do you purge?"

I know Tim was noting the fact that Marcia was a mere nymph even after we'd all witnessed her packing away groceries all day.

"Not of my own volition, but if you keep this up, you're gonna make me hurl." Marcia was getting testy.

"Do you know," Tim informed, "that stomach acid damages the esophagus, eats away the porcelain from your teeth and could cause an electrolyte imbalance?"

"I told you I don't purge," Marcia said. She licked her popsicle stick and tossed it over the roof edge.

Tim said quietly, "Denial is a dangerous thing."

A truck door slammed. Teresa switched off her flashlight. We all froze. I heard the sound of keys in a lock. The front door opened and then closed.

"He has a key," I whispered. "What's he doing in there?"

Tim was close to my ear. "He's *got* to be looking for that ring he gave her. He knows the cops didn't find it, otherwise they'd have him in cuffs by now."

"It's not illegal to give someone a ring," I said.

"Why did she hide it in a banana? Why wasn't she wearing it?" Marcia whispered with her hands cupped around her mouth. I noticed in the moonlight there were rings on all her fingers.

"When we get down from here," I scolded, "you put all of those back."

"Can't," Marcia said, lifting her nose in the air. "I ate the banana."

I rubbed my temples.

The front door slammed and then a truck door.

"He's leaving," Tim whispered. We all leaned out and looked at the truck.

"That didn't take long," Teresa said.

"He knew exactly what he wanted. He wasn't in there long enough for him to be searching for this ring." I patted my chest. Moira's ring nestled itself deeper into my protective cleft.

Marcia imitated me in a sassy tone. "When we get down from here, you put that back."

"This, my friend," I said, "is evidence."

"Evidence you need to do some push-ups," Marcia said.

Teresa gasped. "Do we actually share the same DNA? What's wrong with you?"

Marcia whined. "I'm hungry."

The truck's engine revved and then we watched taillights move off down the driveway. When the truck was a safe distance away, Tim looked despairingly toward the ground — and the ladder. "Now what?"

"Follow me," I said, and ran the roof luge one more time.

Of course, Teresa did something more spectacular than slide off the roof on her belly. She got to the edge of the roof, stood, dove and tucked before executing a double somersault and sticking a perfect landing. She even pointed her toes and kept her legs together the whole while and snapped her arms up when she was done.

Tim lost a belt loop on the way down but he was okay. Marcia found the rope we'd left up there before and rappelled down, until the rope broke a second time. She landed on her back, winded, and lost some Tootsie Rolls.

We hoofed it to the barn and into Tim's SUV.

I took the passenger seat. "By the way, Tim, how did you know for sure that was Mr. Gullikson's truck?"

Tim backed out quickly. "Two weeks ago he had a run-in with one of those industrial-size lumber carts. Took off his back bumper. Last week he was crossing the road and didn't see the concrete median. Took out his muffler. Then a couple of days ago he . . ."

"I get the picture," I said.

Marcia stuck her head between the seats. "Can we stop by Taco Bistro on the way to the lake?"

Chapter Twenty-Two

At the water's edge we found a place to park, and Teresa pulled the tank out of Tim's SUV. We were far enough away from Candy's campground so as not to attract attention, but close enough to make the trek without becoming exhausted. Someone would have to carry the heavy tank. Lucky for me, both Teresa and Marcia could clean and jerk twice their own weight without even tooting, and Tim was no slacker either, although he was so dismayed when we passed a bad case of fire blight that he was in no frame of mind to think straight.

The moon was full, so we didn't need our flashlights for the time being. We still had to navigate through a heavily wooded area with caution, and several times I nearly fell after tripping over roots and stumps. Tim was ahead of me and normally would have stuck out an arm to assist, but he was in a state of dismay.

"Fire blight," he moaned. "A fast-moving bacteria. Affects plants in the rose family and can enter the plant through the blooms, the pruning cuts, and the deer that eat the branches. I hate deer."

I stumbled, caught myself and pushed on. Wow. The wet suit didn't feel as tight, and I could only conclude that it was because I'd sweated off fifteen pounds, at least. "Tim, how can anyone hate deer?"

"Hate 'em. They're eating machines." Tim stopped suddenly and crouched down on one knee. "See this?" He flipped on his flashlight and aimed it at a lower tree branch. "Symptoms. Leaves and twigs turn brown, then black, and curl over in a distinctive shepherd's crook." Tim grabbed the branch and sounded choked up when he said, "It looks like it's been burned. If someone doesn't treat this, it will kill the whole tree, usually in a matter of weeks." Tim stood and shook his head. "What's the world coming to?"

"I suppose this would be a bad time for me to mention I need to use the bushes," I said.

"Come on!" Teresa hissed from up ahead of us. She and Marcia had gained a fair distance while Tim was lamenting, so I had to put off my bathroom needs for the time being. Besides, there was no way I was going to get back into that wet suit once it was down around my ankles. However, I could hardly be held responsible if I lost control once I hit that cold water.

We broke through the forest and walked in pairs along the lake shore. Marcia and Teresa had apparently made up and chatted quietly with Marcia carrying the tank on her shoulder. Up ahead I could see dots of light at the campground. I scratched behind my ears where the plastic of my mask and snorkel rubbed, and I switched my fins from one hand to the other. I counted the lights. One, an orange glow, probably the Hibachi Boys' campfire. Another large white light, obviously from the security lamp near the bait and tackle shop. A third, moving, and I guessed it was probably from a flashlight held by someone on his or her way to the bathroom. Luckyyyy.

"Hey, that's weird," I said softly to Tim. We were within fifty yards of the campground, and one of the lights I'd seen was coming from a window of Robe's camper. "She said she was pulling out today. In fact, she acted a little freaked out about not staying another minute. So why is she still here?"

"Hey, uh, I could hear you better with

288

your mask off."

"Oh." I pushed the mask up onto the top of my head. "I was just thinking to myself."

Tim looked over the top of his glasses. "Is there any other way?"

"Pssst!" I motioned for the girls to come back to us and we all crouched low, lights off. "Remember the plan?"

Marcia put one foot on the tank and unwrapped a fruit roll-up. "One of us has to get the boat first."

"I'll get it," I said. "I know which one it is. But I'll need help once it's in the water. After I'm all tanked up — I mean, suited up, I'll go in and start looking for Moira's car. Not much sense searching over near the wooded area, since you can't drive a car through there, and someone would have probably noticed tire prints in the sand if her car had gone in at the campsite. If we don't find anything here, we'll move over to the southeast side of the lake. Just remember I only have about forty-five minutes on the tank. An hour at most, okay? We all good?" I looked from Marcia to Teresa and then to Tim. They all nodded in turn.

A rustle in the bushes behind us stopped me short. "You hear that?"

Tim's lips framed a tight, thin line. "Golldang deer." He stood, yanked the fruit roll-up from Marcia just as she was about to put an end into her mouth, wadded it up and heaved it into the bushes with so much force I was sure he'd dislocated his shoulder.

"That's a lot of rage, Tim."

Tim wiped sweat from his brow. "I think I'll call the little sick tree Treeva. She should have a name."

Marcia made a raspberry. "Why not Leif? Or Barker? Or Rootie? Equally creative and thoughtful. And by the way. You owe me a roll-up."

The bushes rustled again. A twig snapped. Tim clenched his fists. "Why, I oughta . . ."

"Please, gang, we've got a job to do here, ya know?" I clapped my hands in front of Tim's face. "Keep it together, man." I pushed my mask down, did a test breath through my snorkel and stomped off toward Snack's boat.

As I got close to the campground, I waded out into the shallows until the water was up to my knees. Then I pushed off and dog-paddled my way over toward the dock. The lake was a black, borderless, featureless expanse. And it was bone-jarring cold. The water flooded down my back and into my wet suit. My lungs shrank about four sizes and my bladder expanded about two before everything went numb. I'd left my booties

290

back with Marcia, Teresa, and Tim, and as I passed the dock and kicked toward my waiting boat, little fish mouths nibbled my toes. Even though my head wasn't submerged, I kept the snorkel in my mouth. In the dark it was especially difficult to see through the mask, so I kept the lights on my right and aimed for the bulky shapes, knowing the one on the far end would be my transportation back to my friends.

I found Snack's ride in short order and nearly capsized the boat. Falling off a roof was child's play compared to hefting my water-logged bulk over the side of a moving, aluminum wall. The oars were inside the boat, just as Snack had promised, and although it was fitted with an outboard motor, I knew it would be impossible for me to operate a covert mission using it, so I untied, pushed off, and dug in. I rammed the dock and three other boats before I thought to take off my mask, but after that it was smooth sailing. I bent and pulled, bent and pulled, and when I got to the area where I left the rest of the gang my arms were flaccid noodles.

Teresa stepped into the water and pulled me ashore. "Tim's got your tank strapped into the BCD and checked all the gauges. You're set."

Marcia clamored into the boat and took an oar.

"Hey," Teresa said, "that one's mine. I called it." She jumped in and started a tug-of-war before Tim cleared his throat and stopped the tomfoolery. "Oh, all right." Teresa grabbed the other oar and sat down beside Marcia to sulk.

"Shhhh! You guys, we're not that far from the campers. Keep it down, okay?" I strapped on my weight belt, not too heavy because I was diving in fresh water. Then I spread my feet for stability, and Tim helped me shrug into my BCD, an inflatable vest which, held together with plastic clips, holds the tank and adds a little warmth and protection. I felt around for my regulator. Everything was where it should have been. All I had left to do was put on my booties and fins.

First Tim held out my booties, fully expecting me to slip them on while balancing first on one leg, and then the other. I had at least twenty pounds on my back and ten more around my waist (along with some extra poundage I couldn't take off at the end of the dive) not to mention I was standing on shifting sand. "You've got to be kidding."

"How do you wanna do this?" Tim chewed

on his lip.

I chewed on my nails.

"I've got it." I lowered myself to the ground, shaky legs and all, and sat. Then I stuck my feet in the air. "Just put them on for me."

Tim approached me in the manner of an attentive parent. He went to one knee and felt around for my feet because we were working with whatever meager moonlight reflected off the lake, and it was hard to tell a foot from a rock. He slipped one bootie onto my foot, zipped it up (and thank goodness I'd shaved my legs that morning), then took care of my other foot. He smoothed the booties down with gentle hands and then found my fins and fitted them with a tug at the strap around my ankle. He pressed down on my toes. "How does that feel?" he asked with sincere interest.

"You've worked in a shoe store, haven't you?" I asked. Gravity had taken over and I was lying back on my dive tank, studying the constellations. The only thing that felt good at that moment were Tim's fingers pressing on my piggies. "If we had the time, I'd pay you a million dollars for a foot rub."

"As a matter of fact," Tim said proudly, "I practice acupressure on my spare time, and I think I have a card in here somewhere . . ."

Marcia banged the rim of the boat with her oar. "Helllooooo. We're drifting."

I sat up, struggling, and took a deep, cleansing breath. "Okay. Let's roll."

Tim saluted and vaulted through ankle-deep water toward the boat. "Tim!" I hissed. "That wasn't a figure of speech."

"Oh." Tim splashed back to me and put his strong and capable hands against my side. He pushed and I rolled until I was in the water, then he pushed a few more times and I stuck my regulator in my mouth just as I began to sink to the bottom. Every time I rolled over that tank, I'd added a new bruise to my already battered body. What in the world was I trying to prove? I pulled myself along the muddy lake bottom until I felt myself floating. I adjusted my buoyancy, sucking the pressurized air with as much calm and control as I could muster. There was no time to think about how I was relying on that thing on my back to keep me from drowning or that I was actually breathing under water — an act that goes against every self-preservation reflex — I just had to do a job and get out alive.

I was too low. I pulled a cord on my BCD to allow in a little more air. I shot to the surface and blasted up and out of the lake like a breaching whale. For a moment I identified with Moira — and not in a good way.

The visibility was practically nil under the water: not good in the daytime, and disorienting in the inky blackness of night. Even close to the surface of the water, my eyes were practically useless and my hopes of finding Moira's submerged car dimmed with the ever-receding depths below. Something hard tapped the top of my head. Remembering the blades of the outboard got me thinking I'd drifted directly under the boat and if the girls got any bright ideas about cranking up the motor I'd be combing my hair with a wig brush. Or worse.

Tap, tap, tap. Again with the knock on the noggin. I peered up toward the surface and saw a light wavering within arm's reach. Darn. I'd forgotten my flashlight. That might help. I reached up and held out my hand and someone passed me the torch, one of Ted's industrial types that wouldn't die in the water in case the baggie failed. I just hoped I'd fare as well. I shined the light around. Much better.

As I drifted, the only sounds I heard were strangely alien; my sucking, then blowing, bubbles rising around me, and the occasional bump when an oar struck the side of the boat. I could hear nothing else. I aimed the light down toward the bottom of the lake and occasionally pointed it upwards in order to track the boat as it moved along, oars dipping and pulling in lazy, tandem strokes, and if the girls had followed our predetermined route we were moving in a zigzag pattern along the west bank.

Nothing. Save for some lake weeds and curious minnows, there was nothing of interest at the bottom of the lake. At least not where we were looking. The girls were told only to go out as far as a car would reasonably drift, then cross in front of the dock and start our search on the other side.

I surfaced and shook my head. Marcia aimed her flashlight at her face. "This is my disappointed look," she said.

I pulled the regulator out of my mouth (along with a long stream of drool), and floated in my BCD. "I'll paddle over to you and hang onto the boat while we go to the other side," I said.

Marcia shined the light on my face, blinding me even more completely than when I was in the water without a light. "Stop that," I said, but most of it came out as a garble because I was spitting out rancid water from Moody Lake, the place, I couldn't help but remember, where Moira's bloated, decomposing body had recently floated.

Marcia chuckled and moved the light around my face in circular patterns, then up and down, and then she outlined my body with her light. She drew a line from me to the boat. "Come on, Mrs. List, coooome into the liiiight."

I was fully buoyant at that point which made it easy for me to pull myself along the surface of the lake toward the boat. I got there with little effort, raised my hand up to the edge and heard the first gunshot.

Pop!

Teresa's oar exploded in her hands. She cried out. "Holy Moly!"

Pop!

Something grazed the top of the motor and with a zing ricocheted out to oblivion.

Marcia screamed, "Someone's shooting at us!" She pointed her light toward the shore.

Pop!

I fumbled for the dump-valve cord on my BCD in order to bleed out the air. If I could dive, I'd be out of range of the bullets. "Crank the motor! Start the boat!" I shouted before stuffing the regulator into my mouth. Tim grabbed the cord on the outboard and yanked. The motor sputtered and died. Tim yanked again, and again, and again. Marcia and Teresa shouted encouragement. I searched for my valve as bullets whizzed within inches of the boat but my numb, tired arms failed me and I couldn't find it. I couldn't find it! A bullet whizzed by my shoulder and plunked into the water a few feet away. I grappled and grabbed, and searched. Then I remembered I had another option; a pressure-release valve. I reached for it, put my thumb on the button — and that's when the bullet struck my tank.

CHAPTER TWENTY-THREE

The sound the bullet made when it penetrated the heavy metal wall of my dive tank was deafening. But the time it took for me to even process this was a mere split-second because upon impact I blasted across the lake at rocket speeds. The pressurized air escaped the tank, creating a jet stream behind me. I skipped over the top of that water with no manner of control; neither anchor nor rudder. My regulator ripped out of my mouth, my mask and snorkel were violently torn off of my face, water coursed up my nose, and then I changed direction and whipped around in a spinning, circular motion, me going one way, my legs, arms and stomach going the other. I spun fast, then picked up speed and flipped and spun across the surface of Moody Lake like one of those little Fourth of July novelties that spin out of control when you light them until they land on someone's roof and burn their house down.

As I whipped around, a human centrifuge, I bumped over the small waves, skittering herky-jerky, wigwag, then again with the nauseating spinning. I should have been wondering who in the world was shooting at us. I should have wondered if it had anything to do with the fact we were searching for murdered Moira's car, whether or not Tim, Marcia and Teresa were shot dead in Snack's boat. And I should have been mildly concerned about what I was going to tell the old man tomorrow or what I was going to report to Mikey, but I didn't. I just closed my eyes, held my breath, and prayed for it all to end.

When it did, I was at the edge of the woods where this whole thing started, out of air, without a snorkel and mask, and sinking like a rock. Apparently the bullet had fragmented and pierced my BCD. I grabbed at my weight belt and pulled the quick release. It slipped from my waist. But I was still going down. I fumbled for the clasps on my BCD so I could shed it and paddle for shore. Somehow I got it unfastened and squirmed out of the cumbersome vest. Gone. I threw out one arm in an effort to swim, but I was so tired and dizzy it just flapped in the water. I continued to sink,

sink, sink, and my legs floated down . . . then stopped. My feet touched bottom.

"Oh," I said. I stood up and walked out of the lake.

In the distance I heard the sound of a motor. I breathed a sigh of relief that ended in a grateful sob. The sound was getting closer. That meant someone in the boat was still alive and they'd seen me when I shot off into the distance. I collapsed on the bank and waited.

I saw the dim hulk of the boat approaching at a faster-than-safe speed. It wasn't slowing as it got closer. It wasn't turning, either. I scrambled behind a tree and heard three hard splashes before I watched in amazement as the boat glanced off a floating log, flew up into the air and sailed high up over my head. It soared until it was out of sight. I heard a thunderous crash and saw a large ball of fire shoot into the air. *Now* what was I going to tell Pendersnack?

Tim's voice called out. "May? You okay?" He and the girls waded toward the shore, drenched and shaken, but as far as I could tell, uninjured. Tim scooped up my BCD on his way in, and Marcia held one of my fins. I could say good-bye to my snorkel, mask and weight belt.

Tim thudded the BCD on the ground

beside me and I touched the ragged hole in my rented dive tank. *There goes my deposit.* "I'll take this to the police. I only see one hole, so I'm guessing the bullet is still inside." Teresa lifted the tank as easily as she would a Styrofoam cup and gave it a vigorous shake. A satisfying clatter verified my guess.

Another loud *pop!* brought us to our senses. A tree branch splintered overhead and came crashing down at Tim's feet. "This is an outrage!" he cried.

"And this," Marcia pointed to her backside, "is my rear end beating you back to the truck." She darted off through the woods.

No prodding necessary, Teresa hefted the BCD on her shoulder and, of course, overtook Marcia in seconds. Tim pulled me along by the arm and kept me upright even though I tripped over every branch, bush and pebble on our way to his SUV. A leafy branch slapped me in the face, but Tim reminded me it wasn't the tree's fault, and we kept hauling buns while bullets whizzed over our heads.

We tumbled into Tim's SUV. "Go, go, *go!*" We all shouted. Tim, of course was having trouble finding his keys.

"I thought they were in here, no, here, no,

maybe I put them . . ."

Blam!

Tim's side mirror disintegrated in a spray of glass.

"Go!" Teresa hammered the back of Tim's seat.

"Got 'em!" Tim shoved the key into the ignition and twisted. The engine answered with a sick moan. He turned the key again.

Pop!

A bullet shattered the back window and exited through the front, leaving a hole just above the dashboard. We all grabbed our heads to be sure they were still intact.

I screamed, "Tim! Let's go!"

"It won't turn over!" Tim pumped the gas and tried again.

Out of the corner of my eye I saw a sudden movement — a shadow — and just as I went for the lock, someone wrenched my door open. A large pair of hands reached inside the SUV and grabbed my collar. A man hauled me from the truck and tossed me to the ground.

I struggled and swung and beat my hands against the man's chest. I held out two fingers and aimed for his eyes but he dodged, and I merely jabbed air. I kicked for his groin, but I had lost my booties in the lake and just added two more bruises to my collection when my bare feet were deflected by solid knuckles.

"Relax, May!" My husband held me against him. Another shot rang out and Ted dragged me along the ground to the front of the SUV where Marcia, Teresa, and Tim had already taken cover.

"Thanks for coming to my rescue, guys," I said.

They all looked apologetic, but I can't say I blamed them. After all, I'd wasted no time looking for a retreat when they were sitting vulnerable in the boat. So we were even.

"Ted? What are you doing here?"

"Saving your bacon, I think, May Bell."

"Please don't say that. Makes me a little nauseated." I held my stomach.

During a brief break in the gunfire, when I imagined the shooter was reloading, Ted shouted, "Run, everyone! Get to my Hummer. Stay down. I'm right behind you." Ted pointed, and I found my last reserve of energy.

For the first time, I loved Ted's Hummer. Forget roads; we cut straight through the forest, plowed down a few small trees (and that made Tim hyperventilate until Teresa calmed him down), crawled over rocks, found pavement finally, and made it home in record time.

■ ■ ■ ■

Ted put on some coffee while Tim, Teresa and Marcia went to various rooms in our house to change into some dry clothes I'd provided for them. My cat and dog ignored me and followed Tim, and I was only too happy to get the cold shoulder because I had other things to worry about.

I retreated to my bedroom with Ted. "I'd like to understand," Ted said, while peeling the wet suit off my body, "what in the world you were doing tonight." He grunted and tugged and made a lot of strained expressions while he undressed me, because the wet suit had become a second skin by now.

When he reached for a pair of scissors I held up a hand. "I'll get it," I said, and grunted, and tugged and writhed until the thing was in a heap on the floor. Everything on me relaxed and expanded all at once. I have never felt so relieved. I didn't even have an urgent bladder anymore. All that g-force and cold water took care of that need, albeit without my consent.

"And what I'd like to know," I said, rummaging through my panty drawer, "is how you knew where I was."

"I was quite impressed by the mural on

the wall."

"Oh, yeah. That." Shoot. I'd forgotten to shove the bookcases back in place.

"But it doesn't quite explain why you were there or who those people are, now wearing my pants."

"I only gave Tim your pants. The girls are wearing my sweats."

"Forgive me."

"Let me get some clothes on and we'll talk about it in the dining room. I suppose it's time you know everything."

Ted rubbed his nose, blinked his tired eyes and left the room. Poor thing; but he was used to late nights and sleep deprivation. As soon as he was out of the room I got dressed, then picked up the phone and dialed Officer Murphy's cell number. Certainly someone at the campsite had reported the shooting by now, and when Mikey answered the phone my assumptions were confirmed. I could hear the wail of sirens in the background.

"Can you talk? Are you driving hands-free?" I asked.

"Mrs. List?"

"Listen carefully, Mikey. You're probably responding to a nine-one-one call. Right?"

"What other kind?"

"Are you alone in your car?"

"Yeah . . ."

"Are you on speaker? You can't drive and talk on your cell phone. It's illegal."

"Mrs. List!"

"You're going out to Moody Lake, am I right?" I heard tires squeal.

"I can't talk right now, Mrs. List."

"When you get to Moody Lake, you're going to find an SUV all shot to pieces and you're going to check the license plate and you're going to find out it belongs to one Tim Kholhauff. And if you're worth your stuff, you're going to know Tim works out at the country club and I'm just asking you for two things."

"Can this wait?"

More sounds of tires squealing.

"I'm just asking you to stall before you come to me or Tim or anyone else about what happened out at the lake tonight."

"What do you know, Mrs. List?"

"That's not important right now. The second thing I'm asking is for you to retrieve a blue rubber glove from the SUV. Don't lose what's inside the glove. This is very important."

I heard the warble of sirens and the rumble of a maxed engine. "Mikey! Are you listening?"

"You're gonna give me ulcers."

"No, no, I'm not. Ulcers are usually caused by a bacterium called Helicobacter Pilori. Easily treated with antibiotics. I could give you palpitations, high blood pressure, or migraines, but not an ulcer." Sometimes it's good to be married to a doctor.

The sound of the siren petered out. The engine noises stopped. Mikey whispered into his phone. "We're here."

"Okay. Now remember what I said. Look for a blue rubber glove in the SUV, but don't share, and don't lose what's inside. I'll explain it later. And don't bother looking to question Mr. Kholhauff tonight because he isn't home. And . . . there's a dive tank somewhere out there. You might want to examine it. There's a bullet inside."

I hung up the phone before Mikey could protest, and then I joined my company in the dining room.

By the time we had our third cup of coffee, Ted was up to speed on what we knew so far, which wasn't much. I'd lost the ring when I was shot over Moody Lake like a human projectile, and Marcia didn't have her stolen jewelry either, it was sitting in the ruins of Snack's boat.

"So the whole night was a bust," Teresa said. She sat at my table, her hands wrapped around a steaming cup. Her eyes were

308

bloodshot and she blinked slowly, fighting the same fatigue we all felt.

"Not exactly," I assured her. "We made somebody nervous, and that somebody knew we'd be out at Moody Lake tonight."

"Or maybeeee," Teresa said, "they, or he, didn't know until he followed us from Moira's house."

I slammed my fist into my palm, startling Tim who'd started to doze. "J.G."

"Jeff Gullikson." Marcia sank her teeth into an apple.

I looked around the table. "Are you thinking what I'm thinking?"

"I'm thinking," Teresa said, "the night ain't over yet."

CHAPTER TWENTY-FOUR

We pulled up in front of Jeff Gullikson's house around midnight. I was surprised to see his truck in the driveway and the lights out in his house.

"Maybe it wasn't him," Teresa said.

"Only one way to find out." I got out of my Camaro and slid along its side, around the trunk and up the passenger side until I was next to Gully's truck. I ran over and placed my hands on the truck's hood. I shook my head, and then ran back to the Camaro.

"It's cold."

"Of course it's cold," Tim said. "It's been at least two hours since he used us for target practice."

"Okay. Phase two."

"That was phase one?" Marcia asked.

"We've got to get in his house and find that gun."

"Can't," Marcia said, pulling on a huge

wad of gum. "He doesn't have a fireplace."

"And I don't have a gun."

I shrieked and whirled. Jeff Gullikson stood on his porch, tying a bathrobe sash around his waist.

Tim, Marcia and Teresa ducked out of sight.

Jeff reached around his door and switched on the porch light. I immediately un- clenched my buttocks. His hair was pushed up on one side of his head, he had pillow lines on his left cheek, and the bags under his eyes told me I didn't have to worry about J.G. being our perp. We'd caught him in REM.

I gave a let's go sign. "Get out here, everyone, Gully's not our guy."

Jeff called out, "Can I offer you a bever- age?"

What a nice fella. Even in the middle of the night he was being considerate. I found his hand when I reached the porch and took it in mine, just like he'd done for me when we first met. "Allow me to explain," I said.

"Not out here. I've got a pretty good feel- ing I know what this is all about. I got a call from an Officer Murphy an hour ago."

Ted, Teresa and Marcia shuffled up to the porch, their heads hanging.

"Come on in, then, but don't think you're

gonna get out of the five A.M. staff meeting."

We all found comfortable chairs in Jeff's modest but orderly den. The décor was "everything golf." Our fourth cup of coffee pushed us over from barely awake to completely buzzed and the questions and accusations came fast and furious. No, Jeff wasn't courting Moira in the old-fashioned sense. The ring was a club gift for Mrs. Finch's loyal contributions over the thirty-plus years she'd been a member, and although it was odd that it would be engraved personally by Gully, he said, blushing with embarrassment, that he thought it might pave the way for her to find it in her heart to eschew the ways of the world and yearn for the pearly gates. If only she'd find him a worthy confidant.

And apparently, it had softened her up a bit. She became more talkative when Gully greeted her before her tee times, and they even had lunch together once a week. She was lonely, he said, and her caustic personality was just an unfortunate expression of her disappointment in a sinful world.

"What was she like, Gully? I mean, did she talk to you about her family or friends or hobbies? Did she have any reason to believe someone wanted to kill her?"

312

"Never a word. As for hobbies, she enjoyed gardening . . ."

"Yeah," Teresa said with a snort, "I noticed."

"Oh, I'm sorry, Teresa. I told her she could help herself to any landscaping plants she wanted. She was a big contributor, after all."

"Gee, thanks."

"She, uh . . . tracked birds' migratory patterns, went to Coeur d'Alene every year to photograph bald eagles, she liked to read . . . um, she didn't have any relatives and few friends except for those at the club . . . and she was working on a novel."

"Really?" I liked that. "I've been thinking about writing a book for years. Did she finish it?"

"She didn't talk about it much, but yes. Yes, now that I think about it, she only mentioned it once after it was done. She'd sent it out all over the place and got rejection letter after rejection letter. Since that depressed her I didn't bring it up after that."

Teresa's big blue eyes grew wide. "Rejection letters?"

Marcia squinted her good eye, tilted her head and raised her hand. She pulled an imaginary trigger. "Pow," she said.

"It makes perfect sense." I downed my

313

coffee. "She gets rejection letters over a period of time, takes them out back, pins them to her target and blasts them to smithereens. Even though I've never actually written a book, I've started a lot of them. It's a highly personal undertaking. I could see myself shooting a rejection letter full of holes. Yeah, buddy."

"We'll need to examine that piece of paper we found," Marcia said. She stuck her finger in her eye and then touched the tip of her tongue.

"What's she doing?" I asked Teresa.

"It's her contact lens. It's so she can read, but only with that eye. It messes up her depth perception a little, but she's getting better."

"Don't eat it, Marshmallow," Tim said.

Tim took a solid fist to the temple.

I stretched out my legs, bent over and rubbed the small of my back. "I think I'm starting to get the picture. It sounds like she wasn't that bad after all. Just, like you said, Gully, very lonely and very disappointed. That doesn't sound like someone with serious enemies. I understand that just before she disappeared she teed off on a day she didn't normally golf and she had a guest with her. The weapon used to kill her was from the grounds equipment, but it had disappeared and was unaccounted for until it showed up in Moira's neck."

"Don't forget Buddy," Tim said.

I was surprised he was still conscious. His lids looked like they were tied to horse shoes. Either it was exhaustion or he had a concussion, thanks to Marcia.

"We'll get to him soon enough." I stood and worked out some of the kinks as I pondered. "I'm still not satisfied with everything you've told us, Gully."

Jeff creased his forehead. "Really?"

"You were at Moira's house this evening, weren't you?"

"No," he said without hesitation.

Teresa put her hand on his arm and spoke softly. "But Mr. Gullikson, we saw you. You don't have to be ashamed about getting close to an older woman. It's what life is made of. It keeps us young and vibrant."

Gully looked around the room. "No, I really wasn't at her house today."

Tim stroked his bearded chin. "Your truck was."

"My truck? I . . . I, uh, maybe somebody borrowed it. I always leave the keys in it. You guys know that — it's always there for any of you if you need to use it."

Marcia agreed. "That's true. I always told you it wasn't such a good idea."

"Everyone in the grounds crew knows you leave the keys in your truck?" I asked.

"Sure," Teresa said. "We usually check with Mr. Gullikson first, but I think we've all found a reason to borrow that truck at one time or another."

"We need to take a look at your truck, Gully." I headed for the door. Jeff, Teresa and Marcia followed, but Tim had given up on staying awake and was out cold, head on the back of his chair, snoring softly.

"Wait." I stopped and everyone ran into me. "Sheesh. Personal space, okay?" Everyone backed up a step. "We're gonna need some things, Gully. A flashlight, a lint roller, some cotton swabs, a . . . bottle of water, a couple of baggies, and . . . uh . . ."

"A beef stick," Marcia said.

Gully took care of my needs and held the flashlight while I walked around his truck. "Marcia," I said, "run the lint roller over the upholstery. Then put the whole thing in a baggy. Teresa, come on back here with me. Oh, by the way, Gully, is the truck where you parked it when you got home?"

Mr. Gullikson scratched his head. "I think so. I can't swear to it, but it looks right."

"How can you *not* know if someone takes your truck?" Teresa unlatched the back of the truck. The tailgate was dented and difficult. It made a grinding metallic creek when she lowered it.

"I go to bed around eight, and I always wear earplugs."

"Oh, you do?" I asked. "Then how did you know we were here?" I wasn't buying it.

"When you pulled up, your headlights shined right into my bedroom window."

Oh.

Teresa jumped into the bed of the truck. I handed her a swab and the water bottle. "Aim the light over here, please, Gully."

Jeff leaned over the side of the truck bed and moved his flashlight around. There wasn't much to see except for some sand in the corners and a spare tire.

"Wait. Wait! Over there."

Gully moved the light to the center of the truck bed. There was a brown stain that appeared to be blood covering a large area.

"Been doing any hunting lately, Mr. Gullikson?" I narrowed my eyes.

"I, uh, moved a dead deer off my property last week." Gully's Adam's apple was bobbing. "I'm sure that's what it is."

Marcia moved around in the cab, rocking the truck gently as she gathered fiber evidence. I looked at Teresa, she looked at me, and we were both thinking the same thing.

Gully's little dead-deer story was a little too convenient.

"You're lying, Mr. Gullikson," I said, motioning for Teresa to get out of the truck bed. "What did you do? Get Moira to change her will? Did you find out from Buddy that she was going to donate her whole fortune to the club and you thought, 'Well, I've spent all of this time with her and she's not going to give me a thing'?"

"Of course not." Gully's Adam's apple was *really* jumping.

"And then you killed Buddy to keep him from exposing you? Did he get suspicious? Or did you just need a shortcut up the career ladder?"

Gully's eyes were wide. "No! Why are you being so hateful?"

I stepped backwards and waved my hand at Marcia, trying to get her attention, because Mr. Gullikson's hands rolled into angry fists. I'd really hit a nerve. Marcia didn't notice me, though; she was humming loudly, rolling the upholstery. *Come on, Marcia, look up. Look up!*

Teresa hopped out of the truck. She'd swabbed the blood — just as I'd instructed before we left the house — and now waved the cotton swab under Mr. Gullikson's nose.

"We got you."

"You don't know what you're talking about. Mrs. List —" Gully stepped toward me.

"You just hold on there, Mr. Gullikson," I said firmly. "Stay back."

"You've got it all wrong, Mrs. List. I haven't been anywhere. As God is my witness, I've been asleep all evening."

I waved my hand toward Marcia again. *Look up, for crying out loud!*

"And you want me to believe someone just happened to come along, borrowed your truck, drove it over to Moira's house after you" — I put up my fingers and scratched air quotes — "transported a dead, bloody deer, after Moira was killed with an instrument that you, coincidentally, fashioned out of a golf club?" I put my hands on my hips. "What do you take me for?"

"You're way out of line, Mrs. List." Gully's voice trembled.

"Objection!" Marcia shouted from the cab. "Objection! Come over here, May, I think this might interest you."

I held up a finger. "You just sit tight there, Mr. Gullikson."

Gully ran his fingers through his already mussed hair. He said without much energy, "But I'm standing."

"Whatcha got, Marcia?" I slid my eyes

over to Gully, and then glanced inside the cab. Marcia was sitting behind the wheel. The cab light was on.

"The keys were in it, like he said, but the seat. Look at this." She put her hands on the steering wheel and her right foot on the gas pedal. "See?"

"See what?" Again I cut my eyes over to Gully. He hadn't moved.

"Mr. Gullikson is at least six feet tall. His legs aren't disproportionately short, so there's no way he could have driven this truck and reached the pedals. I'm about five-three and I don't need to adjust the rearview mirror to see out the back. He couldn't have been the last one to drive this truck."

"Just a thought," I said, feeling not just a little bit disappointed. "Turn the key one click. Wait. Use your sleeve. Okay, just one click and then turn the radio on. Again, use your sleeve."

Marcia did as I asked. A seventies rock number blasted through the speakers. "Mr. Gullikson!" I hailed him over. "Is this the station you normally listen to?"

"Oh, like he'd tell you the truth," Marcia said.

"I don't listen to secular music, Mrs. List, especially not rock and roll," Gully said with humble sincerity. "It's an instrument of the devil."

I mumbled, "I'd reserve that title for soil probes and crack hoes."

CHAPTER TWENTY-FIVE

Tim hadn't budged when we went back into the house, and since I was the only one with a car (and I wasn't sure I could drive farther than back to my own place since I was seeing double), Teresa and Marcia were invited to spend the night on the couch at Mr. Gullikson's. Tim had claimed the chair. Because Gully's truck was a crime scene — I was pretty sure of that — I collected all of the evidence and warned him not to drive it to work the next day, but I wasn't in the mood to answer any of Mikey's questions that night, so I agreed to pick everyone up for work at four-thirty. That would give us all about three hours of sleep. Not much on the swab, but the lint roller had picked up some interesting fibers. A lot of little gray curly hairs. Ew, I thought. Did Mr. Gully occasionally drive naked?

I let my Camaro drive me home that night and can't even remember making the necessary turns and stops. All I could think about was how disastrous the evening had been and how close we'd all come to losing our heads. I'd never have forgiven myself if anything had happened to Teresa, Marcia or Tim. Some detective I'd turned out to be. I did take some satisfaction in knowing I'd made someone nervous, and it had to be when we were digging around Moira's house. There wasn't any other reason for someone to be shooting at us out at the lake unless he or she knew we'd been looking for evidence leading to Moira's killer. He or she must have thought we found something or were about to find something out at the lake. So the question was — who had driven Gully's truck out to Moira's? What had we really found in the back of Gully's truck? Was the blood from an animal or a human?

When I finally found my way to my bed, my mind blew a circuit and the breakers flipped off. Whatever I was pondering would have to wait until the next morning.

Which happened to be about two seconds after I closed my eyes. The alarm clock's ringing became part of my dreams, and I was running in a flaming wet suit through the halls of my college, late for class, but I couldn't find the room, couldn't even remember what class I was supposed to be in, for that matter, while the tardy bell rang and rang. Ted nudged me awake.

"I'll put on the coffee," he said.

I showered and dressed with my eyes closed. When I got to the kitchen Ted handed me a thermos. "I made bacon and eggs, too," he said. "Do you have time to eat before you go?"

"I think I'll just have toast, thanks." Torch stood at my feet, tongue hanging out, tail wagging. "He can have mine." I tucked my shirt into my new khaki pants and felt official, all duded out.

"Lookin' good, babe." Ted pulled my car keys off the hook and walked toward the front door.

"You walking me out?" I grabbed a jacket out of the hall closet.

"No, I'm driving you to work."

"What?" I turned to look at him.

"Last night you almost got yourself killed. I don't know what you have going on exactly, but until the police find who was shooting at you, I'm not leaving your side. I've called Dr. Brennan to cover for me until this mess is cleared up."

"This mess?"

Ted opened the door. "You know what I mean. And, yeah, this mess. You may have taken things a little too far this time."

I brushed past Ted, then turned and held out my hand. "I can handle myself." My pulse was racing and a hot flush was working its way up my neck. "Give me the keys."

"No."

"Yes, Ted." I reached for the keys, but Ted pulled them away.

"May, I know this stuff gives you some kind of . . . high. Solving puzzles, fixing problems, bringing bad guys to justice. But you've already done all that. In the last few years you've been shot at by drug dealers, you've been put in prison, for Pete's sake, you've been tied up and nearly blown up, you've confronted criminals who would just as soon grind you up into little bloody pieces than let you walk away, and I just don't know how much more of this I can take."

I looked into Ted's eyes and saw the dark circles, noted the furrows of wrinkles lining his forehead and the way the corners of his mouth pulled down when he paused.

My chest tightened and my eyes burned with tears of frustration. I looked out toward the black sky and then exhaled slowly. "What else do I have, Ted?"

"What else do you have?"

"Yeah. What else?"

"You have me."

"Yes. I know that. And I've been there for you for over thirty years. I've been there for Patty. I've been there for everyone and everything and I have never complained. I'm proud of my role as a mother and a wife and I've enjoyed every minute. Well, most of it. But Patty is gone, you don't really need me anymore, your career is solid and so it's not important for me to host tea parties anymore . . ."

"Hold it. You think I want you around just to cook my meals and wash my clothes and otherwise sit in a chair knitting socks until I get home every evening?"

"I don't know how to knit, but, yeah. That's pretty much it." I lifted my chin while trying to keep it from trembling.

"I just don't want you dead!" Ted's voice went up an octave.

I smiled and spoke softly, trying to hold my tears at bay. "But, Ted, when I'm doing this stuff that you think is crazy — and maybe it is — but when I'm out there, I feel so alive."

Ted nodded, understanding. He studied my face a long minute, and then cupped his hand under my quivering chin. "I'm still driving you to work. I want you to *stay* alive."

Ted explained that after dropping me at

the shop he would catch a few winks in my car until early tee time and then get a game in while he was "in the neighborhood." I know it was his way of keeping an eye on me and I have to say if he hadn't been concerned, I'd be rethinking my vows. He'd expressed worry about my involvement with police business before, but this time he was really worked up. I guess it was selfish of me to add stress to my husband's already busy days, but I had to wonder if he had ever given a moment's thought to the days *I'd* spent trudging through lists of mundane tasks, coming home to an empty house, and thinking my purpose in life had been used up and I was faced with the thought of eventually watching sunsets in my rocking chair. Looking over at him, I believed that at last he understood.

As we passed by a twenty-four-hour department store, I asked Ted to stop. I ran inside and came back in no time with a bulging plastic bag. "I needed to pick up something," I explained. Ted just navigated his way through the parking lot, knowing better than to ask questions.

"We're gonna be late," I said, hinting that Ted might want to drive a little faster, but he cruised along calmly, one hand on the steering wheel, his left arm resting on the window ledge of the door.

"I have a feeling being late is going to be the least of your worries," Ted said. He lifted a finger and pointed to the rotating police lights parked atop the cruisers as we neared the country club maintenance shop.

"Oh, shoot," I said. I thought Mikey might catch up to me, but not so soon. "Oh, shoot!" I sat up straight in my seat. "Maybe there's been another murder!"

Ted slow-rolled up the gravel road and craned his neck around. "No crime-scene tape."

"That's a good sign."

"No coroner's van."

"Another good sign."

"SWAT unit's here."

"What?" I leaned forward and rubbed my hand over the windshield.

"Just kidding."

"Let me out here. No need to get you involved." I opened the door before Ted had a chance to apply the brakes. I was ready to hit the ground running, but I'd forgotten to undo my seat belt, so the car was stopped by the time I got out. I signaled Ted to go, and I jogged, as only an old woman can do, toward the police cars.

I spotted Officer Murphy leaning against his cruiser, clipboard in hand. "What's going on, Mikey?" I huffed and puffed, because the jog was a good fifty yards.

"Oh, there you are. Mr. Gullikson said you'd be in about . . ." Mikey checked his watch. "Fifteen minutes ago."

"I'm late. So fire me."

"Or arrest you."

"Huh?"

"You have a lot of 'splainin' to do, Lucy." Mike lifted an eyebrow and gave me one of his official stares.

I held up a plastic shopping bag. "All right. But, first, why don't you and your boys come on in and have a donut?"

Chapter Twenty-Six

The shop was swarming with cops when I walked in. The grounds staff was sitting, lined up against the hall wall in a palpable state of shock. Mr. Stamper was drooling and reciting assignments in a monotone. "Tim, Teresa, Marcia and May on landscaping . . . Elder, Jim and Jerry on the surrounds . . . Jacob, Brandon, Derek, Travis on bunkers . . ." His eyes bugged out and his dog licked at his face but Stamper was in a zone of the twilight variety and it would take something like a stick of dynamite to blast him back to reality.

Jim the ex-cop cracked his knuckles and insisted on some professional courtesy, but he was ignored. The three cabana boys, James, Jesse and Aaron, fiddled with their portable video games, happy to be out of work, and the college kids dozed. One of them, Matt, had his head on Marcia's shoulder. She pushed him off and he fell over onto Teresa's lap. She rolled her eyes at me and shrugged. Bonnie and Clyde were playing slap hands while Jerry quietly crocheted an afghan, which was folded neatly on his lap. Elder held his deflated football in his lap and wept openly. The guy I'd seen playing craps at the hoedown was now playing cribbage with Tim. Chris moved a slinky back and forth from hand to hand.

"What's going on here?" I turned to Mikey and thought he might not be deserving of any donuts after all.

"You'll need to take your place against the wall."

"Hold on, buster. You can't just tell us to sit on the floor without a darn-good reason."

"This cover it?" Mikey pulled a paper out of his pocket.

"Search warrant. That's pretty good. What are you looking for?" As if I didn't know. I heard clattering and banging coming from the mechanics' shop, and through the glass window I could see cops rummaging around in Dave and Joe's sacred quarters. The two guys were standing nearby, and occasionally their mouths would work, probably explaining the use of the big machinery parked around the shop.

"Please, Mrs. List. Have a seat like everyone else."

"I don't see Mr. Gullikson," I said, my feet planted firmly.

"He's out with Officer Sherman."

"You're looking at his truck, aren't you?"

"I can't really discuss that."

"Oh, criminy, Mikey. Come on. I know I have done a few things that were . . . well, maybe not the smartest things to do, but I can help you here. You've got to believe me."

Mikey reached for his cuffs.

"Wait." I took a few steps down the hall, away from the group. I beckoned Mikey over to me. He glanced around, checking to see if any of the other officers were watching, and followed. I spoke in a low voice and Mikey had to lean in to hear me.

"Did you find that blue glove in the shot-up SUV like I asked?"

"Yeah, I got the glove and the piece of paper inside. It has nothing to do with this case." Mikey reached in his pocket and brought out the glove. "It's all yours."

"It has everything to do with this case! You have to get it over to whoever, or whomever, or whatever you take it to for analysis."

"And what's that going to prove? Where did it come from?"

Mikey was softening a little.

"Did your guys search Moira's house?"

"Yeah. We didn't really find anything."

"Well, I did."

"You searched Moira's house?" Mikey's voice sounded like a girl's. He was so upset he trembled. "When?"

"Not until after you'd done your walk-through, so don't get all crazy on me, okay? Just keep this to yourself and you won't have any problems. Go to Moira's house again and look in the backyard. You'll find some shell casings for a forty-five. I think. Not sure, but I know they're from bullets."

"Moira wasn't killed with a bullet."

"I know that. But — she was shooting something off a target out back, and that little piece of paper is all that's left of what she was venting her rage on. I think it's an important clue, don't you?"

"I doubt it." Mikey put the glove in my hand. "But if it will make you feel any better, we did find a gun in her house when we did the search. And, it was registered and legal. She lives in the country and she can shoot all day if she wants. As long as it's at a non-living target — unless, of course, it's hunting season, but then she'd have to have a license and —"

"I get it," I said, knowing it was useless trying to convince him the paper was worth a look, so I shoved it in my pocket. "You need a donut. Here." I dug around in my bag and came out with a variety pack.

"I really do need one of these," Mikey said. "I don't think I've slept four hours in the last three days. Thanks, Mrs. List."

"You eat up there and I'll put some coffee on in just a minute.

"Okay." Mikey crammed his mouth full like a hungry little boy, giving me a chance to continue.

"It looked like there was some writing on the paper. A letterhead. I'll find out what it said and we'll go from there. Now. Another thing. That shot-up SUV you found, I know you figured out it belongs to Tim Kholhauff over there." We both looked at the bodies against the wall. Tim was jumping his little cribbage pegs along the board. "He was with me when I searched Moira's house."

"Mmm?" Powdered sugar had formed in a circle around Mikey's mouth and sprinkled his chin.

"So were Marcia and Teresa."

Mikey choked. I whacked him on the back until his face regained its natural color.

"While we were at Moira's, someone came in driving Mr. Gullikson's truck. Later, when we were searching the lake, that someone, we figure, followed us and tried to take us all out with a high-powered rifle."

"So now you're a weapons expert?" Mikey reached for another donut.

"We were out in the water. Well, Teresa, Marcia and Tim were in a boat, and I was in a wet suit."

Mikey's pupils constricted.

"And the bullets were screaming around us. It had to be something bigger than a pistol. Had to be. Then one struck my tank and I just *flew* over that water like a skipping stone."

I had Mikey's attention.

"Then, we crashed Mr. Pendersnack's boat, and Ted saved us and we went to Mr. Gullikson's house and found blood in his truck."

I felt the need to jump ahead since Mikey was turning blue again. Some of that donut had lodged itself far down his windpipe, and I shouted for Aric to get the coffee perking. Of all the guys I'd met the day before, Aric showed the most energy, although it was insane, mach-ten energy, and I figured his habit was to guzzle at least fifteen cups of coffee before breakfast, so he was the reasonable choice to act as barista. I'm sure Mikey wasn't happy with the compromise in his crime-scene procedures, but he couldn't say anything with his throat slammed shut.

Aric jumped up and dashed into the break room. On his way he accidentally kicked the cribbage board and pegs flew. Tim, obviously ahead until the game was disassembled, shouted and threw his cards at Aric.

Mikey finally cleared his throat. "Sherman should find the blood. He just started his search, but he's efficient when it counts, and he's got some other guys helping out."

"Sure. Okay. I'm guessing you're here because the murder weapons were both from the grounds crew, right?" I kicked at some of the cards that had landed around my feet.

"Right."

I pulled on my earlobe. "Buddy was embezzling money from the club, and Moira had enough money to pull him out of his dilemma, but he turns up dead, so I'm thinking it had nothing to do with her money. Someone wanted them both dead, but why?" I pulled on my other earlobe. Since I'd been jet-propelled across the lake my ears were a little waterlogged. Oh, my goodness. I hope I didn't have anything living in there. I pulled at both my earlobes. Not much better.

"What's the connection between Moira

and Buddy?" Mikey blew a little white powder when he spoke, making his breath sugary sweet.

"I have no idea."

"Give me another donut."

Sherman hustled in, skidded to a stop when he saw me and adopted an attitude. Mikey held up his hand to say, "No worries."

"Well," Sherman said, holding up a paper bag, "I did a presumptive on the blood in the back of Mr. Gullikson's truck. It's positive for human blood. Paul is taking him down to the station now."

"What? No." I looked from Sherman to Mikey.

"Yesssss." Sherman glared at me. "It makes sense, doesn't it? Did you tell her what we found with the demolished boat out at the lake?"

I looked at Mikey. He said, "It was next to the shore, actually. We used a metal detector to locate all the shell casings there, found your dive tank, complete with a hole in it and aren't you lucky? And we found some jewelry. One ring with the initials J.G. engraved in the band."

"Done deal," Sherman said, and stalked out.

"I wondered where that went." I bit my lip.

Mikey bit his lip, but it was probably to keep himself from shouting something rude. "We would have been here earlier, but the shots apparently woke up the whole campground out at Candy's. The crowd came out and gave us a heck of a time. That woman you call Robe is still mad that we haven't located her computer."

"Wait, Mikey. She told me she'd left it at home."

"Whatever. She's probably the type to enjoy giving cops a hard time. Anyway, crowd control was a problem."

"Wonder if she got any pictures," I said, jokingly.

"That's not a bad idea, May." Mike lit up. "Why didn't I think of that? When we were moving Moira's body, she was clicking away. Maybe she caught something we can use against Mr. Gullikson. The crime-scene guy just took pictures of the body and not much else. I keep telling him —"

"You'd better hurry if you're gonna get anything from her. She was pulling stakes when I saw her yesterday. Anyway, I think you've got the wrong guy."

"Blood in Mr. Gullikson's truck . . ."

"But he said everyone drives it. That was

338

verified by Marcia, Teresa and Tim. He leaves the keys in it and it's available to anyone here." I waved my hand toward the restless crowd.

Aric raced out of the break room just then, holding a steaming cup of coffee in front of him. It sloshed as he ran. "Here you go, officer."

Mikey accepted gratefully.

"So, it could still be anyone here, right?" I asked.

Mikey sipped. "S'pose so."

"Someone with motive, opportunity, means . . ."

"Everyone here has the means. Have you seen all those tools and machines in there?" Mikey looked downright lustful. I have read somewhere that power tools and sex light up the same excitement area in a man's brain. Honestly. It's a study.

"Well, you can't haul everyone down to the station unless you come up with something more than a silly little thing like human blood." Even as I said it, the argument sounded weak at best. But I had to try.

Paul shot through the shop door and ran down the hall toward Mikey. "Found blood in one of the golf carts!" He held up a swab. "Cart number ten. Who drives cart number ten?"

The postal workers, aka Bonnie and Clyde, held up their hands. Paul had them cuffed and escorted them out the door in a blink.

Another officer came through the garage door pushing Dave and Joe ahead of him. They were also cuffed. "Tool marks match the soil probe!" They were pushed out to a waiting cruiser. I heard the rumble of loud car engines and then their ebb as the cruisers left with their prisoners.

"Now, hold on, Mikey. You have nothing. Aren't you getting a little overzealous here? I mean, you've just arrested nearly half the grounds crew. They couldn't all be killers."

Outside, Jake barked furiously, protecting his master. Billips, Mr. Stamper's dog, answered the call and ran past us in aid of his canine friend. More barking and snarling and shouts from the officers (and some barking and snarling from the dogs).

Stamper came alive finally and stopped reciting assignments. "I'm coming, sweetheart!" He yelled and jumped up. He ran past us, followed by the rest of the crew. They all crashed into each other, then into Mikey, then into me, and we were a mob tangled on the floor. I caught sight of Mikey reaching for his gun, and I slammed a knee into his side. He grunted and released his weapon. Teresa and Marcia just ran over the pile and got outside first. Aric came out of the break room a second time, holding four cups of coffee at once. I thought he was going to pass them around, but he took alternating sips, standing out in the parking lot as the sun started to come up over the horizon.

Sherman, attempting riot control, sprayed mace all over, but it was carried away by a merciful stiff breeze — right back into Sherman's face. He coughed and sputtered and went to his knees. Jim, the ex-cop, laughed hysterically, then kissed his biceps and did another bodybuilder's stance, arms in parentheses, swiveling left, then right.

Gully sat in the back of Sherman's car, his face pale, and he looked awful. He had that bent-over appearance like you see when someone's sitting with their hands cuffed behind their back. I tapped on the window and said, "We'll bail you out. Don't worry!"

Out of nowhere, a strapping young man dove onto Sherman's cruiser. He landed spread eagle on the hood, raised his arms and battered the windshield, causing a little crack to spiderweb across it. "Dad! Dad!" the man yelled, peering through the glass.

"Jeffrey! Please! Don't worry, everything will be okay," Gully answered.

I jumped back. Jim lunged forward and hauled Jeffrey off the cop car. He wrapped his arms around the struggling youngster. Wow. Gully has a son?

Fed up with the chaos, Sherman growled, jumped into his car and peeled away toward the police station. Two other police cars had already left with the postal workers and the mechanics. I watched in dismay while Gully looked back through the window, his face the picture of desperation.

Jim dragged Jeffrey back to the shop, Aric handed him a half-finished cup of coffee, and I tossed him a donut. Jeffrey calmed down a little, but not much. Elder took one look at Jeffrey's tortured expression and burst out in a fresh wave of tears. "We'll bust your dad outa there, Jeffrey, don't worry."

Standing in the parking lot I waved away the dust churned up by the disappearing cop cars and turned my attention back to Officer Murphy. "Mikey. Do you even know if Mr. Gullikson owns a gun? He told me he doesn't, and just because he has human blood in his truck means nothing. He might have been oddly close to Moira for whatever reason, but there's nothing that says he killed her, and I know the murder weapons used on Buddy and Moira were hand-tooled by him, here in this very shop, but —"

"What, Mrs. List?" Mikey crossed his arms over his chest.

"I think I'll shut up now."

"Good idea. But I'll see if he has a gun, and we'll compare it to the bullet we found in your dive tank, and if it's not destroyed, that should tell the story."

"But it doesn't answer the all-important question. Why?" I said.

"Who knows? Maybe he'll tell us."

"I just don't know." I shook my head.

Mikey rubbed the back of his neck and then yawned. "I've got to get some sleep. We still haven't figured out how Skinny Carl died, and now this."

"Good luck with all that." I looked away and watched the sun creep up higher, turning the sky a beautiful pink color. It must have matched the pink in my cheeks. I hoped it just looked like a reflection.

"The tox reports came back negative, but he did have a raging case of E.-coli poisoning."

Thank goodness. "That's it, then. The bacon he had in his system! You can put this one to bed, Mikey."

"We'll see."

I stood and enjoyed the dawn while keeping an eye on Mikey. He did look tired. In the distance Billips and Jake barked and barked. "What are they barking at?" I turned my attention to the noise.

"Billips! Come here, baby!" Stamper followed the sound and disappeared over a small hill. He waded through tall grass. "Billips! Jake!" He whistled, but the dogs didn't respond to his call. "Billips!" Mr. Stamper then screamed. "Officer! I think you'd better come over here!"

I looked at Mikey, he looked at me. We both ran.

Buried in a large depression, nearly covered by brush and tall weeds, rested the car of the late, great Moira Finch.

CHAPTER TWENTY-SEVEN

"All right, everyone back!" Officer Murphy spread his arms and moved the mob away, and then he got on his radio. What was left of the grounds crew huddled around and gawked at Moira's car resting there. One big metal crime scene.

"I'll get the yellow tape," Jim said, and lumbered away.

Stamper rounded up the dogs and locked them in the men's bathroom. Then he came back and snapped his fingers, a signal that it was finally time to get to the staff meeting. I looked at Teresa, my eyes saying, "Is he nuts?" But she gave a gesture of submission and herded the group back toward the break room. On her way past me she said, "You find out what you can, and, when we're done, meet me at the twelfth-hole flower bed. I'll make excuses for you."

"Thanks," I whispered.

While Mikey was busy stringing tape

around the car with the help of his buddies in blue, I walked, or rather stumbled, through the tall grass and noticed the twin impressions where the car tires had smashed down the weeds before coming to rest in the shallow valley. It was no wonder it hadn't been spotted before. If the dogs hadn't sounded the alarm, we would have missed it for weeks or months, unless the guys threw an errant football. That reminded me. Mikey was sending out for the evidence guys to do their thing and there wasn't much to see anyway, so I made my way back to the locker room where I'd left the plastic shopping bag.

The group moved off toward their machines and I caught Elder on the way out. "Here," I said. And handed him a brand new football. Elder's eyes lit up and a smile crossed his face. He threw his arms around me. As he left, his sobs were ones of joy and I heard him mumble, "I'll take care of you, little guy. Don't you worry, now."

One good deed done. Now time to finish this case.

I threw tools in my assigned golf cart, shoved my hard hat on my head, and made for hole twelve. Marcia and Teresa were already on their knees pulling weeds when I got there. Jerry was riding a mower nearby, going in expanding circles, and Tim was at work with a weed whacker. When they saw me approach, Teresa gave Marcia a nod, twirled her finger above her head, and Tim shut off the whacker. We huddled under a bushy tree.

"Do you have access to a computer?" I asked Teresa.

"Sure. But the one in my office can be seen by anyone walking by. Do we need something more covert?"

"How about Mr. Gullikson's office?" I asked.

"What's this about, Mrs. List?" Tim absently rubbed his glasses over his shirt.

"I don't know. But I only have one lead that we haven't followed. We need a computer."

"Well, Mr. Gullikson won't be back for a while. I don't think it will be a problem," Teresa said.

Marcia pulled off a chunk of string cheese. "We can lock the door."

"Okay." I glanced out from under the tree. Golfers were making their way onto the course.

"Let's get going."

"All of us?" Tim asked.

"We're in this together, aren't we?" I looked at the three. All looked haggard but motivated.

"Race ya," Marcia said, and she made for her golf cart.

Teresa beat her, naturally. Tim sighed and patted the tree before climbing out from under. My hips locked up, and by the time I limped to my cart, everyone was long gone.

Gully's office was just as I remembered it. Neat, orderly and professional. His Bible was open to Revelation, and I think he was probably reading up on what to expect when the world came to an end. He probably thought he was running out of last days after Sherman photographed, fingerprinted and booked him into the county jail.

I felt sick at the thought of Jeff doing even one minute behind bars.

"Here," I said to Tim. "Take this." I handed him the glove. "Take the paper out, but be careful." I looked over at him. "Oh, my gosh. All of you — go wash your hands." The group had dirt and mud up to their elbows. Or, that is, *soil.*

They all rushed out and as I waited for them to come back I glanced over Gully's office, looked at his desk, and scanned his desk calendar. He had lots of meetings, so there was little time for him to pull off a murder. He'd even had a meeting scheduled with Buddy Shields the morning after I found Moira. Hmmm. The morning Buddy turned up in the pond. I tried to remember whether or not he'd kept that meeting, but the subject hadn't come up. I went to work at the computer and by the time everyone came back looking scrubbed, I'd tried several failed attempts at logging onto the Internet.

"I can't get access," I said to Teresa. "Do you know Gully's password?"

"It's *golfpro,*" Tim said. "He's not a secretive man."

"What's the point in a password, then?" I asked.

"Not secretive to the grounds crew. Nobody else can just walk in here and use his stuff."

I thought his generous nature might have been his undoing.

I typed in the password and went directly to Google. "Okay. What can you see on that paper?"

Tim held the paper under a light. "Not much. A name."

"Mr. Gullikson said that Moira had written a book and that she'd been getting rejection letters. Apparently the rejections had upset her. From what I understand, after you write a book you usually try to find an agent who will then place your book with a publisher. Let's try agents first. If that doesn't pan out, we'll look at publishers. What's the name?"

"Uh, it's just a partial, but I think it says S-t-r-o . . . that's all I can find. And there's a little squiggly thing above the name. Probably a logo or something."

"It's a start. Marcia, would you mind nuking a cup of coffee for me? This could take a while." I typed in *Literary Agents.* Oh, my. This was going to take all day. I shouted toward the door. "You'd better put on a fresh pot, Marcia!"

Tim sat on the corner of Gully's desk. "Maybe I'm new to all of this cloak-and-dagger stuff, but this seems like a waste of time, Mrs. List. Let's say you do find the agency that's on this piece of paper. Then what? And how's that going to help us figure out who killed Moira and Buddy?"

"All is know is that Moira had a very limited number of friends and only a few hobbies. We've thought about Buddy's need to kill her, but that didn't pan out when we found him dead, too. I don't think Mr. Gullikson has any reason at all to kill Moira, mostly because he has nothing to gain. He wasn't involved in the flow of money here at the country club and I can't see him as the jealous type. The only thing left is to find out what she had going on with these literary agents."

"That's stupid," Marcia came through the door with a whole frozen pizza in her hands. "Moira was killed with a tool that came from this shop."

"One that was lost on the golf course, don't forget," Teresa said.

"And she was found out at Moody Lake," Tim added.

"While her car was here all the time," I said, feeling defeated. It was like I'd been given a Rubik's Cube with every square a different color. No matter how I twisted and turned this case, nothing was lining up.

"I've just got to do something," I said. "And one of you should wander over near the crime scene out there to see if you can see what's going on."

"Yeah," Marcia said, munching on a piece of thick crust. "After last night, it's actually comforting to have the police around. I don't much like getting shot at."

I groaned inwardly, thinking it was just a matter of time before Snack tracked me down and demanded his money for the boat.

"Here. Look." I scrolled down through a

list of agents. "Strong and Hammond Literary Agency." I clicked on the link to their Web site.

"No logo," Tim said.

"No go," Marcia said.

I went back to the names. "Denis Stroud Literary Agency."

"No, there was no Denis on the paper." Tim took a piece of pizza from Marcia.

"Stroller and Couch."

"Sounds like a furniture store," Teresa said. "I think I'll take a stroll myself. Keep at it, May. You're doing great."

"Wait!" Tim said. "Click on it."

I went to the Web site.

"Bingo." Tim grinned through his extra cheese.

My mouth fell open. "Stroller and Couch. There it is. The logo is clear as day."

"Is there a phone number?" Teresa reached for a pad and pen.

"Uh . . ." I scrolled. "There are two numbers."

"Give 'em both to me."

I read off the numbers, sat back and looked at Teresa. "Now what?"

Tim handed me his cell phone. "Call them."

"What do I say?"

"You'll think of something. You always

do." Marcia took another huge bite of her pizza.

"Is that coffee almost done?" My chest was tightening up again, and that meant my throat was closing up, too, and if I talked to anyone, it would sound like I was squeaking through a straw.

"Here," Tim said, "I'll do it." He punched numbers and held his finger to his lips.

We all waited.

Tim stood there, his ear to his phone, his eyes darting around the room. He closed the phone. "Nothing. Give me the second number." He dialed again. As he waited, he whispered, "Where is this agency?"

"New York." I knew what he was thinking. It was early still, but the people in the agency had a three-hour head start on the day because they were on the east coast. Not too early for them to be conducting business.

"Ah, yes." Tim was talking and he'd for some odd reason adopted a southern accent. He also lowered his voice to a commanding boom. "This heah is Officer Timothy Kholhauff with the Harvest Police Department in Harvest, Washington."

My mouth dropped and I gestured wildly for Teresa to close the office door.

"I'm investigating the death of one of our

353

citizens by the name of Moira Finch." Tim paused. "Ah, yeah. She was murdered. Tha's right, ma'am. Now we're just trying to follow up some leads here and we've found a letter from your agency whereas I believe you rejected her literary work and we're trying to verify the particulars." Tim paused again. "Ah, yes, I'll wait." Tim covered the mouthpiece and looked at me. "I'm on hold."

I covered my mouth with my hand because I was dangerously close to bursting out with laughter. "They bought it?"

Tim quickly held up a finger. "Yes. Mrs. Moira Finch." Pause. "Oh, she did? How recently? Uh-huh, yes. Yes, ma'am, and would you have that sample still in your possession?" Pause. "I understand. Yes. Can you please fax that over to this number?" Tim waved his hand around and Teresa wrote the club shop's fax number on a piece of paper for him. He read off the number. "Yes. I understand. Yes. Uh-huh. Yes, it was a tragedy. Thank you very much for your help."

Tim snapped his phone closed. He smiled like he'd just swallowed a canary instead of the mouthful of frozen pepperoni and extra cheese smudged over his goatee. "Get this," he said. "They did get a writing sample from Moira and they actually loved her work. But. They said the genre was a problem. She'd called it a science fiction fantasy historical thriller mystery western romance novel and they just couldn't place it. Besides, they said a story nearly identical had just been published by a large house and it wasn't worth their time to shop something so similar right after the first one hit the best-seller list. It would be redundant. And, they actually had suspicions that Moira Finch had plagiarized great portions of the book. They didn't tell her that because there was no proof, but they rejected her work just the same."

"Plagiarism?" I gasped. "Did they tell you who had written the best seller?"

"Forgot to ask," Tim said.

"Well, how many science fiction fantasy historical thriller mystery western romance novels have recently hit the best-seller list?" Teresa asked. "It can't be too hard to track *that* down."

It was incredible. "You think Moira actually stole someone's work? Whose?"

"Pretty good motive to kill her, I guess," Marcia said.

"Except she didn't get her book published," I said. "Why would someone want to kill her even if she had stolen their work?"

"That would really tick me off," Marcia said.

"And don't forget," I added, "someone tried to kill us, too. There must have been something in Moira's house, and whoever drove Gully's truck over there didn't want us to have that something. Maybe we're looking at this backwards."

"How so, Mrs. List?" Tim broke off the last piece of pizza, leaving Marcia with a slender slice.

"I'm just thinking." The fax machine started to hum and paper spit out. "We'll look at this first. Tim, why don't you take over for me here and search through the latest best sellers — whatever might fit into that genre the agency told you about. I've got to get some coffee."

I opened the door to Gully's office and nearly ran over Officer Murphy.

"What are you doing in there?" Mikey frowned.

"Paperwork," I said. "Coffee?"

"Thought you'd never ask."

I walked Mikey to the break room. He was dragging and his shoulders drooped. He was exhausted, and that meant he was vulnerable.

I poured us each a fresh cup. Not bad; at least it was hot and caffeinated. "Any luck out there?" I leaned against the counter.

"How many times do I have to tell you?"

"That you can't tell me anything. What if I say I have a really good lead? Would you tell me something then?"

"I'm afraid to ask."

I sipped at my coffee comfortably, knowing I could help make him lieutenant, or he could just continue to be stubborn and stay on patrol for the rest of his life. "It's realllly good," I said.

Mikey blurted, "We found the club manager's keys."

I nearly squirmed. "Where?"

"In the weeds by Moira's car."

"Do you mean *he* hid Moira's car in the weeds?"

"Possibly," Mikey said. "Her keys were still in the ignition. He could have hidden it there and then hoofed it back to the parking lot."

"But he couldn't drive without his keys and —"

"Decided to spear himself with a crack tool and dive into the club pond?"

"It's another lead." I began to feel a tension headache coming on. Added to all of the aching places on my body I had visions of a long, hot bubble bath in my future. Mikey brought me back to reality.

"And what do you have for me?" he asked.

"When you searched Moira's house did you find a computer?"

"No, nothing like that."

"How about a flash drive or some disks or any papers with writing on them. Even some handwritten."

"All we found were some legal papers, her will, that sort of thing. Nothing personal at all."

"Doesn't that seem strange? No correspondence, no letters, diary, anything like that?"

"Nothing. *I* don't have a diary. And nobody writes letters anymore, May, it's all e-mail, text, video teleconferencing or voice mail these days."

"Stands to reason she'd have a computer, then. And by the way. How did you get into her house and then lock up after you left?"

"Mr. Gullikson had an extra key on his set. He offered."

"He offered." It sure wasn't looking good for Gully.

Sherman wandered in, a travel mug in his hand. He'd made good time getting back after taking Gully to the pokey. "You still here?" He grunted at me and filled his cup from the carafe. "Mr. Gullikson's cooling his heels. We did an initial test on that blood

358

we found in his truck and it came back XO. It's not the female vic's. We tested him for GSR. That came back negative, but he had plenty of time to wash his hands."

"The blood could be the male vic's, right?" Mikey asked.

"Won't know till we get a DNA match."

Mikey rubbed the back of his neck. "That will take months."

"But we know Gully didn't have Moira in his truck at least," I said.

"Why are you still here?" Sherman asked and twisted the top on his travel cup.

I sneered at him.

"By the way," Sherman said, "that girl we arrested out at the lake confessed to stealing everyone's stuff. She posted bond so we had to let her go, but we haven't found it all yet. Someone said they thought they'd seen her poking around Candy's porch and I'm guessing that's where she put it. I'll go out and round it up as soon as I can pry my rear away from all this mess."

I caught Mikey's attention. I lasered his eyes with mine.

"Wait," Mikey said hesitantly, looking from me to Sherman. "I'll get it. I'll log it in. You have enough to worry about right now. Let me take care of it."

"Suit yourself," Sherman said, and lumbered out.

"All right. What's up, Mrs. List?" Mikey leaned against the counter beside me.

"This all started out at the lake, and I don't want Sherm to mess up any evidence. Tie up loose ends here and I'll meet you out there in an hour, okay?"

"You still haven't told me what you got."

"I'll bring it to you and hand it over with a kiss and a ribbon. Is that okay?"

"Just the evidence, Mrs. List."

"Spoilsport."

CHAPTER TWENTY-EIGHT

"I have one little problem," I told Officer Murphy after I was sure Sherman was out the door and out of earshot. "I, uh, don't have a car."

"Don't even think about it."

"I forgot Ted brought me here. He thinks . . . I need protection or something."

"He can't save you from yourself, and you're not taking mine. You even make one move toward my car and I'll drop you with my Taser."

"Very funny. Never mind. I'll find a ride somewhere. Just don't do anything until I get to the lake, okay?"

"Why don't you show me what evidence you have and then we'll play ball."

"Ball?" Elder wandered in with his new toy bundled up in a makeshift sling. It looked cute. Sort of like a sports Snuggly.

"Go throw a few, kiddo," Officer Murphy said in his most official tone.

"I was. I mean, I did. And then I found this." Elder held out a cell phone.

"Where was it?" Officer Murphy took the phone and flipped it open.

"It's dead," Elder said. "But we keep a box of chargers in the supply closet. People drop 'em all over the place and I started collecting them a while back."

"Go!" I yelled, which almost caused him to pass out, but Elder clutched his football protectively and ran off, arm out like he was blocking tackles. Seconds later he was back, and thrust a tangle of chargers in my hands.

I tried a few without success but finally one fit. I plugged the phone in and we were in business.

With all the phone handling, we could forget fingerprints. "Whose is it?" I looked on while Mikey pressed buttons. He scrolled down to an entry entitled ICE.

"I know what that is. In Case of Emergency." I nodded vigorously.

Mikey's eyebrows went up. "It's our vic's."

"Buddy's?"

"Mrs. Finch's. In case of emergency, we are to call Mr. Jeff Gullikson, and the number is . . . uh . . ." Mikey checked his notepad. "It's his work number here at the office."

"Well, that doesn't mean anything," I said.

362

"It could be Gully's phone, for all we know. Where did you find this, Mike?"

"I didn't find it," Mikey said.

"No. Mike. Mike, meet Mikey."

"That's confusing," Mike said.

"Officer Murphy, please," Mikey said as he examined the phone.

"Elder, please," Football Mike said, and then he explained. "I found it by the car after I threw a perfect pitch to Travis. Fumble fingers let it slip right through his hands. I saw Blue go for my little guy here and scooped it up before he could squish it to death. That's when I found the phone."

"I have an idea." I put my hand on Elder's shoulder. "Do you know Mr. Gullikson's cell phone number?"

"Sure."

"Will you go into his office and call it? And then come on back here."

Elder hustled off. I stared at the phone. It didn't ring. Elder hurried back, a look of expectation on his face.

"Okay, now, could you go back and look through Mr. Gullikson's Rolodex? See if you can find a cell phone number for Mrs. Moira Finch, then dial that number."

Again, Elder hurried off. I stared at the phone. It played a cheerful little tune. Bingo.

"Okay," I said to Officer Murphy. "You

363

were right. It's Mrs. Finch's phone."

"Told you, didn't I?"

Sheesh. As the minutes ticked by, Mikey got more and more cranky. "But you couldn't have known."

"Sure I could. She has her name etched across the back here." Mikey turned the phone over. Sure enough, there it was. "Could have saved me some time," I huffed.

"I have limited opportunities for fun on this job," Mikey said.

"So now I'm comic relief?" Lack of sleep was catching up with me, too. Made me quite testy.

"Comic, maybe." Mikey scrolled through the phone some more, not paying much attention to anyone; he was intently looking through the phone numbers and went to the saved voice mail. He pushed the last entry and held it to his ear.

I stared at him, waiting.

"It's a woman's voice," he said. "Calling to confirm . . . our tee time . . . for eight A.M. tomorrow . . . Northside Country Club. Call if there's a problem, otherwise I'll meet you there." Mikey closed the phone. "That's all. The last call made to her phone."

I kept my emotions in check. "Is there a name?"

Mikey looked at the phone. "Just a number."

"Call back," I said, feeling dangerous and excited. "Call the number back, Mikey."

Mikey and I locked eyes. Two weary, bags-and-all, bloodshot eyes. Mikey nodded. He pushed the call return button. I bent my head close to his to listen. Mikey had to stand bent-legged because I was five-four to his six-foot-plus. He was unsteady standing that way, so I supported him with a forearm under his thighs. Mikey put the phone on speaker.

The phone rang once, twice, and then in the middle of the third ring someone picked up. "Candy's Bait and Tackle Shop, how may I help you?"

I couldn't believe it. Candy? I grabbed the phone out of Mikey's hand and slammed it shut.

Mikey scowled at me. His hand was moving toward his utility belt, and I knew his Taser was somewhere in there so I had to talk fast.

"I don't know if Candy has caller ID at her shop, but if she sees Moira is calling her from the grave, especially if Candy was the last golf partner Moira had, she's going to be freaking out right now. She might be hiding evidence as we stand here. Did she think she could get away with this?" I was clench-ing my fists, my jaws and my aching calf muscles.

"Get away with what? Maybe she just planned to have a friendly golf game with Moira. We don't know if she killed her."

"Why didn't she say anything about that when she was so happily steaming up those lattes with Moira's body lying on her sandy beach? Why's that? She never even said she *knew* Moira, did she? She acted like she had no idea who Moira was. And she'd called her days before to schedule a golf game? Did she keep that appointment?"

Mikey looked at me with one eye. The other was fluttering with the attempt to stay open. I, on the other hand, had just found some kind of energy reserve. "Come on, tough guy, keep it together. We've got to get back to the lake. Now."

I grabbed Officer Murphy by the utility belt and dragged him toward his car. His head was nodding. "I guess I'll have to drive, after all," I said, making my way toward the driver's side.

This got Mikey moving. His head jerked up, his eyes flew open and he jumped in between me and the car. "Oh, no you don't. And don't even think about touching my shotgun. Just get in."

I was relieved, actually, because it had been a while since I'd used all those police function buttons, and I never wanted to talk on a police radio again even if my life depended on it. Since I'd apologized a dozen times for destroying the last cruiser I'd driven, I didn't feel it necessary to do it again, so I hopped in the car, feeling the familiar give of police upholstery and the memorable smells of drunks, post-brawl bleeders and meth addicts. That old thrill worked its way up my torso and expanded out over my chest and arms.

"Just like old times," I said, smiling.

"I hope not," Mikey said. He cranked the key and backed out of the parking lot in a hurry. He reached for his radio.

"Do you have to call anyone just yet? Why don't we just wait?"

"I can't do that, Mrs. List, and you'd better keep your head down. Sherman is bound to appear and jump in front of my car if he sees me leaving with you in the front seat."

"You got it." I bent over to hug my knees and whacked my head on the dashboard. Even that felt familiar.

Mikey announced his location into the radio and we sped down the dirt road toward Candy's. I had no idea what to expect when we got there, but the last person to talk to Moira, especially one planning a rendezvous at the country club, was *numero uno* on our suspect list. But Candy? What reason would she have to kill Moira? Or Buddy? There was nothing that had connected her to the two, and she had acted so calm during the investigation, but isn't that just the way things are sometimes? I was feeling certain we were coming closer to the truth.

Officer Murphy drove like the cop he was, ignoring stop signs, flying through red lights, weaving in and out of morning traffic, and it would have served that old lady right if Mikey had rammed her with one of his Precision Immobilization Techniques since she didn't move over even though he used his lights and siren the whole way. Mikey glanced in his rearview mirror.

"Now, who's this?" He was exasperated and in no mood for a tail, but we had one. I craned around and then turned face forward, shocked, but not entirely surprised.

"It's Ted," I said, not loudly enough to be heard over the siren's warble.

"Who?"

Again, I turned around and saw my bright-red Camaro keeping pace with Murphy's cruiser. He stayed with us, swerve for swerve, broken law for broken law.

"It's my husband," I shouted.

"Did you tell him —"

"No! I don't even know how he saw me get into your car!" That man must have radar. Or else he'd hidden binoculars in my glove box.

Murphy took a corner on two wheels. Ted did the same.

"Well, I can't stop now!" Mikey said.

"I'm not asking you to!"

Mikey had to slam his brakes when a bus slowed in front of us. The passengers waiting on the sidewalk ran for cover. Mikey slid sideways, spun his wheel this way and that and got things under control. Not so lucky for Ted, who was working with manual steering and a clutch. The Camaro's fender glanced off the back of the bus. Surprisingly, though, he was behind us again at the next intersection. I turned and shook my fist at my husband, because I know he'd done some damage to my nice chrome bumper. Undeterred, he shot through a red light behind Mikey's cruiser and narrowly missed three guys on motorcycles.

"Oh, my gosh!" I cried. "They're going down!" The motorcycle riders leaned over and put their bikes into the black pavement in controlled slides, ending up in a tangled mess. "No! They're up!" The guys, all in leathers, thank goodness, jumped up and ran after us waving their arms and screaming things I'm sure I'd never heard before.

"Okay. We're almost there." Mikey, feeling the caffeine kick in, turned to me and smiled. I smiled back. We were almost there.

"Turn off the lights and siren," I said.

"Already done." Mikey went to silent mode. He slowed down.

And Ted rammed the back of the cruiser.

I turned again and raised both arms. What was that man doing?

Mikey wasn't even fazed. He had that look in his eyes, the kind a cat gets when it's on the prowl. Focused and tuned in. Thank goodness my old car didn't have airbags, or Ted would be heading off to the dentist.

Mikey pulled over behind some trees and cut the engine. From where we were, we could see Candy's and some activity at the campsite. I heard the Camaro engine go silent.

"I just want to see what we've got here before we go in," Mikey said.

"Stealth," I whispered.

I heard a loud rap on my window and there was my husband. For some reason it reminded me of the time I was in college and my boyfriend Eddie Mildenberger and I were parked behind the grange, just kissing, you understand, and my father figured out where we were and . . . anyway. It didn't feel any better this time.

I rolled down the window. "Ted! We're stealth!"

Mikey bent down and looked over me at my husband. "Get in the back."

Ted hopped in even while I was arguing this was no place for a civilian, but Mikey had other things on his mind. He stared at the campsite. People were coming and going, but we weren't close enough to see faces. "Wish I had some binoculars," Mikey said.

"Wait one," Ted said and hopped out of the cruiser. He came back with a pair of binoculars.

"So you were spying on me."

"I told you I was going to keep an eye on you, didn't I?"

"I can't believe you!" I crossed my arms over my chest and turned to stare out the windshield while Mikey adjusted the focus on the binocs.

"I don't see Candy, but those boys with the hibachi are back at it. I think they're rolling a few blunts right in front of my eyes."

"Who else is out there?" I tried to take

the binoculars from Mikey, but he squirmed away.

"Mr. Pendersnack is fishing off the dock, his buddies are in hip waders standing on the lake's edge, Mrs. Smith looks like she's packing up her gear."

"What?" I grabbed at the binoculars again and this time got a slap on the back of my hand.

"Hey!" Ted said, bristling.

"Not now, Ted! What is it, Mikey?"

"That little frizzy-haired girl is down there. I thought she would be long gone by now."

"Maybe she's in cahoots with Candy! We've got to get to the stuff before she carts it off. Mikey, let's move!" I jumped out of the cruiser and raced through the trees, huffing, puffing, churning my bruises over stumps and logs before Ted and Mikey caught up with me. They each grabbed me by an arm.

"Hold on, Mrs. List. We can't go bursting in on things right now. We've got to be smart about this." Mikey looked earnest and I have to say I was rather worked up, so his professional demeanor calmed me down quite a bit.

At that point, we all turned at the sound of squealing tires coming from the direction of where we'd parked the cruiser and Camaro. A large pickup truck, its bed full of maroon-and-khaki-clad workers shuddered and slid and stopped just as it made solid contact with my Camaro's back bumper. "Oh, geez!" I cried.

One guy — Chris, as I remember — flipped right out of the truck when it slammed to a stop. The other workers jumped from the truck and ran toward us. Chris got to his feet soon enough and followed.

"So much for stealth," Mikey said, looking dismayed.

"Mrs. List! Mrs. List!" Travis, the young man who had fumbled Elder's football earlier, waved me down. Teresa jumped from the cab of the truck, passed Elder and reached me in record time, even for her. I saw Marcia and Tim making good time, and the rest of the crew jogged up behind them. At least most of the crew. It looked like Mr. Gullikson was still doing time at the county jail, the mechanics were more than likely his cell mates, and Bonnie and Clyde were also absent, wards of the warden.

We all knelt in the weeds, and Tim duck-walked up to me. "I found the book!" He was flushed with excitement and dug in his pants pocket. He pulled out a piece of paper. Tim squinted and tried to read it but was having trouble. Marcia snatched it out of his hand and using her good eye, read the name of the book, and its publisher.

"What's the author's name? Who wrote the book?" I was practically having a spasm with the sudden thought that I'd figured this whole thing out. "Was it written by a woman named Candy Schultz by any chance?" Oh, I just knew it would be!

"Let me see. The author's name was . . ." Tim looked again, turned the paper over, looked again, then pulled out another sheet of paper. "I almost forgot to write it down. Had to re-Google it for this."

"What is it already?"

"The author's name is Penelope Peabody."

"You're kiddin' me."

"Some people use a pseudonym," Ted offered.

"That's right, Ted, you're right!" I patted Ted on the arm.

Mikey, still looking through the binoculars, cursed under his breath. "She's trying to move the loot. I can see her little legs sticking out from under the porch there."

"Why the interest in this particular author?" Ted had tired of crouching and was sitting on the wet ground with his arms around his knees.

I plopped down beside him. "When we were all snooping around Moira's house last night . . . oh, where are my manners?" I introduced the landscaping crew to my husband. They smiled warmly and shook hands. Mikey groaned, ran his free hand through his hair, and that was a sign we should all just shut up, which we did. I whispered in Ted's ear. "We found a letter from an agent in Moira's backyard all shot to smithereens. But we could make out part of the letterhead and logo and . . ."

In no time, I had Ted up to date. He looked fairly impressed, although again shocked by everything I'd done while he was totally unaware. I probably should have kept some of the details from him just in case I needed to get myself involved in another homicide investigation, but he'd have to deal with that if and when the time came.

"You think this Candy Schultz got mad at Moira because she was trying to steal her work?"

"Possibly. The call to Moira came from Candy's phone. Moira was found in Candy's lake, they'd planned to golf together and Moira was found with a golf tool stuck through her neck. And Ted, Candy's place was on the garden tour, one that Moira had

375

been a part of every year. She had to know Candy, and maybe they'd talked about writing at one time. Maybe Candy let Moira read her work. It all makes total sense."

"So what's next?" Ted asked me. He paid no attention to Mikey; he didn't even seem to remember that we were surrounded by hunkered-down grounds workers sitting in mud, or that we were in stealth mode at the edge of a crime scene. He was only looking at me. And he was depending on my skills to give him the answers. And . . . it felt good.

I said, "I think we're going to have to retreat."

"What?" Marcia, Teresa and Tim all said in unison. Lots of grumbles and groans.

"Yes. We retreat. We let Mikey go in and confiscate all of the theft evidence that Frizz Head is trying to get out from under the porch. He'll log it into evidence. Doesn't really pertain to our case anyway, and I don't think Candy believes she's under suspicion yet. We have to go find that book written by a Miss Penelope Peabody, and if the author is as pretentious as many seem to be, although I hope I would never get that way and I hear many are really, really nice —"

Ted took me by the shoulders. "What, May Bell? You're killin' me here!"

"Hold on, Ted, when we find a copy of that book, we just . . . look . . . on the back." I held praying hands and opened them slowly for effect, then closed them and turned them over.

"Her picture." Derek had wormed his way over. Travis leaned on Derek's shoulder. Jeffrey sat by, gnawing nervously on his hands.

"Yeah. Her picture would be on the back. Easy breezy," Travis said.

"Easier than you catching a darn pass, my friend," Elder glared at him.

"Let's go play some hoops," the cabana boys said. They loped off toward the truck.

"Hoops? Hoops?" Elder raced after them, and I do believe I heard him whispering words of reassurance and consolation to his football.

All the other guys took off, but Teresa had the truck keys so one guy jogged back. "You will get my dad out of jail, won't you?" It was Gully's son.

"Tell ya what," I said, taking the keys from Teresa and handing them over. "All you guys go down to the police station. The cop with the mustache is named Officer Sherman. He's responsible for most of this mess anyway. I know your dad is innocent, and so are the other guys. We've almost got the evidence we need to close this case down.

Now what I want you to do is go in there, all of you, and make as much noise as you can. Push some pencils around. Just annoy the heck out of Sherman. Don't do anything to get yourselves arrested or anything, but if he gives you any trouble, say something about free speech or that you need to use the bathroom — all of you at once — and that should keep him busy. We need to buy some time. Okay?"

Jeffrey gave me a wide smile. "I think we can manage."

"Okay." I waved him away and soon the truck was gone.

"That's great," Mikey stared at me.

"What?"

"Now how are you going to get back?"

"We have May's car," Ted said, not liking Mikey's tone at all, but Mikey wore the Taser and Ted wore the stethoscope and in an argument I knew who would win.

"Yeah, but there's five of you and only four seat belts in that old car."

"Ooooh, I'm scared." I twirled my finger over my head and pointed toward the Camaro. The gang hurried off before Mikey could cuff us. I turned back to him. "We'll double up," I said.

As I walked away I heard him, fatigue

obvious in his voice, "But that's illegal, you know!"

CHAPTER TWENTY-NINE

Ted drove while I sat in the passenger seat. Tim had a seat belt to himself but Teresa had to sit on Marcia's lap in order for us to stay partially within the law and keep everyone buckled in.

"I don't get it," Teresa squirmed and squirmed. "You nosh all day and still you're a pile of bones. Your knees are cutting into my thighs."

"So why do you call me Marshmallow?" Marcia pushed up with her toes, and Teresa squirmed some more.

"You're doing that on purpose."

"Oops, guess I shouldn't get you too worked up. After all, you're sitting on my lap — Tinkles."

Teresa half stood and came down hard on Marcia's lap.

Marcia grunted.

"Why do you keep calling me Tinkles? It only happened *once.* And I was six years old! And besides, I'd had lots of juice that day and you were tickling me really hard!"

Tim reached over and grabbed the end of the seat belt. He gave it a hard yank and both girls were silent. I don't think they could breathe at all after that, but at least it was peaceful for a few minutes until they started in again.

"What time is it?" I asked Ted.

He glanced at his watch. "About eight."

"Book stores don't open till nine or ten," Tim said. "But we don't have to go to a book store. Just get me to a computer."

"Sure," Ted said. "You can do a bio search of your author, and I'm sure her picture will be there, and if not, we can look at her book cover online, or as a last resort, see if her publisher has a picture. Tell 'em we're doing a promo ad for her, we need a head shot, whatever."

I slid my eyes over to Ted, enjoying the expression on his face. I knew he wasn't just looking out for me; he wanted action as much as I did though he'd never admit to such a thing.

"We can't go back to the shop," Teresa spoke quietly, which was not like her at all. I turned and saw that she and Marcia were a sick shade of blue.

"Loosen the seat belt, Tim, for the love of — !"

"Okay, okay." Tim reluctantly adjusted Marcia and Teresa's seat belt, and I heard them sucking air.

"You're right, though. We can't go back to the shop. Our house is at least twenty minutes away."

"Police station is five," Ted said.

"Riiight." I started to laugh.

"No! He is right." Tim leaned over the seats. "By now, there's probably plenty of distractions at the station. Most of the cops are out doing their cop stuff, and I just need a few minutes at the keyboard."

I looked at Tim, then at the girls recovering in the back, then at Ted. A look of pain briefly clouded his face, but then he nodded, hit the blinker, and said, "Let's go."

As we pulled up in front of the police station, I could tell — even before I got out of my car — that things were going to be crazy inside. The ground workers' truck was taking up two spaces, shadows were moving around on the other side of the windows, and as I got to the station door, I heard shouting and furniture breakage.

I entered, and there stood Sherman. His uniform, usually so neatly pressed, was torn, sweat-stained and rumpled. He slapped his thigh, looking for the gun that wasn't there, and his face was so red I half expected blood to spurt from his eyes.

"You'd better get this group under control!" he shouted at me. "I've got the Spokane SWAT unit on speed dial and I've just called the canine division!"

The whole grounds crew, minus the incarcerated, was there, and if I didn't know better, I'd have thought they had just flown the cuckoo's nest.

Aric stood next to Sherman and talked into the poor man's ear. Nothing specific; he just kept talking, talking, talking, jumping from subject to subject.

Blue had found the coffee cup stash and squished one cup after the other in his fist before dropping the cups at Sherman's feet.

Elder tossed his football within inches of Sherman's nose. Derek caught it and threw it back, grazing Sherman's hair with each pass. They continued the routine over and over.

Stamper sat in a corner with his dog, loudly reciting assignments. "Jacob, Riley, Brandon on bunkers . . . Jesse, Marlin, Chris on surrounds . . . James on irrigation."

It was enough to make anyone crazy.

Travis sang the National Anthem in a

loud, deep vibrato. Ending in a high, extended note — one I never thought any man could reach — he then took a breath and began again. It all made me want to turn and run. Then, when Chris chimed in with "Row, Row, Row Your Boat," my toenails curled.

But Marcia nudged me in the small of the back and I stepped forward. I glanced around quickly.

"Where's Paul?"

"Down at the morgue," Sherman hollered.

"Skinny Carl?" I was certain of it. When were they going to get that guy in the ground already?

"None of your business."

I knew it. "Officer Murphy?" As if I didn't know.

"He's been called out. And just when I need him here. I keep trying to get him on his radio, and of course he's not answering."

"The rest of your guys?"

"Gone. All gone. Doesn't matter, SPD's sending in reinforcements. You'd better just take yourself on outa here."

"Now, Sherm." I sidled up to the mustached officer. "Don't you think you'll look a little foolish? SWAT? Canine unit? SPD? For what?" I waved my hand over the bunch. Aric was still reciting words from the dictionary, and then started reading posters, till I patted the air and he grew quieter, but not totally. "Annoying, yes. But criminal?" The football flew over Sherman's head.

Out of the corner of my eye I saw Tim slip behind the desk. Teresa and Marcia followed.

"And really. Didn't you have a little trouble with some nervous condition? I mean, if you get a bunch of hotheads over here shooting up the place all because you can't get yourself calmed down . . . well . . ."

Blue dropped another cup at Sherman's feet.

I heard the tapping of computer keys.

"It might even look downright unpatriotic."

Travis started again, this time with the "Battle Hymn of the Republic." The cabana boys joined in, a wonderful four-part harmony. Chris accompanied them with a musical instrument he produced from his pocket. A comb covered in tissue paper.

Sherman, as mad as I'd ever seen him, grabbed up his radio and called off the canine division, and canceled SWAT. Then he put a call out to Officer Murphy. Nothing. "I don't get it," Sherman growled.

"Stella!" he screamed.

Oh, my. He's really slipped a gear, I thought, but then I remembered Stella was the name of his new dispatcher. Again, nothing.

"Gone to lunch?"

"Forgot. Doctor's appointment," Sherman said.

"Good for her," Ted said.

"So, uh, who responds if you get a nine-one-one?" I asked.

"Apparently, that would be me." Again, Sherman spoke into his radio, but still no Mikey.

"Is it unusual for Officer Murphy not to answer his calls?" I asked, feeling just a nudge of nervous jitters. Mikey was just going down to collect some stolen items from under Candy's porch. No big deal, nothing complicated, unless . . .

I heard the hum of a printer. Then Tim's head popped up from behind the computer and he gave me a thumbs-up. Marcia and Teresa low-crawled their way out from behind the counter.

"Hey, Mr. Stamper!" I yelled. "Can't you control your men? There's grass to mow and gardens to hoe."

Taking the hint, he snapped his fingers and had the place cleared out in seconds.

I knew Sherman could make a call and have Candy's place swarming with cops in seconds. After all, he had SWAT on speed dial. But, I wasn't so sure that was such a good idea. If Mikey was in trouble, as I was beginning to fear, wouldn't it be more benign if some wannabe "campers" just happened to drive on up to the bait and tackle shop looking for a nice place to hoist a tent? We had to get down there.

I wanted to pay Jeff and the rest of the jailbirds a visit, but there wasn't time. Outside the police station I grabbed Aric's arm. "Get a lawyer down here and get Mr. Gullikson and the other guys out. Then wait about an hour and send the police down to Moody Lake."

"What's going on?" Aric's eyes were wide. He gulped down an energy drink, tossed it aside, and popped open a second.

I grabbed it from his hand and chugged it in three gulps. *Whoa.* "Please. No questions yet. Can you do that for me?"

Aric produced another drink from his pocket. "I'll make it happen."

CHAPTER THIRTY

This time I drove. Ted had done enough damage to my Camaro and besides, I'd just slugged down a whole can of energy drink and if my heart went into arrest, I wanted my doctor's hands free so he could administer compressions. Naturally, in the heat of the moment I hadn't considered the fact that I would be driving during the heart attack. Never mind. Mikey was in trouble. We needed to get to his aid, and fast. I clutched and pressed and bent and swerved and sped toward Candy's as fast as my big ol' engine could take us. I wasn't too concerned about getting a ticket, either, since Sherm was by now choking down a few calming ingredients and the rest of his crew was scattered to the four winds. The road was mine.

"Darn it!" I yelled and the three in my backseat leaned forward.

"What is it, Mrs. List?" Tim's face appeared in my rearview mirror.

"Honey, you okay?" Ted looked concerned.

"We didn't have a chance to go over what you found on our mystery author. Tim, you'll just have to read it to me. Did you get a picture?"

Tim unfolded the printout. "Here's what we've got. A big semi."

"A big what?" I stared at Tim in my mirror.

"Big . . . semi!" Ted braced for impact.

I looked up and cranked the wheel, narrowly avoiding a semi stopped at a red light. I blew through the light, shooting the gap between a fire engine and a logging truck.

"We're good," I said.

Tim cleared his throat. "I got a list of other books by the same author."

"Same genre?" I saw a small bottleneck up ahead and went off-road until we were clear.

"No. It's sort of weird. They're all over the place. A thriller, a mystery, a paranormal romance . . ."

"A paratrooper romance?" Marcia leaned over Tim's shoulder.

"Just let me finish, here, Marshy, okay?"

"Huffy, huffy."

"Maybe she liked to expand her horizons," I said, slamming on brakes for a group of kindergarten kids out walking with their teacher. I waved them over impatiently.

"What's really strange is that she, uh . . . wrote . . . let's see here . . . twenty books over the last ten years."

"That's pretty impressive. When would she even have time to —"

"Crap!" Marcia screamed.

"Please don't use that word!" Teresa shouted, and then she said another word that would have finished my sentence better in the first place, because I hadn't seen the construction worker waving his "slow" sign and I knocked it right out of his hands. No time for apologies.

I looked over at Ted, expecting a reprimand, but he just stared ahead, his face a picture of mental disconnect. Poor guy.

"The picture," I shouted at Tim. "What about the picture?"

"Oh. Here it is. It's the only one I could find." Tim held up a grainy black-and-white photo. I stared at its reflection in my mirror.

"That's not her." I eased my foot off the gas. "That's not Candy. It's a much younger woman, and doesn't look a thing like Candy. Wouldn't be Candy ten years ago."

"You sure?" Teresa asked.

"Sure I'm sure." I slowed, feeling frustrated. Now what? We were nearing the wooded area near Candy's Bait and Tackle Shop. Maybe Officer Murphy was fine after all. Maybe Sherman's radio wasn't working or he'd tried to get in touch with Mikey while Mikey was doing what came naturally.

"Oh, yeah," Tim said, "and all her books were published by different publishers, different states, none here in Washington."

I slowed to a roll. "That doesn't make sense at all."

"What doesn't, honey?" Ted had come around.

I pulled over to the side of the road and cut the engine. "It doesn't make sense that Moira could be accused of stealing someone's work when the author never even lived here."

"But May," Ted said, "Tim wasn't reading her bio. Just because the publisher isn't in Washington doesn't mean the author doesn't live here, or didn't pass through here at one time or another."

"Well, I know that picture isn't Candy." I took the muddy photo from Tim, turned it this way and that. "She does look slightly familiar, though. It's so blurry, it's hard to say." I tossed the photo back. "I don't know. What was the name of the book Moira supposedly plagiarized?"

"It's called *Alien Lovers at High Noon*," Tim said. "Here. I'll read a little excerpt."

Tim started to read but I couldn't get past the first paragraph. There's only so much heavy breathing and two-headed alien necking on horseback a person can take.

"That's all there is, anyway," Tim said. "Not much else in her bio. She grew up in Colorado, was an English teacher for a while, enjoys traveling, mostly in the States, and, oh, yeah. She likes to golf."

Marcia perked up. "That's some sort of koinkidink."

"No," I said softly, and then more firmly, "No, no, no! No koinkidink, Marcia."

Ted perked up. "No kinky what?"

"Give me that picture, Tim." I grabbed the photo out of Tim's hand. Then I smiled. "I do recognize this woman." I waved the paper around.

"I thought you said it wasn't Candy." Ted drew his eyebrows together. They actually touched.

"It isn't, Ted." I smiled some more, letting that warm feeling rush around my veins.

"Then, who, May? Don't make me make Teresa beat it out of you." Marcia glowered.

"I've got to get Sherman on the phone, and fast. Who has a cell phone?"

Lots of blank stares. Then Ted sighed and

handed me his. I dialed nine-one-one.

Sherman came on the line in no big hurry. "What is your emergency? And if this is a crank call, I'm not in the mood."

I put the phone on speaker mode. "Officer Sherman. Don't hang up. It's me. May List."

"Oh, is it now? And *Officer* Sherman? I think I'll just go now."

"Wait! Please. I think Officer Murphy might be in trouble down here at Moody Lake. I need you to get to your computer right now and do something for me."

"If I've got an officer in trouble, I need to get out there."

"Please. Just do this first. Besides, you don't have a gun anyway so how much help do you really think —" Ted stopped me with a quick shake of his head. "Go online and pull up the bio of an author named Penelope Peabody."

"This is a crank call. I'm hanging up now."

"No!" Everyone yelled.

Silence.

"Officer Sherman? Are you there?"

"Yeah, I'm here."

"Just please. Pull up her photo, too. Then check to see if her name is an alias. See if you can find her picture in some wanted posters or something. I'll wait."

"First, this might take a while. And second, I still can't get Officer Murphy on the radio. I'm calling SWAT."

"You might do better to call HRT."

Everyone in the car looked at me and mouthed, "Who?"

"HRT. Hostage Rescue Team. Because I think that's what you've got here, Sherm."

"So now we're back to Sherm."

"Officer Sherman. Are you at your computer?" My stomach now was twisting and turning, and that made me think of Skinny Carl, and where was Paul anyway? Wasn't he supposed to be watching Mikey's six?

Sherman came back on the phone. "How did you know, Mrs. List?" He actually sounded impressed.

"Her picture's on a wanted poster, right?"

"Not exactly, but I do have this name as an alias, along with several others for a woman who —"

"Is wanted in connection with murder! Am I right or am I right?"

"Not until today, we lifted her fingerprints off of . . ."

Oh. That took me by surprise. "Her fingerprints?"

"Yeah. I'm looking at her right here on my monitor. This is the face of the woman who came up when we searched the database for fingerprints we found on our victim's car."

"No kidding."

"No, she was wanted in connection with a B and E down in Texas about eight years ago. Statute of limitations has probably expired on that one. But she was arrested a couple of other times passing bad checks under a host of aliases. No known address currently. She probably skipped town."

"You can see that on your computer?"

"We're linked to AFIS." Sherman sounded proud.

"I'll bet I can tell you her real name, Sherman, and I'll bet she's a killer."

"Give it your best shot," Sherman said.

"Her name is —"

Wham! My front tire blew out.

"Good thing we weren't moving," Ted said, pulling the handle of his door.

"No, Ted!"

POW!

"We're getting shot at again," Marcia said. She spoke in a matter-of-fact tone, like she did this every day.

"Everyone out!" I screamed. "Around the side of my car!" I shoved the cell phone in my pocket when I dove for cover, but I could still hear Sherman shouting.

"I'm calling SWAT!" he said. Then the

phone went dead.

Another round whizzed over our heads and smashed into a tree behind me. A couple of cars drove by, slowing when they saw us all hunkered down beside my car, and then sped off again just as quickly.

Pop! Zing!

Marcia turned whiney. "Who keeps shooting at us?"

"I think I know," I said. "But we can't just stay here. We're sitting geese."

"Ducks." Marcia said, and produced some string cheese. Teresa yanked it away.

Pow!

Then, silence.

"She's reloading!" I shouted. "Now's our chance!"

Ted looked at me like I'd just told him to eat a cactus. "Our chance for what?"

"That!" I pointed toward the road. In the distance, I could see the small approaching form of the maintenance crew truck. "Now, go!"

We all jumped up, ran out to the road and waved them down. The truck, filled with workers (all of them this time) skidded to a halt. Much to my relief, Gully was at the wheel.

"Get in," I ordered. The girls were way ahead of me and grabbed hands of the muscled gentlemen in the back.

Pop! A round blew off Gully's trailer hitch.

That was all the inspiration we needed. Ted and I jumped in the cab, Tim hung onto the dented tailgate, and everyone got as close to the bottom of the truck bed as possible. Gully hit the gas.

I was clutching my ankles. I twisted my neck around and looked up at Gully. He had a good day's worth of stubble and purple circles under his eyes. I thought I caught sight of a prison tattoo, but that was more than likely my imagination.

"Good to see you free, Mr. Gullikson." I smiled wanly.

"God works in mysterious ways."

"Was it hard time?" I asked sympathetically.

Gully drove us away from the campground. "I made some new friends," he said.

"Yeah, I know how that is. Last time I was in the clink I met some really nice girls." The campsite disappeared behind us.

"We are all the same. No better or worse," Gully claimed.

"Some a little worse," I said under my breath. But it was refreshing the way Gully was taking his unjustified incarceration.

The truck cab's little rear window slid open. The two postal workers stuck their heads through.

"I figured out who murdered Moira," I said smugly.

"Who?" they demanded.

I finally felt it was safe to sit upright. I nudged Ted, who did the same. "Not so fast. Hey, Marcia!" I yelled past Bonnie and Clyde. "I need a ride back to the lake."

"What do you want me to do about it?" Marcia spat a handful of sunflower seed shells over the side of the truck.

"We're not going in the same old way. You get my drift?"

"Ahhhh." Marcia nodded and threw another handful of sunflower seeds into her mouth. "No."

"Turn at the next sign, Mr. Gullikson. We're gonna wrap this thing up here and now."

Marcia spat a spray of sunflower shells. They caught the wind and blew away. "Why you lookin' at me like that, Mrs. List?"

We passed a sign. On it was written *Municipal Airport*.

Marcia read the sign, looked at me again, and said, "Oh."

I asked her, "You carry your pilot's license on you?"

"Uh, yeah. But I'm a little rusty."

"How rusty?"

Marcia swallowed. "Corroded?"

I nodded. "That'll do."

399

Marcia hadn't flown for a while, she explained, but it was just like riding a bike. Only harder.

I sent the grounds crew back to the campsite with explicit directions that they should set up a perimeter just to be witnesses if necessary, and not to move until SWAT or HRT or the canine division or the National Guard arrived. I didn't know exactly what Sherman was planning. They actually saluted me before speeding off.

The plane Marcia rented was only big enough to hold four people, so after some quick calculations it was decided Marcia would go (not much of a decision there), I would go (I knew what and who we were looking for), Ted would go (because he wouldn't take no for an answer), and Mr. Gullikson would go (because he'd earned it). Teresa and Tim would make some phone calls. I left them with instructions and we were off.

We were off.

We tried to get off the ground, but Marcia hadn't lied about being rusty and she had to taxi back to the beginning of the runway three times before working out the kinks. Finally, she remembered how fast she needed to move the small airplane before we could get the thing airborne.

"It's really been a while," she apologized.

"How long?" Gully was turning all different shades of green.

"About ten or twenty or . . . thirty years or so."

Gully began to pray. Very loudly.

The noise of the little plane was distracting. I shouted, explaining, "When I saw that picture I was expecting Candy, you see?"

Marcia pulled the yoke and skipped over the tops of trees, grazing a few, but since Tim wasn't there it wasn't a really big deal. I continued. "I wasn't expecting to see anyone else, so I didn't recognize her. At first."

"Come on already, May!" Ted had no color in his face at all. It was quite frightening.

"Lawn-mower Head!"

Marcia turned the plane and everyone shifted. Ted scrambled for an airsick bag.

"Just breathe in through your nose, Ted," I directed.

"Lawn-mower Head? What's that supposed to mean?" Gully opened his eyes.

"Marcia. Do you remember when I said we might be looking at this backwards?"

Marcia was getting the feel of the airplane. She banked, then dove, then did a few maneuvers that had Ted reaching for an airsick bag again.

"Don't tense up, Ted, it will only make things worse."

"This is fun," Marcia said. "It's all coming back to me."

"We had an idea that maybe Moira had been killed because she plagiarized someone's work and it made them mad enough to murder her."

"On account of the fact that she had been getting rejection letters that she was blowing away in her backyard with a pistol," Marcia explained just in case someone had missed that detail.

"And more that I can't go into right now. Anyway, when we found Moira's phone, the last caller was Candy. Or so we thought. The only thing is, the call had been made at Candy's shop. Didn't have to be Candy, but it did have to be someone who had access to the phone during business hours, and it would be someone that Candy would allow to use the phone without it seeming unusual, otherwise she'd probably have said something to the cops when Moira's body turned up."

Gully looked at me expectantly.

I encouraged deeper thought. "More than likely one of the campers?"

"Right. Sure."

Marcia hooted and cranked the yoke. The plane did several rolls. Change fell from Ted's pants pocket, and then there was a heavy thud as a pair of binoculars clattered around the cockpit.

"Ted, where have you been hiding those?"

"Just never you mind," he said.

I looked over at my husband who was now hanging upside down. His full head of hair looked like it was standing on end from my perspective. I felt the blood rushing to my forehead and demanded Marcia right the plane. We had work to do.

"We're almost over the lake, now, Mrs. List."

"Good. Someone. The binoculars."

I peered through the lenses while Marcia did some slow, low passes.

"Hmmmm. No movement. Uh, okay, I see some movement now. All the guys did just as I asked. They're all spread out in a nicely spaced line around the campground. Sort of hard to see through the trees . . . but . . . yeah, there's Jeffrey . . . and Derek, and I can see Joe and Dave. Get lower, Marcia, can you?"

"Sure!" Marcia said.

Marcia circled and came in low enough for me to make out the cribbage board in full play between the mechanics. I called out a status report. "Joe's winning!"

"Back to Miss Lawn-mower Head," Ted said.

"I don't know her real name, it's just what I call her on account of her frizzy hair. Or sometimes I call her Frizz Head, or Frizzy, whatever. I saw her in Candy's the day Moira was pulled from the lake. Now. What if Moira hadn't plagiarized someone else's work? What if someone was plagiarizing *Moira's* work? Huh? What do you think?"

Marcia dove toward the shop and then pulled up in a steep climb. "This is fun," she said again.

"Stop that, Marcia." I peered through my binoculars. I saw Mr. Pendersnack's boat in pieces (reminding me I needed to write a fat check for the damage), and I saw the ruined fish on Candy's porch. I saw the Hibachi Boys' campfire smoking nicely; I saw pieces of the yellow crime tape still tied to the picnic tables. I saw Robe's RV, but I didn't see any bodies alive or dead. "Take me over the parking lot again." I looked through the binoculars, but since that made the ground look really close, I put them in my lap. Darn. The ground really was close. "Pull up, Marcia! For the love of —" I cried.

Ted and Gully were making funny noises, mostly sounds of forced air and strangled groans.

Marcia yanked up on the yoke. We were all pressed back in our seats.

"Mikey's car is still in the parking lot," I said loudly, despite the g-force compressing my body to the size of a flat raisin.

"What?" Ted shouted.

"Officer Murphy's car is still in the parking lot! He never left and he's not answering his calls. No one is moving down there. Something is definitely wrong."

The airplane's engine whined in time with Marcia's expert maneuvering.

"So," Ted said, "let's say this frizzy, er, gal was plagiarizing Moira's work. She got the book published, why would she need to come here and murder Moira?"

"I haven't quite figured that part out yet. But I'm sure now I recognize the woman in that photo. It wasn't a very good picture, but I remember seeing her the morning

Moira's body was pulled out of the lake. She probably put on some makeup for the photo op. I heard the message on the phone confirming the tee time, and I recognize that voice, too. I heard her talking in the coffee shop. I knew I'd heard that voice and seen that face before. It just seemed so familiar."

"And she did get arrested for stealing," Gully said. "There was talk at the police station. Only she didn't do a whole lot of time." I noticed a little bitterness in his tone.

"And," I added, "Sherman said her fingerprints were on Moira's car. He found them in AFIS and matched them to a B and E, and matched those to a woman arrested for passing bad checks, alias Penelope Peabody among others. They never caught the woman because she's had no known address, and the case didn't garner much attention, especially in Washington since she wasn't wanted here. Sherm said the statute of limitations on the B and E probably ran out, so the cops didn't give the case much shoe leather. If she'd golfed with Moira that morning, she had access to the crack tool, and anyone can own a gun these days."

Gully asked, "But how did she get my truck? And when?"

"And why would she need to kill Buddy?"

Marcia asked.

"Still working on that. But since her fingerprints were on Moira's car, it's pretty much a lock. Good thing I called Sherm about that, huh?"

Ted patted my leg. Since he was in front and I was in back, he had to turn to do that, nudging Marcia with his shoulder. She bent sideways, and we all did the same when the plane pitched violently.

"Take me down, Marcia." I pointed toward the parking lot.

"This isn't a helicopter, May," Ted said.

"I've got to get down there, Ted. I think this is a hostage situation."

"Forget it." Ted rolled his eyes. "Ma'am," he said to Marcia, "we can go back to the airport now. Let the cops handle this."

Spittle flew from my lips I was so angry. "We will not!" Marcia snaked through the sky, unsure of what to do. I shouted into her ear. "Take me down!"

Marcia looked over her shoulder at me. We went into a dive. "Where?"

I unbuckled, leaned against the door and shoved it open. The wind caught my hair and nearly blew me out.

"Ted! Take my hand. Marcia, get as close to the water as you can."

Ted looked horrified. "No! May, you'll get

smashed to a million pieces if you jump into that lake."

Gully added, "Not to mention you'll have to swim a long, long way to the shore."

I turned to them all, feeling foolish. "You're right. I just got carried away."

"What?" Marcia turned, the plane canted sideways, and I fell out the door.

CHAPTER THIRTY-TWO

It's natural to grab for something — anything — when you're falling. It rarely works in the movies; the bad guy plummets as the cop leans over the edge of the tall building watching as the goon, futilely scratching at air, smashes on the sidewalk below. However, if it's a good guy, he might get lucky and land on an awning, breaking his fall before the awning rips and deposits him safely in front of a fine Italian restaurant. In the tiny fraction of a second I had when I separated from the airplane, I really hoped I was one of the good guys.

Marcia saved me from smashing into a million pieces. She saw what had happened and cranked the plane over swiftly, nudging me gently with the metal bars that held the wheels in place. I grabbed blindly and closed my hands around one of the bars. Impossible. I was hanging below the airplane now, arms stretched over my head, hair blowing in the wind, quivering muscles ready to give way any minute. Marcia must have known, or it was Ted, giving her the truth about my muscular atrophy. Either way, she only had one option. We were going down.

This was no water plane, so Marcia made the hard decision. She got me as close to the water as she could, flying almost slowly enough to stall the plane, and soon my toes were skimming the surface. My hands slipped from the bar. Since I was still moving forward from the waist up and my toes were dragging the water, I did a horrific belly flop when I hit the lake, and felt a sharp pain in my sternum. I was slightly concerned that I'd separated my ribs or had broken a few. The wind was knocked out of me, and I couldn't breathe. Water shot up my nose, ripped off a few eyelashes and flooded my ears, but I was alive. I rolled over on my back and quickly felt around on my chest. All seemed to be in intact although painfully bruised. Thank goodness I was blessed with plenty of cushioning in that area. I waved that I was okay, and watched as the airplane drew away after Marcia wagged its wings in response. I didn't even want to imagine what my husband was doing during that whole thing, but darn it, he didn't even bother to follow me out the door. Another entry in my diary.

So there I was floating in the middle of the lake, and a darn-good thing Marcia hadn't dropped me at the edge, but I wasn't sure I had the strength to swim to shore. Without the buoyancy compensator, it was much harder to keep my head above water and my hands were so tired, just trying to dog-paddle was a monumental effort. But I had to try.

Still on my back, I stroked and kicked. Eventually I found a rhythm. Stroke, kick. Kick, stroke. Maybe I'll have a stroke, I thought. Is my life insurance paid up? Will my daughter be sad? Patty probably wouldn't waste too many tears; she's devoting her time to helping total strangers down in Belize. Where are those grandbabies she promised me? Quite unfair, and I felt regret at my unpleasantness. I was just feeling sorry for myself. Of course my daughter loved me, and she was a good woman. Married a good man, too. Kick, stroke. Kick, stroke. Man, was I sore.

"May! Over here!"

I lifted my head out of the water, logrolled onto my stomach, and nearly cried out with relief.

"Mikey!" I started to say, but slimy water

filled my mouth and I choked and sputtered. Mikey was rowing like crazy across the lake. Not from Candy's, but from the area where we'd lost Snack's boat. I hadn't even heard him launch, but then again it's hard to hear anything when your ears are flooded.

Mikey put those shoulder muscles to good work. He was shooting across the lake. "Swim to me, Mrs. List. Swim to me! Hurry!"

I did my best, which wasn't worth much. Mikey pulled up alongside me, dropped his oars and grabbed the back of my shirt and the waistband of my jeans. With a mighty pull, he had me over the side of the boat. I thudded hard onto its floor.

"Stay down," Mikey said. His eyes were wide, his hair wild, his nostrils flared. He turned the boat and sped back the way he'd come.

"Your friends in the woods told me who was flying and that you were up there," Mikey said, glancing around nervously as he rowed. He was speaking quietly. "What were you doing hanging from a plane?"

I waved Mikey's question away like I was swatting at flies. I was saving my energy and didn't have any desire to talk.

Mikey brought me up to date. "Your

friend landed on the road out there. That husband of yours ran back to the lake and was up to his neck, ready to swim out after you before I dragged him back and cuffed him to a tree."

"You handcuffed my husband to a tree?"

"All of those country club people out there are going to get someone killed."

"I'm glad you're okay, Mikey, I was worried about you. Thought we had a hostage situation or something."

"We *do* have a hostage situation. I've been watching it all play out. Now you guys come along and mess things up."

"Why didn't you answer your radio? Sherman's been having fits trying to get you. For all we know he's calling SWAT as we speak."

"SWAT?"

"And the HRT, the Canine Division, whatever it takes."

"I couldn't get back to my car," Mikey explained. "And this stupid thing" — he knocked on his portable radio — "is out of batteries or something. Cheap equipment. Maybe if the taxpayers would —"

"Mikey. Mind just explaining what's happening so I can sit up already?"

"No, May. You can't sit up. She's got a gun."

"I knew it. That frizzy-haired girl, right? She killed Moira, didn't she? Who's she holding hostage?"

"What? The frizzy-haired girl? What are you talking about?"

I sat up. "It's not the frizzy-haired girl? That one we saw at the tackle shop?"

Mikey had at last rowed us ashore. He jumped out and I tried to do the same but caught my toe on the edge of the boat and did my second belly flop of the evening, this time on wet sand. It should have hurt, but there wasn't any place left on my body to punish.

"Hurry. Get back into the trees." Mikey grabbed my elbow and pulled me while I stumbled, all squishy, useless knees and grinding hips. Once we were concealed in the lakeside forest we both crouched down, panting, backs against tree trunks.

"What makes you think it was the frizzy-haired girl?" Mikey peered around the tree trunk, trying to get a view of the campsite. He had drawn his gun and held it at the ready.

"Her fingerprints were on Moira's car. Sherman confirmed. And, he figured that out because we gave him the name of the author of the book that was published by the people who rejected Moira's book.

Matched the alias with a woman who was wanted for a B and E and arrested for passing bad checks." I slammed my fist into my palm. "Should have figured it out sooner. Thief, my foot. She's a killer!"

"I have no idea what you're talking about, May. All I know is that I get here and find that frizzy-haired girl trying to move the stolen items. Just as I'm coming around the bait and tackle shop, ready to grab her ankles because she's halfway under the porch, I see something that would make any police officer's blood run cold."

"An empty donut box?"

"You just couldn't help yourself, could you?"

"Sorry."

"No. That Robe lady was standing behind the girl, and she had a rifle aimed at her back."

My heart dropped. Darn. Robe had figured it out before I had. "And you naturally drew your gun."

"I was just about to when the girl crawled back out and handed Robe a computer. They didn't see me."

"Then you drew your gun."

"I was about to, but they both walked into the shop."

"Then you called for backup."

"I was going to, but first I had to see what was happening in the shop. I looked through one of the windows, very quietly, very carefully, and noticed there were people sitting on the floor, hands tied behind their backs. It was dark in there but I could see they had gags in their mouths."

"Then you called the HRT."

"Well, I wanted to, but that's when I saw a rifle aimed at my face."

"Then you ran like blazes."

"You could say that."

"I did say that."

"So, you see, I couldn't shoot with all those innocent civilians there, and I couldn't get back to my car because I had to take cover. And I couldn't call for help. But I was just about to flag down a car on the road when all these guys, friends of yours, started running through the woods and I had to keep them from going to the shop, then you dangled from the underside of an airplane, and, well, here we are."

"And here *we* are," Ted said. He, Marcia, and Gully jogged up to us and, taking the hint, crouched down behind trees.

"So what's the sit rep, May?" Ted asked.

"How'd you get loose?" Mikey looked stunned, but slightly impressed.

"Ted! Sit rep? I'm so proud of you." I gave

him a hug. Then I gave him a slug on the shoulder. "You didn't jump in after me."

"It looked very cold," Ted said, but he looked apologetic so I shrugged and filed the incident away. I'd use it next week when I brought up the need for a new washer and dryer. He looked apologetic at Mikey, too. "Marcia had a handcuff key stashed away," he said. "As it turned out, it came in handy."

Mikey slid down and sat hard on his haunches. I'd forgotten he hadn't slept in a couple of days. "I need a phone. Any of you guys have cell phones?"

Ted patted his breast pocket. He patted his pants pockets. "Oh, yeah, May, you were the last one to use my phone . . . oh." His face fell.

I looked out toward the lake. "It's swimmin' with da fishes."

"No one else?" Mikey looked around.

"Sorry," Marcia said.

"Mine didn't get charged while I was doin' time," Gully said. I do believe his voice had changed overnight — like he was hardened a little by his experience.

"I'm not seeing any movement over there, and I haven't heard any gunshots, so that's good. I'm guessing Frizzy got everyone tied up and was getting ready to take off with the loot when Robe caught up to her. She'll get a citizen's award for sure. But it's strange that she hasn't come out. Anyone can see my police car out there. Maybe Frizzy wrestled the gun away from her. No telling." Mikey poked his head around the tree trunk and checked out Candy's shop. "So, why don't you fill me in, Mrs. List? Sounds like I've missed a few things. Good work with the fingerprints, by the way."

I took a deep breath. I had to make this fast. "This is what I know. Moira was found dead, floating in this lake with a country club soil probe shoved through her neck. The last record of her was a tee time with a mysterious guest who made a call from Candy's to confirm. Moira was shooting literary-agent rejection letters in her backyard. Moira's car was found next to the country club's maintenance shed. Murder weapon was made by Gully here." I indicated Gully and he tipped his head. "But the weapon, uh, tool, had been missing, presumably left on the golf course."

"Where anyone could have found it," Marcia stated.

"Yes." I nodded to Marcia. "No blood found on the golf course or in Moira's car, but according to Sawbones, there must have been buckets of it. There was blood found in Gully's truck — not Moira's blood, probably Buddy's — and none in Moira's car, so she was killed somewhere and transported. But when? And where had she been before she was transported out to the lake?"

"And who made the phone call from Candy's?" Mikey rubbed his chin.

"And while at first we were thinking there was a money link between Buddy and Moira, he was killed too."

"With a homemade crack tool from the country club maintenance shop, and that's why we arrested all you guys." Mikey looked at Gully, still not convinced he wasn't the guilty party, or maybe he just hated to be wrong.

"So," I continued, "Buddy Shields didn't kill Moira. We know that, but I do believe he was killed *because* of Moira."

"Now you lost me, May." Ted looked puzzled.

Gully's mouth dropped. "Buddy had a meeting with me at the shop the morning he was killed. I just remembered that!"

I felt smug. "I noticed that on your desk calendar. I also saw the meeting was supposed to be in your office very early in the morning."

"Always very early," Gully ran his hands over his stubble.

"But he didn't make it, and I'm guessing

it's because he found Moira's car when nobody else could. Maybe Buddy had to take an unscheduled potty break, and couldn't make it to the bathroom, or he noticed the grass all smashed down. Whatever the reason, he must have stumbled across the murderer and how was she going to explain the car?"

"She couldn't," Mikey said, keeping his eyes on Candy's shop. "She had to kill the witness. Plenty of available tools in that shop."

Gully shook his head. "No," he said. "I was the only one there and the shop wasn't open."

"Well, she got the crack tool somehow," Marcia said. "And she needed to hide the body somewhere. She seems to like to dump bodies in the water, and the only place was the pond because . . ."

I jumped in. "All she had to transport the body in was one of the golf carts. She couldn't go far with that."

"I wouldn't have even heard a cart driving out," Gully said. "And Buddy wouldn't have driven to the shop. He'd have just walked down. He liked his morning walks."

I looked at Mikey. "That's why you found blood on one of the carts." I continued. "There was probably a little scuffle," I said, "and that's when he dropped his keys. No one would have been on the course yet. She just drove Buddy on over to the pond, plopped him in and hustled on back."

Ted looked doubtful. "How did Moira end up here at the lake if she was killed on the course, and what was the killer doing hanging around Moira's car? That's the last place she'd want to be."

"Looking for something," I said.

"Something that she didn't find because . . . ," Mikey said.

"It was here all the time." I smiled at Mikey. He smiled at me.

A rustle in the bushes startled us all. Teresa and Tim rushed in and crouched down beside us. "What are we looking at?" Tim asked.

I jerked my head toward Candy's. "Hostage situation. You make those calls?"

"Yeah," Tim said. "Interesting stuff. Sorry it took so long."

Mikey worked some kinks out of his shoulders but kept his gun out. "What calls?"

Tim produced some papers. "We called all the publishers on this list, all who published Penelope's books. We asked for her mailing address like you told us to and, sorry, officer, but I had to use a ruse. Said I was in homicide and blah, blah, blah, they were pretty cooperative."

Mikey frowned. "Never works that way for me."

I patted his arm. The gun arm. His trigger finger was pretty tired and he flinched, causing one round to shoot off into the woods. "May!"

"Oh, darn. Think that blew our cover?"

Suddenly there was a lot of activity around the bait shop. Not to mention in the woods. The grounds crew thought they were being shot at, and they abandoned their posts. The cabana boys were in a line, crashing past us, not even bothering to apologize or explain, and Chris was close behind them. Blue wasn't running for anybody, but he walked like his pants were smoking. The college boys scattered, Mr. Stamper got within a few feet of us and then passed out, facedown. Tim ran out and threw some branches over him. Joe and Dave ran past and shook a ring of keys at us. Soon I heard the rumble of an engine, and the mechanics took off in the truck with Aric in pursuit, shouting and screaming. Jim, the ex-cop, and the postal workers went down on one knee and pulled out pistols. Mikey demanded they holster their weapons, and their faces fell, but they complied. Like disappointed kids they shuffled off toward the road.

"The door opened!" Teresa had Ted's binoculars aimed at Candy's shop.

Mikey, all business, raised his gun. "Where is that hostage team anyway?"

"You know Sherm," I said. "But don't worry; we've got your back."

Mikey shook his head. "No you don't. I'll handle this."

"Sure, Mikey." I went to pat him on the shoulder, but then remembered it wasn't such a good idea with his itchy trigger finger. "Probably could have used Bonnie and Clyde here, but no. You sent them away."

"Who?" Mikey asked.

"Dave and Marlin. Never mind."

Teresa whispered loudly. "Someone with really awful hair is moving out. Another woman is behind her with a gun aimed at her head."

"What's the woman wearing, Teresa?" I squinted but only saw blurs of color.

"Uh, it's hard to see, she's pushing the frizzy-haired girl in front of her. She's wearing, uh . . ."

"A robe?"

"Yeah. How did you know?"

Mikey was sweating. "Where is everyone?"

He banged on his radio.

"Does the frizzy-haired girl have something in her hand by chance?" I asked.

"Yeah, yeah. Looks like a laptop. Yeah. I think that's what it is."

"Of course it is." I wanted to punch the air.

Mikey stood up. "I have to do something. She's going to get away."

Teresa said, "No, no. Looks like Robe has her in custody. Probably gonna take her down to the station. Yup. They're now getting into her RV. Uh, looks like she's got the girl in the front seat, and . . . now . . . oh, no! That frizzy-haired girl is wrestling with the lady in the robe! She's grabbing the gun!"

Teresa gave us a blow-by-blow. "The woman in the robe is trying to get away but now that frizzy-haired girl has the rifle aimed at her!"

"Not on my watch!" Mikey jumped out from behind the tree and took off in a sprint.

I looked at Ted, Marcia, Teresa, Tim and Gully in turn. "It's showtime, guys."

"Let's go!" Ted jumped up and started to run after Mikey. The cuffs dangled from one wrist.

Marcia looked at me and shrugged when I noticed the cuffs. "He wouldn't hold still."

"Never mind." I was up and chasing after the guys. I heard the thunder of feet behind me, but not for long. Teresa stretched out and passed Mikey in a flash. Ted was breathing hard when I caught up to him. Marcia drafted off of Tim, using his broad shoulders to block the wind.

When we got to the edge of the woods we all dropped to the ground again.

"She's not leaving," Teresa said.

Mikey took aim on the front windshield of the RV. "What's she doing in there?"

"Uh-oh. The frizzy-haired girl just punched the lady in the robe on the side of the head! Oh, my gosh. Robe's down. Can't see her anymore."

I caught Mikey's eyes, pointed to my own, then to his, and then jabbed a finger toward the shop.

Mikey frowned. He whispered, "What are you doing, May?"

Sheesh. Again, I pointed to my eyes with two fingers, then to his, and then I pointed toward the shop. When I could see he really wasn't getting it, I sighed and said, "Go around the shop, get your car and call for backup. Then, you've got to drive around the front of the RV and block it off. We can't let her get away. Go on, now, pull up in front of the RV."

"She's got a gun in there, May." Mikey looked at me like I was crazy.

"Fine." I stood and brushed off my knees. "Then I'll do it."

"Wait." Teresa grabbed my pant leg and tugged. I crouched down again. "The door's opening on the camper. Oh, snap. The girl just punched Robe in the face. Wait . . . wait . . . Oh! She's just pushed that poor woman out the door. No sign of life. Frizz Head's behind the wheel!"

"I didn't hear a gunshot," I said. "She's probably just knocked out."

"Just?" Ted had his doctor face on. "She's gonna need attention."

"She's gonna run for it!" Teresa said. The RV's engine revved.

Marcia peeled back a bag of cookies. "I can sit here all day."

Now *I* was sweating. "We've got hostages in there, two murders, a civilian down, and the perp is getting away. Mikey?"

"Nobody does anything till we get backup." Mikey's jaw was set.

"What happened to *not on my watch?*" I stared him down.

"I could have been premature."

Oh, for pity's sake. Now the RV was pulling out. I had to think fast, so I came up with a ruse. "Hey, everyone, look who's back." I turned quickly and pointed into the empty woods. When all eyes turned, I jumped up. It was only a few yards to the RV, and I was in the clear. And — I was in a clearing. No cover whatsoever. I had to serpentine just in case bullets flew. I looked up at the RV's window and saw the wild eyes of Frizzy. I waved my hands and raced back and forth, shouting at her. "Exit the vehicle!"

CHAPTER THIRTY-THREE

Everyone screamed at me. "May!" "Mrs. List!" "Maybe Baby!" "You idiot!" That last one was probably from Mikey, but he'd thank me later. The RV skidded to a stop. Hah! I had her. Oops. Slowly the driver's window went down, and Frizzy thrust the barrel of a gun through.

"May!" That was my husband.

I dodged, ducked, rolled, and came up on the other side of a picnic table. A shot rang out. The table's bench seat splintered. I popped my head up. "Missed me!"

Pounding feet. I shot a glance over to my left. Here came Ted. Guess I would scratch that last diary entry. The handcuff clanked around by his side, his hair flew back away from his terrified face, and his eyes were mostly white. I've never seen that man's legs actually *blur* before. He was moving so fast. Another shot rang out. This time it sounded different. That would be from Mikey. Ted dropped down beside me.

"Hi, Ted. Good to see ya."

"I'm going to have you committed!" Ted's face was bright red and he was sucking wind.

"We'll talk about that later." I peeked up from behind the picnic table again. "Mikey's keeping her busy. Now's our chance."

"Our chance for what?" Ted clutched at his chest.

"Come on!"

Again, I was up and running. Ted shouted something indecent, but he followed just the same. I could hear the metal clatter of his cuff. I got to the RV and slammed my back against its side opposite the driver. Ted slammed up beside me. I knew Frizzy must have heard that, but she couldn't shoot us unless she came out. Or . . . if she shot through the walls.

"Hey," I asked Ted. "Do you think those bullets can go through these walls?"

"They went through your dive tank, didn't they?"

"Oh, snap."

Blam!

A bullet flew through the wall. In, not out. That was from Mikey. "Hey!" I shouted.

I heard a groan and remembered Mrs. Robe. She lay on the ground dangerously close to the trailer's back wheels. "Cover me," I said to Ted.

"With what?" Ted raised his arms.

I leapt toward the woman and dragged her around to the back of the camper while Mikey pinged bullets at Frizz Head. Ted slid along the camper wall and joined us in the back.

"Take care of her, Ted."

The woman in the robe groaned loudly. Ted lifted her wrist and checked his watch. "Pulse is good."

With my back against the RV, I slid along the driver's side, hoping Mikey was distracting Frizzy long enough for me to get a chance at disabling her. Again, I heard Ted at my heels. I glanced over at him and glowered. He glared back. Together we slid along. In the side mirror I could see the face of Frizzy. She was positively white and she looked terrified. Not surprising; she was going down for a double homicide. Her window was still open, and as I inched my way forward I developed a plan. I reached out and took my husband's hand in mine. His was clammy, understandably. I could hear his breath fast and ragged near my neck. Since he was a good deal taller than me, I imagine he was sliding along, crouched somewhat, and if we weren't in such a precarious position it probably would have looked ridiculous. But there we were. I sidestepped, slid, sidestepped, and pulled my husband beside me, our hands firmly entwined.

As I got next to the driver's-side window, Frizzy turned and caught my reflection. Her mouth dropped open, her face went a shade whiter, and she thrust the gun out awkwardly trying to crank it around to take aim at us. I jerked Ted's hand up, grabbed the dangling handcuff and locked it over Frizzy's wrist. Startled, she released her grip on the rifle, and I wrenched it away. "Ha!" I screamed. "Ha, ha, ha!"

Frizzy screamed too, but not with joy. She screamed like she was in mortal danger. Gave me a good case of goose bumps, and it wasn't at all what I expected. She didn't sound like a hardened criminal, she sounded like a scared little girl. Now it was her turn to give me the heebie-jeebies.

Screaming still, Frizzy panicked. Should have thought through my big plan a little better. She tromped on the gas pedal and pulled away fast. Ted had to run beside the RV to keep up, both of them still attached at the wrist. His long stork-like legs churned and his elbow banged against the side of the RV. "May!" he screamed. "May! Do

431

something!"

I looked around wildly, finally remembering I had a rifle in my hands. Duh. I got down on one knee like I'd seen the postal workers do. I put my cheek down to the stock, closed an eye, and I took aim.

Pop!

I shot out the left rear tire. The RV swerved wildly. Ted's feet came off the ground and he swung around, and then landed solidly, still running. I aimed again.

Blam!

I shot out the other rear tire, and by the sound of things, probably busted an eardrum. The RV fishtailed, my poor husband flew into the air again, banged against the side of the RV, and then all was quiet.

I ran up to my husband first. "You all right?"

Ted looked woozy, but okay. I aimed the rifle at Frizzy.

Then I heard the sirens.

Mikey ran up to me and removed the rifle from my kung-fu grip. The maintenance crew had doubled back when they saw the approaching police protection and they swarmed the scene. All four Harvest PD cop cars rolled up, lights spinning, and so much confusion that even the ducks on the lake took flight. Some of the cops were ordered by Mikey to check out the situation in the shop. "Take everyone back to the police station and get statements," he said. "Keep 'em separated until everything's sorted out. Don't let 'em say a thing till they're downtown."

"You're under arrest," I said to the frizzy-haired girl. "Arrest, arrest, arrest."

"It's not me!" She was blubbering. "I didn't do anything!"

"Sure. Tell it to a jury," I said. "I got you fair and square, Miss Penelope Peabody."

"Who? What? I'm trying to tell you, that woman was going to kill me!" Frizz Head looked back at Robe.

"You should be ashamed of yourself," I said to the girl as I stroked Ted's back, waiting for someone to come over with a handcuff key. "Why'd you have to go and kill Moira? She find out what you were up to?"

"I don't know what you're talking about." Frizzy squirted tears. She wiped the back of her hand over her nose. "That lady made me get into her RV. She was going to kidnap me!"

I held up my hand. "I suggest you just don't say anything else until you get yourself a good lawyer."

Mikey came over, undid the cuffs and took the gun from me. Ted rubbed his wrist and then put his hand under my chin. "Good job, May, but next time why don't you let me in on your idea for catching the criminal, okay?"

"You got it, hon. You might want to go over and check your patient. She's conscious now but might have a concussion or something."

Ted winked at me and went to do some doctor duties. He carried Robe over to a picnic table and laid her down carefully. Soon the lady was sitting up cradling her head. She closed her eyes and grimaced when Ted examined the gash near her temple. "Probably won't need stitches," Ted called to me, "but she might need a bandage."

"I've got some in my RV," Robe said. "Just help me up, and I can take care of it."

Officer Murphy was on the job, reading Frizzy her rights. He walked her back to his car, and all the while she protested her innocence. Mikey turned and called to me, "Good job, Mrs. List." He considered Robe. "You want me to call out an ambulance?"

I waved at him and smiled. "I think Ted's got everything under control. But, hey. I'll be expecting a citizen's award at your next roll call!"

Mikey winked at me. "You'll all need to

come down to the station and give us a statement, but take care of her first." He nodded toward Robe as he pushed Frizzy toward the car. I could hear the gal bawling and making up loud excuses all the way until she was locked in back of Mikey's cruiser. And away they went.

Soon the maintenance crew grew tired of watching the show, especially after all the hostages had been loaded up in the police cars. I saw Mr. Pendersnack and all his fishing buddies load up first, then Candy, then the Hibachi Boys. Within seconds the campground was quiet.

Mrs. Robe, with my help, climbed the steps to her RV. "Ma'am," Ted asked, "why don't I make some calls and get you some new tires? It's the least I can do after my wife . . ."

I gave him a look.

"I don't have a phone in here," Robe said, "but you can go use the one in Candy's shop."

Ted turned to go, but I suggested he look around for a first-aid kit while he was over making his calls. "We'll need to take care of this gash." I held a tissue up to Mrs. Robe's head. "Here." He dug around in his pockets and found my Camaro keys. "If you get tired, just go ahead over to the station and then go on home. I can take care of things here and take a taxi over to the police station." I kissed Ted and took the keys. He wandered back to Candy's.

I followed Robe into her RV. When I entered, I heard a low growl. Sitting on one of the chairs was the poodle I'd seen the day I brought Robe her latte. He was small and not too scary, a cute little gray thing.

"It's okay, baby," Robe said.

"Oh, what a sweetheart." I reached out my hand and nearly got it taken off by his cute little itty-bitty teeth. "Feisty little thing."

The poodle tucked its tail between its legs, curled up and glowered at me.

Tim, Teresa, Marcia and Gully hovered around the door to the RV. "You need us for anything here?" Gully said, "Because if it's all the same, it's been a really bad day."

I waved them off. "No, you all can go home now. Thanks for all your help."

"What about this stuff you wanted me to get?" Tim had the list of publishers in his hand.

"Guess it doesn't matter anymore," I told Tim. "Here. I'll take it."

Tim handed me the papers, looking relieved. The poodle barked, barked, barked, until Robe calmed him down.

"Okay, everybody, nothing to see here. Go on home. Don't be surprised if you get a call from Officer Murphy, though. He likes to tie up loose ends."

"Like Columbo," Marcia said. She snapped off the end of a carrot and crunched loudly.

"Like a light bulb," Teresa said cheerfully.

"What?" Marcia said. "Why do you always have to say random things like that?" They both walked away. Although I couldn't make out the words, I could tell they were arguing within seconds. However, they had their arms around each other, so they were going to be okay. Tim followed.

I was alone with Mrs. Smith. I'd stopped thinking of her as Robe because I didn't want to accidentally call her that. I remembered what she'd told me when we were introduced. Mrs. Smith was so much nicer. She was looking exhausted and haggard, and her face was a sick shade of green. I helped her into her living space and assisted her into a chair beside her poodle.

"Thank you," Mrs. Smith said softly. "I think I can manage from here."

"No, ma'am," I said firmly. "My husband is a doctor. He'll come back in a few minutes, and I think, until he does, you might want to just take a rest."

"Oh," Mrs. Smith said. Her eyes grew wide. "I'm not feeling well."

I rested my hand on her knee. "I wouldn't be surprised if you have a mild concussion. Sometimes it makes you nauseated. Do you want to throw up?"

"I think I do," Mrs. Smith said in such a tiny voice it was hard to hear. "Oh!" Robe jumped up and dashed out of the RV. She hurried off toward the public bathrooms. The poodle barked.

I let Mrs. Smith have her privacy. I stood, stretched, and massaged the small of my back. It had been a tough case, all right, but we'd put it all together. I glanced around Mrs. Smith's RV. On the passenger seat I noticed the laptop that Mower Head had stolen. It was nice to see Mrs. Smith wouldn't go home without it. I lifted it up, thinking Mikey would want to log it in as recovered property. When I turned it over, though, I was momentarily confused. This wasn't Mrs. Smith's computer. In fact, it wasn't a computer stolen from the campsite at all. I peered at the scratch marks on the back of the computer. The same tool used to etch Moira's name on the back of her phone was used on the computer. Moira's computer?

I lifted the lid and ran my finger around

the touch pad. Moira was meticulous and organized. In her documents file I found not one book she'd written, but several. And then I found copies of her rejection letters. She's blown away the originals in her backyard, but she'd scanned copies onto her computer. In another file labeled "acceptance letters" I found one. Only one, from a Fleetwood Literary Agency. I read it, curious because I thought Gully had said Moira had been rejected repeatedly. Her work had never been accepted by an agent, let alone published.

The letter was short, upbeat, encouraging. The agency was enticed by her query, loved her first two chapters, and wanted to see her entire manuscript, but would not take simultaneous submissions. They were adamant. If the manuscript has been sent to any other agencies they were not interested.

Poor Moira. She never got a chance to get that book published. But the publisher who'd rejected her book — the one we spoke with — did say someone had sold them a book almost identical. I was confused. Mrs. Robe had claimed this was her computer. She'd even refused to leave the lake until it had been found. She'd claimed it had been stolen. Then I had an awful thought.

I felt a cold electric jolt race through my heart. The first book written by Penelope was ten years ago. Mower Head? She was maybe twenty-three years old. Twenty-five at the most. A plagiarizing book thief at thirteen? I knew then I'd made a terrible mistake.

I looked out the window and saw Robe stumble out of the bathroom. She paused, put her hand over her mouth then raced back in.

How could you have been so stupid, May? I looked toward Candy's. Ted must be calling around for deals. I should have known better than to send him shopping for tires. The first time I'd seen the girl with the wild hair, she'd been wearing a phone thing in her ear. Why would she need to use Candy's phone? I looked around. No phone to be found in Mrs. Smith's RV. If that really was her name.

I looked out the front window again. Robe was slowly making her way back. I glanced around quickly. There were some drawers under the small bed in back. I jerked open one drawer. Nothing but clothes. Then I noticed something poking out from under the mattress. I pulled it out. A photo album. I opened it and felt weak in the knees. Morbid, macabre, horrible and sickening.

Photos of crime scenes. Murder scenes to be exact; amateur shots that looked like they'd been taken by the same camera. I slammed the album shut and clapped my hand over my mouth to hold back the shrieks. I looked out the front window again, my heart hammering wildly. Mrs. Smith was almost at the front of the RV. I pulled out another drawer and found an accordion folder.

Mrs. Smith was at the steps. Her little dog stood up and wagged his tail.

I unwound the string and pulled up the flap. My pulse was pounding in my ears.

Mrs. Smith turned the knob.

I lifted out a sheet of white paper. At the top of the paper was the logo: Fleetwood Literary Agency. Then I remembered something. Marcia had used my lint roller in Gully's truck. What had she found? Gray, curly fibers . . . I looked at the poodle.

Mrs. Smith walked into the RV. I spun around, the paper in my hand.

"I see you finally put it all together, didn't you, Miss Smarty Britches?"

"You're looking much better," I said, my insides twisting. I was shaking so hard that even my stomach muscles were quivering.

"Ah, I was faking it." Mrs. Smith squinted. "I just needed an excuse to go get this."

She brought her hand out from around her back and held up a pistol. "Compliments of the guys from Vegas," she said.

"The Hibachi Boys."

"Whatever. I got my hands on it, and they probably thought that girl stole it with the rest of our stuff, but they couldn't exactly report it, since it had its serial numbers filed off."

And was, therefore, untraceable, I thought. I glanced quickly out the window. *Ted, what's taking so long?*

"Looking for your husband? He's still in there probably looking for tires, and good luck with that. These things have to be custom-ordered. I should know. This has been my home for years. Lotta miles under this thing, yessiree. Lotta miles."

I motioned toward the laptop. "That's not yours."

"Nah, it's not. And I would have been long gone if it hadn't been for that stupid girl who stole it while I was in the john first night here. Of course I couldn't leave without it."

"You stole it from Moira."

"Yeah, I did. But it was necessary. It's always necessary to take the evidence. That's what's kept me in the money all this time."

I looked around me at the humble digs. "In the money?"

"I'm makin' it, okay?"

"How? What did you do, exactly? Steal Mrs. Finch's book and sell it as your own?"

"You did figure it out. Bravo. But you can't make a living off one book. If it were only that easy!"

"I saw your, uh, photo album."

"Yes, I like to keep reminders."

"You killed them all?"

"It was necessary. Not at first, no, and it's sad, really." Mrs. Smith put her gun elbow in her other hand and walked around the small space. I backed up and sat on the bed. "New writers are so desperate and so insecure," Robe said. (I was back to Robe. My distaste for the woman was growing by the minute.) "*So* insecure that they jump at the chance to get their stuff published. They practically give it away. And some of them are really good, but they don't have the confidence to believe in their own talent."

"You wrote a book didn't you? But you couldn't get it published." I thought I'd gotten a good idea of this woman, and sadly, she could have been hundreds of us with a deflated dream.

"It was good. But none of the publishers thought so."

"So what did you do?" I looked through the side window quickly. The place looked deserted. *Where are you, Ted?* I discreetly looked around for a weapon.

"No need to try to escape. You'll just stay put until those tires get here, and then I'll be on my way. You'll be staying, of course. I just have to find my camera." Mrs. Smith looked around. "Oh, well, that can keep. As I was saying, you just have to know people's vulnerabilities. It's really quite simple."

"You set yourself up as a literary agent, didn't you?" I still had the paper in my hand.

"Again. Bravo. You're quite good. Too bad you're gonna be dead and no one else figured it out. Not even the publishers who bought the books I stole from those simple-minded authors."

"*Trusting* authors."

"Yeah, yeah. It did take some thought. I had to be choosy, and with hundreds of manuscripts coming in I worked hard. First I had to find the books I thought could be marketable with a little work here and there. Had to be sure they hadn't been placed with any other agents, and then after I got them published I had to meet with the authors. That's why I live in my RV. It helps me move around."

"Then you stole their hard copies, their computers, their discs, flash drives, thumb drives, whatever would prove they'd written the books . . . and you killed them."

"Well, I wasn't going to kill Moira at first, but her book was going big. It was only a matter of time before she saw it in one of the grocery stores. I changed the title, of course, but, yeah. I had to kill them all, as it turns out. If they'd seen their work, they could have sued!"

"Naturally. So just humor me. I've got to understand before you kill me off."

"That's fair," Robe said. After all, she had nothing to lose by explaining things to me — I'd be dead before I could tell anyone.

I kept listening for the sound of Candy's creaky back door, but nothing. *Please, Ted. Hurry!* "You pretend to be an agent. How do you get clients? A Web site could be traced as well as an ad."

"Writers' conferences, dear girl. Conferences. They come in droves. The poor, the illiterate, the brilliant, the hopeful." Robe's eyes were growing more and more evil by the second. No sign at all she was suffering from a head wound. I sized her up. We were about the same; she was just a little bigger. Maybe I could take her. I kept talking.

"So you go to these conferences. Writers'

conferences. Then you what? Set up interviews?"

"Sure. The writers are usually required to bring samples of their work."

"And when you see something you like, then what?"

"I don't have time to go into every situation, so I'll tell you what you really want to know. Mrs. Finch didn't go to any conference, but there are other ways to get manuscripts. I got pretty good at sneaking around the trash bins behind New York agencies. I usually don't find much, but once in a while there are some things that look promising."

"You dug Mrs. Finch's manuscript out of a trash bin?"

"It had been rejected. I thought it had promise. I got it published, didn't I?"

I shook my head. *Didn't they shred that stuff?* "I thought you didn't take simultaneous submissions."

"Shouldn't have," Robe said. "But I really needed the money and I got careless. Now I think your husband has been gone quite a long time looking for tires. Maybe he's calling the cops."

I grew worried, first that Ted wasn't coming back, and then that he was. I just didn't know what to do. I talked fast. "It always takes him a long time to pick out tires. He's rather indecisive about that kind of thing. Please humor me. Okay. You got Moira's book published. Then what?"

"I didn't really want to kill her. It was all getting rather tiring. This killing and stealing. I had to drive all over the country. But I needed to find Moira, pretend to be interested as an agent, make up some story about how I'd been referred by another agency, some such thing."

"Because you couldn't take the chance that she'd have any evidence of her book."

"Naturally. I found out where she lived, drove on over, parked my RV and called her. She said she golfed most days, and invited me along. Since I like to golf and could take in a little fresh air, it was the perfect opportunity to cozy up to her. Put her off guard and act interested in her work."

"You killed her with a tool you found on the golf course. Why didn't you just shoot her?"

"Shooting is messy."

"And a soil probe through the carotid isn't?" I couldn't believe what this woman was telling me. *Ted, where are you?*

"And there's the matter of ballistics, and so on. Guns are noisy and risky. I always find a weapon of opportunity because it's nearly impossible to trace back to me. I've gotten away with it for nearly ten years, haven't I?"

"Help me understand. You're on the golf course having a wonderful time, telling Moira you love her book and want to represent her, right?" All the while I was thinking, *you miserable excuse for a human being.*

"Yup. Made her day."

"Then, what?"

"Then she just goes all cranky on me. She sees this tool that, in her words, was litter left by those blasted groundskeepers. She grabbed it and started to put it in her bag, but I offered to put it in my golf bag."

"How very kind of you," I said with as much sarcasm as I could manage around a mouthful of nerves.

"I then — very politely, mind you — invited her back to my RV for some tea while we went over her contract. I'd already asked her to bring all of her material to the golf course, which she'd promised she would, so we could do some last-minute edits or what have you. I really can't remember what I said. She offered to drive back here, which worked out well for me since I'd taken a taxi to the country club."

It all became very clear at that point, and I didn't want my imagination to work as well as it usually did because the vision was just too horrible. However, I pressed on if for no other reason than to buy myself another ten or fifteen minutes of life. "You kept her here in your RV until it was late probably, am I right? Waiting for everyone to go to bed, telling her of the wonderful things that would happen with her book, the money and notoriety she'd receive, what the cover would look like, how great it was going to be as she started her writing career and how you would be her cheerleader."

"A walk in the park."

"It gets dark and you take her for a midnight stroll on the beach."

Robe scoffed. "No, more like a late-night boat ride. I grabbed the tool she picked up on the golf course, hid it in the boat, we got in, rowed out to the middle of the lake, and Yah! Right through the neck. It was like slicing pudding. Only juicier."

I gasped and covered my mouth with my hands. Then I gathered my composure as best I could, but I really had the shakes at that point.

"Then I washed out the boat, tied it up, drove Moira's car back to the golf course and hid it in the weeds to give me time to get out of town before she was missed, caught a taxi back, took a quick shower and went off to bed."

"You stole Moira's stuff, but then it was stolen from you."

"I didn't know who stole it at first, but then I saw that crazy-looking girl digging around under the porch and I knew where it was."

"And you were going to kill her, too?"

"Well, she'd seen it."

"And what about Buddy? The man you dumped in the pond?"

"I almost went crazy. Two days I looked for that computer. We were all missing things and couldn't find the thief. All that time Moira's body's floating out there. Then I thought maybe I'd just left the computer in Moira's car. I went back to check and that guy caught me there. I pretended I was lost, looked for a weapon of opportunity, and that's when I saw the golf cart parked by the fence. The crooked tool, looked like a one-pronged rake, was in the back of the golf cart. I grabbed it, swung, and . . . you know the rest. A really good shot, too. Right in the heart. He went down like a soft wedge shot. Plop."

"And you took him to the pond in the golf cart."

Mrs. Smith touched her nose and pointed at me. "When I didn't find the computer in

450

Moira's car, I went back to her house to look. I couldn't very well drive my RV over, so I took that big truck I'd seen parked in front of the shop. I'd seen the keys in it, along with Moira's house key and I know that because she had this cute little picture key chain hanging off of it, and you wouldn't believe who's in the picture."

"Her dead husband?"

"Nope. She had a picture of herself! Can you be that conceited? Anyway, I went through the glove box and found the address for the guy who owned the truck. I just caught a taxi about a mile from his house the next night and" — Robe chuckled — "he never even knew it was gone. And he never knew I'd thrown my bloody clothes under the tarp after I killed Buddy. I took those out after I saw you guys jump off Moira's roof. Thought you might have something that would hang me."

"And that's how Buddy's blood got in the truck and in the golf cart. And that's why you were shooting at us."

"Yeah, but I had to return the truck in case you called the guy who owned it. Figured you'd know whose it was. Anyway, I finally found the computer, and that girl thief is going down for murder, so I think it's time we just put a period to the end of

451

this sentence." Robe lifted the gun and pointed it at my forehead. "I really hate to get brain matter in my RV, but Moira's book is doing so well I can afford a new one. When your husband gets back, I'll tell him you said good-bye, then I'll send him on to join you."

I said quickly, "You left your fingerprints on Moira's car."

Mrs. Smith stopped in her tracks. Her face drained of all color. "I did?"

"And they matched them with some fingerprints they found at a B and E."

Mrs. Smith snapped her fingers. "Darn it! That was probably one of my firsts. I didn't kill the writer that time because I couldn't sell her book after all. Phooey. Should have done her when I had the chance."

"They'll know soon enough that young woman they took in for the murder doesn't have matching prints, and they'll be back."

"Hmm. I guess you're right. So. We should get this show on the road, huh?"

Really bright, May Bell. Mrs. Smith raised the gun. "Wait." I held up a hand. "There's nothing to gain by killing me. I can help you get away from here. The cops already know who you are."

"But I have no address. I'll be invisible."

"Not in this thing." I looked around the

RV. "But if you take another car and leave, they won't be able to find you. You can take my car." I searched in my pocket and brought out my keys. "And I won't tell them you have it until you've had time to find another one. You can change your name, your business address, and" — I held out the papers — "I see you get your checks at different PO boxes. You can get new ones. No one can find you. You could go off the grid!"

I could see I was making an impression. Out of the corner of my eye I saw movement out the window but I didn't dare look away from Robe.

"Where's your car?"

"It's just up the hill. Go through the woods. You can't miss it."

Mrs. Smith lunged forward, trying to fake me out, as it was, and she did a good job of it. I cried out and threw my keys at her. She caught them, smiled, and turned on her heel. She called for her dog and put her hand on the door.

"I got the bandages!" Ted wrenched the door open.

Mrs. Smith, off balance, fell forward, stepped awkwardly, and plunged headfirst down the steps.

"Oh, my goodness!" Ted stepped aside,

not even bothering to break Robe's fall.

I was moving at the speed of sound. I know this because I left my shouts behind me when I dove down the stairs after Mrs. Robe.

"Oh, my goodness, May!" Ted reached out then and tried to break my fall, but I shoved him away and got my knee on Robe's neck as she reached for the gun that had fallen away when she hit the ground.

Ted took it all in. He kicked the gun away and grabbed handcuffs from his back pocket. He thrust them my way. "Here, May Bell," he said, his voice all quivery.

I grabbed the cuffs and locked up Mrs. Robe in a flash. I brushed the hair out of my eyes, looked at my husband and, gasping for breath, gave him a satisfied nod. "You were there all the time, weren't you?"

And then the SWAT team arrived.

CHAPTER THIRTY-FOUR

Down at the police station Officer Murphy actually hugged me after I'd completed my written statement. I think he was going on three days without sleep and he would have hugged the break-room refrigerator if I'd suggested it, but it was good to get his affirmation for a job well done. While he was in a fragile state, I confessed. I had been the one who'd messed up the autopsy of Skinny Carl. The stomach contents in evidence were mine, not Carl's.

Mikey got the giggles. Tears actually streamed from his eyes. Then he hugged me again. "You know what you did, May?"

"I'm so sorry." I lowered my head.

"No! If we hadn't checked the tox results more closely, we'd have never figured it out. I guess you haven't heard. Skinny Carl did have E. coli, that's true. But, he also had a lethal dose of antifreeze in his system, courtesy of his girlfriend who had been

455

nursing' him through his illness. She just mixed it in his sweet tea. She'd also written the ransom note, collected the money and had the gall after we *persuaded* a confession out of her to ask for the reward money Carl's parents had put up for his return."

"Did she give a reason for shooting him after he was dead?"

"She hated his guts."

"My guts."

"I didn't know you were acquainted."

"Coroner humor."

Sherman walked by and sneered. "Oh, you're sooo funny."

Mikey and I locked our bloodshot eyes and laughed so hard we both lost a little bladder control.

The grounds crew was grateful to get out of the whole ordeal without losing any limbs (at least that's what Tim said, and I'm not sure if he was talking about human or tree).

The next weekend, with Stamper giving assignments and Mr. Gullikson taking a much-needed break on my porch, the crew showed their appreciation by cleaning up my yard using their tools and machines. Jeffrey, Mr. Gullikson's son, hovered nearby, probably nervous about letting his father out of his sight. I finally waved him over and soon he and his father were building a warm father-son bond. They talked for hours.

Bonnie and Clyde chopped wood, played thumb wars, chopped wood, played thumb wars, chopped wood, and finished out their assignments with plenty of calluses. Some from chopping wood.

Jim, the ex-cop, carried boulders around, not really doing much with them, but his muscles got huge!

Elder had fashioned a new sling for his football and caressed it occasionally as he pushed a lawn mower back and forth.

The cabana boys, Aaron, Jesse and James, dug a huge hole with pickaxes, singing prison songs as they worked. They lined the hole, filled it with water and designed a gurgling waterfall.

The college kids ran down to the nearby stream and came back with buckets of fish to put into the pond. Derek had a toad he dropped in as well, but it hopped out and disappeared. Derek looked dismayed until I told him he could go find another and he ran off hooting with glee. Aric leaned against a shovel and kept up a running commentary on the whole process. Billips and Jake chased squirrels. Dave and Joe were busy keeping the machines running then gave up and played cribbage on my back deck. A strategic move, because they weren't missed for several hours — after all the hard work was done.

I didn't see Chris for a long time until he appeared suddenly, covered from head to toe in a white, dusty material. He explained it was cement residue, because he'd just finished pouring a full-size basketball court in my backyard. He also said he'd lowered the hoops — just for me. Maybe I'll adopt him.

Blue grumbled a lot, but when he presented me with four loaves of bread he'd made just for me, I caught a glimmer of kindness and softened toward him a great deal. Jerry then tried to upstage Blue by presenting me with a new BCD and a bouquet of flowers that he'd stolen from the club's garden. Teresa ordered Stamper to write him up, but Gully shook his head and all was well.

Travis, Matt, Jacob, Brandon and Riley decided it was time to try out the pond after a hard day's work and dove in after stripping down to their boxers. The fish died immediately.

All the while, Teresa and Marcia were generously landscaping the mountainous area around my house, and when they were finished it was incredible. The trees, bushes and flowers added so much personality and beauty that I was again moved to tears, this time of the good emotional variety.

We all bade our fond farewells after I was forced to promise everyone I'd be back to work with them a few hours each week. I think I can handle that.

That evening a herd of deer came through and ate everything Marcia and Teresa planted. I haven't told them yet.

As I lay in bed with my husband that night, heating pads and ice packs covering our bruises, I stared at the ceiling and thought what a wonderful day it had been. Day, heck; it had been an awesome week! Ted moved one of his own ice packs from his knee to his forehead. Trixie was curled up beside me purring happily. This day was full of surprises.

"You did real good, Maybe Baby."

"Yeah, it all turned out pretty well, didn't it?"

"The guilty one is in jail, the innocent are back on their mowers and blowers and rakers."

"They're good people, Ted. I think I'll finish out the summer working with my new friends."

"Might not be a bad idea."

"Oh, criminy, Ted. I have been so busy, I forgot. Patty sent a package."

"I know. I saw it on the counter. You want me to get it?"

"No, you stay. I'll get it."

I rolled out from under the covers. My little dog took the warm spot, and I gave him a pat on the head before shuffling off down the hallway. As I passed the family photos along the wall, I paused at the wedding photo of Patty and Jack. I hadn't seen them in over three years. I felt a lump rise in my throat.

Downstairs, I lifted the small package. It wasn't heavy; probably a scarf from Belize. I already had a closet full, but it was a thoughtful gesture anyway. I carried the package upstairs and sat on the bed beside Ted. He saw the glisten in my eye, and his expression softened. "Why don't you call her?"

I laughed softly. "This time of night?"

"Well, then, open it. You can call tomorrow and say thanks."

I nodded my head, slipped my finger under the tape and pried away the flap. When I opened the box I was confused at first. Just an envelope with some tissue paper filling the box. Ted and I exchanged quizzical looks. I opened the envelope and squinted. "It's just a couple of receipts. I don't have my reading glasses. Can you make them out?"

Ted took the papers and grinned broadly. "They're coming home. These are copies of airline tickets."

I squealed and bounced up and down on the bed. "When Ted? When?"

Ted peeled away a little sticky note. "It says we should look at the picture."

"What picture?" I dug through the tissue paper and found a photo of Patty and Jack, standing with their backs to a beautiful blue ocean, their bare feet in white sand. I frowned. "Patty sure has put on weight since she's been gone."

I showed Ted the picture and he roared with laughter. "Take another look, grandma."

I looked again, more closely. I looked at my husband, my eyes flooding with tears. "Grandma?" There stood Patty, her husband's hand proudly on her swollen belly. *"Grandma!"* My whole body healed of every bruise, every hurt, every bump and ache. I am going to be a grandma! I fell on my husband and cried delicious, ecstatic tears. I pushed away, looked at his eyes, saw the tender way he loved me, and collapsed again in laughing sobs, my face buried in his chest.

Ted wrapped his arms around me.

"Oh, my," I said, my voice muffled. "Now I've gotta learn to knit."

ABOUT THE AUTHOR

Dawn Richard was born in Texas, but her family eventually settled in Montana's Bitterroot Valley. She grew up there enjoying the life of a kid who loves the outdoors: hiking, fishing, camping and horseback riding. Later, she joined the U.S. Army and lived in Bremerhaven, Germany, working as a combat medic. Afterward, she attended the Defense Language Institute as a Russian linguist for the Army. After her discharge, she worked as a curriculum specialist for the U.S. Air Force, once again in Texas, where she met her husband, a tanker pilot. Dawn currently writes full-time, and lives north of Spokane, Washington.

Par for the Corpse is the fourth in the May List Mystery series. Her other books include *Death for Dessert, Digging up Otis,* and *A Wrinkle in Crime.*

The employees of Thorndike Press hope you have enjoyed this Large Print book. All our Thorndike, Wheeler, and Kennebec Large Print titles are designed for easy reading, and all our books are made to last. Other Thorndike Press Large Print books are available at your library, through selected bookstores, or directly from us.

For information about titles, please call:
(800) 223-1244

or visit our Web site at:
http://gale.cengage.com/thorndike

To share your comments, please write:
Publisher
Thorndike Press
10 Water St., Suite 310
Waterville, ME 04901